UBER MAN

For Ikiru and his kindred,
the coming race.

UBER MAN

JASON REZA JORJANI

ARKTOS
LONDON 2022

ISBN	978-1-914208-76-8 (Paperback)
	978-1-914208-77-5 (Hardback)
	978-1-914208-78-2 (Ebook)

| **EDITING** | Constantin von Hoffmeister |

⊕ Arktos.com   🅕 fb.com/Arktos   ◉ @arktosmedia   ◎ arktosmedia

CONTENTS

"The pen is mightier than the sword."

— Sir Edward Bulwer-Lytton

"I'm a writer, but sometimes I feel like I was written. 'You see that guy,' they say, 'he's a real character.' But maybe I wrote myself."

— Jean-Michel Basquiat

CHAPTER 1

DANA AVALON

T HE SKYSCRAPERS of Gotham were so massive that they looked like slabs of black granite as they exploded into a twilight cut through by lethal neon laser beams. That was the impression I had every time that the vibrations shook me out of the trance, and I slipped back into this time and place long enough for my gaze to fix itself on the view from the horizontal window cut out of this colossal bunker of a building. The architectural drafts of Hugh Ferriss had been a major inspiration for the design of our new city that stands atop the Palisades, from Englewood Cliffs all the way up into the Hudson Highlands, overlooking the storm-battered towers of Manhattan as they rise from out of the waves of the Atlantic Ocean.

These towers, growing like crystals from the cliffs and hillsides, seamlessly fused Neo-Deco with Brutalist and Modernist elements in a self-conscious embrace and synthesis of those features of New York's architectural heritage that stood most defiantly against the reimposition of Tradition in the world. Now the city's defense perimeter, which once extended for a couple of hundred miles in every direction, had been breached by soaring armadas of sleek Olympian attack ships, and these pillars of defiance were being brought down, one by one. I could hear a steady cascade of shattered glass pouring onto the empty streets. Empty because the city had already been almost completely evacuated.

A week ago, when the first Olympian stealth scouts were sighted inside the defense perimeter at night, Gotham's last holdouts began to reluctantly pack into transport ships headed for the Prometheist colonies carved out of large asteroids in the belt between Mars and Jupiter, where finding them would be like searching for a needle in a haystack. There, they were undoubtedly welcomed as tragically defeated heroes by off-world Prometheists who saw Gotham — the only living metropolis left on Earth — as the last bastion of terrestrial resistance against the so-called "Golden Dawn" of Tradition and the ultimate symbolic repudiation of the Olympian Imperium. As the transport ships dove beneath the waves of the Atlantic Ocean and il-luminated the submerged streets of Manhattan in their searchlights, the fugitive Gothamites must have identified with the last denizens of Atlantis.

The attendant adjusted the electrodes fastened to my forehead as I focused on the commands of her hypnotic voice, and I went under again as my floating body relaxed back into the cathedral darkness of the Regression Room. It was an uncannily seamless transition to be-ing in the womb, until I felt the umbilical cord strangling my neck like a noose. In retrospect, I wonder why the imminence of death did not abruptly catapult me back here — into the Gotham of the fall of 2112. Instead, I found myself floating high above Booth Memorial Hospital on a crisp late winter day in February of 1981, looking in the direc-tion of the Terrace on the Park and the old World's Fair grounds in Flushing Meadows. Then, I focused downwards to see my father — or the man who would become my father — walk out of the hospital for a smoke, as my would-be mother entered her twentieth hour of labor.

This was the last of my regression sessions. That was the usual protocol, to end with one's birth in a previous life. But these sessions were much more intensively immersive than the standard past life regressions that every Prometheist went through in young adult-hood. I had gone through that before, not without causing a scandal that subjected me to nearly shattering stress. This second round of regressions, which was drawing to a close, was intended to prepare me to operationally take charge of the mission that I had already initiated. My task was to flip from past life recall to an out-of-body experience of the world of my previous incarnation, astral projecting from out of static memories into a dynamic experience and exploration of New York City in the 1980s.

As the reincarnation of the founder of the Prometheist movement, I had grimly arrived at a fateful decision a few years ago. Before the close of the first decade of the 22nd century, it had become clear to me that the battle against the Olympian Imperium was lost in the present and that the only way to win the war would be in the past. Of course, I kept this information strictly classified, sharing it only with a small think tank, whose members unfortunately confirmed my analysis, and an elite cadre of the most superbly trained time travelers in the Prometheist Resistance. According to our analytical models and projections, the decade of the 1980s was the last possible historical moment wherein an alteration in the chain of events could probably avert something like the presently unfolding defeat of Prometheism by the tyrannical forces of Tradition. Specifically, we determined that the collapse of the Soviet Union from 1989–1991 was the fulcrum that, should it be prevented, could tip world history back into an ascendant trajectory for long enough to build a viable Prometheist Resistance against the mid-21st century Olympian re-conquest of Earth.

So, I developed an elaborate plan for a series of key alterations in the chain of events that would take place in the course of the 1980s. In order to provide a resource base for this operation, the elite cadre of Prometheist time travelers was deployed as a spearhead. I had them sent back to 1977, giving them several years of lead time to amass resources by building a pharmaceutical company on Long Island that would market at least a dozen breakthrough drugs whose chemical formulas I had sent back in time with them. These were phenomenally marketable drugs which, on our timeline, would not be invented until the 1990s or the early years of the 21st century. They were trained to set up insider trading as well, so as to make a secondary profit on the skyrocketing stock of the publicly traded drug company. I also set them to work forging false documentation to construct my supposed biography as a corporate executive woman of the late 20th century, a task for the accomplishment of which they drew extensively from the Soviet KGB playbook of placing deep cover spies in foreign countries, such as the United States.

My plan is to join them in 1980, with Manhattan as the international hub for my attempt to reshape the timeline. Of course, what this means is that the original timeline will be overwritten. The world that I have known in this lifetime, and for that matter much of my immediately preceding incarnation as I lived it, would melt into non-existence — except for in the personal memories of the time travelers sent on this mission. It is my prerogative to make the determination that the situation is so hopelessly desperate that such drastic measures are called for. The responsibility rests on my broad shoulders alone. My name is Dana Avalon, and I have Phenomenal Authorization.

I am a native of Gotham, and my parents played a significant role in building this city. My mother, Brenda Wells, was an architect, and my father, Richard Avalon, was what, in the last couple of centuries, would have been called a "real estate developer." To speak of "real estate" in the context of the pseudo-economy that we have in this enclave makes little sense. I suppose you could say that he was in "construction." Dick was already in his early sixties when I was born, in late January of 2077. (Yes, I'm an Aquarian.) Career-wise, he cut his teeth on Simulacra construction in the 2040s. This was a relatively short-lived trend of building habitats or "total environments" that were reconstructions of particular past eras. Imagine highly fortified gated communities with an entirely consistent and cohesive style. More authentic and less gaudy than simulacra of various places at the casino resort hotels of old Las Vegas.

By then the world had been completely devastated by convergent catastrophes, from pandemics to super-volcano eruptions and multiple mega-tsunamis produced by tremendous earthquakes. There had also been catastrophic climate change, resulting in droughts, deep-freezes, and mass starvation. Most of the severely diminished population was disease-ridden and desperate. Under these appalling conditions, many of the superrich retreated into micro-cities that were modeled on the aesthetic and lifestyle of one or another past epoch of relative peace and prosperity. The majority of those who could afford to live in such places opted for modern conveniences, so simulacra of the 1950s were more popular than reconstructions of the Wild West or Victorian Britain.

The *most popular* of all of the "total environments" were communities modeled on 1980s America, which is the type of construction that my father specialized in. It is how he met my mother, who was an architecture student researching her doctoral thesis by doing an on-site study of a small-scale urban reconstruction of an Eighties American cityscape that he was building (there were also suburban simulacra). She recruited him into Prometheism. She appealed to his practical sensibilities, motivated by her own opportunism. "The movement" (as she was fond of calling it) had always valorized "the Eighties" of the previous century as the zenith of social development and cultural innovation. In the 2040s, many of the wealthy individuals who opted to live in simulacra of that era were Prometheists. In fact, the dominant Traditionalist discourse had by then framed Prometheism as an ideological superstructure intended to morally justify the greed and deviance of reactionaries who wanted to salvage the evils of Capitalism, albeit by dealing in cryptocurrencies after the global abolition of "filthy" money. This, despite the strong Communist currents in the thought of Jorjani — but I am getting ahead of myself.

Richard Avalon "converted" to Prometheism because he saw construction opportunities and business deals with individuals who, at least implicitly, still believed in personal wealth over the putatively "greater good" of so-called "public welfare." Meanwhile, my mother became Brenda Avalon because my father (who was already twice divorced and too old for her) was an insurance policy that she wouldn't wind up a "paper architect" in a world where 99% of architecture firms had gone out of business and almost all construction projects were run by the state. They were both career-driven enough that they waited two decades into their marriage to decide to carry a pregnancy to term, and this was only because by then my mother was in her mid-forties and this was her last opportunity to give the great Dick Avalon a flesh and blood bearer of his legacy as the world's last great builder.

I was born in Gotham, only about a dozen years after the groundbreaking of the project — which was the crowning glory of my parents' collaborative enterprise. No mere micro-city or gated simulacrum, Gotham was the first new full-scale metropolis constructed since The Arrival in 2048. As such, the building project could not but be considered an act of insurrection on a titanic scale. That the construction was completed at all was, in truth, a testimony to the confidence of the Olympian Imperium, which decided to use it as a dark crystallization — a tumor, epitomizing everything that they considered wicked and depraved about what was fast becoming "the old world" of Modernity. Gotham was their Sodom, with its many Towers of Babel that they left to rise up for a time with the intention to topple them later in an all the more dramatic demonstration of Divine Judgment descending on sinners.

What can I say about my childhood? I was always a tomboy, but then so were most girls here in Gotham by the standards of gender norms that had been reimposed worldwide by Traditionalists under the paternalistic guidance of Olympian Overlords. But my boyishness went above and beyond the average, even for Gothamite girls. I took up scuba diving by the time I was old enough to carry the weight of a sizeable oxygen tank on my back, and I abused the privilege of my parents' access to the restricted area of Manhattan to dive on the ruins of the old city.

The Avalon Corporation was cleared for entry into that part of New York Harbor so that its team could draw inspiration from studying, photographing, and modeling the details of the decaying skyscrapers. Their partly shattered hulls were being steadily worn away by the waves of the Atlantic Ocean, which broke around them before pressing on up the Harbor through the geometric grid of channels that had been the streets of Manhattan. After the last remnants of the Antarctic ice sheet melted, laying bare the ruins of Atlantis, the sea-level had risen up to about the 30th floor of the Empire State Building. Her spire, originally built as a Zeppelin dock, still stood as a monolithic sentinel over the dead city that Gotham was modeled on.

One of the most unforgettable dives that I did, together with my mother, in the last year before my relationship with her fell apart, was on the Guggenheim. I had grown up surrounded by Frank Lloyd Wright designs, and blueprints for new buildings with decorative details that were partly inspired by the archeo-futuristic elements of his Deco period. Though my parents attempted to shelter me as much as possible from the world of the Olympian Imperium, outside the defense perimeter of Gotham, I knew that the Traditionalist state that had consolidated control over most of the planet branded Wright as one of the principal degenerates of the so-called "Kali Yuga." Children were taught that he was a "murderer" whose architectural designs were a product of his evident mental derangement. All of that was in the back of my mind when we dove through the shattered glass dome of the Guggenheim that day, casting our flashlights onto corroding Modernist sculptures that crouched inside the guardrail of the spiral walkway like demonic totems. The Guggenheim's atrium had become a kind of self-contained aquarium for slithering, shimmering fish, and a feeding tank for a couple of geriatric sharks who we had to put out of their misery.

I was also an avid skier. The plans for Gotham were actually first drawn up at a reclaimed ski resort about 120 miles north of the ruins of Manhattan. Once known as Hunter Mountain, this area of the Catskills had enough existing infrastructure that the Prometheist movement had chosen the Avalon Corporation to build an Eighties-style community at this location, and to reconstruct the ski lifts and lodges for the use of those who settled there. Our paramilitary forces filled the dense forest surrounding the designated area with fortifications capable of mounting significant anti-aircraft fire.

After a few skirmishes, on the level of partisan warfare, those locals in the Catskills who were loyal to the Olympian Imperium decided to put enough distance between themselves and our mountain enclave. The landing of a few armed electro-gravitic vessels and personnel transports at a makeshift spaceport that had been built on a peak adjacent to the Hunter Mountain summit, was enough to spook them into believing that our "rebel" forces were considerably more formidable than was in fact the case. In point of fact, our connection to the Asteroid Belt colonies was tenuous, and we wondered if the Imperium would cut this Prometheist lifeline at any moment. But, meanwhile, we skied — mainly as a means of clearing and refreshing our minds.

My parents had the largest chalet in the community, built from out of the deep infrastructure of an old, ruined hotel, on a hill diagonally across from the mountain. It was in the skylit and sunbathed studio on the upper floor of this chalet that, I am told, the blueprints for the construction of the first set of buildings in Gotham were drawn up by a small group of architects and engineers overseen by my parents. These were the towers furthest south along the Palisades Cliffs, with the clearest and most breathtaking views over the partly submerged skyscrapers of Manhattan. Prime real estate, which Imperium propaganda portrayed as belonging to the Devil himself. Funny to think that this had once been New Jersey. Maybe it was the Jersey Devil.

"You little devil" is a phrase that I often heard throughout my childhood and adolescence. I stopped hearing it only because at a certain point my mischievous antics and rebellious contrarianism were no longer amusing, especially to such scions of respectability as my parents were in "the movement." I was a talented artist and, around the age of eleven, the content of my drawings began to shock them. They wondered what prurient influence I had come under, and where all the spectacular violence in these images was coming from — as if we weren't living in a world that had just gone through a global holocaust ending in the brutal imposition of a totalitarian socio-political order.

I was fascinated by history and literature, which were my strongest subjects in middle school. Digging my claws into every book that I understood to be banned by the regime reigning outside my relatively sheltered environment became an obsessive mission. My rebellion never took the form of affirming the Traditionalism of the outside world, which was after all the ideology of the majority of sheeple on Earth. Rather, I was radicalized in the opposite direction. My reaction to living under the shadow of such prominent Prometheists was to become "holier than the Pope." I started to express contempt for their construction endeavors as a superficial and rootless misunderstanding of the Promethean ethos. Like most Prometheist households, our library included the complete works of Jorjani. I began by holding these up as mirrors to the shortcomings of the Prometheists of our time, but then I turned on the "canon" itself. By the end of my high school years, I was reading Jorjani against himself.

That's when the terrible break with my mother took place. My father was blessed to have already died of heart failure during my junior year, because otherwise I would probably bear the guilt of killing him with the stress that this scandal caused for our family. The worst that he had lived to see was my starting to date girls more often than boys, and it was hardly appropriate for someone so prominently associated with Prometheism to express any displeasure over his daughter turning out to be a lesbian, or at least bisexual. I can tell you that my mother wasn't all that pleased by it, even though she tried to keep that to herself and find other excuses for expressing her disapproval. Things were never the same after she caught me and my first girlfriend making out.

The breaking point in my tense relationship with her came when, like all young adults in the movement, I underwent the past life regression sessions that were expected of anyone between the ages of 18 and 22. The therapist and attendants involved in my regression hypnosis sessions violated their confidentiality oaths by gossiping about the content of the memories that had been unlocked from my subconscious. Rumors spread like wildfire, and scandal engulfed the "Avalon" name over my father's fresh corpse. Dana Avalon, it was said, claims to remember having been Jason Reza Jorjani — the movement's martyred founder. This, in turn, meant that she was also claiming to have been a number of other figures of historical significance, which were believed to be previous incarnations of Jorjani.

I will never forget the first of my past life regression sessions, at the age of 18. When I came back to my room that evening, I took a long hard look at myself in the mirror. Then, for the first time, I understood in much more tangible terms what Ian Stevenson had been on about when he pointed to morphological resonance across lifetimes. My face looks more than a little like Jason's countenance as I had seen it in historical photographs of him as a young man. My eyes are the same amber-tinged hazel color, and my right eyebrow arches almost as high above the left one as his did. My undyed hair is the same shade of brown as Jorjani's and even its natural texture is alike, just wavier as his would have been had it grown out longer.

I found the resemblance to be quite striking — accounting for the basic difference between typically male and female bone structure. I noticed that even my somewhat boyish body is similar to his at that time in his life when he was thinnest and most fit. I am somewhat more curvaceous — but not nearly as much as you would expect for a girl. I have really tiny tits — albeit with huge, and aggravatingly excitable nipples, which, together with my hypertrophied clitoris, became the butt of many cruel jokes made by mean-spirited girls in the high school locker room (especially after I came out as more interested in girls than guys). My shoulders were actually broader than Jason's. (I guess I'd have made a better rugby player.) Overall, I definitely had an androgynous look — but in a sleekly pretty way, not at all butch.

I digress in the direction of vanity. My first session in a Regression Room was unforgettable. I was already familiar with the procedure, in theory, but nothing can really prepare you for the experience of surrendering your naked body to the saltwater of the tank in the middle of the dark room, with a ceiling so high that it makes your heart sink to look up into its pitch blackness.

As the psychoactive drugs were administered through water-resistant adhesive patches, which also fastened the pulsed neural recalibration electrodes to my forehead, the therapist guided me, with her hypnotic voice, into a vivid visualization of what my subconscious knew to be the most traumatically significant event in my immediately preceding incarnation. That was the established method. Not to begin with one's death, even if it was a traumatic or violent one (as I eventually discovered that mine had been), but to zero in on the single most significant nexus and trace its branches of longer-term effects and root causes out from there, like tracing the dendrites in neurons as they light up during a brain scan.

The first thing that appeared from out of the darkness while I floated in the Regression Room was the ethereal image of a jellyfish, glowing with shades of blue light. Specifically, it appeared to be a huge man o' war. At first, it was floating with its tentacles reaching down toward my head and its bell just under the ceiling, giving me the impression that I was under water.

Jellyfish predate the dinosaurs by hundreds of millions of years, and they may outlive man. A jellyfish can lay up to 45,000 eggs in a single night. The cells of the immortal jellyfish change identity under stress, shedding tentacles and transforming into a polyp that perfectly clones the creature. Jellyfish are thriving under the same ecological stresses that threaten the survival of other animals in Earth's oceans. In fact, research has revealed that they are the dark energy of the Oceans.

Wind and tides (influenced by the Moon) cannot account for the amount of energy required for the degree of water-mixing that we observe. Bioengineers have used fluorescent dyes and underwater cameras to film the interaction between fluid and the pressure differentials in front of and behind the body of a jellyfish. What they found is that when the fluid moves from the high-pressure field in front of the jellyfish to the low-pressure field behind it, the water is trapped at the rear end of the jellyfish and moves along with it. On a large enough scale, significant oceanic turbulence and water-mixing is caused by the interaction between this displaced water and the cross-currents that eventually dislodge it. In other words, what appear to be miniscule forces that one imagines would be absorbed into the wind and tidal friction of the seas are actually capable of stirring up storms and possibly even climate change on a planetary level. It is relevant in this regard that some jellyfish are even longer than a blue whale, the largest surviving mammal on Earth.

Despite lacking a brain and spinal cord, the neural net around the inner margin of the jellyfish "bell" allows it to form images and see color through its 24 eyes, some of which are on stalks and capable of peering above the water. It is the only creature with a 360° field of vision. Jellyfish also afford us the ability to illuminate the invisible. The gene for the Green Florescent Protein (GFP) that makes them glow in the dark when they are agitated was isolated and used to develop florescent tracers for research on the progression of Alzheimer's disease and cancer.

They are deadly, and you usually cannot see them surrounding you. Harpoon-like cells lining the bell deliver their venom with a pressure hundreds of times stronger than the punch of a professional boxer. While some jellyfish stings only tingle, others can kill a person in under five minutes or leave their victim badly disfigured.

When the spectral jellyfish floating above me in the Regression Room wrapped its tentacles around my brain and body, a flood of memories came back to me. It was from a period in the life of Jason

Reza Jorjani that extended between 2016 and 2018. I processed these disturbing and convoluted memories for several weeks by writing out extensive notes. The vivid recall, over many regression sessions, was augmented by a treasure trove of Jorjani's correspondences that I secured from a closely guarded archive maintained by loyalists. Prior to my regression, I had never been afforded the opportunity to go through these. But once rumors of my being the reincarnation of Jason leaked out, one of these esoteric Prometheists who respected the Avalon family name let me go through them at my leisure. I read and reread my notes based on the past life regressions and reconstructions from reams of Jorjani's private letters, until their basic elements were branded in my mind. Their lines acted as cyphers to bring scenes from my past life into a present recollection that was at least as vivid as reliving incidents from my childhood. My notes, which I colorfully titled "Riding Satan's Ass," read something like the following…

CHAPTER 2

RIDING SATAN'S ASS

L IKE SOME ACCURSED LAIR of the fairy folk, the inside of the majestic building seemed incomprehensibly vaster than the space it took up along the street of this posh neighborhood in London. It had a central atrium *surrounded by numerous libraries*. I do not remember seeing a single other person while we were there, besides the security at the imposing front door. The place reminded me of the Illuminati estate depicted in Stanley Kubrick's *Eyes Wide Shut*. It is in one of the many dimly lit libraries cavernously encircling this mansion's central atrium that I had my first extensive meeting with Frederick Boulder.

Incongruously dressed in a bow-tied shirt and black leather jacket, Frederick Boulder struck me as a lanky, long-limbed man with mischievously wild eyes that darted around intensely to follow the Monarch butterfly of his mind. His closely trimmed, pointy beard made him look a bit like the Devil. There was a third man at the meeting. Frederick had put me in touch with Darius Guppy some months earlier. Unlike Frederick, Darius was a polished letter writer and we kept up a considerable correspondence until I had the pleasure of meeting him in person when he attended my talk at the London Forum a day before we reconvened in this quiet and cavernous mansion.

When Darius walked into the London Forum meeting, I spotted him immediately, and after I made my way through the crowd, we embraced in Persian fashion with kisses on both cheeks. The man certainly stands out. In fact, I would say he is the most handsome man that I've ever met. His mother, Shusha Guppy, is an illustrious Persian singer and writer of Bakhtiari descent. The Bakhtiari are known for their height and robust stature. But it is not just his looks. Darius has an aura about him, penetratingly intelligent but also profoundly charismatic. During my lecture on Heidegger, his eyes were closed in deep concentration. Occasionally he would nod approvingly, with a bit of a smirk. "That was brilliant!" he remarked, as the police burst into the venue at the end of my talk and escorted us out of the building with choppers overhead.

Later that evening, when we were cramped into a sort of safe house and right-wing salon, I noticed that Shahin Nezhad, the leader of the Iranian Renaissance, was looking across the room intently at Darius, who was sitting next to me. Shahin said, "Jason dear, Darius looks awfully familiar. I think I've seen him somewhere before." I replied, "No, you're remembering him from James Bond movies. He looks exactly like Sean Connery playing 007." Shahin's eyes widened in surprise behind those thick bifocals, and, after a bit of stunned silence, he blurted out, "You're right!" Darius smiled. In that charming British accent of his, he said, "I think I'll not comment on that."

It had been the question of Iran's future that made me take Frederick Boulder seriously in the first place. He had contacted me in the summer of 2016, praising *Prometheus and Atlas* to high heaven — or perhaps he was shouting its praises up from the depths of hell. Frederick introduced himself to me as the head of the British branch of the Vril Society — the occult group in which esoteric German aerospace projects had their earliest origins. I found what he was writing to me hard to believe, and his atrocious spelling and poorly punctuated messages did not help me to take him seriously. So, I would rarely respond to him. Then he offered to concretely assist my work with the Iranian Renaissance movement by putting me in touch with Michael Bagley, the President of Jellyfish Inc., which Frederick described as a private security and intelligence agency working with the Trump team to prepare a new United States policy regarding Iran and the Islamic world. I was told that General Michael Flynn clandestinely worked for Jellyfish, and I appreciated Flynn's position on how to deal with the Islamic threat. In fact, one of the close associates of the Iranian Renaissance, Erfan Ghaneifard, had translated Flynn's book into Persian.

I figured that engaging with Bagley would be a way to find out whether Frederick was a crank or whether other things he was telling me might be true. It turned out that Michael's clients mostly consisted of the chief executives of Fortune 500 companies. I first met with him months before the 2016 presidential election and then again in the early days of the new administration. Michael claimed that he would see President Trump on a regular basis, and he introduced me to others with even more access, including Walid Phares, who Michael described as "the shadow Secretary of State." He said that Rex Tillerson was just supposed to be a front man, and that when I spoke to Phares I should assume that I am essentially speaking directly to President Trump. He also explicitly stated that Walid was "Deep State" and had built his reputation in the intelligence community during the Lebanese Civil War.

I met Walid Phares and discussed Iran policy with him. Later on, I wrote him a very substantive letter warning the Trump administration not to go down the pro-Saudi path that it wound up choosing to pursue with respect to regime change in Iran. This was the secret plan that Hillary Clinton had for dividing and conquering Iran, and the main reason that I and so many others within the Iranian Renaissance movement supported Donald Trump was to make sure that it never actually became US foreign policy. The one thing that could turn the largely pro-American Persian people against the United States was American support for a Saudi-led Arab war against Iran.

The hook that Michael reeled me in with was a proposal that I act as a liaison who provides media content produced by the Iranian

Renaissance for Jellyfish to broadcast into the Islamic Republic of Iran from a facility in Croatia. But Frederick and Michael's interest in me was not limited to what we called "the Iran project." Frederick's group was the hidden virtual audience for my October 2016 Identitarian Ideas conference speech in Stockholm, "Occult Science and the Organic State," which secured me the position of Editor-in-Chief of Arktos within a week of having delivered it (so quickly that by the time the video footage was processed, the title appeared next to my name). At a meeting we had in Washington in an annex of the Old Ebbitt Grill, just across the street from the White House, which Michael only half-jokingly described as his "office," Bagley proposed to "take Richard [Spencer] out" and install me as the leader of the Alt-Right.

By then, I had met and befriended Richard Spencer during the infamous NPI 2016 "Hailgate" conference. I naively counter-proposed that Spencer (who I still hadn't gotten to know well enough) was a reasonable guy who would accept direction from above if it meant that, through a figurehead other than himself, he could have access to the President. Steve Bannon was known to be a reader of Arktos books and Michael's plan was to send me into the White House to cultivate a relationship with Bannon, and through him, to influence President Trump.

At the time, my main reason for wanting to have such influence was to help determine Iran policy. Michael claimed to have gotten at least one of my letters on this subject into the hands of the President. I wrote the letter, but it was co-signed by Shahin Nezhad. In it, on behalf of the Iranian Renaissance, I explicitly warned Trump not to pursue a pro-Saudi or generally pro-Arab strategy for regime change in Iran. In retrospect, I suppose that through that letter the President and his policymakers also acquired some fairly substantive intelligence on the outlook, intentions, and capabilities of the Iranian Renaissance movement.

Together with Frederick and Michael, a plan was hammered out to secure my position as the leader of the Alt-Right by creating a

corporate structure that unified the major institutions of the move-
ment, in both North America and Europe, bringing Richard Spencer's
National Policy Institute think tank together with Daniel Friberg's
European Arktos publishing house, and the Red Ice Radio and
Television network founded by Henrik Palmgren. A major investment
would allow me to become a majority shareholder both in this new
Alt-Right Corporation and in its would-be subsidiary, Arktos Media,
replacing Daniel Friberg as its CEO. When I expressed concern to
Michael about what this plan would mean for my academic career, he
replied, "What do you need an academic job for? You've been there
and done that. Now it's time for us to put some money in your pocket." When a man who routinely does work on contract for Fortune
500 executives says that, it certainly seems like an assurance that one
will not be thrown under the bus. Unless, as I later realized, the whole
thing was a set-up.

I was still very far from this realization when, in mid-December of
2016, Richard Spencer visited New York for a few days. His right-hand
man, former *Radix* journal editor 'Hannibal Bateman', slept over in
my Upper West Side apartment and Richard and I got to spend a lot
of time together. Between a business lunch at Persepolis on one day,
and a long evening that ended with a Dionysian, intoxicated hours-
long conversation in my living room, I seeded into Richard's psyche
the idea for a corporatist unification of the major institutions of the
Alt-Right movement. But Richard did not know something about this
act of inception, which I commemorated by leaving an Easter egg for
the future in a picture that I suggested we take in front of a statue of
Hermes, the Trickster, on that evening of December 17.

What Richard did not know I disclosed to him about a month
later, during a late-night dinner at the Hamilton restaurant in DC.
By then we had decided against renting an office in a Manhattan
skyscraper, in favor of a more private shared workspace in a townhouse in Alexandria, just outside of Washington, which would also
be Richard's apartment. I told him about my backers and that they

were going to provide me with a startup capital investment for our proposed business venture as part of a larger black budget project to be implemented by the Trump administration. With the birds of the Hamilton's taxidermy aviary as the only eavesdroppers, I whispered to Richard that this project involved the construction of a vast constellation of "micro-cities" in North Africa and Western Anatolia to contain the flow of migrants from the Islamic world, and to act as resettlement areas for illegal migrants expelled from Europe.

I was fully aware of the catastrophic damage that these migrants were doing to the social fabric of European countries: increasingly frequent acts of terror, molestation of women and children, and the spread of no-go zones where *sharia* law is enforced in ghettos of cities like London, Paris, and Frankfurt. So, I would have had no problem sleeping at night knowing that I was profiting from a project that would relocate these mostly military-aged Muslim men to places where they cannot volunteer to act as a fifth column for the Islamic State (IS). This was especially the case since I had been forced to helplessly witness IS destruction of the irreplaceable Iranian heritage in regions of northern Iraq and Syria that were once cultural centers of the Persian Empire. Not to mention the rape, enslavement, and genocide of the Yezidis.

After listening to my explanation of who my potential backers were, and of what capabilities they had, Richard agreed that granted such an investment would be forthcoming I would be on point. What was especially compelling to him was the promise of engagement, through me, with people inside the White House, such as Steve Bannon. I explained to Richard that my backers suggested that I could do this but that it would not be possible with Richard at the helm. He said, "I get it. All I want is not to be cut out."

The next day, Monday, January 16, 2017, which happened to be Martin Luther King Day, at the then secret HQ on King Street in Alexandria, with no furniture and Richard's belongings strewn across the upstairs bedroom in open suitcases, we co-founded the Alt-Right

Corporation. The other partners had not signed on yet. We called Daniel Friberg and Henrik Palmgren while perched on a windowsill, with nowhere to sit. Rosie Gray's photograph of us for her piece in *The Atlantic* was taken late that afternoon. She's right that the only thing to drink in the kitchen was a half empty bottle of whiskey. Well, half empty by the time she showed up.

I went on to discuss the plan for the capital investment and my leadership of the corporate unification of the Alt-Right with every single core board member of our company, including Arktos CEO Daniel Friberg. Daniel and I even shook on the deal in February of 2017, as captured by a photograph that is really haunting in retrospect. We are in front of a huge sunken ship that was famously looted while it spent years partly exposed in Stockholm's harbor. I used the lead-in to my speech at the Identitarian Ideas IX conference to hint at my central role in forming the Alt-Right Corporation. That policy speech, in February of 2017, just weeks after the formation of the corporation in late January, was supposed to be a prelude to the investment that I was promised would come later the same month.

The startup capital for the Alt-Right Corporation did not come through, as promised, in February. Michael told me that the funds would be available by March. Then Frederick explained to me why there would have to be another delay until May. Allegedly, both Neo-Cons and Neo-Liberals at high levels conspired to ensure that President Trump never authorized the construction of what they considered glorified concentration camps, even though Michael and Frederick assured me that the funding for the "micro-cities" had already been allocated. Another excuse was that there was a sustained campaign to purge the Trump administration of everyone connected to Jellyfish and potentially open to a secret policy dialogue with the Alt-Right. This began, in February, with the dismissal and threatened prosecution of General Michael Flynn, included the ouster of Sebastian Gorka, and ended with the forced resignation of Steve

Bannon in August — not coincidentally, the same month that I would leave the Alt-Right.

By then I was already under surveillance. As early as my October 2016 trip to Stockholm, I noticed I was being directly monitored by intelligence agents. One night when I came back to my hotel at 2 am, there was a man dressed in black sitting on a wheeled rotating chair in the hallway a few doors down from my room. Before scribbling some notes on his pad, he gave me a look like he was bored to death, and I was long overdue (the conference had started very late and ended hours later than expected). At first, I thought maybe he was a Swedish secret police agent who was tracking me because during this trip I visited the home of the notorious broadcaster Omid Dana, who is something like the Iranian Alex Jones. In retrospect, I changed my mind, because by the late summer of 2017, almost every time I would make a reservation at a restaurant in Manhattan using my telephone, someone who was all too obviously a spy would show up at the table next to mine. This was so evident, and so disturbing, that some of my friends stopped wanting to be seen with me in public out of a concern that these agents, usually sitting at the bar or at the next table over, would clandestinely photograph us together or record our conversation.

Months before my resignation from the Alt-Right I began writing letters to Frederick warning that I was losing control of my partners and influence over the direction of the corporation. I wrote that I would be forced to take drastic measures if he and Michael allowed me to be humiliated in front of them on account of hollow promises and repeated, false assurances that the obstacles had been cleared and the capital would finally reach us. That never happened before I was defamed in *The New York Times* on September 19th, 2017. I contacted both Frederick and Michael and gave them a final opportunity to do right by me. I would never have been in that pub being surreptitiously recorded by Patrik Hermansson (aka 'Erik Hellberg') if they had not set me up as an Alt-Right leader. Frederick later confessed that, although Hermansson was posing as a far-right student doing a dissertation on the suppression of free speech in academia, and although claiming that this was his cover for infiltration on behalf of an Antifa organization, the "Hope Not Hate" group that Hermansson supposedly worked for is a front for British intelligence.

Why did the promised funding for their plan never materialize? Is it because Michael really ran into trouble selling his North African concentration camps to the Trump administration, especially after Flynn and Bannon were purged? Perhaps motive can be reconstructed from consequences. What was the consequence of the investment not having come through? I became publicly identified as the unifier of the Alt-Right, a business partner of Richard Spencer, without being able to make a living out of it. At the same time, as Frederick and Michael made excuses and renewed their false promises, month after month, I was humiliated in front of my Alt-Right business partners and then sidelined by them. My association with the Alt-Right was also used to tar the reputation of the Iranian Renaissance.

Mr. Hermansson was sent my way by people closely connected with Frederick Boulder. It was Frederick who contacted the coordinators of the London Forum, Jez Turner and Stead Steadman, to set up that talk for me at the Forum on Saturday, February 4th, 2017, where Hermansson first set his sights on me. He also secured an invitation for Shahin Nezhad to give a speech as well. You see, Frederick Boulder co-founded the British New Right. It launched at a gathering with almost thirty people in Central London on January 16th, 2005.

By the time I spoke at the London Forum, twelve years later, Frederick's pedigree was impeccably established in British right-wing circles, including a leadership role in the Center for Anti-Marxist Studies at the London Club. This is remarkable, because in 2004, only a year before founding the British New Right, Frederick was writing letters to fellow "comrades" claiming to be a Communist who supports "the ideas of Stalin, Mao, Hoxha, Lenin." He would close these letters with the phrase, "All things Soviet." Unfortunately, I discovered this only after cutting ties with him.

Frederick was the London office head of Jellyfish Europe Limited, located at 4 Huntington House Street on Saint Paul's Avenue in Willesden Green. Although American journalists have described the founders of Jellyfish as the "sons of Blackwater," and it is true that Michael used to run intelligence operations for Blackwater founder Erik Prince, it seems that Jellyfish was more than the salvaged intelligence directorate of Blackwater. It is also relevant in this regard that at one of our meetings Michael told me that he had a bad falling out with Erik Prince, whose quasi-exile from the United States he considered well deserved.

So, Jellyfish was not, as some had assumed, a direct successor to Blackwater in the way that Xe was. It had another predecessor as well, a European group called g3i that was based in Rome and, at any given time, had 20 to 49 employees. Frederick was the UK representative of the g3i group, which he described as a "security company... with top level projects for oil and intelligence agencies." The company was particularly involved in "offshore" oil projects, which is interesting in light of the water element evoked by Jellyfish. Of course, "Blackwater" also suggests the blackness of oil mixed with the water surrounding offshore platforms — perhaps including platforms operating outside of the jurisdiction of any sovereign nation. From our earliest communications Frederick had emphasized Jellyfish's connections to offshore oil projects. He told me that OilPrice.com is a Jellyfish front.

On April 2nd of 2017, several months before the revolt against the Maduro government in Venezuela, Frederick sent me a nearly $1-billion itemized oil contract and business plan to pass on to Shahin Nezhad, whose day job was as a top-notch engineer at one of the world's largest oil companies. Frederick had confessed to me that his people were planning to overthrow the socialist government of Venezuela and that they needed to get into the oil industry there before doing so. Fortunately, Shahin came back and said that Occidental Petroleum was not capable of the project. This was fortunate because the attempted coup in Venezuela failed, and how curious that

President Nicolás Maduro's primary target in successfully resisting his engineered ouster was to go after oil bosses in a graft purge.

Venezuela was not the only failed coup that Jellyfish was involved in. While devouring his favorite Persian food at a lunch we had during one of his Manhattan business trips, Michael hinted to me that Jellyfish was behind the July 2016 Gülenist coup d'état in Turkey. He was exasperated and outraged at President Obama for helping to restore Erdogan to power. Erdogan went on to unleash a bloodbath of reprisals against the coup plotters and every conceivable collaborator. Later on, I learned that Frederick was involved with Fetullah Gülen.

That was not Frederick's only high-level contact in the Islamic world. The Emir of Qatar, Hamad bin Khalifa Al-Thani, was also an associate of his. It is during this Emir's rule from 1995 to 2013 that, due to a drastic engineering expansion of the small emirate's offshore oil and gas industry, Qatar was able to rise from third world status to become the richest country on Earth. Al-Thani brought both the Asian Games and the World Cup to Qatar. He hosted the UN Climate Change Conference in 2012. By 2013 his international investments exceeded $100 billion, including in The Shard, Barclays Bank, Heathrow Airport, Harrods, Paris Saint-Germain F.C., Volkswagen, Sicmens and Royal Dutch Shell. The Emir also founded Al Jazeera, the Arab world's most influential media group. He has been linked to the Islamic Republic of Iran and is a supporter of Hamas, which is why his son and successor came under pressure from Saudi Arabia. A man in Frederick's position who has business ties with the Emir of Qatar and deals in billion-dollar offshore oil projects should easily have been able to come through with the $1-million promised investment in the Alt-Right Corporation.

After bringing me to the London Forum, Frederick did not attend the talk himself. He complained about the Antifa demonstrators who surrounded the venue. To be fair, the protest was so large that there were even police helicopters circling the high-rise building, oddly enough, during my lecture on Heidegger and Technology. However, at the start of the event, Frederick was actually in the lobby of the conference hotel, and he sent up a certain Kroptin Mehrzad. Mehrzad is well-known as a leftist in London circles, who takes left-leaning positions in television interviews. This troubled Shahin and me, as well as our close associate Aria (Ali) Salehi Pamenari — a member of the board of trustees of the Iranian Renaissance. That is because we had encountered Kroptin a day or two earlier at an Iranian Renaissance event in London. He was not there as a sympathetic audience member but as a person carrying out surveillance, sitting alone in the back of the room with a disapproving look on his face. Kroptin did the same thing at the London Forum event where Shahin and I spoke. He came in, checked things out, reviewed the book stand, and then left grumbling about how we were a bunch of "Mosleyite Fascists."

What was a leftist like Kroptin doing at either event? Why was he an associate of Frederick, a scion of the British New Right and someone seemingly interested in facilitating the aims of the right-wing Iranian Renaissance? Frederick claimed to have left the conference hotel to meet Darius and bring him back inside. Darius was coming straight from the airport. He had flown in from South Africa, first-class, just to meet me in person. When Darius arrived, he was able to walk straight past Antifa and police into the hotel, "bold as brass" as he put it, like any other hotel guest. Frederick refused to go back inside with him, claiming that Kroptin had told him "it isn't safe." Why was a founder of the British New Right using someone who is rumored to be an asset of Scotland Yard to scope a place out? Kroptin also has connections to the Mojaheddin-e-Khalq Organization, radical left-wing Maoist-Islamists who are even worse than the Islamic Republic.

Where does the MEK (or MKO) get its money? Tel Aviv and the Israel Lobby in the United States. The Mossad trained the group's operatives to carry out assassinations of nuclear scientists in Iran and clandestinely gather intelligence on Iranian nuclear facilities. Meanwhile, the American Israeli Public Affairs Committee (AIPAC) successfully strong-armed Hillary Clinton's State Department to remove the Mojaheddin from its list of terrorist groups. Elie Wiesel and Alan Dershowitz were among the group's most prominent advocates.

Would it surprise you to learn that Frederick Boulder was also a Zionist? He put me in touch with Avi Churkin, an agent of the Mossad who divides his time between Jerusalem and Moscow and was a key liaison of the State of Israel to the government of South Africa. In a conversation we had late in the spring of 2017, Churkin, who was involved with the "micro-cities" project, nonchalantly mentioned to me that Frederick worked for British intelligence. He did not mean to reveal this. It was in the course of a conversation about something else that Churkin said, as if he assumed that I should already know it, "He's done some pretty impressive work for MI6." I made sure not to react with surprise, but I was deeply disturbed.

British intelligence had been involved in the occult since its inception. After all, Her Majesty's Secret Service was founded during the Renaissance by John Dee, Queen Elizabeth's court magician, who also set up the British Royal Navy. Satanist Aleister Crowley, the self-proclaimed "wickedest man in the world," waged an occult war against the Nazis for MI6. The motto of the secret intelligence service was "Semper Occultus."

At the age of 27, Frederick Boulder had been the director of the Association for the Scientific Study of Anomalous Phenomena located at Hatton Garden in London. It was founded in 1986 and he ran it from 11/27/1993 until 11/21/1994. About a year earlier, at the age of 26, Frederick had become chairman of the Rennes-le-Château research society. The society's activities at the mysterious village were the primary source for the book *The Templar Revelation*. Why did Frederick resign from the Association for the Scientific Study of Anomalous Phenomena only a year after assuming its directorship? He was subjected to investigation by MI6 for his connection to the French far-right and the Priory of Sion secret society at the heart of the mystery of Rennes-le-Château. MI6 suspected him of being involved in a plot to restore the Merovingian dynasty across all of Europe (an obvious danger to the British throne). At that point, he was caught up in this investigation and was probably either sincerely turned or coercively convinced to join British intelligence himself as an infiltrator of various groups with diverse ideological orientations. The only common denominator was that they were the most radical political groups, especially ones that defied clean-cut ideological definitions. They were those groups most threatening to the reigning Establishment.

It would be convenient to claim that my concern for the future of Iran was the only Achilles heel that Frederick aimed for when he set me up with the Alt-Right. But that would be a lie. As I've said, when he first introduced himself to me, it was in his capacity as the head of the London branch of the Vril Society. I would go on to discover, both through conversations with him and my own digging into his background, that the Vril was only one of many occult orders that Frederick belonged to. Just to give a few examples, he was a Freemason, a member of the Double Horizon Lodge of the United Grand Lodge of England, the Group of Thebes, the Osiridean Egyptian Orient, the Universal Grand Lodge of Argentina, and P2. (At one point, he wanted me to set up a New York branch of P2 for him by working together with members of Italians For Trump.) What I learned from Frederick, fairly early on in our communications, was that all of these esoteric societies were connected by an international network that transcended exoteric cultural, religious, and ideological boundaries, and that had been in place not for decades, but for centuries. Those who belonged to it were called "Illuminati."

In *Confessions of an Illuminati*, Leo Zagami came straight out and identified (by his real name) Frederick Boulder, his former associate and close friend, as a fellow member of the Illuminati. On at least a couple of occasions, Frederick told me that he was a member of the Illuminati and in one of these instances his remark suggested that he was recruiting me. Frederick publicly listed his profession as a "freelance librarian." Later, I learned that the term "librarian" has an esoteric meaning. Not long after Adam Weishaupt founded the Order of the Illuminati, in 1785 the Bavarian government outlawed the organization. The concern was that its members, who were also called "invisibles," were infiltrating numerous European regimes and institutions. When the Elector of Bavaria forced the Illuminati underground, they survived the ban on their activities by setting up libraries and disguising themselves as a network of book clubs. These "librarians" chose an owl above an open book as the seal of their secret society. A few years later they were implicated in catalyzing the bloodbath of the French Revolution, which dialectically led to the unification and modernization of Europe under the aegis of Emperor Napoleon Bonaparte. Later, they engineered the rise of Adolf Hitler. But they aren't Nazis. The owls are not what they seem.

The "esoteric projects" that Frederick invited me into were what was really irresistible. In retrospect, I realize that was undoubtedly by design. The most interesting of these was a clandestine exotic energy and propulsion project. This project was headed by a former NASA Jet Propulsion Laboratory scientist with an impressive resume who also had an interest in parapsychological phenomena. Frederick introduced me to this scientist because ever since *Prometheus and Atlas* won the 2016 Parapsychological Association (PA) book award, I had cultivated connections with prominent researchers in the PA and the related Society for Scientific Exploration (SSE).

Frederick had seen my personal photographs with men like Colonel John B. Alexander and Jacques Vallée, well-respected individuals with PhDs who were not only involved with paranormal research but had worked on classified military intelligence projects. Dr. Alexander's dissertation, at Harvard, was on "Thanatology," or the science of death, knowledge he would apply as he went on to become an advocate for the development of non-lethal weapons. I befriended Dr. Alexander and his wife Victoria through Jeffrey Mishlove, the parapsychologist who hosts the *New Thinking Allowed* program that I have appeared on many times. Frederick had probably seen the cheerful photograph I posted with John and Victoria Alexander during a visit to their home in July of 2016.

They had moved to Las Vegas around the same time as Mishlove to work on a paranormal research project funded by Robert Bigelow, the eccentric billionaire who would later award Mishlove half a million dollars for research that made the case for the soul's survival of bodily death. Bob Bigelow funded an interdisciplinary group of scientific researchers, including Colonel Alexander, to study the anomalous phenomena at the Skinwalker Ranch. In addition to his expertise in PsyOps and non-lethal weapons, in the 1980s John Alexander led an internal intelligence investigation into the alleged MJ–12 group. The conclusions of his investigation, and his view of the UFO phenomenon as a manifestation of the Trickster, can be found in the book *UFOs: Myths, Conspiracies, and Realities*. The book's foreword was written by John's close friend Dr. Jacques Vallée, who, despite decades of studying UFOs, is still a successful venture capitalist.

Jacques Vallée invited me to his San Francisco home on Saturday, April 8, 2017. Across from the sofa I sat on was a spectacular view of the skyline, with the Transamerica Pyramid right at the center of it. Jacques' second wife, Flamine, made us a delightful dinner. Frederick saw me post the photo that Flamine took of Jacques and I in his living room, and he wanted me to see if Vallée was interested in contributing to the project. Meanwhile, given the repeated funding delays, I was beginning to revert to my initial skepticism regarding Frederick despite his impressive connections. So, I was also interested in introducing Jacques to the ex-JPL engineer in order to get Jacques' advice on whether I was being manipulated by tricksters of the kind that he discusses at length in his book *Messengers of Deception*. Unfortunately, Jacques came down with an ear canal problem and he had scheduled surgery for later in the same week we had set the meeting with the project engineer. Jacques' daughter was staying at his apartment to look after him post-op, so we never got to regroup after the meeting to privately discuss his impressions of the project.

When I asked Frederick about the origins of this technology, he told me to read the works of Joseph P. Farrell on Project Chronos. He seemed to be amused by how close Dr. Farrell had gotten to the truth about *die Glocke*, the Nazi "Bell" device. That background research on my part culminated in the essay "Black Sunrise" published in *Lovers of Sophia* (Manticore 2017, republished by Arktos in 2019) and later expanded upon both in *Prometheism* (2020) and *Closer Encounters* (2021). I think that the concept I first defined at the core of that essay, namely "destructive departure in worldview warfare" (*Abbauender Aufbruch im Weltanschauungskrieg*), adequately grasps the aims, motivation, and modus operandi of the Illuminati network that Frederick belongs to. It is not, as I suggested in "Black Sunrise," a strictly Fascist organization, but one that uses Fascism and many other ideologies that would appear to contradict each other.

The "Bell" was a Zero Point Energy (ZPE) and propulsion device based on electro-magnetically powered torsion of a Mercury-Thorium serum. Hal Puthoff, a physicist who did decades of classified research for Naval intelligence and the National Security Agency, and who worked on contract for the CIA at the Stanford Research Institute, went on to research ZPE at his Institute of Advanced Studies in Austin, Texas. He was the next person in the SSE that I was going to reach out to, through Jacques who knew him well, to see if he would consult on the project. Dr. Puthoff knew that ZPE devices could be miniaturized for use in a wide variety of vehicles, or even for installation in anyone's backyard. However, if such a ZPE system were to be weaponized there would be "enough energy in the volume of your coffee cup to evaporate all the world's oceans many times over."

Jacques and I met with the power and propulsion project engineer over brunch at the Fairmont Hotel on Nob Hill in San Francisco on Monday, August 14, 2017. He showed us the blueprints for what was allegedly a retrofitting update of the 1940s Nazi "Bell" design, reconstructed to contemporary technological standards and miniaturized to fit inside of a car. The project was a system for electron harvesting

from a Mercury-Thorium "battery" for power and propulsion purposes. The presentation that was made to Vallée — in his guise as a
venture capitalist — pitched it as a clean energy alternative to coal-
burning plants, nuclear power, and other power generation systems
that adversely impact the environment.

Unlike these systems, the device did not need to be connected
to the power grid, thereby allowing for decentralized "off the grid"
operation of electrically powered devices and vehicles, within homes
and offices or traversing land, flying in the air, or navigating at sea.
The device had a modular design that made it scalable for power generation at various levels, from a small automobile to the largest cargo
ship. It could also power drones, provided that the casing of the drone
incorporated ceramic insulation of the Mercury-Thorium power cell.
This ceramic insulation had been a prominent part of the German
design of the Bell in Project Chronos.

Finally, just as in the nuclear industry, where applications included
electrical power, atomic weapons, and nuclear medicine, there were
also potential medical applications of this technology. The Mercury-
Thorium reactor could be used for treatment of cancers, since it
generates electrical impulses of a type that are destructive to cancer
cells (with less deleterious effects than in chemotherapy). For obvious
reasons, this venture capital-oriented presentation did not get into the
weapons application of the technology (which would not have been
lost on Puthoff).

After the meeting with Dr. Jacques Vallée in San Francisco I flew
to Newport Beach to visit with Dr. Fariborz Maseeh, an MIT-educated
Iranian innovator whose breakthroughs in micro-electro-mechanical
systems (MEMS), i.e. nanotechnology, allowed him to become a billionaire and "venture philanthropist" in the year 2000 at the age of
41. The previous summer Dr. Maseeh had flown me out to Newport
Beach to privately teach him the *Gathas* of Zarathustra. We had
met at the Pacific Club, next to the Duke Hotel where he put me up
for several nights. This time his secret proposal was to fund me to

write Iran's next constitution. When he contacted me, I was actually already in Los Angeles for the meetings where my colleagues in the Iranian Renaissance and I formed the Iranian United Front. Quite a synchronicity.

I told Fariborz that I had a date set to meet with Jacques Vallée in San Francisco but that I could return to the LA area after that if he wanted to meet while I was still on the West Coast. So, he flew me from San Francisco back to Newport Beach. I am mentioning the meeting with him in Newport Beach now because it figures in the other "esoteric project" that Frederick tried to involve me with. It was also based in Newport Beach and, given Fariborz's expertise in nano-technology and his venture philanthropy, Frederick wanted me to see if he would be willing to get involved. As it turns out, I did not pitch it to him, partly because Maseeh's proposal that I become Iran's Thomas Jefferson stunned me and I did not want to divert him from this.

The Illuminati project at Newport Beach revolved around race and genetic modification. This pet project of theirs was actually based in India, but a Vedic institute in Newport Beach played an important R&D role. During my second set of face-to-face meetings with him in London, in the week of May 22, 2017, Frederick explained that this project involved the excavation and collection of remains of a group of very tall hominins with naturally elongated skulls. Frederick and his associates were obsessed with the idea of "Atlantis" and interpreted these finds as remains of the Atlantean engineers of the civilizations of Peru, Mexico, Egypt, Mesopotamia, and of equally titanic ruins as of yet unearthed in the Gobi Desert. The things that Frederick shared with me suggested that they were trying to redevelop this phenotype along with the psychical abilities that set these early humans apart from us. Their ultimate aim was a hybridization of that form of early humanity together with modern man, who has certain analytical and creative cognitive capacities that these giants lacked. After the hit pieces in *The New York Times*, *Newsweek*, and other mainstream media outlets in September, my letters to venture philanthropist Fariborz Maseeh went unanswered. Before the defamation, Maseeh had planned to bring me out to his ranch in the fall of 2017 to have in-depth discussions about my work on the proposed Persian Constitution. So much for becoming Iran's Thomas Jefferson.

Why was I continually encouraged to present policies to the shadow Secretary of State, in person, and to the President of the United States, in writing, which Michael had already told Frederick were unacceptable? How could this have been allowed to go on for so long that, on August 11 of 2017, we formed the Iranian United Front (*Jebheyé Irângarâyân*) in Los Angeles, unifying the most established patriotic political parties opposed to the Islamic Republic, including the Pan-Iranist Party, under the false assumption that the Trump administration would give us a serious hearing? Perhaps because certain agencies wanted the Iranian Renaissance to put all of its eggs in one basket, so that they could break them all at once. Perhaps they wanted to do the same thing to the Alt-Right.

As the youngest and most intellectual member of the new coalition, I was the one who named it *Jebheyé Irângarâyan* (literally "Iranist Front") during one of the several days and nights of meetings we had in Los Angeles from August 11 to 13, while my Alt-Right partners were making a mess in Charlottesville. My speech introduced the coalition to the English-speaking world. Tarring me could potentially be used to destroy the whole coalition. On September 28, 2017, the mainstream Persian media outlet *Radio Zamaneh* ran a hit piece on me even more libelous than that of *The New York Times*, titled "In America, an intellectual leader of Iranian Fascism has been dismissed from teaching." The Iranian (Persian) Renaissance Foundation is referred to as an imperialistic "fascist" organization, and its fate is explicitly and irrevocably tied to mine. This was done to take us out of the picture when the key moment arrived, sooner than some expected, in the winter of 2017–2018.

The Iranian uprising against the Islamic Republic began in late December of 2017. I had been staying at Shahin Nezhad's home during the *Yalda* (Mithraic Christmas) holiday, so I bore witness to some of his initial communications with people inside the country. By the time I was back in New York, the demonstrations had become much more fearsome and widespread. No one in the mainstream media seems to have noticed that the uprising in Iran took place six months after the most well-established Iranian opposition groups were unified for the first time in 38 years of theocratic tyranny. Or maybe they were told not to notice. I will never forget that late summer night in Los Angeles when we, the founders of the Iranian United Front, sat in a circle, with our faces illumined only by the light of a pool of fire in a dark courtyard. By the year's end, that fire spread to 70 Iranian cities.

For some time, a faction within the so-called "hardliners" of the Islamic Republic had been considering embracing the idea of an Iranian Renaissance in order to salvage some of the core structures of the Islamic Republic that protect Iran's banking system from globalist control and secure Iran's territorial integrity in the face of foreign-backed separatist agitators. This faction was centered around Esfandiar Rahim Mashaei, who briefly served as Mahmoud Ahmadinejad's Vice President and was unsuccessfully backed by Ahmadinejad to run against Rouhani (because the Guardian Council deemed Mashaei a "deviationist" for his nationalism). Mashaei's circle had been reading Iranian Renaissance texts, such as *Aryan Imperial Political Thought* by Shahin Nezhad. As part of the core structure of the Islamic Republic themselves, these hardliners were able to secure permits for demonstrations against worsening economic conditions and corruption. Ahmadinejad gave a speech threatening the regime's corrupt establishment shortly before the protests began, and in very short order he was arrested by the Islamic Republic for provoking unrest. The slogans of the Ahmadinejad-associated protests condemned the so-called "reformist" Rouhani administration for its broken promise that Iran's concessions in the nuclear deal would raise living standards. These legal demonstrations were organized in the city of

Mashhad, the hometown of Shahin Nezhad, which is also where the grand Shi'ite shrine of Imam Reza is located.

At the same time, the Iranian Renaissance planned a celebration for Ferdowsi's birthday. The event was originally scheduled for the 27th of Âzar (his actual birthday), but then Shahin rescheduled it for the 2nd of Dây (the date that he gives for his birth, not adjusted to changes in the calendar system), or December 23, 2017. The tomb of the author of the Persian national epic, the Shâhnâmeh, is in Tous, just outside of Mashhad. The idea was to replicate our Cyrus Day event, when hundreds of thousands gathered at the tomb of Cyrus the Great on October 29, 2016. Once busloads of ultra-nationalists arrived at the tomb, they were informed that their rally permit was revoked. These angry ultra-nationalists were diverted to Mashhad where they encountered the legal hardliner demonstrations, and joined them, shifting the slogans in a nationalist direction. Then they went back home to the smaller cities and towns where the Renaissance had its largest following, rather than in more Westernized major metropolitan areas. The rest is history.

The violent protests that engulfed more than 70 Iranian cities and towns from December of 2017 through January of 2018 were fundamentally different from the Green Movement of 2009. Back then I was a solidarity demonstration organizer and a human rights activist running the New York Chapter of *Iran Crime Watch*, an organization set up by Akbar Moarefy. My primary responsibility was lobbying the ambassadors of the member states of the United Nations Security Council. I also wrote a letter to then US Secretary of State Hillary Rodham Clinton. Unlike in 2009, no one was asking "where is my vote?" and not so much as a green handkerchief could be seen on the streets during this uprising. The slogans were not calling for democracy or demanding so-called 'free elections.' Instead, masses of protesters were yelling: "We are Aryans, we don't worship Arabs!" "Islam and the Quran, we sacrifice them both to Iran!" "Whether by cannons, guns, or tanks—the clergy have to go!" and "Reza Shah, may your soul rejoice!" By the first week of January 2018, the protesters chanting his name were burning down mosques and setting fire to the religious schools that train mullahs and produce the regime's reigning ayatollahs.

Reza Shah came from the rural working class, and contrary to the more peaceful nature of the upper-class 2009 protest movement, this working-class uprising was a violent insurrection spread across the countryside rather than concentrated in large cities. People in the streets were not demanding a chaotic 'democratic' revolution, one that would decimate the nation's industries and threaten its territorial integrity. Rather, they were inviting a military coup and removal of the ayatollahs under martial law conditions. It is safe to say that it resembled a "color revolution" in no way whatsoever. In fact, I knew from having discussed the situation at length with Avi Churkin that the Mossad was taken completely by surprise. Churkin informed me that the Mossad was tracking the uprising at more than 1,200 distinct flashpoints across the country (on a 'big board' that synthesizes data from various sources, including hacked CCTV cameras), but they had no hand in catalyzing the protests and were unable to control them. Meanwhile, the Trump administration had not yet even formulated, let alone implemented, a cohesive plan for how to effect regime change in Iran.

I know that because I played the largest single role in drafting the first such plan, and we were still in the process of conveying it to the President when the uprising began. After my defamation in September of 2017 resulted in a cutting of ties with Jellyfish, through which we had initially hoped to amplify our ability to organize the opposition within Iran, the secret triumvirate within the Iranian Renaissance decided to salvage our political project and use a different angle of approach to the Trump administration.

I call it a triumvirate because during the time we were dealing with Michael Bagley and Frederick Boulder, it consisted only of Shahin Nezhad, Aria Salehi Pamenari, and myself. Although Shahin and

Aria participated in one video conference call with Michael and met Frederick in London on a couple of occasions during our February 2017 London Forum visit, I was the agreed upon point of contact with these operatives. Due to the charter of our 501c3 cultural organization, none of these political activities were approved by the board of trustees or the board of directors of the Persian (Iranian) Renaissance Foundation. They were secret.

In October of 2017, Siegfried Shahram Aryan, was brought into this secret group. Shahram was a rocket scientist with a PhD in theoretical Physics, and an advanced degree in biomedical science. He also knew six or seven languages, including Ancient Greek, Latin, Pahlavi, and Old Persian. The man was a polymath. He was the single largest contributor to the Iranian Renaissance think tank, regularly delivering erudite and captivating lectures on Iranian history. Much of what I learned about racial differences in IQ and genocidal miscegenation as a factor in the decline of Iranian Civilization came from his think tank lectures. S. S. Aryan would often joke that he himself was a descendent of the Turkic peoples most responsible for this decline.

Since Aria is not an ideas man, Shahram was brought in to collaborate with Shahin and me on drafting a proposal for regime change in Iran. The proposal would then be conveyed to Vice President Michael Pence via a certain Texas billionaire who was a business partner of Donald Trump. This man had told Aria that Pence, not Trump, was responsible for coming up with an Iran policy. Whatever Pence decided on would be approved by the President. This made some sense to me considering the fact that back in 2009, it was Pence who most sternly chastised Obama for not backing the protesters and gave a most rousing speech in Congress calling for America to help free Iran. We were assured, in no uncertain terms, that despite Trump's infamous "Arabian Gulf" speech, a definitive and detailed Trump Iran policy did not yet exist (in November).

During November and December of 2017, Shahin, Shahram, and I wrote a detailed proposal for US Vice President Michael Pence. The document is, without exaggeration, about 70% my work. In the draft stage Shahram was assigned with writing the "Historical Analysis," I wrote the "Analysis of the Regional Situation," and Shahin wrote the "Sociological and Demographic Analysis." However, given their poor English, their sections had to be reworked, and I was instructed to edit them into a stylistic harmony with each other and with my section. Most importantly, I wrote the "Executive Summary" (then we nit-picked it as a group and I repeatedly revised it accordingly). Although, of the four people who signed the document, only Aria's contact information is listed in the final draft, since he was, via the Texas bil-lionaire, the point of contact with Vice President Pence, Aria played absolutely no role in formulating the contents of the proposal. I even-tually presented this proposal to a member of the National Security Council at a bunker underneath Capitol Hill, in late February of 2018. Shahin Nezhad, Aria Salehi, and President Trump's business partner were all in attendance. The Texan flew in and met us at Capitol Hill. In my first meeting with him, I clearly impressed this Davos summit core member. A man of few words, who is not easily impressed, he turned to Aria and Shahin and said, "I *like* this guy."

One night in early 2018, Shahin Nezhad called and asked me to replace Dr. Ali Akbar Jafarey as his doctoral dissertation advisor. John Morgan of Arktos was visiting at the time, and even though he could not understand the conversation that Shahin and I had in Persian, I am sure that he remembers the impression that it made on me. Perhaps he could also tell that I was somewhat at a loss for words. I be-lieved Shahin when, on numerous occasions, he had referred to me as a member of his family, but I was still not prepared for such an honor, especially given the standing that Dr. Jafarey had as the person who effectively began the Neo-Zoroastrian movement. He was probably the most revered spiritual teacher in the entire Iranian community, not including ayatollahs and their devotees. It was his revolutionary translation of the *Gathas*, made in the 1980s, that introduced me to the thought of Zarathustra when I was a teenager. Later, while visiting

Tehran, I had acquired Jafarey's Persian edition, which deepened my understanding of the spiritual fountainhead of Iranian Civilization. Shahin formally converted to Zoroastrianism under the guidance of Jafarey, who officiated at his wedding with Artemis. So, when he asked me, I replied, only half-jokingly, "Godfather, it's an offer that I can't refuse." That is not to say that I did not try to have him reconsider, or at least consider the consequences for his own reputation. Conferring a doctorate on someone is not a joke, I explained to him, and how it would look if a "fascist" approved his. He said, "Jason dear, as far as they're concerned, we're all fascists."

I immediately perceived that Shahin had several secret aims. The most significant, and the most gracious, of them was to use this project to bolster my resume for any future Persian political career. The second was to help reestablish my academic standing in the wake of the defamation that threatened to destroy my career teaching at American universities. The third was to bring me under the influence of the man who was his own idol, Ardeshir Babakan (180–242), founder of the Sassanian dynasty and the third and final Persian Empire before the Islamic Conquest of Iran. Shahin so revered Ardeshir that when, during my Christmas (i.e. *Yalda*) season stay at his home, I brought him and his wife Artemis a matching pair of cufflinks and earrings based on a Sassanian coin, he was convinced that the portrait was one of Ardeshir.

That the leader of the Iranian Renaissance would write a dissertation on the political philosophy of the founder of the Sassanian dynasty is not surprising. It was a perfect follow-up to Shahin's two previous books, and I have reason to believe that it was a preface to a planned drafting of Iran's future constitution. Shahin's first book, *Dramatic Climax before the Decline*, is one of only two texts that aims to be for the third Persian Empire what Gibbon's *Decline and Fall* was for understanding the collapse of the Roman Empire. Shahin's second book was titled *Imperial Aryan Political Thought*. The term "Imperial Aryan" here, namely *Iranshahri* (or, more precisely, *Iranshahrig*) in

Middle Persian, is the adjectival form of *Iranshahr*, a contraction of the Ancient Persian *Aryana Khashatra* or "Aryan Imperium" — the official name of Iran during the Sassanian period, beginning with Ardeshir I.

I had reason to believe that Shahin Nezhad would position me to be his successor and propel me into a leadership role in Iran that would, on the face of it, seem very unlikely. Maybe "reason" is not the right word here. Beyond the nature of our relationship and the potential that I saw in the Iranian Renaissance at the time, as well as my ancestral pedigree as the great grandson of a Qajar monarch, there was an experience that I had in Iran during my stay there in the summer of 2004 that rendered this possibility more realistic to me than it would be based only on these other factors.

During my first three nights in Tehran, which were the first nights that I had spent in Iran (in this lifetime), I had a recurring dream. A huge griffin would sweep down over me with the sun blazing behind it, making it cast its shadow over me. When the *homa* (Persian royal griffin) got close, screeching loudly, I felt a heat so intense that it was like I was going to burst into flames. Then my body would hurl upwards in bed, ready to throw up onto the floor. That is how I was jolted out of the exact same dream, three nights in a row. The nausea was intense, as if it were caused by radiation exposure.

I had no idea what this recurring dream meant until years later. When I was doing research in the New York Public Library for my study of Sadegh Hedayat's *The Blind Owl*, namely the book that eventually became *Novel Folklore*, I came across a fascinating passage buried in one of Hedayat's obscure books about Iranian folklore. Hedayat writes that there is a folk tradition according to which: "If the griffin casts its shadow upon you by night, then you shall reign by divine right." How does a *homa* cast a shadow over you *at night*? In a dream, where the sun is shining behind the griffin.

That was not the only strange experience I had during that trip to Iran. Another occurred on the night after hiking all the way up to the

Cave of Shapur in the mountains of the southern Fars province, where a grotto atop the mountain features a rock-hewn sculpture of the Sassanid Emperor Shapur I, the son of Ardeshir Babakan and patron of the Gnostic prophet Mani. Not a soul was in sight. After we paid our respects to Shapur in the eerie silence of the dark cave, my driver, who had volunteered to climb with me, suggested that we make haste back down the very steep boulder-filled slope when, around sunset, we heard the growls of mountain lions pursuing us at a distance. When he finally dropped me off back at my hotel in Shiraz, it was well after midnight. With all of the restaurants closed, the only thing for me to eat or drink was a large frozen bunch of Shiraz wine grapes that I had been keeping in the refrigerator. While gorging on these, I fell asleep from exhaustion with the lights still on.

When I woke up, everything in my hotel room was exactly the same. Except that the room was full of men in black suits, wearing black ties over white shirts, with some of them holding black hats in their hands. I was so alarmed that my first reaction was to reach toward the phone to call security, but then I noticed that the Men In Black were gathered around the bathroom and curiosity compelled me to scope out what was going on in there. I got up and walked to the open bathroom door, at which point I could see, from in between the bodies of the MIBs, that Mohammad Mossadegh was lying in my bathtub. He was old and frail, and he gestured in such a way as to wave them off to the sides — so that we could see each other clearly — and he pointed toward me with his bony index finger. The Men In Black turned their heads back to look at me, and looked at each other in annoyance as well, as if they were all opportunistic suitors who had just been brushed aside in favor of some unknown person. A couple of the men helped him out of the tub and wrapped him in a towel, then brought him to sit on the bedside. It was one of those rooms with two beds, separated by a night table, so I was sitting on the edge of the other bed, facing him.

At this point, all of the men in suits disappeared — and Mossadegh transformed into a woman. She was a beautiful older woman, younger than Mossadegh, but still with a wizened look. She had a lot of grey and white in her wavy hair, which curled at the ends. There was profound wisdom, acceptance, and invitation in her gaze. I saw the best of myself in her, but she knew more about me than I did. The towel had fallen around her waist, and I got up and placed the palm of my hand on one of her breasts. I felt the most intense sense of communion with this woman. It was as if we melted into one. It was an intensely erotic experience with an ecstasy beyond the merely sexual. Then I woke up, lying on that bed, with the no longer frozen Shiraz grapes next to me.

I eventually met this woman, albeit at a much younger age than she appeared in that hotel room in Shiraz. Nassim Nouri reached out to me on Facebook after hearing my interview on *Prometheus and Atlas* with Red Ice Radio in 2016. She did not know that, while we were Facebook friends, I had amassed an archive of photos of her because I was fascinated by her resemblance to the woman in the Shiraz hotel room — albeit, about 25 years younger in appearance. We had exchanged only a handful of Facebook messages. Then, on the night of August 11, 2017, after my keynote speech at the event forming the Iranian United Front in Los Angeles, I was out in Westwood (the Persian District of LA) with Shahin Nezhad, Aria Salehi, and a handful of other people from the Iranian Renaissance. We were supposed to go to Sholeh (The Flame) Restaurant, but we decided to have Persian Pizza instead. Sitting at the bench of the Persian Pizza sidewalk café in "Tehrangeles" I suddenly heard someone call out my name. I turned around and it was Nassim, heading to meet some friends at Sholeh restaurant for dinner. (Had we gone there, as planned, I would also have run into her.) I got up and walked over to her. We stood silently transfixed with an invisible electricity coursing between us that was more magnetically intense than anything that I have ever felt with anyone. Fascinatingly, although Nassim and I did not hug and kiss, Kourosh Aladdin, one of the members of the Renaissance, who was intently watching us, swears that he saw us do that. He must have seen the aura or spectral essence of the event.

Considering the fact that I met Nassim in the flesh during the most important event ever held by the Iranian Renaissance, it is ironic that my relationship with her would end my work with them. Within a year of having met Nassim, incidents involving Shahin and Aria, and dealings with Reza Pahlavi, the CIA, the Trump administration, and so forth, had convinced me that even the best elements of the so-called "opposition" to the Islamic Republic of Iran were at the very least unreliable. There was, in my view, a serious possibility that any regime change spearheaded by these external forces, and the foreign interests on which I now realized that even the best of them were dependent, would lead to the territorial disintegration of Iran. This view was implicitly reflected in my book *Iranian Leviathan*, which was released in the late summer of 2018. I wrote the book in a way that would promote a political solution from within Iran itself, in an attempt to reach out to that faction around Esfandiar Mashaei, who had reached out to Shahin Nezhad and been rebuffed.

For their part, the leadership circle of the Iranian Renaissance saw my proposal for a hybrid Aryan-Shi'ite transition in Iran, and my somewhat sympathetic treatment of Ayatollah Khomeini (a shrewd overture on my part to nationalists within the IRGC), as evidence that I was being manipulated by the Islamic Republic. Unfortunately, they did not have the decency to directly (albeit falsely) accuse me of having made a deal with the intelligence services of the regime. Instead, word reached me that the leadership of the Renaissance had (deludedly) come to believe that Nassim, who by then had become my fiancée, was an agent of the Islamic Revolutionary Guard Corps Intelligence Directorate, and that she was subjecting me to psychological manipulation and had seduced me into collaborating with the regime. Anyone who knows the least bit about Nassim would recognize how utterly preposterous this allegation is. It was also tremendously disrespectful in its disregard for my level of intellect, scholarship, and discernment.

In October of 2018, select members of the Iranian Renaissance had planned to go to Tajikistan to attend a scholarly conference on Iranian Studies and to privately meet with President Emomali Rahmon. Considering the financial consequences of my defamation, the travel expenses and hotel room had already been paid for by one of my staunchest supporters in the movement. Without having the backbone to tell me upfront that they were not going to take me (the only actual scholar of the group) together with them to the conference and the meeting with the Tajik President, they unilaterally cancelled my participation by simply disengaging with me and leaving for Tajikistan. I could, and initially did, accept this as an understandable response to the content of *Iranian Leviathan*, which had after all been written with funding from individuals in the leadership of the Iranian Renaissance. But when I found out that in secret discussions, they had decided not to take me along because they believed that I was under the thumb of Nassim, and that whatever I heard at the meeting with President Rahmon would be conveyed, via her, to IRGC Intelligence, I immediately resigned in protest from my position as Senior Advisor to the Persian Renaissance Foundation (without publicly stating my reasons).

Their suspicions were particularly absurd considering the work that I had done to engage elements within the Israeli government. The hidden subtext of my public discourse of "Iranian Zionism" was a very private attempt to engage with pro-Iranian elements within Israel who, on account of their zealous religious faith, see Iran as a divinely chosen land that could once again play the role that Cyrus the *Moschiach* and other Persian kings such as Xerxes had played in protecting the Jewish people. There was a faction to the right of Netanyahu who held such views, and they had managed to maneuver one of their own, Avigdor Lieberman, into the position of Israeli Defense Minister. I wrote a letter to Lieberman. I received confirmation that this letter made it to his desk, via a certain Mossad agent on the Greek island of Kos. Unfortunately, the coalition government of

Israel fell apart and Prime Minister Netanyahu took over the duties of Lieberman, simultaneously serving as Defense Minister.

Once Netanyahu consolidated power, I attended a meeting with two Jewish New York businessmen who I was given to understand were also high-level Mossad operatives and close friends of "Bibi" Netanyahu. An associate of mine set up the meeting, at a posh Italian restaurant in midtown Manhattan, but I was the one who made the pitch to them that a strong nationalist regime in Iran was actually to the benefit of Israel. I cannot say who these two individuals were, because they threatened my life (no less than three times) if I were to reveal their identities. What I can say is that despite being impressed with me at the meeting, when the two of them got back to my associate later on, they told him that their background check had revealed that I was under the surveillance not only of their own Mossad, but of at least three other intelligence agencies based in America, Britain, and Iran. "We don't know what this guy's done," they said, "but we've never seen anyone under this kind of surveillance before. Don't bring him to another meeting. They'll close all the doors on you."

"Come down from off of Satan's ass!" (*Az kharé Shâytân biyâ pây-in!*) This is a Persian expression that was directed at me far more than once in my life, including by my colleagues in the Iranian Renaissance. In the Persian language, a person who is, as it were, *riding Satan's ass* is someone up to no good, but in a very particular way. To ride Satan's ass means to engage in recklessly dangerous and often morally questionable behavior, usually motivated by outrageous or outlandish ideas. This ride is not supposed to end well. It is possible to ride Satan's ass all the way into hell. But this is not at all the same kind of expression as "the path to hell is paved with good intentions." Nor is this a path to hell that consists of a long series of mere blunders that eventually lead one, haphazardly, into a morass that becomes inescapable. There is a certain defiant, perhaps even haughty, pride to the rider of Satan's ass. While he realizes that he may appear foolish to some, he is a trickster convinced of his own cunning intelligence. Yet, in the eyes of most people, he is a fool — possibly even a lunatic. So, they tell him to come down off the infernal ass before irreparable harm is done. I never listened. After all, I have Phenomenal Authorization.

CHAPTER 3

PHENOMENAL AUTHORIZATION

A FTER MY FIRST few sessions of past life regressions, my mother forced me to undergo special psychiatric evaluations. Instead of being proud that her daughter was the reincarnation of the founder of the movement that she had devoted her life to designing buildings for, my mother was full of jealousy and resentful rage. She also seemed to be terrified that these claims would tarnish the Avalon family name. Terrible catfights broke out between us — in the course of which many architectural blueprints of hers and many drawings of mine were destroyed. She also attempted to erase the extensive notes that I had taken, and which I've largely reproduced in the preceding narrative of the catastrophic period in Jorjani's life from 2016 to 2018. I could see why Prometheists wait until after high school to undergo past life regression, because had I still been surrounded by the boys — and especially the girls — in my school when this happened, I doubt that I would have survived the added stress of the violent resentment and vicious humiliations that would undoubtedly have been directed at me. In the end, the most esteemed psychiatrists and parapsychologists in the movement grudgingly came to a consensus assessment that I was, in all likelihood, the reincarnation of Jorjani. But the damage was done as far as my relationship with my mother was concerned. We never spoke again, and I refused to appear with her at any function.

Though I lost my mother, I gained others who brought me under protective wings that were much needed in the wake of this scandal. Had I continued living on the campus of Gotham University during my college years, I suspect that there would have been a considerable threat to my personal safety. I do not mean from agents of the Imperium so much as from within the movement itself. In every ideological or religious movement there are self-appointed guardians who, one or two generations after the death of the founder, come to see themselves as gatekeepers to, and guarantors of, his legacy at the same time as they betray the founder's ethos at the most fundamental level. Prometheism was no exception. It reminded me of the story of the Grand Inquisitor in Dostoyevsky's *Brothers Karamazov*. Sadly, my mother was one of these inquisitors.

The gatekeepers of Prometheism saw the potential Return of Jorjani as their worst nightmare. They were ready to murder me, ostensibly to protect my own legacy. But there were others, a secret society of rogues, who claimed to possess an esoteric interpretation of the thought of Jorjani, and who were ready to help me better understand myself and steal back the fire that I started nearly a century ago. We would have meetings late into the night at an apartment that they helped me to secure with the substantial cryptocurrency that I had inherited from my father. Meanwhile, at the university, I double majored in Philosophy and History, graduating with highest honors despite being sleep-deprived during most of my classes.

This rogue council of esoteric Prometheists became the occulted advisors that reviewed and critiqued my philosophical writing as I went on to four years of graduate studies at Gotham University, ending with a doctoral degree obtained in 2103 at the relatively young age of 26. Within a year (thanks to the facilitation of the secret group), this infamous dissertation was published with the title *Chaos, Order, and Progress*. Infamous because it was an ontological and epistemological critique of Jorjani's thought, coming from a young PhD who was now widely known within "the movement" to have turned out to be the reincarnation of Jason when she underwent that Prometheist rite of passage that is past life regression.

In my dissertation, I argued that Jorjani's conception of "Order" and his formulation of its relationship with "Chaos" was problematic in terms of the idea of social and historical "Progress" that he wanted to affirm. (Forgive me if I tend to refer to myself in the third person here, as I obviously did when I wrote *Chaos, Order, and Progress.*) Traditionalists see Chaos as a mere degradation of Order. To them, Order — which is called *Rta* in Sanskrit and *Cosmos* in Greek — is an eternal structure of Being. This is conceived of as a Macrocosm, which may be mirrored (or distorted) to a greater or lesser degree of fidelity by the Microcosm of the individual person and the collectivity of a society. The Order itself never changes. Even its variant instantiations on the Microcosmic level follow fixed patterns of increasingly degraded fidelity, until "the gods" (the Hindu *Devas*, or Greek Olympians) restore order at the end of every cycle. By contrast, the essence of Modern thought about the relationship between Order and Chaos is that emergent and determinate Order draws from out of a background of indeterminate Chaos as a wellspring of innovative Creativity, thereby yielding Progress in all domains — albeit not necessarily in anything resembling a straight line, and potentially admitting of many dialectical regresses and triangulations within an overall forward-oriented developmental trajectory. All legitimately Modern thought is teleological (goal-directed) in this way.

Jorjani fell short by failing to provide a coherent and cohesive definition of "Order" as distinct from the pure potentiality of Chaos from which it draws so as to be dynamic, and therefore Progressive, rather than static in the way that *Rta* is conceived of as being. This, despite the fact that in *Iranian Leviathan* he had provided himself with the resources to do so in the course of his explication of the hypostatization of primordial Chaos as *Âz* and his discussion of its relationship with *Ashâ Vahishtâ* as the ordering-principle at work in the evolutionary force of *Spentâ Mainyu*. All he had to — I mean that I had to do — was read these ideas back into the ontological framework developed in *Prometheus and Atlas* and *Prometheism*. The explanation of the psychical/biological unfolding of the *imago* of superhuman existence from out of the *larval* form of humanity, which culminates the argument of *Novel Folklore* (again advanced in the context of ancient Iranian theosophy) and the exploration of the modus operandi of the "Prometheaion" as a re-programmer of the quantum computational Cosmos in *Closer Encounters*, could also have been drawn from for the sake of providing a positive definition of "Order" qua *Ashâ* as a "progressive" (*spentâma*) structure over and above the Chaos that creative evolution requires as an inexhaustible background of undefined potential.

Thinking of history with a view to a purposive aim, unfolding progressively on the way to a projected "end of history" — inevitably framed as a Utopia — is something that we first see in Zarathustra. In my dissertation, I argued that the ancient Iranian prophet is, strictly speaking, the first "Modern" thinker (in the post-Atlantean historical record that has been left to us). Zarathustra's understanding of the relationship between Chaos, Order, and Progress reemerges, perhaps not coincidentally, after the late 18th-century French translation of the *Avesta*. Georg Hegel clearly owes a debt to it, and thus, so does Karl Marx, at least indirectly. But it can already be seen in the writings of the Marquis de Condorcet and, especially, the philosophical project of Auguste Comte. My thesis argued that Jorjani ought to have taken Comte more seriously and looked past Comte's patronizing and paternalistic attitude toward women (which is ironic, since I was now incarnated *as* a woman).

Whether or not he realized it, Comte was channeling and refining Zarathustra. Comte's "Religion of Humanity" is closer to what Zarathustra was trying to articulate than the travesty that Zoroastrianism became by the Sassanian period in Imperial Iranian history. As in the case of the gospel of the Superman preached by Friedrich Nietzsche, who adopted Zarathustra as his mouthpiece for good reason, the "Religion of Humanity" presupposes the death — no, the murder — of any transcendent God akin to the Macrocosmic Brahman of the Traditionalists. Instead, what Counter-Traditional Modernists deify is Humanity's own Promethean power of industrious and innovative self-perfection that stops at nothing short of the recreation of Man — as an ungodly self-creation, in *Frankenstein*. Shelley aptly intended to title that masterpiece "The Modern Prometheus."

This brings me to another problem with Jorjani's thought, which became the focus of my second book, published in 2105, and titled *The Future of Modernity*. (Okay, I'm going to stop referring to myself in the third person.) In *Prometheus and Atlas*, fresh out of doctoral studies and still under the spell of contemporary Continental "Philosophy" (so-called), I made the mistake of putting the title "The Postmodern Prometheus" on the chapter wherein *Frankenstein* features prominently as part of an attempted revival of the archetypal power of Prometheus. In my second book — in *this life* as Dana Avalon — with the hindsight of the appalling history of the 21st century, I have come around to realizing that there is nothing "Postmodern" about what I wrote there. In fact, there is nothing to "Postmodernism" at all — other than a cynical psychological warfare and social engineering project that aims to "deconstruct" the Modern just so that Tradition can prevail again. Of course, the vast majority of its proponents, in the late 20th and early 21st century, did not realize that they were suckers being used for this — being used by people who took Evola's *Ride the Tiger* to heart, or who thought along similar "Accelerationist" lines about hastening the supposedly inevitable collapse of the Modern world.

My second book begins with a look at early-to-mid-20th-century visions of "Futurama" or "the World of Tomorrow." A robotic workforce, personal flying cars, cities under the sea, colonies in space, and many other innovations that were expected by "the year 2000" or earlier are surveyed as the surface layer of a deep Futurism that spanned from Italy to America, and then extended to Japan in the decades after Hiroshima. Even the Russian Cosmists of the 1920s were part of this global project to soar headlong into the ever-expanding horizon of the Modern age. The Soviet Union embraced its own vision of this Promethean ambition, in a bid to rival Capitalism with a promise of a more just and universal Utopia. Psychotronics (Soviet Parapsychology) was part of this Modernist vanguardism.

Contrary to what many theorists of the "Modern" assume, this worldwide movement — or constellation of movements — was not reductively materialist. This is especially clear when one examines the work of a number of leading modern artists and literary figures, from Wassily Kandinsky to André Breton and Franz Kafka. Their work is steeped in the occult, even if it represents a radical revolt against Tradition. In the realm of science, Psychical Research and its successor, Parapsychology, were uncompromisingly scientific in their methodology and entirely consistent with what actually characterizes the modern mindset. Judging by the empirical rigor of research in the field, and the complexity of data analysis, Parapsychology has a more legitimate claim to being a modern science than Psychology or Sociology do.

The reason why many theorists have missed this when formulating a phenomenology of the "Modern" or of "Modernism" is that they have mistakenly drawn an equivalence between Modernity and Anti-Tradition. The latter is a term introduced by the Traditionalist French writer René Guénon in order to designate the atheistic and materialistic form of modern thought that rose to prominence during the French Revolution and was eventually embraced by the scientific establishment of the Western world. In his book *The Reign of Quantity and the Sign of the Times*, Guénon contrasts this "Anti-Tradition" with a different modality of Modernity, one which he has noticed heralds of, as he is writing in the 1920s, but which he believes is yet to come to its culmination. Guénon calls this the "Counter-Tradition." Unlike the reductively materialist and atheistically secular "Anti-Tradition" that was epitomized by the French Cult of Reason and the Marquis de Sade, the Counter-Tradition is profoundly spiritual. Guénon, writing as a staunch defender of Perennial Tradition, sees the Counter-Tradition as the ideology of the coming Antichrist. It is the full flowering of Modernity. *Prometheus and Atlas* made the mistake of conflating Modernity in general with the Anti-Tradition, and of confusing the Counter-Tradition that Prometheism represented with something "Postmodern" rather than the *fully* Modern. Looking back from the year 2112, after the almost complete destruction of the Modern world, there is no ambiguity about this. My writings as Jorjani actually represented the zenith of Modernity.

In *The Future of Modernity*, I examined the distinction between the two types of Modernity that Guénon differentiated from one another. Therein I affirm Guénon's claim that there really are only two types of worlds — a world of Tradition and a Modern world. A period like the Italian Renaissance, or for that matter Hellenistic Alexandria, is an example of a world in transition between Tradition and Modernity (in the Alexandrian case the transition was aborted by the institutionalization of Christianity, and in the case of the Renaissance it was retarded by the Vatican). Moreover, as Guénon rightly suspects, *our* Modernity may not be the first "Modern world." There may have been at least one Modern age before ours, the Modernity of an "Atlantis" that (in its final phase of civilization) spearheaded a global revolt against the Traditional world order of Olympus. The Modernity of Atlantis was erased, or more literally drowned, by the forces of Tradition — as our own Modern Age will also be when its last bastion of Gotham falls.

I drew on the writings of Julius Evola, especially his *Revolt against the Modern World* and *Ride the Tiger*, to flesh out this epochal and ontological distinction between Modernity and Tradition. Evola was a cynical supporter of certain currents of Modernism, having even been a Dadaist painter in his youth, because he thought that the collapse of the Modern world ought to be accelerated. From his Traditionalist perspective, which is most closely aligned with Hindu notions of *Yugas* (world ages) and the caste hierarchy of a world that ought to be ruled by the *Devas* (the "gods"), Modernity is simply the *Kali Yuga* — the last and darkest age of deviant degeneracy in a perennially repeating cycle of world ages. Bringing this age to an end sooner, by intensifying its destructive forces, would, therefore, accelerate the advent of the new golden age or the next *Satya Yuga*. The term "New Age" is a source of a great deal of confusion because to some people it signifies this dawning of a new golden age, which is an entirely Traditionalist idea, whereas to others it means what it did to German intellectuals who used *die neue Zeit*, literally "the New Age," as the term for "the Modern Age" in the German language.

In *The Future of Modernity*, I argued in favor of the latter, namely that Modernity is the age defined by the very idea of "the new." Guénon, after all, saw the New Age movement, which had already begun in his epoch, as the rising Counter-Tradition, wherein the spiritual takes the form of the "psychical" that can be grasped scientifically. Guénon thought that a scientific approach to the occult was quintessentially Modern, and that the Antichrist would come to power by means of the technological production of "miracles." In hindsight, this is exactly what Prometheism has done and on account of which it has been recognized by the Olympian Imperium as the only real opposition to their restoration of Tradition.

At the heart of *The Future of Modernity* was a Deconstruction of Postmodernity or a turning of so-called "Deconstruction" on itself. The distinction between "Modernism" and "Postmodernism" in architecture, the arts (including cinema), and literature was examined with a view to demonstrating that there is nothing positively or substantively new about putatively "Postmodern" works that was not already there in "Modern" works. For example, so-called "Postmodern" architecture is just "Neo-Deco" when it is not trash, and Dada (which was sometimes literally trash) is at least as de-constructively engaged in satirical and absurdist parody as anything "Postmodern." Is Frank Lloyd Wright a "Postmodern" architect simply because he fuses

Modernist geometric rationalism with ancient decorative motifs from various cultures? Of course not! Wright is absolutely Modern. Anyone who thinks that the line between Modern and Postmodern art and literature is drawn by some rejection of the Rational or by a supposed commitment to linear Progress, is clearly ignorant of the place of the irrational and the archaic in Surrealist art and poetry — which is radically Modern.

What was really at the bottom of the advent of putatively "bottomless" (or anti-foundational) Postmodernism is the paradox of Simulacra that are lacking an original. In other words, the idea of an all-encompassing Simulacrum. This idea was responsible for so much of the nihilistic irony and all-pervasive aversion to authenticity in the allegedly "Postmodern" epoch of the late 20th and early 21st century, shaped by the delusion that since nothing is real, nothing really matters. I argued that, even in the Gotham of 2112, this delusion still needed to be destroyed — in Martin Heidegger's still uncorrupted sense of "destruction." To this end, I "deconstructed" the writings of Jean-François Lyotard and Jean Baudrillard, two leading theorists of Postmodernism, in a clearer fashion than the "deconstructions" that Jacques Derrida and Michel Foucault engaged in. I demonstrated that the all-pervasive Simulacrum idea is a perversion of the perfectly legitimate conception of a Cyberspace coextensive with the Cosmos, i.e., an observer-dependent and potentially programmable quantum-computing "Holographic Universe" with fractal-generating Chaos as its unfathomable and unpredictable background. There is nothing "Postmodern" about this idea, which was developed by serious thinkers and writers such as David Bohm, Michael Talbot, and Philip K. Dick in the 1980s — at the zenith of Modernity.

The Future of Modernity concluded by exploring the double entendre of its title. It means both reaffirming Modernity *as* the future and retrieving the future that was envisioned by Modernity. To this end, I investigated the connection between Futurism and "Transhumanism" — the brainchild of Iranian Futurist Fereydoun M.

Esfandiari (better known as F. M. 2030). The soullessly reductive materialism that was the dominant trend in the Transhumanist movement was harshly critiqued by me, and I rejected this "Anti-Traditional" Transhumanism in favor of a "Counter-Traditional" Transhumanism that resumes the Promethean project of occult alchemists from Faust onwards. To paint a portrait or sculpt the image of this Counter-Traditional reaffirmation of Modernity as the future in the highest fidelity possible, raw material was drawn from a plethora of visionaries in the period preceding the decline that set in during the 1990s.

I made an argument that the era of 1977 to 1999 was the zenith of Modernity, with 1988 as the single year that marks the peak of the entire Modern age. In other words, one year before the precipitous collapse and disintegration of the Soviet Union from 1989–1991. Without a Communist rival in the Russians, and a worldwide ideological war with these easternmost Europeans that was so dead serious it could literally have ended in the nuclear holocaust of all mankind, a seemingly triumphant capitalist West gave in to self-destructive decadence and nihilistic decay. Meanwhile, a no longer Communist China, increasingly reembracing Traditionalist Confucianism, rose to fill the vacuum of the USSR as the new superpower rivaling a rapidly declining United States. Not a rival competing with us to build a better Utopia than the Promethean Soviets believed Capitalism capable of offering to mankind, but an Ancestor-worshipping culture that fundamentally fears the future and considers all Utopian projects of Progress — including the Maoist one that still owed something to Marx — as vainglorious and ruinous folly lacking "the Mandate of Heaven."

Looking back at the leading edge of our emerging global Modern culture, from New York and Hollywood to Paris and Tokyo, in the years '77 to '99, *The Future of Modernity* aimed to give its readers not only a sense of what we lost, but also of the kind of future that we want to reclaim as our destiny. A Transhuman future, which is Counter-Traditional and not merely Anti-Tradition. A future of Robotics,

Eugenics, Psychotronics, and Cyberspace — with a final frontier that is not only the colonization of space but also the conquest of time. That is the terminator (the horizon) of Modernity. Beyond Left and Right, the book insisted that now the only way forward is Up instead of Down. It set forth "*Cosmopolis Excelsior*" as a motto for Prometheism as a movement, and for Gotham as a city-state standing in rebellion against the reactionary Imperium of Tradition.

When I wrote *The Future of Modernity*, I was still relatively optimistic that what we were building in Gotham could expand outward and reconquer the globe. That would turn out to be a short-lived optimism, fueled partly by the rapturous enthusiasm that had electrified me on account of realizing that I was the reincarnation of Jorjani and that, with the help of my well-placed counselors, I was going to take back the Prometheist movement from corrupt gatekeepers. Well, I *did* do that. But my enthusiasm about fulfilling the destiny of Prometheism by reclaiming the Modern "Future" for the world at large waned rapidly — in proportion to the degree of control that I actually gained over the movement, and the amount of information and analytical power that came along with that.

Five years after *The Future of Modernity*, I finally completed my third book. Published in 2110, at the age of 33, *Phenomenal Authorization* is the work that I am most widely recognized for, and the one that, unbeknown to all but a small group of elite Prometheist operatives, became the conceptual basis for the desperate time travel project now underway. Most Prometheists — and, fortunately, also most people in the Imperium — see the book as theoretical, perhaps even fantastical, with no inkling that its core ideas are now operational axioms.

Whereas my first two books were intended to be constructive criticisms of Jorjani's thought, my third book aimed to forward the philosophical project that I embarked upon in my life as Jason. Three ideas central to his corpus became points of departure for developing a new concept. The first of these ideas was "Novel Folklore." The second was "Destructive Departure in Worldview Warfare." The third and final one was the trickster dubbed the "Prometheaion" and her machinations on a fifth-dimensional level, reprogramming the quantum computational Cosmos. Consequently, it could be said that what I came to call "Phenomenal Authorization" was already implicit in the canon of Prometheism, but this book rendered it more cohesive and explicit. The text explored the relationship between Authorship, Authorization, and Authority.

Very much in line with the post-structuralist hermeneutics developed from out of Heidegger's thought, and implicit even in the Kabbalistic dimension of Kafka's writing, the "worldhood of the world" (to use Heidegger's phrase) was recognized as proto-textual in nature. This is actually what was intended from the very first philosophical usage of the term *Logos* by Heraclitus of Ephesus, long before that term was retroactively associated with reductively mathematical or analytical "logic." Originally, the idea of *Logos* was that the structure on account of which our universe is referred to as a *Cosmos* or "ordered array" is akin to the warp and weft of a grand narrative or super story. Stories, like dreams, can involve absurd elements that are "illogical" from the perspective of a quasi-mathematical or reductively analytic logic, but that make sense narratively — at least on a subconscious level — and are therefore encompassed by the original conception of *Logos*. Surrealist poetry is still *Logos*, and events can transpire in our Cosmos that are more akin to Surrealist poetry than they are to anything "logically" analyzable or describable in terms of a chain of causality that can be mathematically schematized.

As I had argued in two of the essays on Free Will in *Lovers of Sophia*, individual persons are at least potentially co-authors over the narrative structure of the Cosmos. But clearly, Authorship is the prerogative of only a few, since most people are no better than Non-Player Characters (NPCs) in the Massively Multiplayer Online Roleplaying Games of the early 21st century (which I had discussed in *Prometheism*). Authorship belongs not only to "authors" in the literal sense of writers, but to any creator who reshapes the "worldhood" of our world at the most fundamental level, namely the level of the folklore that conditions the substratum of the collective and personal unconscious of people in one or another society of a world increasingly globalized by technological enframing (to use another Heideggerian term). Not all authors are "authors" in this sense. In fact, most writers definitely are *not*. But a number of filmmakers, painters, even graphic novelists (like Alan Moore or Grant Morrison), and musicians are "authors" in this sense.

What determines who is or is not an "author" contributing to weaving the tapestry of the *Logos* that makes a *Cosmos* from out of *Chaos* is a double-sided or bi-directional function of "Authorization." Authorship can "authorize" what phenomena are accepted as possible experiences, and what other phenomena are suppressed from — at least widespread — manifestation on account of being deemed "impossible" and pushed to the "fringe" or margins of whatever "reality" is thereby defined. For example, there is no question that the authorship of Stephen King in the late 20th century was working at cross-purposes with the entrenched materialist and mechanistic paradigm of the scientific establishment. It is not a question of what one personally feels about the aesthetic merit of King's novels or the lack thereof. His influence, including through film adaptations, was quite literally *phenomenal,* and it operated on a society-wide scale precisely on the subconscious stratum of folklore. The same was true of Whitley Strieber, for better or for worse. What the case of Strieber highlights is the flip side of this function of Authorization. Those whose authorship authorizes the forms taken by phenomenal manifestation are in turn "authorized" by something. Their process of phenomenal authorship is either initiated by what authorizes them, or their creative endeavors are of a kind such as to solicit the vital interest and active concern of an authorizing force that allows them to act as a *medium* for the reshaping of "reality."

This brings us to the final element in the constellation of three author-related terms, namely Authority. Whoever happens to be in an explicit position of political, economic, or even social power is not necessarily the true "authority" in the world. By the early 21st century, no one with half a brain believed that the elected representatives of any government were really the powers that be. While this might be more believable of corporate executives, the volatile rise and fall and vicious turns of fortune in the lives of such men (and they *were* mostly men) strains the credibility of such a proposition — especially since the only "power" that these men had was their (often undeserved) fortune. Finally, social power was eventually held mostly by social media influencers and trendsetters, who were essentially no better than the premier gossip peddlers of late 19th-century women's salon attendees. This can hardly be counted as "authority." Real authority within the context of one or another world is the authority to define the limits of that world, or at least to play a significant role in defining those parameters that determine what is or is not "possible." The first accurate image of ultimate authority in the history of Philosophy is Plato's allegorical depiction of the puppet masters on the plank above the shackled prisoners who can only see the shadow play on the cave wall in front of them. The Authors who Authorize Phenomena are the Authorities who are Phenomenally Authorized to do so. These very rare individuals have Phenomenal Authorization.

It is in the development of this concept, or the excavation of it from out of the corpus that I had composed in my life as Jorjani, that the secret group of esoteric Prometheists was most helpful. I realized that this idea was already there in the writings of Jorjani on an occulted level. It *was* the esoteric message. There were many seeming contradictions and apparent paradoxes in the books that I wrote during that lifetime. These were keys to open up an esoteric dimension of Prometheism. Consider a few examples.

In *Prometheus and Atlas*, what could possibly have been meant by saying that Mercury mirrors Prometheus and there is probably no

Zeus because Mercury murdered Zeus a long time ago and has pretended to be Zeus by wearing his mask ever since? How could Islam be a creation of Mithraic Parthians, putatively for the purpose of inoculating Sassanian Iran against totalitarian ways of thinking and being, as is argued in *Iranian Leviathan*, if Islam is one of the Abrahamic "revelations" promulgated by the tyrannical leader of the Elohim or Devas (the being called Yahweh, Zeus, or Indra) as is claimed in both *Prometheus and Atlas* and *Closer Encounters*? Why use Whitley Strieber's *Communion* as a principal example of "Novel Folklore" in the book by that name, if Whitley Strieber is as much a victim of theologizing mind control as Betty Andreasson who was taken by the Grays to meet Nordic angels who introduced her to the white light of God and who promised the imminent return of Jesus the Messiah? Is the Gnostic Christ in fact Mithra, as suggested in *Iranian Leviathan*, or is Gnosticism just another variant of the cognitive dissonance that we have been subjected to by the "gods" or "angels"? What is the connection between the appearance of Artemis in the essay on Kafka in *Lovers of Sophia* and the reappearance of Artemis, sometimes in passages reproduced verbatim, in the context of the discussion of early Mithraism in *Iranian Leviathan*, and why is the symbolism of a black dog sacrifice to Artemis at the esoteric core of *Faustian Futurist*? More questions of this kind could be formulated, and every such question holds a key to the esoteric truth of Phenomenal Authorization.

The truth that those authors who have the authority have principally authorized the phenomena of world history. Jorjani, probably when drunk, would occasionally tweet one or another variation of "God is an invention of the Devil." But he never cared to explain this diabolical aphorism in any of his actual philosophical writings. What it means is that the Devas did not create the revealed Abrahamic religions. Reread the chapter on "Iranian Zionism" in *Iranian Leviathan* (the one comically titled "Tekel, Tekel, Mene Shekel"). Put it next to *Closer Encounters*. The Abrahamic "revelations" were invented by Prometheus to shatter the divine power of the Devas with their quasi-philosophically justified totalitarian caste system based on rarefied notions such as the mirroring of the Macrocosm of Brahman in the Microcosm of Atman and the Cosmic Order of *Rta* in the divinely ordered society of the *Satya Yuga*. This is not to say that the Devas did not *become* the Elohim and play into this new theological framework. But as soon as they did so, they were playing a game whose rules were being set by Prometheus for the sake of the ultimate undermining of all "faith" in what comes down from on high based on paternalistic authority and sanctified tradition.

Look back at the metaphor of the "funhouse mirror" in the discussion of Hermes in the closing chapter on "Mercurial Hermeneutics" in *Prometheus and Atlas*. The Abrahamic "revelations" were intended to be a farcical self-deconstructing mockery of a system of hierarchical divine command and servile human obedience. Their purpose was only able to be perverted, by Devas who played into this narrative, because it turns out that the vast majority of people actually want to be enslaved. They hate freedom and they loathe those who want to be free. Just as Plato had already suggested in the Allegory of the Cave at the core of *Republic*, the mob is always ready to lynch whoever has the bright idea of trying to free their fellows from enslaving illusions and delusions. Who would *actually* worship "Yahweh" or "Allah" for centuries? *Nothing* "human." That's for sure. Definitely creatures who are far more contemptible than any wild beast. *Nothing* — I won't even say no *one* — who deserves a future, or who can be trusted to be part of a future built on the basis of open access to potentially very dangerous Singularity-level technologies and psychic techniques. The Devil invented the meta-narrative of the Abrahamic "God" as a Noble Lie to *test* the "humanity" of Man. The verdict is that Man must be replaced. Prometheus was the father and long-suffering advocate of an undeserving and ungrateful creature, who proved to be monstrous by *choosing* to serve an incredibly grotesque Scarecrow. Prometheus will now return to his laboratory and fashion a new, posthuman progeny.

The enemy is real. The Devas are real. They really did embrace the image of being angelic Elohim. They are denizens of a Traditionalist, time-traveling Breakaway Civilization that is sadistically tyrannical and that attempts to provide philosophical justifications for a static hierarchical structure that stifles social progress and the creative evolution of the individual. But the enemy only *re*-acts. We are the *actors*. We have been the Authorized. They are not Authorized. We Authorized them, as the black pieces on *our* chessboard. Yes, the black and white squared board preserved, from Atlantean times, by the Freemasonic Order. It is Mithra the Mediator who authorizes Ahriman to move against Ahura Mazda, so that there can be the constraint that is a precondition for constructive order. For every action of ours, the enemy engages in some reaction that forwards a game whose aim and end they have never properly grasped: maximal and indefinitely extended Creation, the categorical imperative of the Prometheaion. S/he is the authorizer of the authority of the authors of phenomena.

I would know, since I have had Phenomenal Authorization in more than one lifetime. The past incarnation of mine that is most relevant to understanding the esoteric purpose of the putatively "Abrahamic" so-called "revelations" is my life as David. When I was Jorjani, during my graduate studies at New York University, I met a young woman named Marie. She was Parisian, although her ancestry was not purely French but rather from a fairly prominent Jewish family that had emigrated, generations ago, from Spain. She was a deep thinker and an extraordinarily expressive writer, a woman capable of ascetic austerity and also of insatiable harlotry — an irresistible seducer of both men and women.

One night when she was having sex with one of her girlfriends in her apartment around Washington Square Park, I was so intensely focused on her from miles away, in my room on the Upper East Side, that she saw my spectral form appear in front of her for a moment. Fortunately, her lover was facing the other direction. She confronted me about it the next day, and astonished that she had also experienced it from her own perspective, I confessed. "I have nothing to hide from you," she said, "I just wanted you to know that I can see you when you do that."

Marie was at NYU studying both Drama and Philosophy. (Career-wise, she went on to become a journalist in Paris.) Not incidentally, it was in the period when I met Marie that the majority of my past life memories of Nikola Tesla came back to me — the memories that I incorporated, in a somewhat embroidered form, into the narrative of *Faustian Futurist*. This is undoubtedly because her presence triggered them, on account of the fact that she was the reincarnation of Sarah Bernhardt.

I began to have dreams wherein Marie was an actress. I would meet her backstage after her performances and call her "Sarah." On a night that culminated with us rubbing noses atop the Empire State Building in the midst of tremendous windshear, I confronted her about this, and she told me certain intimate secrets that very clearly confirmed it and explained her strong interest in drama, once again, in this lifetime. But what is more relevant here are the memories that *she had* of the other lifetime that we spent together, a life wherein she was "Queen" Bathsheba and I was King David of Israel. The karma of that life was quite palpable to her and cast a shadow over our rapport. On some level, she still resented that I had her Hittite husband murdered so that she could become my consort.

Sir Ridley Scott gave David, both the android and the Michelangelo sculpture, such a prominent role in his film *Prometheus* and its sequel *Alien: Covenant*, because Scott is clearly in the know about who David really was and what aim he was esoterically serving. The symbolism of David's confrontation with Goliath, and the machination by means of which he prevails against apparently superior brute force, is an elementally Promethean image. Before David was sanctified as a prophet or a king, the man was first and foremost an artist — a poet and musician. The seal that he vouchsafed to his son, King Solomon, who built the principal Temple of Israel on that old abandoned megalithic Atlantean platform, is an epitome of the occult project of "revelation" or of the relationship between "revelation" and occultation. The upward-facing triangle is supposed to be white, and the downward-facing triangle that is interwoven with it, should be depicted as black. The latter is what the Tantric Hindus and Buddhists have preserved as the "Shakti Yantra." The Star of David that became the Seal of Solomon is an Atlantean symbol of the necessity of "evil" as a catalytic force in a dialectical process of creative evolution.

David's relationship with "God" was always a rapport with the Shekinah, in other words, the Prometheaion. Despite how his story was rewritten by the rabbis and cohanim in order to obscure this, one can still discern it from between the lines of what has survived in the Bible. Abraham, Moses, Jesus, and Muhammad were all pawns. King David and, before him, the wizard Melchizedek, are the true founders of Judaism. Just as John the Baptist and Mary Magdalene really invented Christianity. The true Gabriel of Islam was Salman the Persian, and the Assassin leader Hassan Sabbah was the real Seal of Prophecy. These promulgators of necessary evils are the "spiritual princes and nobles" of the "initiatory chain of gnosis" that I wrote and preached about during my life in Sassanian Iran as the martyred Mazdak.

Even the most tragic figures among the Authors of Phenomena — the revolutionary martyrs, the impoverished inventors, and the visionary starving artists — have been akin to the "Coyote" trickster of the American Indians, who plays dead in order to get the upper hand, albeit not necessarily in the same lifetime, and not for him or herself alone, but for the Prometheaion who is the Creatrix of the Cosmic Game. S/he confers Phenomenal Authorization. That is why we esoteric Prometheists are now ready, willing, and able to rewrite history in a way that preempts the re-conquest of Earth by the Olympian Imperium. This is, after all, not the first time that the matrix of the world has been recoded. I made that much clear when I wrote *Faustian Futurist*.

One pivotal experience that I had in my life as Jason speaks to what the Shekinah or Prometheaion is really like in Herself, beneath and beyond the various phenomenal appearances that she veils herself with through the wonders worked by those with Phenomenal Authorization. The formless form of Her that I encountered was what the German Romantics called "The Blue Light," as in the Leni Riefenstahl film by that name. To them, this amorphous blue glow was a symbol of the Impossible. In two closely connected experiences, I was given to understand that this being that is nothing definite, and that can be encountered as a pregnant darkness that destroys what one takes oneself to be, is the so-called "alien" intelligence that we are attempting to contact.

In the first of these experiences, I was at a summer sleep-away camp at Amherst College that was also like a prep school program between middle school and high school. Warren, my best friend at the time, came with me and had a room down the hall from mine. One night as I was sleeping, I became aware of my heartbeat. I was conscious but still asleep and not dreaming. It seemed that it was beating slower and slower, but it may also have been that the timeframe of my consciousness was being altered to the point that I began to sink into the space between two heartbeats. When that happened, when it seemed like my heart had stopped beating, I fell out of my body through the bottom of my feet. I was being pulled by a tremendous gravitational force toward the dark heart of a vortex of oblivion.

I said to myself that if I cannot somehow pull myself back, the camp counselors will find my corpse in the morning. Then, as I struggled to break free from the event horizon of this vortex, I saw the following scene: there is a revolt or uprising. I see rioters around a barbed-wire fence. In the midst of this violent chaos, I see my own corpse on the ground. My face is chalk white and there are deep black rings under my eyes. Then, to my horror, I notice that my corpse is being propped up by my father. I'm in his arms, but he is also dead. His corpse is holding mine.

The shock of this finally brought me back to myself. I was ice cold. When I looked into the open closet that was across from the foot of the bed, the darkness inside it reminded me of the black hole that I had almost been swallowed by. "Reminded" is not strong enough. It was the same blackness and it seemed alive and capable of devouring me. Not able to stand being alone in that room any longer, I went down the hall to my friend and turned the light on in his room. Once Warren woke up and looked at me, his face suddenly twisted into the most horrified expression I've ever seen. He recoiled and hid himself under his blanket. Already unsettled, this reaction of his disturbed me more than if I had just stayed in my own room. I remember saying to him, over and over again, "What is it? Why are you doing that? It's just *me*. It's just *me!*" After a while he cautiously looked up from out of the covers, and then said, "Oh, it *is* you." When I asked him why he initially reacted that way, he said: "Your eyes! Your eyes! They weren't *your* eyes. It was as if they were looking right through me, seeing through my whole being."

For a long time, I couldn't tell anybody about this experience. Every time I was about to, I would be overcome with emotion and had to stop myself so that I would not start crying uncontrollably. On a couple of occasions, I just said, "One night I died, and then came back to life." I started high school, months passed, and I tried very hard to forget the whole thing. Then, one night during the first winter after that summer, I was lying in bed looking at the digital clock when — without my really falling asleep — the room fell away, and I found myself outside under the night sky walking on a vast path of gravel lightly dusted with snow.

The wide path was situated between two rows of titanic radio telescopes, the ones that are used for the Search for Extraterrestrial Intelligence — one after the other, extending to the horizon on each side of the path I'm walking down. I noticed that all of the gigantic SETI dishes were burnt and shattered, as if they had received a signal that was too powerful. Then I had a sinking feeling in my stomach and, as on that night in camp, began to notice my heartbeat, with a longer and longer interval between each beat, as if my heart were going to stop again. Meanwhile, a huge blue light began to coalesce in the night sky ahead of me and above the gravel path. That was the Prometheaion, unveiled. The "alien" intelligence that no merely mechanical device could be used to communicate with, and a force that, when "contacted," rewrites the fabric of your being. I looked into the spherical blue glow and said, "Alright, alright, I get it! Just don't make me have to see that again!" Then I was back in my bed, with my hand on my chest checking for my heartbeat. My eyes had been open the whole time. It was a vision, not a dream. My life was never the same again after that night.

I mentioned that the concept developed in *Phenomenal Authorization*, my third book as Dana Avalon, had been applied operationally. In the two years since the book came out in 2110, definitively securing my position as the leader of the Prometheist movement and the widely recognized reincarnation of its founder, I managed to maneuver members of the esoteric group that had been secretly advising me into key positions with access to our most sensitive technology. Most of the corrupt gatekeepers of Prometheism withdrew into their private lives in Gotham without risking a violent confrontation, or the potential loss of their lucrative mining industries in the Asteroid Belt colonies. Those few who were not shrewd enough to cut their losses were easily dealt with by the younger and more energetic members of our faction. The latter were both adept operatives and fanatical devotees who, regardless of my change of sex across lifetimes, sometimes referred to me as "Chairman Jorjani" despite my repeated requests that they refrain from doing so.

It is these Prometheist Assassins (in the Alamut sense) that we trained, from 2110 to 2112, to become the spearhead of the time travel mission to rewrite the course of events in the 1980s. They are the operatives that I sent ahead of me, to set up the pharmaceutical company in 1977 and to also start raising capital through insider trading of its stock that would be soaring by 1980. Avalon Pharmaceutical was meant to be a cash cow for a larger company that the group would be tasked with setting up, named AtlantiCorp, of which it would be a subsidiary. A few members of this vanguard were given period-specific paramilitary training as well, which I participated in. I especially excelled in sharpshooting with sniper rifles. Of course, I also had to learn how to manually drive an automobile, since our hovercars here in Gotham basically piloted themselves.

The group had also been authorized to negotiate the purchase of a property that was to be my residence: the penthouse apartment of 55 Central Park West in Manhattan. I had even given them specifications for what style of furniture to acquire for the apartment, and what kind of women's wardrobe to fill the closets with. Finally, I requested that they acquire one of the original DeLorean prototypes designed by William T. Collins in late 1970s America, before John DeLorean settled on mass-manufacturing an inferior model in Ireland. I asked them to have the car's stainless-steel frame painted matt black and to replace the interior upholstery with black leather.

It wouldn't be long before I found out how much of these plans had been successfully executed. We used a corridor in what had been the East River as our staging ground for time travel operations. Maritime traffic was directed up the Hudson River, which was closer to the Englewood Cliffs that Gotham had been built upon. By the time I was rushing to the submersible saucer that was to warp space time around it as it dove into the East River, what remained of Gotham's skyscrapers were exploding all throughout the skyline of the city. As I made my way down the building, I noticed that the nanotechnological "utility fog" that would produce solid walls with an architectural design that changed on a weekly, or even a daily basis, was starting to malfunction. I was afraid that I would get stuck in the elevator that traveled, not just vertically, but made diagonal turns on its way to the streets, as the elevators of many of our skyscrapers with curved bases did.

The night sky was full of Olympian Predators, and it's a wonder I wasn't exposed to their laser blasts in open stretches between the tunnels and covered walkways that led to the silvery saucer awaiting me on a cliffside hanger deck. I'd have run faster if I didn't have to carry the suitcases that contained carefully chosen information documenting certain events on this timeline, relevant to a number of the operations that I had planned to carry out in the late 20th century. There were a couple of aids and a couple of security personnel with me, who were helping to get all of this luggage to the saucer. I was already wearing my wetsuit, but 1980s diving gear (which we replicated) was pretty heavy. The plan was for me to leave the saucer through the airlock in my diving suit, after using a satellite phone to call a team that would rush to meet me at Pier 42 on the Lower East Side of Manhattan, between the Williamsburg and Manhattan Bridges, across from the Brooklyn Navy Yard.

We loaded the saucer and I bid a rushed farewell to those who helped me load it. Fortunately, they were not cleared for knowledge of the fact that I was about to erase them together with their timeline. That would endow the documents that, unbeknown to them, they helped to load, with the magical quality of being from a world — from a future — that no longer existed. Just as the portal was about to close, my regression hypnotist showed up. Now *she* knew. I've never seen both wistful resignation and grim affirmation so inextricably conflated in a single gaze and facial expression before. As I looked her in the eyes, and the saucer's entryway closed, I put my hands together prayerfully, in a *namaste*, and touched them to the *ajna chakra* in my forehead.

As the saucer lifted off the hanger deck and glided over the cliff above the Hudson River, heading southeast toward the skyline of sunken Manhattan, I looked back at Gotham one last time. The mesmerizingly beautiful neon light of the laser beams blasting and cutting the city to bits was aesthetically discordant with the destruction of Earth's last bastion of Liberty. That was my last thought as I strapped myself in and prepared for the deep dive into the fluid darkness of time. I could already feel the gravity wave forming around the shell of the craft like an envelope that would slice right through the moonlit waves of the Atlantic Ocean. It didn't cause any physical vibrations, but I could feel it in the pit of my stomach, nonetheless. To experience this for the first time was like the psychical equivalent of having my umbilical cord cut. I lost myself completely for a few moments.

The pitch, yaw, and rate of rotation of the saucer determined the precise degree to which the fabric of space-time around it would be warped by the Zero Point Energy drive shielded at the core of the vessel. Once the space-time warping engine or "warp core" of the vessel shut off, and I got reoriented, I turned on the searchlights, which only lit up the garbage at the bottom of the river. Then I released a small spherical probe from the side of the vessel, which was equipped with cameras, sonar, and LADAR. It sped to the surface, rose above the water of the East River, and began sending back data that included a stunning view of the United Nations building and mapped the rest of the skyline around it. It certainly seemed like 1980s Manhattan. I sent up another probe that was designed to pick up old radio frequencies. The first thing I heard, loud and clear, was a news bulletin being broadcast from the top of the Empire State Building, announcing that an eruption had begun on Mount St. Helens in Washington state. I scanned the frequencies again, and the next thing blaring loudly inside the saucer was the Blondie song "Call Me."

I reached nervously for the satellite phone, and then dialed the designated number. (Just figuring out what that number would be and how to make sure that the vanguard would secure it in 1980 New York took some serious planning.) I could barely breathe to respond when a familiar voice answered on the other end of the line. "I'm here," I said. "Dana?" "Yes, Johnny. I'm here."

As they undoubtedly ran numerous red lights to get to the docked ship that they were going to use to retrieve me, I piloted the saucer further south along the East River to get as close as possible to Pier

42. The suitcases all had a design feature that allowed them to float straight upwards. Once I got a call back on the satellite phone, letting me know that the team had arrived, I released these suitcases, and then climbed through the portal myself with the saucer's remote-controlled self-destruct mechanism in my hand. Even though spring had started, and this wetsuit provided good insulation, I could feel that the water was still pretty cold.

As soon as I broke the surface, I squinted in the searchlight of a ship. It was Johnny's boat, which had already spotted the suitcases and headed toward them. The small team that was with him helped to load the floating luggage onto the boat, as I climbed aboard myself. All he said as we sped back to Pier 42 was, "I can't believe that you're finally here." I was dazed and didn't respond. I just kept staring at the bright light of all the buildings along the river, including both the Chrysler and the Empire State spires that could be seen on the skyline.

We ran as fast as we could from the boat to the waiting black stretch limousine, packing the suitcases both into the trunk and the spacious backseat of the car itself. It did not appear that anyone saw us. After all, it was the middle of the night. I hit the remote-control detonator and turned back briefly when I heard a loud splash in the water behind us. Hopefully, no other ships had been crossing that stretch of the river when the saucer exploded into small shards on the river bed. The driver sped through the streets, occasionally eying me curiously in the rearview mirror. I stared out the tinted window, my eye caught by the lights of Katz's Delicatessen. "What's the date?" Johnny looked at me, smiling in relief at hearing me finally open my mouth. He replied, "March 27th, 1980. Thor's Day."

Johnny pridefully, and almost gleefully, explained to me that everything had gone according to plan. We were headed to 55 Central Park West, where my furnished penthouse apartment was waiting for me, and my black DeLorean was parked on the street across from Tavern on the Green. The rest of the crew on the boat, who I did not recognize, had taken another car, so Johnny and I were alone. "You should probably change out of that," he said. "I don't think you want to show up to your fancy building for the first time wearing a wet suit. The doorman might say something to the board."

Johnny had been one of the operatives in the spearhead group that I had spent the most time with during their training for the vanguard mission. We would buddy up during martial arts lessons and do other combat sparring together, and he would often shoot right beside me during our target practice sessions. But he never flirted with me too much, since I overemphasized my interest in women so that he would get the idea that I was a lipstick lesbian (rather than bisexual, which is closer to the truth). Besides, although he had all the respect in the world for me (every member of the vanguard did), I don't think I was his type. It probably also didn't help that he knew I was the reincarnation of a man whose writings and biography he, like all of the other spearhead operatives, had been immersed in. Johnny was straight as an arrow. I don't think he'd have been able to keep it up with the thought repeatedly resurfacing that the chick he was banging is a reincarnation of Jorjani. So, I stripped off the wetsuit right there in the back of the limo. I had stuffed a single era-appropriate change of clothes with me in one of the suitcases. It was a simple, knee high one-piece black dress that I easily slipped on. "No underwear?" Johnny asked, while smirking. "I don't think the doorman will have an opportunity to check," I said. He looked happy to see that I was adjusting enough to regain my sense of humor. There was a pair of high heels in the suitcase too, and I put these shoes on as the limo pulled up to the building.

The driver got out of the car and opened the door for me. This was the first time that I got a good look at him. He was a tall, bony black man with a couple of scars on his face. As the car crossed Central Park South, Johnny had whispered to me that he was ex-DIA. Military intelligence. He had served in Vietnam *and the jungles of Cambodia.* He was also an unconventional practitioner of voodoo, with a particularly Promethean caste of mind. Jean-Pierre was his name. He was from New Orleans, and there was still a hint of Creole in his accent. As he held the car door open, Jean-Pierre also motioned commandingly to the building's doorman to bring the cart. Meanwhile, Johnny unloaded all of the luggage onto the sidewalk, before placing it onto the cart together with the doorman, into whose palm he slipped a wad of cash. I could smell the dewy night air of Central Park, the smell of dirt and a hint of evergreens, in the moment before I stepped into the magnificent art deco lobby. I stopped for a moment to close my eyes and breathe in deeply.

The doorman caught up with me, and slid the cart packed with suitcases into the lobby. At this late hour — it was almost 2 am — he was the only one on duty, so Johnny took the cart from there. Through the still open door of the lobby, I waved goodnight to Jean-Pierre, who nodded and saluted me in turn, as he climbed back into the limo with a slight knowing smile on his face. Johnny told me that he would be my driver whenever I needed to show up to a meeting or event where it would not be appropriate for me to pull up solo in a DeLorean. Apparently, Johnny had been to the apartment enough times, including on this doorman's night shift, that the guy didn't ask any questions before he pressed the elevator button at the front desk to unlock access to the penthouse.

Johnny handed me the keys and gestured for me to go ahead of him, as he pulled the cart out of the elevator. It had been *a long time* since I handled old metal keys like these. A lifetime, in fact. He stared at me somewhat amused as I fiddled with them and finally got the door open. The apartment was spectacular. It far exceeded my expectations. I walked from the entry foyer down into the sunken living room as Johnny unloaded the suitcases. "I'll leave you to have a look around while I take this cart back downstairs," he said. I looked at him, hardly able to contain my excitement. "Welcome home, Dana. Welcome *back*, Chairman..." He couldn't resist adding that.

Before checking out the rest of the house, I hurried up the staircase to the top floor of the duplex. It was an uncanny feeling to see the hybrid Gothic-and Art Deco-style stone turret up close for the first time after walking out of its doorway onto my terrace and turning around to face it. The structure was more magnificent than I had even imagined based on photographs that I'd seen of it. The whole white stone façade was bathed in spotlights that were set up on the roof, so that it shone with an aura of magic and mystery against the night sky. The crown jewel of the building, its deco details reminded me at once of Arthurian legends of the Round Table Knights and the temples erected at the top of ancient Mesopotamian ziggurats, where the high priestess of Ishtar playing the Whore of Babylon would grant supplicant kings benediction beneath her open thighs.

I looked over the edge of the terrace, leaning against one of the stone pillars that rose up from the line of the wall. My mind briefly flashed back to what this place looks like in the early 22nd century. I had seen it up close several times, including the day that I dove on the Guggenheim with my mother. It was a seething pool of ocean waves, roughly enclosed by decrepit skyscrapers on three sides, where the currents that were channeled through the streets of lower Manhattan converged for a stretch of a few miles before flowing more freely upwards toward Harlem and the South Bronx, the open side of the imperfect rectangle, where almost no buildings were tall enough to rise above the waves. But now the even more breathtaking vista of Central Park extended out before me like a blanket of dense trees, framed by the sparkling skyline of the Upper East Side and of Central Park South, where none of those eyesore matchsticks of "Billionaire's Row" had been built yet to mar the grandeur of the grand old New York buildings facing into the park, like the Essex House. After being mesmerized for a moment by the lights of all the buildings, I looked straight down and saw the rooftop of Tavern on the Green across the street. Even the lights in the finely sculpted shrubbery of their outdoor dining space could be discerned from here. I decided that I would go there for brunch tomorrow, after a morning walk in the park. Maybe I'd walk across to the Guggenheim on 5th Avenue.

I heard Johnny come back in, and I went downstairs to say goodnight to him. "I can't thank you enough for what you've done here," I said, as I gave him a huge hug. "Don't forget these, Dana." He handed me the keys to the DeLorean. "It's parked downstairs, next to the Gothic stone church with the red door." I smiled and nodded as I placed them on a small tabletop in the entry foyer. As he headed out the door, Johnny said, "I'll let you just settle in tomorrow, and then the day after, Jean-Pierre will drive you out to the pharmaceutical company on Long Island, for a full briefing from the team at the SCIF (Secure Facility) that we've built underground there." "Thank you, again, Johnny. You all really came through." He smiled back at me proudly, and gave me a military salute, as he got onto the elevator.

I was so pumped with adrenaline that I wasn't tired at all. So I opened the suitcases right there in the entry foyer, rather than dragging them through the apartment. Before bringing the sensitive documents upstairs, I checked that the hidden combination lock vault had been properly installed behind a panel in the library that lined the interior walls of the roof turret — as I had specified when we planned the apartment. Once I confirmed this, I carried the documents up by the handful. Each stack was relevant to one of my planned operations to alter key events in the timeline. Then I emptied some of the other items in the suitcases into my closets, at which point I realized that my requested fashionable '80s women's wardrobe had been acquired. Presumably one of the women on our team, who was closest to my size, had tried at least some of the items on. (I certainly hope that it was a woman who had filled one of the dresser drawers with a variety of women's underwear, including quite a few rather risqué thongs.) There was also a set of shoes of various types in my size, from sneakers to super high heels, lining the floor of one of the closets.

By the time I was done packing and storing the suitcases themselves, I was a little less high-strung, but still too excited by being here to be able to fall asleep. It was 3 am, and I was starting to worry that I'd be a zombie tomorrow if I didn't get some shut eye. So I went into the bathroom of the master bedroom, and turned the water of the "hot tub" on. (I mean, it was little more than a large bathtub.) Then I slipped the black dress off, hanging it on the knob of the bathroom door because a bathrobe was already suspended from the hook. I noted that it was a Calvin Klein bathrobe, which I found ironic, since in the timeline that I came from, Mr. Klein would purchase this apartment in 1983 for only $1 million and nearly destroy it by knocking down all of the interior walls. The board could rest assured that if or when he came around, I wouldn't sell for any price.

I slipped into the hot tub and bent my knees until my whole body sank beneath the steaming warm water up to my chin. Then I started touching myself, trying to get back into my skin in this strange time and place. Now the value of the regression hypnosis sessions became very clear to me. Despite having lived in New York during this era, had it not been for immersion in my memories of that life, the experience of being here would be almost unbearably uncanny. I could tell from how long it took me to come that my body had been very tense. Once I did, I felt every muscle relax from the release of the prolonged tension. I drained the water out of the tub, turned on the shower, and lathered my body. When I shampooed my hair, I let the hot water run over my head and face for a while. Then, I dried off and got under the covers of my bed with its tall Gatsby-style headboard. Sometime before the indigo hour, I fell asleep.

CHAPTER 4

OPERATION NEQAB

THE BLARE OF HONKING yellow cab horns woke me up in the morning. Apparently, they could be heard even from the 20th floor. *Ah, New York.* On account of the fact that I had forgotten to draw the curtains closed properly, the morning light that bathed the room made it so that I could not put myself back to sleep. Once I walked over to the curtains and looked down at the checkered taxis that were making all the noise, I decided to pull them all the way open instead of closing them. I glanced at the digital clock on the bedside table. It was 9:30 am. On a Friday morning the Tavern wouldn't be open for another hour and a half. I got dressed in clothes that were elegant enough to dine there but wore shoes comfortable enough to take a walk across Central Park before doing so. I stopped to say hello to the morning doorman on my way out. "I'm Dana Avalon, the owner of the penthouse apartment," I said, introducing myself. "So *you're* the mystery woman everyone's been talking about." *Just great,* I thought. The last thing I needed was to draw too much unwanted attention to myself. But such are the hazards when you have corporate proxies purchase a million-dollar penthouse apartment at a prime location in Manhattan for you, without ever showing up yourself. "No big mystery — Tom, is it? I was just tied up on business abroad."

Before heading into the park, I went around the corner to check out the DeLorean. Damn impressive. Everything was to specifications.

With its matt black finish and black leather interior, the thing looked like some kind of futuristic Batmobile when its door wings were popped open. I probably should have gone for a more low-key car, but I just couldn't resist. A time traveler *has* to drive a DeLorean, even if no one would understand why for another five years.

When I was done playing with the car, I walked across the street and entered Central Park through the gate that led up to Tavern on the Green. It was 10 am. They were still setting up. So I headed toward the Upper East Side. I walked north across Sheep Meadow to the Bethesda Terrace, where I lingered for a while taking in the sculpture of the angel and walking to the water's edge for a spectacular view of the Loeb Boathouse. There were already a few people out row boating on the lake. Then, I walked up along the East Drive, past the Conservatory pool and visited the bronze Alice in Wonderland sculptures, where I watched a couple of children who were too young to be in school climbing up and down the mushrooms and onto Alice's dress, or playing with the Mad Hatter, with their babysitters making sure that they didn't fall.

I continued on up the East Drive, until I reached the obelisk across from the Metropolitan Museum of Art. Here I lingered a while again, reminiscing on the regular pilgrimages that I used to make to this monument in my lifetime as Jason. This obelisk was one of the few monuments that we had rescued from beneath the waters, and it had proved at least as difficult as the retrieval of the Prometheus and Atlas statues at Rockefeller Center. They had all been erected in the same city center of Gotham, which was something like a sacred precinct, surrounded by some of the first skyscrapers that rose up on the Englewood Cliffs in the 2070s.

I continued a little further up along the East Drive until I got to the exit at 90th Street and Fifth Avenue. I walked up the steps to the Reservoir for a moment and looked across at the skyline of the Upper West Side, seeing if I could spot the rooftop of my new home from here. Then, I walked out onto Fifth Avenue and strolled one block south on the cobblestone street next to the park until I was standing across the street from the Guggenheim.

As I took the building in, I kept having flashbacks of what it looked like under water. I wanted to see it from the inside. I walked across the street. Unfortunately, the museum wasn't open yet. I'd have to come back soon. You might not believe it if I told you that the highlight of this walk was standing there on the street corner, next to this Frank Lloyd Wright masterpiece, and smelling the smoke from the Sabrett fast food cart that was cooking up hot dogs and salted pretzels. There is nothing like the sense of smell to situate you in a place or bring a lost world back to life. This scent, mixed with the exhaust from the traffic along Fifth Avenue, was what finally grounded me here in the Manhattan of March 1980. There are some things about New York that we never managed to replicate in Gotham. I was tempted to have a pretzel with mustard, but I decided to head back to Tavern on the Green for brunch rather than kill my appetite at this food cart.

I walked back by crossing the Great Lawn, on the south side where I could take a close look at Belvedere Castle and pass by the Shakespeare Theater, on my way to the restaurant. By the time I got back to the Tavern it was 11:30, so a few other people were already seated at their tables and were being served. I sat right next to the floor-to-ceiling wall of glass windows that looked onto the outdoor dining space with its large shrubbery trees shaped into the form of various animals. When the waiter came over, I ordered a black coffee and an eggs benedict with smoked salmon. As I sipped the coffee, I began to gather my thoughts concerning what would be my first mission. It was a very challenging operation.

In about four and a half months, on July 9th of 1980, there would be a coup attempt in Iran against the nascent Islamic Republic. It was called Operation *Neqab*, with *Neqab* (Niqab), the word for a face veil, being a secret acronym for the phrase *Nejaté Qiamé Bozorg*, or "Saving the Great Uprising." In other words, saving the constitutional-ist and secular/progressive aims of the Iranian Revolution from being hijacked by regressive religious forces. On the timeline that I was from, this coup would fail disastrously. Hundreds of military officers would be arrested, 144 of them executed, and about 4,000 more servicemen would be expelled from various branches of the military. What is worse is that this would serve to decapitate the command-and-control functions of what had been, under the Shah, the fifth most powerful military in the world, just a couple of months before Saddam Hussein would order Iraqi forces to invade, leading to an eight-year war of attrition that cemented the Islamic Republic as the regressive regime of a besieged Iran. Furthermore, the exposure of the coup attempt within the regular military would justify its being sidelined in favor of a so-called "Islamic Revolutionary Guard Corps," whose principal loyalty was to the ayatollahs. Eventually, this IRGC would become the military-industrial backbone of the Islamic Republic of Iran, leading the reconstruction effort after the eight-year war with Iraq.

The hidden purpose of this war of attrition, which had been set up by the CIA and MI6, was to solidify the Islamic Republic as a militant theocratic Muslim regime that would block the path of the Soviet Union to the oil resources of the Persian Gulf that could have saved the economy of the USSR from the collapse that it eventually faced from 1989 to 1991. Soviet forces had occupied Persian-speaking Afghanistan in 1979, ostensibly to shore up their proxy Communist government there, and so they had considerably extended their already long border with Iran, giving them another staging ground for marching to the oil wells in Khuzestan, seizing the strategic Strait of Hormuz, and key warm water shipping ports like Abadan, Bandar Abbas, and Chah Bahar. My first mission was to ensure that the *Neqab* coup succeeded, thereby preventing the Iraqi invasion of Iran in September of 1980 by placing a right-wing nationalist dictatorship in power. This would antagonize Iranian Communist parties and leftist guerrilla fighters, while also emboldening them by destroying their theocratic Islamist rivals. These Communists, together with ethnic separatists in the outer provinces (who had also been a part of the coup plot), would then act as a fifth column for a Soviet invasion force entering Iran from both sides of the Caspian Sea as well as from Afghanistan. Soviet control over Iranian oil, early in the 1980s, would go a long way to *ensuring the survival of the USSR, including by keeping Cold War tensions high.* That would set the stage for further operations of mine in service of the same aim.

I thought about Operation Neqab throughout my brunch, but I let it slip into the back of my mind for the rest of the day. Since I would have to travel to Paris before too long to meet with the exiled Iranian Prime Minister Shapour Bakhtiar, who was the figurehead of the coup that I knew was already being planned, I resolved to enjoy as much of New York as I could. I did not plan to be in Paris for long, but I did not appreciate being dislocated so soon after arriving here. So I spent the rest of the day zipping all around Manhattan in taxis, visiting as many of the places that had been most significant to me in my lifetime as Jorjani. If you're wondering how I paid for breakfast or for the cabs, I neglected to mention that Johnny, or someone on the team, had left a stack of hundred-dollar bills inside the hidden vault of the turret library. This was to hold me over until the operatives who had been tasked with setting up the pharmaceutical company, and profiting on its stock through insider trading, fully briefed me on both my personal bank account and corporate financial information.

That was actually the first item on the agenda when we met at the Long Island SCIF the next day. This Secure Facility had been built in a Brutalist concrete bunker-style, beneath Avalon Pharmaceutical in Stony Brook, Long Island. Being so involved in the medical industry, the decision had been made to situate the company as close as possible to the new hospital that had just been built at Stony Brook, and to cultivate a relationship with its doctors and researchers. The site of our corporate compound was also selected with a view to its proximity to Brookhaven National Laboratory. On a personal level, I appreciated how close it was to Wardenclyffe, where I built that ill-fated World Wireless tower three lifetimes ago.

Jean-Pierre picked me up in the black limo at 9:45 that Saturday morning, and on account of it being a weekend with no commuter traffic, we made it to the pharmaceutical company by 11 am. Both the pharma and stock-trading teams were there to meet me, although the general policy was for these two groups to have as little direct contact with each other as possible so as to stay under the radar of the Securities and Exchange Commission. Fortunately, since it was a Saturday, none of the rank-and-file workers were at the company. After a brief tour of the main building, we went down into the SCIF through a hidden tunnel that led underground.

Like all such facilities, it was protected from surveillance of any kind — well, of any *conventional* kind. I had also left the team with instructions for a measure intended to limit *unconventional* surveillance, such as Remote Viewing of what went on inside the facility. This was a technique we applied in the early 21st century, and it was fascinating to see it implemented here in 1980s New York. The concrete walls had been imprinted with row upon row of small numbers. You see, numbers are notoriously difficult for clairvoyants to read, even though they are drawn to deciphering them. So, the inscriptions were meant to act as a kind of confusing attractor, weakening any potential remote viewers' capacity to concentrate on the content of meetings at the facility. There were also, at regular intervals, stretches of concrete wall that lacked overhead lighting and were painted silver. Projectors were set up to fill these silver "screens" with hardcore pornographic images and scenes of ultra-violence. There was no audio, so we tried to just block them out as part of the background while we were having a meeting. But a remote viewer who was attempting to clairvoyantly surveil us would tend to get sucked into these psychic traps. Between these shocking images and the enigmatic numbers inscribed in the walls, the data that they would deliver to whoever was tasking them would most likely be garbage.

Small sandwiches and other hors d'oeuvres had been set up on the massive granite boardroom table. I picked at these, and drank coffee and tea, during a several-hour briefing on everything that had been achieved since the vanguard arrived here in 1977. We did *not* discuss Operation Neqab, or any specific operation aiming to change some feature of the timeline, because the details of these was highly compartmentalized information handled on a need-to-know basis. For example, there was no reason for the people who were setting up my meeting with Prime Minister Bakhtiar in Paris to know that I planned to assassinate the poor man once the coup he was leading was successful.

I left for Paris about a week after this meeting on Long Island. It was early April. The Iranian military coup to overthrow the Islamic Republic was planned for July 9–10. I stayed at a hotel near the Louvre, and while I waited to meet with Shapour Bakhtiar, I walked around the museum for a while. It was interesting to see it without the glass pyramid that would become so iconic. The Grand Louvre renovation project would not begin for another year, and that pyramid wouldn't be built until 1989. The inverted pyramid would be built even later, in the early '90s. Unlike the museums of the submerged island of Manhattan, the Louvre and Paris as a whole would survive the deluge because it was far enough inland and just barely high enough above sea level (35 meters on average, as compared to 10 meters on Manhattan Island). True to the city's darkly prophetic motto, Paris would be tossed by the waves, but she would not sink. What destroyed Paris wasn't the flood waters. It was years of civil war between native Parisians and increasingly fundamentalist Muslim migrants who, by 2040, declared a sharia-based Islamic State in France, albeit one that never managed to control the countryside before The Arrival ended it in 2048.

Which brings me back to Shapour Bakhtiar, who had been in exile for almost exactly one year. The Islamic Republic of Iran had just celebrated its first anniversary on April 1, 1980. I knew to set my meeting with the last Prime Minister of the dying Shah shortly after that, since Bakhtiar would likely be both incensed and imbued with a sense of urgency by the anniversary. Bakhtiar had been told that I was a private contractor with a corporate intelligence agency that occasionally collaborated with the CIA on certain operations. I knew that he would not check with the CIA because, contrary to what he told the military men in Iran who were part of his coup plot, Bakhtiar had endeavored to keep the entire operation hidden from the United States since American diplomats were still being held hostage by Islamist forces in Tehran, and such an attempted coup against the theocratic regime would likely be seen as posing a serious danger to their safety. Bakhtiar had been given assurances that my only contacts in the CIA relevant to Iran were rogue elements who considered the hostages expendable if it meant restoring a pro-US regime there. AtlantiCorp had already transferred significant funds to Bakhtiar's Swiss bank account, with the understanding that it would be used as "lubricant" to facilitate broader participation in the operation (we learned not to use the word "coup" with him).

It was the evening of Friday, April 4th, when I sat down to dinner with Prime Minister Bakhtiar at the dining table of my own luxurious suite at the Hausmannian-style Grand Hôtel du Louvre (built in 1855), which those who arranged the meeting, on both sides, determined to be the safest location from a security and counter-surveillance standpoint. No one would see him with me in a public place. The Prime Minister's joint three-man security team, consisting of one of his own most trusted men, one French secret service officer, and a member of the AtlantiCorp security force that had flown with me to Paris as my personal bodyguard, even had instructions to take the elevator to the wrong floor, then walk up the stairs to the right one.

When I opened the door and greeted Bakhtiar, I apologized to him for this protocol. With a wave of his hand, he told me to think nothing of it. We shook hands and exchanged pleasantries for a moment, as he smiled while nervously fingering his mustache and bobbing his head. The security men went ahead and scoped out the entire suite. Then, one of them stationed himself in the hallway, outside the door, wearing an earpiece that he could use to communicate with us. Another went back down to the lobby, carefully watching everyone headed in and out of the hotel. The third sat on a chair near the window, keeping his eye on the terrace. Then, after sipping glasses of wine that I poured us in the kitchen, Bakhtiar and I sat down at the dining table together. The hotel restaurant had sent up a room service tray stacked with a three-course meal. I knew I could bank on classic French food, since Bakhtiar had spent so many years of his youth in Paris — including fighting the Nazis as part of the Resistance during the occupation.

This militantly Anti-Fascist resume would make some of what I had to say a very hard sell. You see, Shapour Bakhtiar was a consummate Social Democrat. When Bakhtiar was studying in Paris in 1934, his father was executed by Reza Shah — the father of Shah Mohammad Reza Pahlavi. So, when the latter appointed Bakhtiar Prime Minister, as a last resort, at the height of the Iranian Revolution of 1979, he was appointing someone who had spent decades as an opposition figure and member of the National Front of Prime Minister Mohammad Mossadegh, in whose government Bakhtiar had served, when Mossadegh briefly overthrew the Shah, before the latter was restored (and Mossadegh arrested) in the MI6- and CIA-backed military coup of 1953.

Subsequently, Bakhtiar was repeatedly imprisoned, spending a total of six years in jail for his secular democratic opposition to the autocratic rule of the very Shah who he would agree to serve as Prime Minister in January of 1979, when Islamist theocrats and armed Communist guerrillas were on the verge of taking over the country. Bakhtiar's vision for a political solution in Iran had always been full restoration of the Persian Constitution of 1906, which would reduce the monarch to a ceremonial figurehead, and secure the full range of civil liberties, freedom of expression, and democratic political representation to all citizens. His attempt to implement such a platform after he came into office, in the midst of what by then was a violent revolution, with measures such as total freedom of the press and the release of all political prisoners, dramatically precipitated the total collapse of the Pahlavi regime within only thirty-six days. Once the general staff of the military swore allegiance to Ayatollah Khomeini, Bakhtiar fled to Paris where he had been busy building up a secular democratic opposition to the Islamic Republic and where, secretly, he had also been coordinating with second-tier military officers and opposition groups sidelined or betrayed by the ayatollahs to carry out Operation Neqab.

The point is that the last thing Bakhtiar wanted to see from out of this operation, which he did not consider a "coup" (since its leaders were no longer actually in power), was for a military dictatorship to seize control of Iran. To him, the military officers involved in the plot were only a spearhead in the service of democratization. His goal remained the same: an Iranian parliamentary democracy, with the broad participation of all political constituencies who were willing to achieve their aims within the legal parameters of the Constitution rather than by means of partisan violence. My unenviable task was to convince Bakhtiar that he had to appoint Mohsen Pezeshkpour as his Deputy Prime Minister. Pezeshkpour was the leader of the ultra-nationalist, one might even say Fascist, Pan-Iranist Party, which had been the loyal opposition to the Shah in parliament until, in 1975, the Shah abolished even this loyal opposition to establish a one-party system. In 1971, Pezeshkpour had used his position in parliament to loudly protest the Shah's willingness to relinquish Iran's claim to Bahrain.

Those charmed by his charisma considered his speeches impassioned, while critics and enemies saw Pezeshkpour as a raving lunatic. He was certainly the closest thing that Iran had to a Hitleresque political figure. He was a staunch anti-Communist and a strong supporter of the Imperial Iranian Military, which it was his ultimate ambition to use for a reconquest of all of the ethnically Iranian territories of the great Persian Empires of the past — someday, including those inside the Soviet Union (the Azerbaijani, Turkmen, Uzbek, and Tajik SSRs) and, of course, Afghanistan, which had been Eastern Iran until the 1800s. Pezeshkpour had a 180-degree opposite view of the Shah to that of Bakhtiar. He saw Mohammad Reza Pahlavi as a weak and ineffectual bureaucrat, all talk and no action. In the last days of the Pahlavi regime, after the Shah had already left Iran, Pezeshkpour delivered a fiery speech from the podium of the Parliament, wherein he accused the Shah of having been at the head of a "bureaucratic totalitarianism." Pezeshkpour, who had shaved his moustache and now bore a darkly comical resemblance to Peter Sellers playing Dr. Strangelove, pounded the podium as he ranted about how this was the worst form of government known to man. He was essentially quoting Carl Schmitt. According to Pezeshkpour, a military dictatorship would be far less corrupt. Unlike Bakhtiar, he refused to flee Iran. In fact, on the timeline that I was from, Pezeshkpour proved to be such a patriot that he effectively lived under house arrest and perpetual surveillance in the Islamic Republic rather than go into exile.

Since I knew that Pezeshkpour would be such a hard sell, I started by giving Bakhtiar some intelligence that would be even more valuable than the funds provided to him by AtlantiCorp. (Of course, he was entirely misled about how I had obtained all this information.) There was a member of the coup-planning group inside of Iran by the name of Farhad Nasirkhani who would turn out to be an asset of Iraqi intelligence. The information provided to the Iraqis by this fellow, ostensibly to secure their support for the coup, would actually be leaked to the ayatollahs by Saddam Hussein himself. In the timeline that I came from, this is something that the Islamic Republic, which considered the secular Baathist Saddam an arch-enemy even before Iraq invaded Iran in September of 1980, never admitted publicly.

The reason that Saddam passed on this information to the Iranian regime was because he knew that their crackdown on the coup plotters would destroy the nerve center of Iran's military, and introduce an incoherent division of power between the no longer trusted regular military and the newly formed Islamic Revolutionary Guard Corps.

This would significantly facilitate an Iraqi invasion of Iran. On the other hand, Saddam knew that if the coup were to succeed, and a nationalist military government were to replace the Islamic Republic as the regime of Iran, any Iraqi invasion would be easily thwarted by the remnants of the Shah's military. Bakhtiar said that he didn't even know who this guy was. I told him to make sure that the coup-planning team inside of Iran got rid of Nasirkhani, and that no one else involved in Operation Neqab approach any individual or organ of the Iraqi government. Bakhtiar nodded very affirmatively and said, "Yes, absolutely. I will definitely see to that, Ms. Avalon. Thank you." The Prime Minister's English was not bad, and where it faltered, I switched to French so that he could more fluently express himself in that language that he knew so well.

Next, I told Bakhtiar that one of the Air Force officers involved in the coup planning had a wife who was untrustworthy and that, perhaps on account of personal marital problems that they had, this woman would likely reveal to authorities of the theocratic regime what she knew about the secret meetings that her husband attended. I did not tell him that because the Islamic Republic never revealed the name of this woman (and even claimed, falsely, that it was her husband who had given up his collaborators, the night before the coup was supposed to take place), we had to use remote viewers to identify her. I told Bakhtiar that we would take her out of the picture. (In point of fact, I would have both her and, for good measure, also her husband poisoned to death months before she would decide to reveal anything.) Bakhtiar was more concerned by this variable than by the informant for Iraq, but he also expressed even more gratitude, bowing his head with his hand on his heart as he thanked me for getting ahead of this potential disaster.

Finally, I broached the subject of Pezeshkpour. I led into it by explaining to him that, unfortunately, as he knew full well, the possibility that the coup would fail or be reversed even *after* he returned to Iran could not be eliminated. Especially since his expeditious return to Iran would be key to its success, and yet this would also mean that he was all the more vulnerable to a potential reversal of the coup by Islamist forces. I told Bakhtiar that I knew that he hadn't told the nationalist military men involved in the coup plot that, democrat that he was, he had also negotiated the participation of Communist factions and even leftist guerrillas who had been betrayed by Khomeini after helping him to seize power, as well as certain insiders of the Islamic Republic who were of a more intellectual and technocratic bent, and did not want to see the promised "Republic" element of the regime become a hollow shell under a Khomeini-led theocracy. The leader of this last group was none other than the Islamic Republic's Foreign Minister, Sadegh Ghotbzadeh, who Bakhtiar had promised to recognize as the leader of an Islamic Party with the freedom to field candidates in parliamentary elections. He had made the same promises of full political participation, within the limits of the law, to the Communist parties, including the Tudeh Party, which was essentially an asset of the Soviet Union. Bakhtiar looked somewhat alarmed when I laid all this out, and I had to gently remind him that I ran a private intelligence agency (a lie, of course).

Bakhtiar accepted my proposition that if—Heaven forbid—he were to be assassinated shortly after the military takeover, the coalition that he had put together, which these officers didn't even know about, would rapidly disintegrate with the Communists turning on the military men who had led the coup, and vice versa, and the moderate Islamic faction turning on both of them and potentially allying itself with the Mojaheddin-e-Khalq (MEK). The MEK was just barely still part of the Islamic Republic regime but was seriously considering turning on Khomeini, who had severely sidelined them after using their muscle to topple the Shah. The MEK was not a part of Bakhtiar's coup coalition and represented a dangerous variable if the coalition were to unravel. The leader of this cultish 'Islamic' Maoist group, Massoud Rajavi, had his own ambitions to lead Iran. (What no one knew at the time is that Rajavi was so hell-bent on this that he would even ally himself with Saddam Hussein, and defect to Iraq with an entire tank battalion, during the Iran-Iraq War — a war that, on this revised timeline, it was my objective to prevent.)

In any case, I had Bakhtiar convinced, albeit grudgingly, that the coalition would not survive his death, and that there would be a very serious threat to Iran's cohesion as a nation. I let him know that, at AtlantiCorp, we were also apprised of his plan to use coup committees in the Azerbaijan, Kurdistan, Khuzestan, and Baluchistan provinces to help topple the Islamic Republic. All of these were border provinces demographically dominated by ethnic minorities with some aspirations for autonomy. There was a real danger that, if Bakhtiar was not there to form a parliamentary government wherein they all felt adequately represented, the very same people in these provinces who had volunteered to help him topple the ayatollahs, would lead a secession of their provinces from Iran, leaving only a rump state of "Persia" (the Persian-speaking part of Iran) that would be an economically devastated nation, especially without the oil that came almost exclusively from the Khuzestan province with its largely Arab population (who called the region "Al-Ahwaz").

So, I reasoned with Bakhtiar, that in the event — however unlikely — that such a nightmare scenario would unfold, there ought to be *some* designated civilian leader to replace him, but one who could work seamlessly with the military in order to crush the Marxists and the 'Islamic' Maoists, who would certainly stage an armed uprising, and above all, to secure the territorial integrity of Iran against potential secessions of those provinces with a Persian minority demographic. Bakhtiar very grimly followed the logic of all of this, but he still broke his characteristic gentlemanly cool and started shrilly shouting in French when I proposed that the only man capable of doing this was Mohsen Pezeshkpour. I told Bakhtiar that he ought to inform the military leaders of the coup that Pezeshkpour is his designated Deputy Prime Minster, without letting the leftists and moderate Islamists in the coalition know this. "He's a Fascist!" Bakhtiar shouted, in French.

His voice would become rather high-pitched when he raised it. I winced. The security man at the window also came over to make sure everything was alright. "I spent my youth here, in France, fighting Fascists! My father was killed by a Fascist like him!"

I began to address him in fluent Persian. *This* he was not expecting. I had saved it as my ace card. When I studied the writings of Jorjani in depth during my college years, and before I went on to write a dissertation critiquing them, I also began re-learning the Persian language. I say re-learning because I think that the many past life regression sessions that I had, which for obvious reasons wound up being more intensive than those of most Prometheists, helped me to regain some of Jason's linguistic abilities. I was able to start speaking Persian fluently much faster than most people who have no prior knowledge of the language. I went back over the key points of the very well-reasoned argument that I had made, but in Persian, and with a tone of more personal concern, adding colorful asides that demonstrated extraordinary insights into both the political history of Iran and the character of certain key individuals and groups, like Pezeshkpour, Ghotbzadeh, Rajavi, and the leader the Communist Tudeh Party, Noureddin Kianouri.

Bakhtiar stared at me with the most wide-eyed expression that I've ever seen on anyone's face. I asked him if he could, in all honesty, think of a single other politician who had served in a prominent position in parliament, or who held some cabinet level post in any of the Pahlavi administrations, who would be able to work as effectively with the military leaders of the coup to hold the country together if he were to meet with an untimely demise upon his return. After shaking his head and grumbling for a while, Bakhtiar admitted that he could think of no one other than Pezeshkpour. Then I asked him whether an outright military dictatorship with *no* civilian leader whatsoever, and potentially no parliament, would be preferable to an administration led by a man who — for decades — headed the parliament's second largest political party in Pahlavi Iran. *"To ki hasti?!"* (Who *are* you?!)

he shouted at me, indignantly, in Persian, before finally caving in as he shook his head, covering his downcast eyes. Whoever I may have been, the logic of the argument was sound, and whatever else Shapour Bakhtiar may have been, he was above all, a *logical* man.

All of this happened before we had dessert. I poured Bakhtiar a sweet wine to go with our crème brûlée and dark chocolate tarts with berries. "How did you learn such fluent Persian?" he asked, returning to a normal tone of voice, and sounding a little embarrassed at his earlier outburst. I couldn't even consider telling him the truth. Bakhtiar was as averse to metaphysical speculations as he was to religious scholasticism. "In the field of intelligence, Iran is my principal expertise." He rocked a bit, bobbing his head to the side, like a Muppet, and said, "*Clearly*, mademoiselle." After a moment's silence, he leaned in to me, with his dessert fork twirled in the air, "You know, there is no one — no politician —, in all the years I have been fighting for liberty in Iran, who could ever have convinced me to do what you ask me to do." My rejoinder was, "Prime Minister Bakhtiar, there has never been, in the long history of Iran, such a perilous time as this one. Not when the Greeks invaded, or even the Arabs, Turks, and Mongols, who sought to conquer your country. You are called upon to make an extraordinary sacrifice, because the very survival of Iran is at stake. It is our hope that you will lead the people of your country into a new era of Social Democracy and personal liberties. But, in any case, you must ensure the *survival* of the nation. I'm sure that you do not want to be remembered as the *last* Prime Minister of Iran." Bakhtiar stared at me somberly, "You are right, Ms. Avalon. I will *do* it." Shortly thereafter, we bid each other goodnight. The next day I visited the grave of Sadegh Hedayat at Père-Lachaise, laying a bouquet of red roses on the black stone pyramid inscribed with his name and the etching of an owl.

My flight back to New York left from Charles de Gaulle that night. It was a British Airways Concord. When we landed at JFK, earlier in the evening of the same day than we had left Paris, I reflected on how absurd it was that supersonic civilian flights would end in 2003 and would not resume, on a large scale, until the 2030s — at least in the world that I came from. Maybe that was something about history that we could change as well. Going through customs was a tiresome experience, and by the time that Jean-Pierre picked me up I was weary enough to lie across the back seat of the limousine. He was good about not bothering me with small talk, especially when he could see that I was tired. I dozed off until just before we reached the 59th Street Bridge, at which point I rolled down the window and gawked at the spectacular cityscape of midtown Manhattan. I used to love the view across this bridge, in particular, with the United Nations and the Chrysler Building clearly in sight. Jean-Pierre was a little unsettled by the fact that I kept the window rolled down as we entered the heart of the city, but it was a tinted window, and I was hungry to see as much as I could of those neighborhoods that were on our way home.

When we approached Central Park South, I asked Jean-Pierre if he would wait for me while I went to get a drink at The Plaza. Of course he obliged. He would loiter in the area and come check back at the front steps for me in twenty minutes, then again in half an hour, and so forth. I walked up to the Palm Court and sat at the bar island beneath the glass ceiling. I wanted to sit alone, but it was fairly crowded, and by the time that I was halfway through my Martini, a rather overconfident middle-aged man with an Italian accent was hitting on me. Clearly a hotel guest, I think he was entertaining delusions about getting me to come upstairs with him after a few more drinks. I told him that I had just flown back from Paris, had jet lag, and was headed back home. He was all pouty, disappointed that I was a New Yorker and didn't have a room at The Plaza. I caught Jean-Pierre up front on his second loop around the hotel. From my mood, I think he could tell that I regretted stopping for the drink and he surmised what had happened. The man was very intuitive. Did I mention that he was a practitioner of voodoo? He donned a black suit and black necktie as a uniform, but he also always wore a creepy bone wristband that

I gathered was a voodoo charm. I leaned on his shoulder slightly as I got out of the limo at 55 Central Park West. Once I got upstairs, I took a quick shower, just to wash the airplane off of me. Then I collapsed into bed and slept like the dead until late into the next morning.

In the weeks that followed, I checked back repeatedly with Prime Minister Bakhtiar on a secure phone line that we set up, to make sure that things were going according to plan. I told him that we had, for our part, eliminated the threat of the treacherous housewife. He told me that all potential ties to the Iraqis had been severed, and, most importantly, that Mohsen Pezeshkpour had been approached in Tehran and had agreed to become Deputy Prime Minister of the putatively "provisional" government that would be installed by Operation Neqab. On April 25th, when news of Operation Eagle Claw broke across the international media, Bakhtiar called me in a panic asking what I knew about this disaster that took place at Tabas in the Iranian desert.

Ayatollah Khomeini was portraying the incident as an "act of God" that demonstrated divine support for Iran's Islamic Revolution and its resistance against the "Great Satan" of America. I told Bakhtiar that, based on what I could surmise from my CIA contacts, black ops men under the orders of Director of Central Intelligence George H. W. Bush had sabotaged two of the helicopters involved in the mission. USAF field operations commander Colonel James H. Kyle may also have been acting on prior directives from Bush when he aborted the mission despite having a minimum of the resources necessary to carry it out, after the loss of the two sabotaged choppers and another one that went into an unexpected sandstorm. I told Bakhtiar that I didn't think that the crash of one of the retreating helicopters into a transport plane, which caused an explosion killing eight American servicemen, was an accident either. (Later, we would see that this failed attempt to rescue the US hostages in Tehran became the single most significant factor that cost Jimmy Carter his reelection and ensured that George

H. W. Bush would go from being the head of the CIA to Vice President of the United States under Ronald Reagan.)

Bakhtiar asked how I thought this would affect Neqab, and I said that if the American hostages were still being held at the US embassy when the operation was carried out, it should be one of the mission priorities to send an Iranian special forces team to storm the US embassy early in the operation so as to free the hostages and save as many of their lives as possible, taking them into custody as leverage to ensure that the United States would accept the new provisional government. The hostage-takers should then be publicly executed as "terrorists," with this being broadcast on American television.

When I turned on the television on the morning of May 18, I saw that an earthquake on Mount St. Helens in Washington state had triggered a massive landslide that caused the northern flank of the volcano to collapse. The mountain suddenly entered a catastrophic new stage of eruption. I was sleeping in because it was a Sunday, and I had been dancing the night away to disco music at Studio 54. I had a bit of a hangover too. As I watched the television coverage, I thought it was a good thing that I didn't let that cute girl I had met by the end of the night come home with me. (Instead, we finger fucked each other in a dark corner of the upstairs balcony, after snorting a line of coke.) She would have been a nuisance to deal with right now. I was particularly fixated on the images that were being broadcast, because I had arrived here, in this time, on the night that the eruption of Mount St. Helens started to simmer (about two months and ten days ago).

The volcano was billowing smoke, and as the day unfolded, and I remained glued to the news reports, I saw how this became a huge black column not unlike that of a mushroom cloud at a nuclear blast site. This is not an exaggerated comparison, since the thermal energy released by the eruption was reported to have reached 26 megatons — equivalent to the yield of a large nuclear warhead. The volcano, in the Pacific Northwest, dumped ash over no less than eleven American states and several Canadian provinces. Fifty-seven people were killed, including a couple of photographers and a geologist who were on-site and could not get out of harm's way fast enough when the landslide and major eruption took place. Hundreds of square miles were reduced to a wasteland, and thousands of animals were killed. When the dust settled, it was assessed that the damage to American and Canadian farmers was in the billions of dollars.

The majestic mountain scenery of the Pacific Northwest reminded me of scenes from *The Shining*, which I remembered was just about to be released. In two lifetimes now, it had been one of my favorite films. It would really be something to see it on the big screen when it first came out in theaters. I couldn't resist the pun of making plans to go see it together with "Johnny" on opening night. He was into horror films, after all. But before that, I had the pleasure of going to see another classic by myself, on the first full day that *it* was released. I went to a morning showing so as not to have to wait in lines that rounded the street corners. Lines wherein fans waiting to see the movie were often subjected to the spoiler shouted by overexcited people exiting the theater. "Vader is Luke's father," they would inconsiderately shout. Yes, I went to the Ziegfeld Theater on 54th Street to see the release of *The Empire Strikes Back*. By the way, I listened for it carefully, and the line was definitely "*No*, I am your father." (At least on *this* timeline.)

I had a VHS player hooked to the big CRT projector TV in my living room, and I began to amass a collection of videotapes of all of my favorite movies. That TV was also hooked up to cable, so that when CNN hit the airwaves for the first time, on June 1st of 1980, it became my preferred news outlet. These were the days back when the relatively radical Ted Turner ran the independent Cable News Network himself, and Larry King had just gotten his own televised show, long before its decline into another outlet of Newspeak. It came to mind just now because James Earl Jones, the voice of Darth Vader, did the recurring audio clip that would announce: "*This* is CNN." It was CNN, with its then unprecedented 24-hour news cycle, that I had on the day that I was waiting for breaking news on the coup attempt in Iran.

I had set my alarm clock for 5 am, which was already 1:30 pm in Tehran. But I could not sleep soundly, and I found myself already lying wide awake and anxious at 4 am, just after noontime in Iran. I threw on my bathrobe and went into the living room to turn on CNN. There was a commercial break, which I took as an opportunity to quickly put on a pot of coffee in the kitchen. As I waited for it to brew, I sat down on the sofa in front of the television. Sure enough, there it was. The first item once coverage resumed, with the banner "Breaking News" running across the bottom of the screen.

"These are scenes broadcast today by Iranian National Radio and Television, which was seized several hours ago by the leaders of what appears to be an ongoing military coup," a voice said over footage of Iranian Brigadier General Ayat Mohagheghi delivering a speech in a stern tone from behind a desk with a Lion and Sun flag sitting on it. Then the feed cut to a videotaped statement from Ayatollah Shariatmadari, who was the most high-ranking mullah in Iran, delivering a religious ruling or *fatwa* that what Ayatollah Khomeini had done since he returned to Iran in early 1979 had been a disgrace to Islam and the legacy of the imams. Shariatmadari reaffirmed the traditional Shi'ite stance that the clergy ought not to tarnish its moral authority by becoming directly involved in the political affairs of the country. In addition to these speeches, there was footage of certain buildings in and around Tehran consumed by flames. Then CNN cut to a reporter who was outside of Shapour Bakhtiar's home in Paris, where it was mid-morning. "The exiled Prime Minister has yet to make any statement, or to receive anyone from the media. His aids are, however, assuring us that a press conference *will* be held in a few hours. The security here is very tight. French police and gendarmerie have surrounded Mr. Bakhtiar's home." I didn't even consider calling him in the midst of all this. For now, all I could do was wait and watch.

Bits and pieces of information, together with a lot of repetition, and a few other news stories, came in over the next several hours. Then, finally, at 7 am, CNN's morning news anchor presented a fairly comprehensive overview. It was 3:30 in the afternoon in Tehran. Apparently, the coup had begun with airstrikes launched from Shahrokhi Air Force Base in Hamadan on key targets of the government of the Islamic Republic in Tehran. The most prominent of these was the home of Ayatollah Khomeini in the Jamaran neighborhood of northern Tehran, which was not only struck by Phoenix missiles from an F-14, but also became the target of a nearly simultaneous kamikaze strike by a martyred F-4 Phantom jet pilot. The Supreme Leader of the Islamic Republic, and the figurehead of the 1979 Revolution that brought the theocratic regime to power, was believed to have been immolated in the compound, which was still burning.

The so-called "Islamic Assembly," which had replaced Iran's national parliament, was also bombed. Immediately following the initial strikes in Tehran, jets took to the air from Air Force bases in Shiraz, Dezful, and Bushehr as well, hitting targets in the south and southwest of the country. All in all, it appeared that around fifty F-4 Phantoms and F-14 Tomcats were part of the aerial campaign. Coup committees in the West Azerbaijan, Kurdistan, Khuzestan, Baluchistan, and Khorasan provinces, as well as in Tehran itself, and in the Imperial Iranian Navy stationed at key ports in the Persian Gulf, carried out purges of those top brass officers who had committed treason against the Constitution, and the Bakhtiar administration, by swearing their allegiance to Khomeini and his fellow ayatollahs. Some of them were arrested, others were shot on the spot. The 23rd Commando Division, the 1st Infantry Division, the 92nd Armored Division, and the 1st Marine Battalion acted as the spearhead of a nationwide imposition of martial law in Iran. From the start of the coup, at least 5,000 rank-and-file soldiers put their boots on the ground to back it. Many of them pulled down flags of the Islamic Republic and burned them in the streets, raising the old Lion and Sun banner back up on the poles over government buildings and city squares.

The most important piece of news, at least for an American audience to wake up to on this Wednesday morning, was revealed, rather strategically, when Prime Minister Bakhtiar finally gave a statement to a few select members of the press at noon in Paris. "At the very beginning of the operation, a team of our Special Forces commandos raided the US embassy in Tehran and were able to free the majority of American hostages held there. Unfortunately, a dozen of the 52 hostages were killed during the operation and some others were also injured. The 40 survivors are in protective custody now and those who require it are receiving medical attention. The provisional military government in Iran is in communication with Washington to secure their transport back to the United States as soon as possible. Maybe even later today, or tomorrow at the latest." With his head somewhat downcast, Prime Minister Bakhtiar went on to add, "I should also report that, although it was my preference that they stand trial for their crimes, it appears that all of the hostage takers who survived the initial commando assault have now been executed as stateless terrorists." The CNN newscast cut to footage of these executions carried out by Iranian commandos with their own handguns, against the wall of the US embassy. Despite the brutality of that footage, it would air over and over again, on prime time American television, albeit always with a warning. That would go a long way in redeeming Iran's image, regardless of Bakhtiar's own reservations.

"Mr. Bakhtiar, who is in control in Iran?" shouted one of the journalists, as CNN cut back to the press conference in Paris. "For the moment, patriots of our military are in control. But it is my understanding that they await my return. These brave men have given every assurance that they will recognize me as Prime Minister when I arrive in Tehran shortly." When I heard these words, I picked up the phone without delay and called the pilot of the Learjet that I had ostensibly bought for conducting AtlantiCorp business. But it had no corporate logo painted on the side of it. I had deliberately left it unmarked. Meanwhile, I got a hold of Manuchehr Ghorbanifar, who had been on AtlantiCorp's payroll for the last month for his "shipping services" and he informed me of exactly when on the next day, and on what private

plane, which belonged to Ghorbanifar's company, Prime Minister
Bakhtiar would be leaving Paris for Tehran. Despite Bakhtiar's iden-
tification with Charles de Gaulle on account of his days in the French
Resistance, the decision had been made to divert potential assassins
or terrorists that the ayatollahs might send, by having the private
plane depart from Orly airport, while a much more high-profile flight
carrying aids of Bakhtiar would fly out of Charles de Gaulle, with the
press having been misinformed that the Prime Minister was also on
that flight.

I had, in advance, located the most isolated and desolate private
airfield on the outskirts of Paris that I could find. On the night of
July 9th, my Learjet left New York from the relatively obscure Stewart
Airport, a former Air Force base that was located about 60 miles
north of Manhattan and landed in that rural French airfield early the
next day. I slept on the plane. Jean-Pierre, whose French turned out to
be not bad, despite his Creole accent, was the only passenger on the
plane besides the AtlantiCorp pilot. Jean-Pierre took a taxi from the
airfield to the nearest auto rental place, and then drove back to the
airfield with the car that would be used for this operation. It had been
decided, when we planned this at a select meeting in the SCIF, that
no driver in France could be trusted more than my personal chauf-
feur — an ex-commando —, who should be brought along for the job.
Besides, my life was already in his hands on a regular basis anyhow.

When Jean-Pierre picked me up, he noticed that I slipped a very
long bag into the trunk of the car, but neither did he remark upon
this, nor upon the fact that I was dressed in a black chador complete
with a neqab (a face veil). The expression that he had on his face when
he would note things silently with a look in the rearview mirror sometimes reminded me of the Observer in the *Silver Surfer* comics. He
drove me to a wooded field with a few clearings between the trees,
somewhere between the towns of Orly and Villeneuve-le-Roi, suburbs
of Paris that were near Orly Airport. When Ghorbanifar gave me
the flight information, I had determined the trajectory of the plane's

departure from Orly on its way to Tehran. The long black bag, which I slung around my shoulder as I left the car parked on the side of the road to trudge into the field, contained a prototype FIM-92 Stinger missile designed by General Dynamics and acquired by AtlantiCorp from a corrupt defense contractor at Raytheon. Now that I was alone in the field, I pulled down the neqab to breathe more freely, but kept the chador wrapped around me, as I dragged the black bag through the field. I was wearing gloves, so as not to leave fingerprints, because my plan was to discard the weapon here after using it.

I checked my Swiss watch. We had made it with little time to spare. I also checked my compass and oriented myself perfectly toward Orly Airport, where the target should have been lifting off at that moment. Then I pulled the Stinger missile out of the bag and mounted it on my shoulder. It was a good thing that I had been working out regularly. The line of cocaine that I snorted when I woke up on the Learjet also helped me to focus. After a nerve-racking delay, in the course of which I picked up and set down the launcher a few times, and even crouched down in the field, increasingly concerned that I'd be caught out here in broad daylight, Bakhtiar's private plane finally came into view. They had left about 20 minutes late. (Still, not bad for Persian time.)

I checked through the scope to confirm that the markings on the plane were those of Ghorbanifar's company. Then, in what remains to this day the hardest decision that I have ever made, besides the one to come to this time in the first place, I pulled the trigger to launch the heat-seeking missile that sped toward the signature of the plane's engine exhaust. I had barely laid down the Stinger when the plane exploded, and its burning debris started to fall not all that far ahead of me in this field. I lost my cool and ran to the car as fast as I could, discarding the chador in the field along the way. I had planned to wear it back onto the plane so that no one at the airport could identify me as anything other than "some Muslim woman." As soon as I jumped in the backseat Jean-Pierre sped back to the airfield without a single word, let alone a question. Within half an hour of the explosion, my

Learjet, which had refueled while I was in the field, was lifting off to head back to New York. Jean-Pierre didn't bother to return the car he rented under a false name. He just left it on the tarmac. He stared at me a few times, as I scanned the radio for news during the flight home. Finally, the reports came in on news services. Shapour Bakhtiar was dead.

When I got back to my apartment, I signaled those cleared for full knowledge of Operation Neqab that I was home, and then I collapsed in bed for hours. Once I finally got up, and put CNN on the TV, I learned that French police had already carried out an investigation of the field near Orly and discovered both the Stinger missile *and the chador and neqab*. Based on this information, the military men that had seized power in Iran announced on National Radio and Television that Prime Minister Bakhtiar had been assassinated by an agent of the overthrown Islamic Republic, potentially a devout Muslim woman. In the same broadcast, they revealed that Bakhtiar had designated Mohsen Pezeshkpour as his Deputy, and that consequently, Pezeshkpour, who was already in Tehran, would be recognized by them as the acting Prime Minister of Iran. By the time that Prime Minister Pezeshkpour delivered a fiery speech at a podium flanked by military officers, at some undisclosed location, probably Shahrokhi Air Base, the socio-political constituencies of the fractious coup coalition that Bakhtiar was supposed to bring together, with his promise of broadly representative Social Democracy, was rapidly unraveling. Marxist Tudeh party members and the 'Islamic' Maoists guerrillas of the Mojaheddin-e-Khalq were already challenging martial law in the streets. All the King's men would not be able to put it back together again.

Speaking of the King, or his successor, my business was unfinished. The Shah was dying of cancer in Cairo, where his wife, Empress Farah, and his children were holding his hand in what would certainly be his last days. I had to ensure that Crown Prince Reza Pahlavi would never be put on the throne by the officers who had carried out the coup, who were after all claiming legitimacy in the name of the old Imperial

Iranian military. I knew how this young man's character would unfold, and he would never consent to a strong military dictatorship in
Iran for any significant period of time. Moreover, those in Iran who
were similarly leery of such a prospect, but who were not committed
to any of the leftist factions either, might look to him as the figurehead
for a parliamentary democracy of the kind that Bakhtiar had wanted
to build.

The Shah was confined to Maadi Hospital, on the banks of the Nile
River, in a suburb of Cairo. The Crown Prince would occasionally
come and go, commuting between the hospital and the home where
the Pahlavi family was residing in Cairo under President Anwar
Sadat's protection. In that short space of time, he was inside of a readily identifiable car that was relatively unprotected — at least against an
RPG rocket launched at it from a rooftop. I thought that I'd be pushing my luck to attempt this myself, and besides I doubted my ability
to operate as effectively in Arab Egypt as in a European country like
France. But I could remotely facilitate escape for an Egyptian mercenary who might be led to believe that he was doing this in the name
of Islam. Although Egypt had not been a Shi'ite country since the days
of the Fatimid Caliphate, there were still some devout Shi'ites there
who lionized Ayatollah Khomeini — even more so now that he had
been "martyred." I knew that, on my timeline, the Shah would die at
Maadi Hospital on July 27. Perhaps the success of the coup would put
him in better spirits and extend his life by a bit, but we certainly had a
very narrow window of time to carry this out while the Crown Prince
would still be visiting his father's hospital bed.

By July 21, we had found our man in Cairo. He was approached by
an operative of AtlantiCorp who spoke Arabic, and who could pass
for an Iranian when he went without shaving. Antonio Belluzzo was
actually Italian and, before my vanguard had recruited him, he had
been a dealer of arms to Italian loyalists in Libya who were planning
a future attempt to overthrow Ghaddafi. On Tuesday, July 22, 1980,
the well-paid Shi'ite mercenary that was hired by the Italian, posing as a vengeful fugitive IRGC commander, who had supplied him

with an RPG and trained him to use it, stood on a rooftop along the mapped-out route of Crown Prince Reza's car ride back home from the hospital. It was after sunset, so he was at least able to take his firing position under the cover of dark. He hit the car, alright. Then, having left the RPG on the rooftop, the mercenary ran down the steps of the building and out its back door to a truck that was waiting on one end of an alleyway.

What our Italian operative, Belluzzo, had failed to tell the fanatical Arab was that the back of the truck, into which he had climbed, was rigged with a fast-acting poison gas, and its door could be locked from the driver's seat. Belluzzo gassed the Arab as he drove, and the man was dead before the truck was out of the suburb. The Italian, all the while wearing black leather gloves that would leave no prints behind, abandoned the truck on a street where he had parked a Mercedes. He quickly shaved with a battery-powered electric razor, and then headed back to his hotel in Cairo to pick up his bags before taking a flight to Rome, from where he would report these details to us in an encrypted telegraph message. The Shah of Iran, heartbroken by his eldest son's death, expired in his hospital bed within 72 hours, only a day after they finally decided to tell him, when he demanded to know why no one in his immediate family had visited him for two days.

The military government led by Mohsen Pezeshkpour was now free to fend for itself in the face of a leftist uprising, sympathetic to the Soviet Union, and ethnic separatist movements that had begun in the Azerbaijan, Kurdistan, Khuzestan, and Baluchistan provinces — two of which (Azerbaijan and Kurdistan) had previously been occupied by the USSR (from 1941 to 1946), and one of which (Khuzestan) contained almost all of the oil reserves that were the lifeblood of the Iranian economy. Meanwhile, Baluchistan was located just to the southwest of Soviet forces occupying Afghanistan, and it featured a strategically significant port called Chah Bahar, on the Sea of Oman that tankers pass through on approach to the vital choke point of the Strait of Hormuz. The USSR did not have any warm water ports, and the Soviets desperately wanted them. I had set the stage for just the kind of conflict in, and over, Iran that would heighten Cold War tensions and, ultimately, if it were played out right, save the economy of the Soviet Union from collapse.

The Pezeshkpour regime's first challenge was, however, confronting an uprising of the pro-Khomeini clergy across the country, including at established Shi'ite seminaries in Qom, Mashhad, and even Isfahan. Those mullahs who had served in prominent positions in the Islamic Republic had mostly been arrested or hunted down selectively so that the state would not have to bother with their prosecution or incarceration. But there were a much larger group of mullahs sympathetic to the regime, who considered Ayatollah Khomeini a martyr, and these clerics martialed about two million *Hezbollahis* (religious vigilante thugs) across the country, especially in Iran's two largest cities, Tehran and Mashhad.

The military capitalized on the anger of the secular segment of the population, especially a significant percentage of urban women, who had deeply resented the nine months or more that they had to live under a medieval Islamic theocracy, with mandatory veiling, and a severe curtailing of their civil rights. Pezeshkpour ordered his soldiers into the seminaries and mosques, to gun down anti-government mullahs in bloodbath after bloodbath on supposedly "sacred ground." Meanwhile, the Iranian Air Force used attack helicopters to mow down thousands of *Hezbollahi* hooligans marching in the street with clubs and chains. The press was bad, but the government survived it, including with the support of most Americans, who regained their respect for Iran. Carter's idiotic statements on "genocide" having been committed by the nationalist military regime in Iran during the late summer of 1980 would cost him reelection, despite the resolution of the hostage crisis — no thanks to him. By contrast, for a brief period, both the Communists of Iran and Soviet officials in Moscow remained silent.

CHAPTER 5

STAR CHILD

B Y 1982, the Communists and Maoists of Iran, consisting of members of the Tudeh Party, the Fedayeen guerrillas, and the Mojaheddin-e-Khalq, had broken their tacit truce with Pezeshkpour's nationalist military junta. This was only ever a one-sided truce anyhow, since they were not offered any participation in the new regime, which had not held parliamentary elections in the two years since the coup, and the Pan-Iranist junta considered them enemies of the state that were aiding and abetting the various ethnic separatists who were intent on tearing Iran apart. This suspicion on the part of Pezeshkpour and his generals proved to be right. As soon as the various leftist factions resumed their violent resistance of the regime in the streets of Iran's major cities, late in 1981, there was a clearly coordinated intensification of the partisan warfare waged by the ethnic separatists. The hammer and sickle flags of the Tudeh and Fedayeen were seen in Azerbaijan and Khuzestan, and the Mojaheddin had made some deal with the Kurds according to which a Rajavi-led regime in Tehran would recognize Kurdish independence.

In December of 1981, Soviet General Dmitry Yazov was transferred from Czechoslovakia, another ethnically fractious country, to the Caspian region with orders to prepare for a Soviet invasion of Iran in support of the secessionists. He was to closely coordinate with the Soviet command in Afghanistan, which would enter the country from the east, while Yazov's forces would march down Western Iran — through a series of secessionist provinces, from Azerbaijan and Kurdistan down to Khuzestan, the oil reserves of which were the primary objective of the invasion. That, and seizure of warm water ports at Abadan on the Persian Gulf and Chah Bahar on the Sea of Oman, which would be carried out by the Soviet Navy once ground forces reached the coastline. General Yazov had a long and distinguished military career, having been one of the Soviet officers who commanded ground forces in Cuba, and personally worked with Castro, during the Cuban Missile Crisis in 1962. At that time, his unit had orders to be the spearhead of a nuclear strike on United States territory in the event that the crisis could not be resolved. In other words, Khrushchev trusted this man to have the nerve to start a war that would leave only cockroaches alive on Earth.

In January of 1982, the ethnic separatists declared independence in all of their respective provinces, while leftist demonstrators and insurgents kept the military tied up on the city streets of Tehran, Mashhad, Isfahan, and Shiraz. The Soviet Union immediately recognized their declarations of independence, sending ambassadors who were really KGB coordinators to the provisional governments of South Azerbaijan, Kurdistan, Khuzestan, and Baluchistan. TASS began to refer to what was left of Iran as "Persia" in all of its official news reports, expressing Soviet support for the "the comrades struggling against fascism in Persia." In March, as the snow started to melt in the Zagros and Alborz Mountains of northwestern Iran, but while it was still relatively cool in the eastern deserts that Soviet forces in Afghanistan would have to cross to reach Baluchistan in the southwest, the Soviet Union invaded Iran. Despite Pezeshkpour's show of giving a speech from beside a *Haft-Sin*, hardly anyone was celebrating Persian New Year on March 21, 1982. There was a curfew in effect in "Persia" as the military struggled to crush the Communist fifth column, so that it could focus on repelling the invading Soviet Army.

This turned out to be a losing proposition. Pezeshkpour prioritized the defeat of the fifth column but having largely succeeded in this objective and secured the Persian core of Iran from a Communist overthrow of his nationalist junta, he also lost the outer provinces to the USSR. By late May of 1982, after several months of heavy fighting, four former Iranian provinces were incorporated into the USSR as Soviet Socialist Republics. For the sake of geographical contiguity, from Central Asia to the seized port at Chah Bahar in Baluchistan, Afghanistan was also declared an SSR. Dmitry Yazov was widely praised as the face and fist of this tremendous victory. The General was promoted to Marshal of the Soviet Union, the highest-ranking military officer in the chain of command of the USSR. He also became the man most feared by the US government.

The Politburo consisted largely of aging and ailing men. Brezhnev was dying, and it was known by the CIA that Andropov, who was due to succeed him as General Secretary, was also in ill health and would not last long. The next in line of succession, by seniority in the Politburo, would be Chernenko, but his health was also rapidly failing. This potentially destabilizing rapid succession of Politburo men as weak leaders of the USSR deeply concerned the new head of the KGB, Vladimir Kryuchkov. He had been the KGB *rezident* in Kabul during the Soviet takeover of Afghanistan and considered holding both Afghanistan and the seized provinces of Iran as a non-negotiable long-term strategic priority. Kryuchkov and men loyal to him at the KGB were considering maneuvering Marshal Yazov into position as the leader of the Soviet Union. They faced one principal obstacle — a young reformer who had come under the wing of Andropov and was being groomed by him as the future General Secretary: Mikhail Gorbachev.

The elimination of Mikhail Gorbachev was among my highest priorities and primary objectives since the politics of *glasnost* and *perestroika* that he had it in mind to forward would prove to be the downfall of the Soviet Union. Moreover, as soon as I began planning this operation, I realized that Gorbachev needed to be taken out *before* he could become General Secretary of the Soviet Union. A hardliner coup against him, of the kind that had been attempted in the terminal phase of the USSR's collapse, in August of 1991, might be more successful if it were staged years earlier, say in 1987 or '88. But *any* old-guard Communist Party coup against reformist policies, such as those that Gorbachev would champion, ran the risk of inflaming public opinion against the regime and dangerously amplifying dissent in the longer run. Someone like Boris Yeltsin could still come along and take up the torch of reform, so that the Soviet Union might fall later but still not make it into the 21st century. The best thing would be for Gorbachev to exit stage left before the common people of the USSR and the leading politicians of the West ever really took notice of him. An assassination, by any conventional methods, would draw too much attention to him. He was, after all, already a member of the Politburo. Also, AtlantiCorp did not have that kind of reach into Russia, and Gorbachev had not begun to travel internationally with the frequency that he did after he assumed leadership (on my timeline). No, something more stealthy and untraceable was called for here. For that, I had only to look at the playbook of the Soviet Union itself.

Specifically, to Soviet Psychotronics research. The Russians were training adept practitioners of psychokinesis (PK) to have a direct mental influence on living systems (DMILS). They practiced by stopping the hearts of mice. They would carry out these tests in Soviet submarines, with the idea that the harmful PK field might be better shielded that way. I had obtained a dangerously full dossier of information about their specific methods and practices, which, on my timeline, had been acquired by the CIA after the fall of the Soviet Union. Once the United States itself disintegrated, the Prometheist movement was able to obtain certain treasure troves of formerly classified information by hiring sympathetic ex-US government officials who had been party to secret Psionic espionage and psychic warfare programs.

I began training in the use of these DMILS techniques of Soviet Psychotronics when I was in my twenties. I admit that I carried out a couple of successful tests on members of the Prometheist Old Guard that considered the reincarnation of Jorjani a threat to their corrupt entrenchment as gatekeepers of the movement. I managed to give one of them a stroke and induced an arrythmia leading to heart failure in another. The training was not all negative. It also taught me to regulate my own healing processes in order to recover from injuries and illnesses more quickly, or even correct imbalances in certain organs.

For the sake of public safety, I will not detail the clairvoyant visualization and telekinetic resonance methods involved in "staring someone dead" even at great distances. Suffice it to say that I had to begin by clairvoyantly surveilling Gorbachev for days on end and establishing a kind of telepathic hypnosis to entrance him at a distance. When his thoughts and feelings about his wife, Raisa Gorbacheva, a cultured woman who had deeply studied Philosophy, bled back into my mind, I found it difficult to continue but I did manage to persist. Despite being a member of the Politburo, Gorbachev would still drive his own car. One time he even rushed to personally bring a packed meal to Raisa at the lecture hall of the class that she taught at Moscow State University, because his wife had been running late that morning and had missed breakfast.

I decided that if Gorbachev were to have a heart attack and a stroke *while* he was driving alone during the morning rush hour, this would be optimal since it would likely result in a car crash that would add a third factor contributing to an almost definite fatality. The prospect of collateral damage to other drivers bothered me, but not when compared to the scale of misery that Gorbachev himself would wind up inflicting upon his own people for decades after the catastrophic failure of his policies. So, one gray and rainy morning in late May of 1982, Mikhail Gorbachev keeled over the wheel of his car as it was totaled on a Moscow highway. After I received confirmation through

TASS, which AtlantiCorp was monitoring closely, I collapsed and was bedridden for nearly a week before I managed to rebound.

By March of 1985, after the NATO exercise Able Archer 83 terrified both the Soviet high command and the KGB, and the deaths in rapid succession of Politburo-based leaders Andropov and Chernenko, Dimitry Yazov was installed as the strongman leader of the USSR. In that time, I managed to use an AtlantiCorp asset in Washington, who was a rather attractive Russian woman, to leak two key pieces of information to the KGB via their Science and Technology man at the Soviet embassy. In January of 1983, two months before Reagan announced the Strategic Defense Initiative (SDI) that would go on to be dubbed the "Star Wars" program, my Russian-speaking liaison, Irena, provided Oleg Burov with a briefcase full of the blueprints for SDI. I had brought these back with me in one of those suitcases that had been loaded onto the saucer. What I told Irena to convey to Burov, so that he could get it across to the KGB back in Moscow, was that SDI was a ruse intended to bankrupt the Soviet Union by scaring the Russians into spending vast sums of money that they didn't have on building something comparable to the space-based laser defense system against incoming nuclear missiles. Washington was not serious about actually building this system, and there was no reason for the Soviets to try to compete.

I had no way to know whether Moscow got the message and believed this, but after Reagan delivered his SDI speech from the Oval Office on March 23, 1983, Burov trusted Irena enough so that I could convey another piece of vital information that the Soviet leadership would certainly act on. I passed on detailed notes about the Chernobyl nuclear power plant meltdown that, on my timeline, would take place on April 26 of 1986. The detailed notes, including diagrams, were obtained from the "Stargate" remote viewing program of the US government. The USSR knew of the existence of this program, which was similar to one of their own that also engaged in precognitive clairvoyance. Burov was, of course, not told that these documents had been smuggled back from far in the future where Prometheists had obtained reproductions of them. They had also been among the contents that I emptied from the buoyant suitcases into my hidden vault on the night that I arrived at my apartment. The Chernobyl catastrophe and the scandal that ensued from it caused deep internal divisions in the Soviet leadership, eroded legitimacy in the eyes of the populace, and played a major contributing factor in the dissolution of the USSR. Preventing that meltdown from taking place would, therefore, also help to preserve the Soviet Union.

Irena Akhmatova was not hired by Johnny or anyone else on the vanguard team that I had sent ahead of me to set up Avalon Pharmaceutical and AtlantiCorp, the parent company for which it principally supplied capital. I had recruited her myself. She had been working at the EastWest Institute at 10 Grand Central on 44th street. EWI was a public policy think tank dedicated to international conflict resolution and back-channel dialogue between the Eastern bloc countries of the Warsaw Pact and that part of the Western world bound together by NATO. I had set up a meeting with John Edwin Mroz, who co-founded the Institute here in New York in 1980. Mroz had brought Akhmatova with him to the meeting, the purpose of which was to discuss prospects for long-term American and Soviet collaboration in space, including a possible joint Mars mission. Irena was there because she was a Russian Cosmist. In particular, she was a standard-bearer of the legacy of Konstantin Tsiolkovsky, the most Promethean of these early 20th-century futurists in Russia, and the only one of the first generation of Cosmists who was anti-Christian enough to wind up working for the USSR. He became the grandfather of the Soviet rocket program, and spiritual father of the Cosmonauts. Tsiolkovsky was also a panpsychist and a eugenicist, positions that made the Politburo uneasy about him and his legacy.

Irena's published writings furthered his project, but in a direction that was too radical for her to be able to work in the Soviet Union. Thanks to the EastWest Institute she was able to occasionally travel back to Moscow from Manhattan, where she had emigrated after a borderline defection. The KGB had sent her to a doctoral program in the Philosophy of Science at Princeton University, but when her 1979 dissertation on "Cosmonauts as Soviet Supermen" ruffled feathers back in Moscow, and she was condemned instead of praised for advocating implementation of eugenic embryo-selection and eventually genetic engineering as part of the Soviet space program, especially with a view to colonization of the Moon and Mars, she decided to stay here. She approached Mroz when he founded EWI a year later, and he facilitated her receiving the right of residency in the United States without forfeiting her Soviet citizenship.

That is what she explained to me when I hired her away from him early in June of 1982. I relocated her to the branch office that AtlantiCorp discretely maintained in the Watergate Office Building in Washington DC. The main purpose of that was for her to cultivate a relationship with the KGB's Directorate X department operative at the Soviet embassy. Directorate X was the KGB's division of Scientific and Technological Intelligence. The secondary purpose of that relocation was to make sure that she did not become my girlfriend. You see, to be honest, my interest in Ms. Akhmatova was not strictly professional. When she showed up to that meeting with Mroz, I was immediately attracted to her. After a few lunch meetings, purportedly for the purpose of discussing potential areas of US-USSR space cooperation, it became clear to me both from her body language and from the telepathic impressions that I received that Irena was bisexual. At one lunch meeting that we had, during a downpour, at Wolf's Delicatessen in midtown, I saw her checking out a handsome man at a nearby booth whose shirt had been soaked through, so I knew that she wasn't strictly a lesbian. There was chemistry between us, but I didn't want to get involved in anything very serious with her that would compromise our work together or put me in a position where I felt compelled to reveal too much to her about who I really am.

However, when she would occasionally come back to New York to attend those few meetings at the SCIF on Long Island for which she was cleared, I would invite her to stay in one of the guestrooms at my penthouse rather than to be put up at a hotel by the company. I knew she preferred the view. Irena liked to get up early and do Yoga on the rooftop terrace as the sun was rising over Manhattan. The first time that I caught her doing this, it was an especially hot and humid day in late August of 1982 — on her second trip back to Manhattan from the Washington office. She broke her routine when she saw me walk naked through the door of the turret, carrying a Yoga mat in my arms. Then, as I unrolled it, and started to strike a posture next to her, she smiled and nodded with a typically Russian expression that said, "*well then*," and she stripped off her own Yoga pants and tank top. We synchronized our *asanas* together throughout the sunrise.

Then, I started to do things that Irena didn't recognize. You see, in Gotham of the early 21st century, the Prometheist movement had developed a form of combined exercise and meditation that synthesized elements of Yoga with Tai-Chi and Capoeira. After she stood there for a moment, both bewildered and aroused by my naked body flowing dynamically through these movements and postures, she asked me what this was and whether I could teach it to her. I stopped, sweating by now in the muggy morning weather, and placed my hands on her hips, held her thighs up, and guided her arms with my grasp, as I taught her what we called "Promethean Yoga." After that session we took the first of many showers together.

On days when she would wake up at my place, I would tell Jean-Pierre to take a break so that I could drive Irena around in my black DeLorean. She loved to listen to contemporary pop music on my car's cassette player. Partly, she wanted to improve her English, which although formally excellent, was not colloquial enough. I told her that I'd be sad if she lost her sexy Russian accent. I had all of the harder-edged and more haunting hits of the early '80s on tape. Irena's favorites were Eurythmics' "Sweet Dreams," Bonnie Tyler's "Total

Eclipse of the Heart," and numerous songs of Laura Branigan, who she was smitten with, and whose music videos she confessed to thinking about when she fingered herself. (I really couldn't blame her. I wanted to see what Irena would do when "Self Control" came out.) We'd put one after another in as we ran red lights crisscrossing the city for both business and pleasure.

The most important business meeting that I took her to was at Trump Tower in March of 1983, with none other than the Don himself. It was set up under the pretext that AtlantiCorp was considering acquiring an entire floor of Trump Tower for its new corporate headquarters. We drove to that meeting in the DeLorean, blasting "Gloria" on the tape deck. I knew that Donald Trump appreciated Slavic women, and with my nearly flat chest and somewhat androgynous looks, I wasn't exactly his type. But Irena definitely was. She looked a lot like the woman that Trump would wind up with, after two divorces, on my timeline. Specifically, Irena bore a striking resemblance to the young Melania Knauss back when she was a black-haired Slovenian model. Irena's breasts weren't quite as big, but they were natural.

I ruled out trying to set her up with him, although that would have served my purposes well, and saved him from the mishap with Marla, because Irena was way too intelligent for him to be comfortable with. Trump claimed to respect "smart" women, but there is a hell of a difference between a housewife who is not a bimbo and a hyper-intellectual woman with a doctorate in Philosophy of Science who works for think tanks. This meeting would be the first of many that I would manage to secure with the real estate magnate, in order to start convincing him to run in the 1988 US presidential election. I justified Irena's presence by seeding in Trump's mind the idea of a potential "grand bargain" between the USA and USSR — a deal that Trump boasted only he could make — involving a joint manned mission to Mars before the year 2000.

On my timeline, Trump had done the interview circuit from Larry King to Orpah Winfrey during a brief period in 1987 when he appeared to be seriously considering running for President, despite his repeated tongue-in-cheek denials that he had no plans to announce his candidacy. He seemed to drop this when, sometime in 1988, Vice President Bush did something to secure Trump's support for his own candidacy. But up until Bush talked (or paid?) him out of entering the electoral fray, Trump certainly appeared to be campaigning, on every issue from the problem of poverty and homelessness, to funding for education, and our failing infrastructure. Where would the money come from? Nothing less than imperial tribute from protected "allies."

One of the documents that I had smuggled with me from the future past was a full-page ad that Donald Trump had paid nearly $100,000 to print in *The New York Times* on September 2, 1987. The headline, printed in bold, read "There's nothing wrong with America's Foreign Defense Policy that a little backbone can't cure." Beneath that, in somewhat smaller print, was a sub-heading that identified the one-page shadow-offset document printed below it as "[a]n open letter from Donald J. Trump on why America should stop paying to defend countries that can afford to defend themselves." Then there was the body of the "letter" itself.

In essence, the piece argued that economic powerhouses like Japan and Saudi Arabia should be paying the United States to defend them from potential enemies like Iran in the Persian Gulf or North Korea in the Sea of Japan. He lamented that the Japanese were outcompeting us, and buying up all of our best real estate, with wealth that we were creating for them by covering their defense costs. He also insisted that we didn't really need Saudi oil, especially not if the Arabs were going to deny us use of their embarrassingly superior mine sweepers to protect tankers in the Persian Gulf. Our so-called "allies" outside of the Western world, and even some in NATO, should start paying the United States of America something akin to imperial taxes, Trump argued unabashedly. I prepared my talking points for this meeting with him based on what Trump himself had printed there, in a political statement that he wouldn't make for another four years, in a future that had already been significantly altered by the ripples of Operation Neqab and the strengthening of the USSR — especially through its seizure of what had been Iran's oil reserves and seaports.

There was a much more personal, but not unintended, consequence of the success of Operation Neqab and the subsequent Soviet invasion of Iran. Stopping the collapse of the Soviet Union was not my only mission here. Influencing and redirecting the life of Jason Reza Jorjani was certainly also part of my agenda. One of the consequences of Neqab significantly facilitated this other mission.

In June of 1982, Jason's father, Fereidun Qajar Jorjani, would come back home in a rage after having watched *E.T. the Extra-Terrestrial*. It was immediately apparent to him that the film had been plagiarized, scene for scene, from a screenplay that he had co-authored around the time that Jason was conceived. The script was called *Star Child*. Every attorney in a law office that Fereidun contacted immediately after the release of *E.T.* concluded that Steven Spielberg's film, which would go on to become the highest grossing movie of all time, was a reworked version of *Star Child*.

All of the most innovative elements of the film were already in Fereidun Jorjani's script, such as the main theme of making an extra-terrestrial entity some*one* (rather than some*thing*) so childlike and vulnerable that the audience would not only identify with him but want to embrace and protect the E.T. in the way that the boy Eliot does. This was a new and unique idea in science-fiction films, which had thus far depicted aliens as either monstrously inhuman (e.g., *Alien*, 1979) or enigmatically ethereal (e.g., *The Man Who Fell to Earth*, 1976). Every detail is there, from the alien raiding the fridge for Reese's pieces in the middle of the night, to the military's hospitalization and quarantine of the Star Child. Even the bulbous body, lanky arms, and long neck of the alien entity were the same.

The sketch accompanying the screenplay had been drawn by Fereidun's collaborator. The co-author of *Star Child* was a Persian painter by the name of Khosrow Yahyai, a man whose sordid past proved to be detrimental to the case that Jason's father quickly built against Spielberg. The linchpin of this case was that at the conclusion of E.T. there is a "special thanks to Melissa Matheson." Rumors aside that she was Spielberg's girlfriend at the time, Ms. Matheson happened to be the typist who prepared the final draft of *Star Child* for Fereidun and Khosrow — neither of whom were very proficient in English. The law office enlisted by Jason's father was prepared to serve Spielberg papers, having tracked the director's movements carefully enough to know when he would be transiting through a certain airport. But Khosrow, who had filed for their joint copyright on the screenplay, refused to give his consent. On the timeline that I come from, in 1981 he had gone back to Tehran, and shortly thereafter started a family of his own. He did not want the attention of the nascent government of the Islamic Republic of Iran to be drawn to him.

You see, when the Revolution took place in 1979, a lot of legal dossiers and police reports from the Pahlavi period fell through the cracks. The late Shah of Iran had been trying to build a casino resort on Kharg Island in the Persian Gulf, but he had problems with a local mobster and quasi-feudal landowner. Khosrow had a rapport with the Shah's wife, Empress Farah Pahlavi, who awarded gold medals to his extraordinary paintings. Fereidun had heard that Khosrow was believed to have pushed this mobster off a cliff into the shark-infested waters of the Persian Gulf, perhaps after having drugged him. Khosrow was himself an avid user of LSD, which is reflected in the bewitchingly surreal imagery of his artwork.

Khosrow smuggled a number of his award-winning paintings out of Iran in the late 1970s, fleeing to America in order to avoid an increasingly likely prosecution. It is then that, for a brief period, he took up residence as a guest of Jason's father and mother (who did not appreciate catering to him). So, whereas many Iranians fled the country after the Shah was overthrown, in 1981, a year before *E.T.* was released, Khosrow went in the other direction — returning to an Islamic Republic, where he believed that his record had been wiped clean by the chaos of the revolution and the confusion following Saddam Hussein's surprise invasion of Iran in the fall of 1980. Now that Operation Neqab had succeeded, that would not take place. Khosrow would remain in New York City up to the time when *E.T.* was released in the summer of 1982.

However, on the original timeline, Khosrow's brother later hinted to Fereidun that, before heading back to Iran, the painter had facilitated Melissa Matheson's transfer of *Star Child* to Steven Spielberg — by whatever, direct or indirect, means all of the key elements of this story reached him and were incorporated into the blockbuster film *E.T.* This same brother gave two of Khosrow's award-winning paintings to Jason's father, in a lame attempt at an apology for Khosrow's treachery. These haunting pieces hung on the walls of the apartments that Jason grew up in, and his father vouchsafed them to him so that, in his adulthood, they hung on the walls of Jason's own secession of apartments. Frankly, I have never seen a more successful attempt at modern art that is quintessentially Persian and as occult as the alchemical works of Max Ernst.

In the now overwritten world where the Islamic Republic survived, and Khosrow went back to Iran, Fereidun remained determined to sue Spielberg for *E.T.* Lawyers were advising him on how to secure the sole rights to the *Star Child* screenplay in order to do so. Around the time that Jason entered the half-French Fleming School in New York, an incident took place that forced Fereidun to reconsider and drop the legal action. One morning, as per his usual routine in 1987, he went to pick up the blue Cadillac to drive Jason to the Fleming School building at 10 East 62nd Street, and to also drop off his mother, Susan Power, at her office in the garment district of downtown Manhattan, when he met with a very unpleasant surprise. As Fereidun opened the front door of the Cadillac, a pile of fish fell from the front seat onto the sidewalk. This was an old mafia symbol used to warn troublemakers that if they did not cease and desist, they would soon be "sleeping with the fishes."

That morning, Susan took Jason to school by train. When Fereidun got the car back from the carwash, the stink of the rotting fish still lingered on the blue upholstery. Around the same time, he received a threatening anonymous phone call, with the voice on the other end of the line reminding him that he had a family and sternly insisting that he "drop it." So, after a heated conversation with his wife, Susan, who was horrified by all this and feared for their son's safety, Fereidun did drop it. He was always convinced that Spielberg had put someone up to making these threats. But I suspected that both the fish incident and the phone call came from another group of people, individuals who were aware of the *Star Child* case, and what a multi-million-dollar settlement of it would mean for how Jason's life would unfold, quite differently from how it did develop in the face of financial hardships later suffered by Fereidun and Susan.

Steven Spielberg may or may not be above using such crude tactics to intimidate someone. But for all I know, Spielberg was never even made aware of the potential lawsuit. The reason why I doubt that he was behind the intimidation is because two utterly bizarre incidents that took place during Jason's young adulthood suggested that Jason had been the target of both surveillance and manipulation long before anyone should even have known who he was or why that might some-day be justified. From these two incidents it would appear that — potentially, both beneficent and malevolent — forces *with access to the future* were very interested in the course that Jason's life would take.

I believe that I can put a date on the day of the first incident, because it was when a firm had just been chosen to design the new World Trade Center. February 27, 2003. In my lifetime as Jason, I was 22 years old at the time. New York's newspapers had printed 3-D models of proposed designs on their front pages, above the fold. I had just emerged from the subway station on the northeast corner of 86th Street and Lexington Avenue when these caught my eye at the news-stand there. I was at the tail end of my regular commute back home from New York University. As I stood inspecting one of the graphics for the proposed Freedom Tower, I noticed someone standing behind me and off to the left-hand side. He had been staring at me intently. As soon as he realized that I had noticed him, he said: "So, what do you think?" I shook my head in frustration and replied, "They should have gone up twice as high to send a message! We have the materials and technology to do that now. Put a permanent fighter detail around it at a fixed perimeter if necessary!" He smiled, and the next words out of his mouth were: "You *would* say that."

I'd never seen the man before in my life, but he was strangely compelling. When he asked if I had a few minutes to spare for a little chat, I readily agreed and crossed the street with him to stand under the marquee of an abandoned movie theater that used to be on the west side of 86th street, heading toward Park Avenue. We spent about half an hour talking there that afternoon. At no point did he ask my name, nor did he volunteer his. What is stranger is that with this man I never felt the need for such a proper introduction. He had me at a disadvantage, because apparently, he already knew who I was — or who I would be, someday. Again, I had just turned 22. I was nobody, really, at least as far as the world was concerned. But this mystery man was able to lead the conversation from one subject of interest to me on to every single other topic, field, and area that I would wind up involved with for the rest of my life up to the present time.

Again, I had barely dipped my toe into some of these subjects at the time of the conversation, but he spoke to me as if these were long-standing interests and he took a critical attitude toward my (future) approach to them without my having volunteered any information on the basis of which he could have drawn inferences. For example, he knew Hafez by heart and he warned me that my emphasis on Mithraism was going to scare some people who "won't understand." It is only after publishing *Iranian Leviathan* in 2019 that I figured out what he was talking about. He had one message over all: "Don't forget your American side." He repeated this several times, once adding, "Emerson, Whitman, Thoreau, remember that they are your heritage too," and another time reassuring me that "you're going to be great! Just don't forget your American side." While I bizarrely did not ask him *who* he was, I had thought to ask *what* he did. He replied, "We maintain a library." That's all. Again, strangely, I did not think to ask him for any elaboration on that cryptic remark. "We," he said, not I. "*We* maintain a library."

Now, this may have been a benevolent man with access to the future. Whereas the other incident was almost certainly orchestrated by malevolent forces with at least as much, if not more, access to events that had not yet transpired. I do not simply mean foreknowledge of the future, which could be sufficient to explain the "librarian" above, but in this case the ability to actually retrieve and move information from the future to the past in a very sophisticated way. The story is a difficult one to tell, but I will endeavor to be perfectly honest.

You see, for a number of reasons, mostly related to the disruption that the Coronavirus pandemic caused in 2020–2021, Nassim Nouri and I remained in a bi-coastal relationship for a long time after she became my fiancée. I would fly to Los Angeles, where I would spend months at a time with her, and she would occasionally come and stay with me in New York. But, as you can imagine, spending months of the year away from each other, we often had rather extensive phone calls of an intimate nature.

Late one night, many years earlier, around the same time as the aforementioned incident with the librarian in 2003, a woman with whom I had been having a relationship called me in a panic. Emma started out by saying, "Why were you talking to me like that?!" When I explained to her that I had no idea what she was on about, she said that she had just been on the phone with me for fifteen minutes, over the course of which I had supposedly coaxed her into a sexual scenario that became more and more explicit, to the point where I was saying things that she considered very uncharacteristic of me and that shocked and disturbed her. In fact, I had not called Emma.

Apparently, in 2003, long before anyone but the likes of the NSA and the Mossad had voice emulation technology, someone with *exactly* my voice had called Emma. Moreover, it was not simply a replication of my voice, which would have been within the technological capabilities of a few top-notch intelligence agencies at that time. This person was able to produce my personality and speech pattern accurately enough to carry on a convincing conversation with a woman who knew me *very* well, before the last five minutes of that conversation went somewhere that she found unsettlingly unexpected.

The clincher is that this did not happen only once. It happened *several* more times, after this first phone call. Each time, the voice that sounded like it was mine was so convincing, and the personality so adaptive and true to my own, that Emma was manipulated into lowering her guard to the point of having an intimate exchange with this person purporting to be me, until the vocabulary and attitude being expressed took a turn that she thought was, to say the least, uncharacteristic of me — as she had known me, then, in my early twenties. When the last of these incidents occurred, Emma was so disturbed that she called the police and filed a report with the NYPD alleging that she had been phone "raped" by someone imitating her boyfriend. I, for my part, had become so incensed that I grabbed a large knife from the kitchen cupboard of my apartment and ran through the dark streets to her building, in case whoever did this might be lurking there when I arrived. That is how badly I was unhinged by these phone calls.

It was only much later in my lifetime as Jason, a couple of years into my relationship with Nassim, that it first occurred to me that the kind of thing that Emma had been describing could easily have been reconstructed from bits and pieces of my many erotically explicit conversations with Nassim (much more explicit than anything I would have said, to anyone, over a phoneline when I was in my early twenties). Emma, who was a discerning and very intuitive person, had been so badly manipulated and violated, on several occasions no less, because the voice in those phone calls was not an *emulation* of mine.

It *was mine* — just from the future, remixed from out of extensive material mined from conversations that I had with my fiancée on the opposite coast of the country.

This would mean that recordings of these conversations were transported at least sixteen years into the past, and at that by people with a level of Artificial Intelligence that no one ought to have had in 2003. To take these tens of hours of recordings and rearrange phrases from them in ways that are so complex that the voice — *my* voice — could be convincingly responsive to someone who knows me *very* well for the span of *a fifteen-minute* phone call would require a level of Artificial Intelligence that was not achieved until the 2030s.

One might ask that if malevolent time travelers with this level of technology were interfering with my life as Jason, why is it that I got anywhere at all in that lifetime. First of all, as the encounter with the man on the street corner of 86th and Lexington suggests, there may have been both malevolent *and benevolent* forces from the future intervening in Jason's life. Secondly, there is one other incident that does strongly suggest that an attempt was made to prevent him from ever even coming on the scene as a public intellectual. I never revealed this in my life as Jorjani because I was concerned that detractors would use it to question my soundness of mind. Shortly after *Prometheus and Atlas* was published in early 2016, and a few months before I was contacted by Frederick Boulder, I began to have totally unprecedented debilitating headaches. These were accompanied by a pain on the upper left side of my neck. The first time that this happened, suddenly, in the middle of the night, I was in so much pain that I literally had to *crawl* to the bathroom to take a bunch of Advil and aspirin (which didn't help *these* types of headaches much).

Eventually, it got so bad that I had a battery of neurological tests done on me, because I was beginning to become concerned that I might have a brain tumor or something. CAT scans and EEGs revealed nothing, and the NYU neurologist could come to no diagnosis at all, especially since the headaches did *not* fit the pattern of migraines. However, she did tell me that the two places I was pointing to are the electrical nerve center of the brain and the carotid artery (the main artery responsible for carrying blood from the heart to the brain). These are the two points in the head and neck that are closest to being "kill switches" that someone who intended to cause a stroke would principally target if they possessed either some highly focused directed energy weapon or a psychotronic technique. Interestingly, these headaches (and the throbbing pain in my carotid artery) went away after the defamation that Jellyfish set me up for had succeeded in destroying my academic career, damaging my relationship with the Iranian Renaissance, and compelling professionals in Parapsychology, Ufology, and other edge science fields to cut their ties with me.

Forgive me for what may appear to have been a long tangent in my discussion of how the success of Operation Neqab altered the course of events surrounding Spielberg's seeming plagiarism of the *Star Child* screenplay in the production of *E.T.* It really is not a tangent at all, because all of these strange occurrences suggested to me that a very deliberate effort had been made by certain interests — other than Spielberg and Company — to ensure that Fereidun Jorjani did not pursue legal action to the point of receiving a settlement so substantial that, even if he had to also sign a non-disclosure agreement, Jason would grow up wealthy. Had I, in my lifetime as Jorjani, grown up with considerable family money at my disposal, rather than in an atmosphere of perpetual financial insecurity, the $1 million dangled in front of me by Frederick would never have made a sufficient impression to entice me to get involved with the Alt-Right as part of a Jellyfish plan to supposedly influence Trump on Iran Policy via Steve Bannon.

The success of Operation Neqab meant that the Islamic Republic was overthrown in July of 1980. Given the restoration of the Pahlavi legal order in Persia (even if without a Pahlavi monarch on the throne), and the Soviet invasion of the rest of Iran, Khosrow Yahyai never left New York to return to Iran. He *had* secretly handed *Star Child* over to Melissa Matheson, who testified to that when Fereidun's attorneys served Steven Spielberg with a lawsuit in early 1983. Spielberg gave a sworn but confidential deposition in the course of which he claimed that he had never heard of Jorjani or his *Star Child* script, and that Matheson had given him the core ideas of *E.T.* verbally, in the course of personal conversations, which is why he had put a "special thanks" to her in the credits of the film. Having been thrown under the bus by Spielberg, Melissa Matheson in turn gave a deposition to the effect that Yahyai had portrayed himself as the sole author of the script when he made a deal to hand it over to her for a certain amount of untraceable cash. So, Fereidun Jorjani's lawyers next served Yahyai, who was put between the rock and the hard place of admitting what he had done or lying under oath. Yahyai gave a deposition that contradicted that of Matheson, claiming that she must have shared details of *Star Child* with Spielberg simply on the basis of having been the script's typist. He swore that he had made no deal with her.

One of them was committing perjury. It did not matter which, although Fereidun would never trust Khosrow again and this certainly brought their friendship to an end. Several years of legal proceedings were enough to make it clear to Spielberg how catastrophic a potential public scandal over this could be. So, he had his attorneys offer a settlement to Fereidun Jorjani, contingent on non-disclosure of the matter. By then, *E.T.* had become one of the highest-grossing films of all time during its theatrical release. The settlement, the details of which were worked out in October of 1987, made Jorjani a multi-millionaire overnight. Unfortunately, the stress of the legal battle had destroyed his already volatile marriage.

Fereidun's fights with Susan were so bad that neighbors had summoned the police to their apartment several times in the mid-1980s. Jason, who was even more traumatized by this violent atmosphere than he had been — I mean than *I* had been — in the timeline that I come from, was probably relieved when Susan Power filed for a divorce from Fereidun Jorjani in November of 1987. She managed to secure custody of Jason, and significant child support and other damages from the now wealthy Fereidun. In view of the threat that she would seek a restraining order against him, Fereidun Jorjani voluntarily moved to Los Angeles, California, where he had more friends and business contacts than in New York, anyhow, and where he would attempt to pursue his directorial ambitions in Hollywood. He would travel back to New York on a regular basis to visit his son, and when Jason would grow older, his mother let him travel to Los Angeles during his summer breaks from school, to spend longer stretches with his father and his Persian grandmother, who had also relocated there.

It was in that one-month interval in 1987, between the October settlement and the November divorce, that I finagled my way into having a prominent place in Jason Jorjani's life. He was in his first semester at The Fleming School and, because of all the chaos at home, he was having difficulties doing his homework despite his innate aptitude. AtlantiCorp had established a working relationship with David Nahmad, a French-speaking Jewish Lebanese billionaire from Monaco who used his position as one of Manhattan's most prominent art dealers in order to move large sums of money around, if you take my meaning. (On my timeline, his son Helly would later be arrested and imprisoned for getting reckless with the family business.) David's daughter, Marielle Nahmad, was a classmate of Jason's at The Fleming School. I went to the trouble of befriending Marielle's mother Colette and convincing her to hire me as a tutor for both Marielle and Helly (who, although a couple of years ahead of him, was in Jason's Judo class at Fleming). My colleagues at AtlantiCorp had helped me to put together a resume as a part-time tutor with false, but checkable, references that seemed impressive on paper. Once I was tutoring the Nahmad children, and I had gained the confidence of Colette to the point where she would sometimes send me in her stead to Fleming functions at which parents were expected, I managed to meet Fereidun Jorjani and charm him into hiring me as Jason's tutor. After tutoring

Jason for a few months, I made excuses to the Nahmad family and dropped both Marielle and Helly.

Attending that 1987 Halloween party at 10 East 62nd Street, to which parents were invited, was one of the most uncanny experiences of my life. Marielle, who I had accompanied, was dressed as a witch, and Jason's costume that year was the tin man from *The Wizard of Oz*. What made it so uncanny was that the building that was then The Fleming School, specifically its lower school, would eventually become both my residence and the place where I would be killed in my lifetime as Jorjani. Known as "Versailles of the Upper East Side" after the Fleming School vacated it in 1992, this Beaux Arts building was remodeled as a townhouse triplex apartment. The marble spiral staircase and the mirrored French Imperial-style room with wood floors, a magnificent painted ceiling, and a fireplace, which had been the weekly assembly room of Fleming, was left untouched. I used this room as an audience hall for important meetings. I had strong-armed the government of Persia to acquire the building as their UN Mission, after I was appointed Persian Ambassador to the United Nations in 2036. Consequently, my place of residence, the exquisitely elegant townhouse, whose ornate hallways and antique light fixtures were reminiscent of a fairy lair, became the unofficial headquarters of Prometheism. Since Persia had become a bastion of the movement, no one in the government of Persia dared to object.

The bombing of 10 East 62nd Street by Islamic terrorists in 2039 was a past life memory that I explored in my hypnotic regression sessions back in Gotham of 2112; as the death of Jorjani, that memory kept resurfacing throughout my first set of sessions. That's why being back there in 1987, on Halloween no less, was such a haunting experience. As I walked up that spiral staircase to the Versailles-style room on the second floor (above ground), looking down at the sunburst pattern of beige-gold diamonds set into the ivory marble in the lobby, I really felt like I was in the Twilight Zone. That song by Golden Earring kept playing in my head as the black high heels I was wearing reverberated on the inlaid crosshatched pattern of the landing that led to the assembly chamber. This feeling only intensified when I saw myself reflected in the chamber's mirrors with their gilded moldings. The echo in that room didn't make it any less unsettling, either. I walked over to the three floor-to-ceiling windows looking out over 62nd between Fifth and Madison. I opened the middle one by the handle, to get some air, checking that no children were around me.

The past few weeks had been very stressful. I had been working hard on Donald Trump, trying to convince him to run for President in the 1988 election. In the end, I basically bribed him to run by promising to save his real estate empire from a collapse that would otherwise be in store for him within a couple of years. We brought him to the SCIF on Long Island and gave him a briefing in the course of which he was misled into believing that we had an intelligence agency which, like the CIA, used remote viewing of the future, but for the sake of corporate investments and stock trading. Trump was given to understand that, by 1990, he could either be bankrupt, and hundreds of millions in debt, or be President of the United States with a new corporate investor injecting enough capital into his failing businesses to keep him from ever going under.

This briefing was in September of 1987, and in addition to sharing with him details of the catastrophic financial situation that he would find himself in within several years, I volunteered specific information about the Stock Market Crash of October 19, 1987. When that event did in fact take place, exactly as predicted, he got over his resentment of our forecasting of his financial demise, which, initially, had really rubbed the eternal optimist and advocate of positive thinking the wrong way. Now, Trump was ready for another meeting with me. It helped that I paid him handsomely to acquire a headquarters for AtlantiCorp on the 55th floor of Trump Tower.

Donald's own office was on the 26th floor of the Modernist masterpiece, which was a 58-story skyscraper. I asked him why he hadn't chosen a higher floor. Trump said that he preferred the view from here, because it was more level with the tops of the buildings on the skyline of the west side of Central Park and also let you look down into the park from a height where it was still possible to discern people sitting in the fields or walking on the paths through the trees. I looked for my building, but it was blocked by the top of the Plaza Hotel, which was off to the left, and very close to the window. My own office was high enough above this floor so that it looked *over* the top of the Plaza, and I could see my penthouse from it through the telescope that I had pointed at my turret library.

Trump's office was junkier than it had been during my first visit here, with Irena back in '83. I had noticed that, over the years, it accumulated clutter on account of how sentimental Trump was about the memorabilia that famous people gave him or sent to him. All kinds of awards and other small sculptures and statues, as well as sports memorabilia, lined the surfaces along the windowsills. Every bit of the wall space was covered with photographs or framed magazine covers. Trump caught me looking at a portrait of the Shah of Iran that he had on the wall. "It's a shame what happened to that guy and to his country. *I mean* having to see your eldest son be killed like that when you're rotting away of cancer as your *ungrateful* country burns. You know back in '78 I was about to build a casino there, in some resort town called Ramsar. It was on the coast of the Caspian Sea. We also had plans on the drawing board for construction of a *yuge* hotel at one of the ski resorts, you know in those mountains just north of Tehran. The Shah told me that he was going to bid to host the Winter Olympics there. *This* year's Olympics actually. *Imagine that.* Tehran '88 instead of Calgary. Then the shit hit the fan." Trump leaned back in his chair, shaking his head while slapping the desk in front of him, as he added, "The Communists are gonna take over that *whole* fucking country, Dana. *They've already got the oil.* Notice how they went for that *first.*" Then he looked me in the eyes and said, "Where's that Russian broad that you used to come around here with?" I told him that I had sent her to work at our office in Washington. He registered the fact that AtlantiCorp had the resources to maintain an office in the Foggy Bottom area of DC, in addition to the corporate headquarters that I had secured for us here at Trump Tower.

"Speaking of Washington, Donald," I said as I opened into the subject matter that I had really come down from the 55th floor to discuss with him. "Now that the market has crashed and saving the economy is at the top of people's minds, don't you think that you ought to announce that you're running?" I looked over at Trump's framed and signed photo with Ronald Reagan. "I bet that if you do it sooner, rather than later, you'll become the front runner fast and President Reagan will even endorse you as his preferred successor. You know he never trusted Bush. The CIA forced Reagan to pick him as VP back in '80." Trump clasped his hands together, leaning over his desk, and pursing his lips a bit. "Who would I pick to run with me?" he finally asked.

I averted eye contact, looking over his shoulder at the green blanket of trees in Central Park, as I slid a dossier across his desk. I had come prepared. It was the resume of General Alexander Haig, including a number of striking photos both from his time as NATO's Supreme Allied Commander and as Secretary of State, before he was forced to resign over his perceived attempt to seize power during the March 30, 1981 assassination attempt on President Reagan. Haig himself had been the target of a failed attempt on the part of the Communist Red Army Faction to use a land mine to assassinate him on June 25, 1979, during his regular car commute to NATO's SHAPE facility in Mons, Belgium.

As Trump looked over the files, I added, "Just don't let President Reagan know until you've secured his endorsement. You won't have to announce your running mate until the Republican National Convention in August of next year, anyhow." Having placed a photo of General Haig in full military uniform, wearing his numerous decorations, with the NATO flag behind him, on the top of the papers in the folder, Trump looked up and said, "I've always liked him. He's very tough on the Russians. That's the kind of guy I'd want in charge in case, you know, something unfortunate happened to me. I don't like to think that way, but when you're picking a Vice President you've gotta consider it."

"So, when will you announce?" I asked. Trump turned his head to the side, resting his chin on his hand. Then he swiveled in his chair a bit to look over the park for a moment. "I'll let my family know tonight, and I'll set the announcement for the end of this week. It'll be *right here*, in Trump Tower, coming down the escalator to the atrium." My rejoinder, while smiling approvingly, was, "It *is* a spectacular backdrop. Titanic, really, with that waterfall coming down over the illuminated rock wall." Grinning with self-satisfaction, Trump said, "You *like* that? I designed it myself." I very much doubted that he *had*, but I shot back with, "Yeah, it's what really sold me on this place as the headquarters for AtlantiCorp. Well, besides *your* being here."

CHAPTER 6

EIGHTY-EIGHT

I N THE FALL of 1987, I started to pick up Jason after school at Fleming on certain days and bring him home to where he lived at 200 East 90th street for his tutoring sessions. In the hours before his parents came back home from work, and especially on some long nights where they were embroiled in divorce-related proceedings, beginning in November, they left me home alone with him as a kind of babysitter. Once we were done with homework, I would engage him in playing with his entire toy collection. Some days it was his *Star Wars* toys, which he would pull out of the C-3PO and Darth Vader carrying cases on his bookshelf, sometimes it was the Marvel *Secret Wars* and DC *Super Powers* action figures, or the *Star Trek* figures from both *The Original Series* (the Mego ones) and *The Next Generation*, but his favorites were the figures from the Kenner toy line based on *The Real Ghostbusters*. Jason was enthralled as I came up with all kinds of story lines involving these figures and the worlds of the shows that they were based on. Admittedly, many of the narratives were drawn from plotlines that I knew would unfold in future shows or movie sequels (and prequels) of these franchises.

I noticed that Jason had the Japanese version of the *Voltron* toy, so I asked him whether he had seen the original *GoLion* anime that had been adapted into *Voltron* for an American audience. He had not, so one day I brought a cassette of it over, which had been subtitled in English for export, and we watched it on his VHS player before his parents got home. It was much more violent and intense than the censored version that was developed for release in the United States, but Jason noticed how the plotline was also a lot more coherent. As our relationship developed, I would wind up introducing him to a lot of Japanese anime acquired at a shop catering to immigrants from Japan down on East 9th street. They would import everything from Tokyo and Osaka as soon as it was released. We would ultimately watch *Akira*, *Goku Midnight Eye*, and *Angel Cop* together, in the privacy of my penthouse where no one knew what kind of "cartoons" I was showing a seven-year-old. I also exposed him to the "comics" in *Heavy Metal* magazines, so that in his own drawings he would try to imitate the art of the French illustrators Moebius, Druillet, and Caza. I pulled the *Heavy Metal* stack out after playing a bootleg VHS of the 1981 animated movie for him. He loved it! I got him a bedside lamp to take home that looked exactly like the Loc-Nar.

You see, after Fereidun Jorjani left for Los Angeles, I convinced Susan Power to let me bring Jason over to my apartment to tutor him here after school instead. I explained that the splendor of the apartment, which I had to invite her to check out, was a family inheritance (so that she would not inquire into what I really did for a living). Both of Jason's parents had already been told that I tutored not because I needed the money, but because I enjoyed doing it now and then to make sure that particularly promising children did not fall through the cracks because of certain environmental stresses and contingent circumstances. I showed Susan a degree in Psychology that I also claimed to have, expertly forged of course. Given what Jason had been through, she considered this more than a fringe benefit of my being his tutor.

So, by early 1988, at seven years of age, Jason was frequenting my penthouse at 55 Central Park West. He never got over the fact that his tutor lived in the *Ghostbusters* building and that her name was "Dana." (The 1984 film was by then his favorite movie, and he was a fan of

The Real Ghostbusters animated show airing weekly on television.) I confess that I chose this penthouse by design, with him in mind. I could have impressed all those geopolitical and corporate persons of interest that I've wined and dined — and occasionally fucked and drugged (not necessarily in that order) — just as well by living in any number of even more upscale buildings in Manhattan. See, I also had to be sure that there was no chance Jason would even entertain the possibility of moving to Los Angeles to live with his father. That was already unlikely, but I had to render it impossible. So, yes, in a sense I was seducing him from the start. That "Dana" tutored him at "Spook Central" would also guarantee that he insisted his mother keep paying for him to come here even after he became, albeit with my help, a nearly straight-A student.

The very first time that Jason came over, while he was working out his math homework on scrap paper for a while, he noticed that I was finishing up typing and saving a document on my Macintosh. (I had heavily invested in Apple stock from the moment that it became available on the stock market, and throughout the 80s that had paid off handsomely. Sometimes, I would even wear the little Macintosh logo lapel pin that the company sent me, as a veiled reference to biting the apple gifted to Eve by the Satanic serpent in Eden. Besides, since I was queer, the rainbow color scheme seemed to be a cute, veiled reference too.) Jason asked what I was writing. I saw this as a perfect opportunity to start to have deeper conversations with him, so I went ahead and tried to explain the book that I had begun researching and writing — a book with which I intended to launch Prometheism decades ahead of when it had been launched in the world that I came from.

"It's called *Uber Man*, Jason. *Über* is the German word for 'over' or 'above.' *Übermensch* means 'Superman' in German." Now I had him intrigued. "You're writing a book about Superman?!" This was going to be really interesting. I had to explain the thesis and structure of *Uber Man* to a seven-year-old boy, using only examples that he would already be able to understand. I remembered being him at that age, so

I knew just what those would be. Actually, I had quite a lot of references that I could work with.

"Well, kind of. It's not about *the* Superman from Krypton, but it *is* about how we can develop superpowers — like superheroes or supervillains — to become more than human in the future." Jason looked at me wide-eyed. "How *far* in the future?" he asked with great excitement. "It depends on the specific inventions and abilities. I write about a bunch of different ones, and what will make them possible before too long," I explained. "Like what? Which ones?!" he exclaimed, as a prompt for me to explain what techno-scientific developments were going to be central to the book's vision of evolution beyond the human condition. "Genetics, Nanotechnics, Cybernetics, Robotics, and Psionics. I'll explain what kinds of superpowers each of them could give us, and how they can totally change the way that we live." Jason sat there captivated, looking up at me eagerly with his hands folded under his chin.

"You remember Khan in *Star Trek II*, and in that old episode of the series where he takes over the Enterprise?" I asked. "Yeah, *of course!*" he shot back, sounding almost insulted that I would even ask. I smiled. "Well, he's a product of Genetic Engineering." "Yeah, *I know,*" Jason said. "So, you know, Genetic Engineering is when scientists change the genes, the code, that people get from their parents, to give them abilities or powers that they would not have had if they were just born normally." Before I could go on, he added, "Like being super smart or super strong, or living longer." "Exactly, that's what I mean by Genetics as a path to superpowers," I replied as I realized that this was going to be even easier than I expected.

"How about Nano... what'd you say... Nano*technics*?" he asked. "'Nano' means super small. Something so tiny that you can't see it with your naked eye. Have you ever seen an old computer? Like the ones that Dr. Banner uses in *The Incredible Hulk*. You know, they were big, like the size of walls or bookshelves, right?" Jason searched his memory for a moment, then came back with, "Yeah, with lots of blinking lights. The Hulk smashes those sometimes." "Well, look at this computer that I'm writing my book on," I said, as I showed him the original Macintosh model that I had bought when it first came out in 1984. "This computer here probably has more power than most of the ones that Dr. Banner was using. But see how much smaller it is?" "Yeah, how come?" he asked. "Because the more scientists learn over time, and the smarter inventors get, the tinier the pieces that they can build a computer with. Computers get smaller and smaller but have more power than the bigger ones of the past. There are boards inside of computers that have little things stuck to them like Legos. They're called microchips. I'll show you sometime."

He retorted, "I *know* what a micro*chip* is. I took apart a Nintendo game cartridge once, after it broke." "What game was it?" I asked. "*Rad Racer*," he said. "So, if computers and other kinds of electronics, like Nintendo games, get smaller and smaller, you can imagine how sometime in the future, the microchips that are sawdered — like *glued*, you know, welded — to those green boards would be *so* tiny that you could only see them under a microscope, the way that you look at cells under a microscope in Science class." He followed what I was saying but seemed a bit incredulous about cell-sized microchips. So, I took a risk to make Moore's Law more tangible to him, and to be honest, also to deepen his clearly growing fascination with me.

"I'll tell you a secret, if you promise to keep it," I said. Jason implored me to tell him. "Don't go telling all your friends, okay?" He promised. "Next year, they're going to come out with a Nintendo that you can carry around everywhere in your hand and even fit into your jacket pocket. The microchips will be so small, that the game cartridges inside it will be a quarter of the size of the ones that you put in your NES now." "No *way!*" he exclaimed, "*next* year?!" "Yeah, I'll get you one if you keep working with me to do all your homework right." (In point of fact, I did deliver on this promise to get him a *Game Boy* as soon as it was released.) "So, Nanotechnics means when electronics can be made so small that machines like computers shrink so much that... they're like... microscopic. So that you could put them inside someone's body like in that movie *Fantastic Voyage* — except not with the silly shrinking people, just the submarine being a 'nano' machine?" *He* said this, not me. "Yes, Jason, that's precisely what I mean. Now imagine what could be done with gadgets like that in surgery, manufacturing, or construction."

"Wait, wait!" he started shouting excitedly. "Isn't that how replicators and the Holodeck work on Captain Picard's Enterprise-D?" The example couldn't have been more perfect. I ought to have thought of it myself. He had now been watching *Star Trek: The Next Generation* for a couple of years. "You've got it! That's *exactly* how they work. They build the replicated food and all of the simulated places and objects on the Holodeck using 'nanites' — like nano-scale building blocks that are smart and can be programmed by a computer." Jason marveled as that sunk in. "In your book, how far do you say that we are from having something like that?" he finally asked. "Well, I'll tell you this much, Jason, it certainly won't take until the 23rd century, like in *Star Trek*. We may have it when you're as old as your grandparents are now." His head slowly slid to the side as I could see he was thinking, "*Wow.*"

"How about Cybernetics, you want to know about that?" I asked, cutting into his reverie. "Oh, I know about cyborgs," he said, "like Robocop, or the Terminator." "Your parents let you watch those movies?" I asked, already knowing the answer. Jason looked up at me a bit bashfully, with his head slightly downcast and turned aside. "Well, I watched them on a sleepover. One of my friends lives at the Waldorf. His father is the hotel manager. They have all kinds of movies on their TV, from the hotel. His parents are never around when I come over, so..." I laughed, which put him at ease. He giggled back. "Then, you remember in *The Terminator* how the computer network in the future decided on its own to start World War III? How all the war machines — the planes and missiles and stuff — were all networked, all linked together, and controlled by a super computer, and that computer… like *woke up*, and started to think for itself, and then defended itself when people tried to pull the plug on it?" "Yeah, I remember that's what the time traveler from the future told that lady…" "Sarah Connor," I said. "Well, Cybernetics doesn't mean cyborgs — like robots — it means smart computer networks that control things without needing people to tell them what to do," I explained. "Isn't that really dangerous?" he asked. "Yes, it could be, Jason. Which is why we need to start thinking about it seriously now, about how to control systems like that so that they give us more power instead of taking things over in a way that we don't want." He nodded at me affirmatively.

"But how about *real* robots? Like Data or C-3PO. Your book is about them too?" he asked. "Yes, I write about how in the future robots will do all the kinds of work that people don't want to do." Underwhelmed he said, "You mean like being garbage men." I replied, "Not just jobs like that, but *all* repetitive labor on assembly lines. All manufacturing, and transportation." His eyes lit up. "You mean like robot planes, cars, and trucks that can fly or drive themselves, like in *Transformers*?!" I was really enjoying this. "Yup. *That's right*, and some of them will even be able to change shape like Transformers, too. Imagine robots that are built out of the nano-scale parts that we were talking about earlier. See how with parts that small they could rearrange themselves into any shape, to do a bunch of different kinds of jobs?" Jason said, "makes sense" with a brooding expression on his face, the meaning of which I discerned when, a moment later, he added, as if with genuine concern, "but doesn't that mean that they could also be soldiers? We wouldn't stand a chance against shape-shifting robot soldiers, would we?" My eyes locked onto his in a steady gaze, as I answered, "That's why the right people — like superheroes, or Jedi — need to build them first, and have to be able to control them, because you don't want any robots or cyborgs like Brainiac on the loose."

"What about the powers that *Jedi* have? Will science discover *those* too, and will people in the future be able to learn how to use them?"

Jason asked, anticipating the last — but certainly not the least — of the techno-scientific developments central to the thesis of *Uber Man*. "Yeah, that's what Psionics is about. Psionics is like technology — you know, gadgets and also techniques or skills — based on the science of Parapsychology." Jason's enthusiasm now reached a fever pitch. "Like Dr. Venkman and Egon and Ray! The Ghostbusters are scientists who do Parapsychology, and they use it to build gadgets like their proton packs, and ghost traps, and stuff. Well, *except* Winston. He's *not* a scientist. Mr. Spock is a scientist, and he can read people's minds too." I shook my head, laughing, with tears in my eyes. "That's right, Jason. Parapsychology is a real science, and in the future gadgets will be invented, like the ones that the Ghostbusters build, and techniques will also be developed, to make it easier to learn the kinds of abilities that the Jedi have, or that Spock has. It will be like learning a martial art, someday."

Then Jason, always seeing the dark side, added, "But what about Darth Vader? Couldn't it be dangerous if bad people learned to use those kinds of abilities? Wouldn't a lot of people be tempted to use them the wrong way?" Not bad for a seven-year-old. "Actually, that brings me to the main point of my book, Jason. Human psychology — the way that we think, and feel, and act — has to change in a big way if we are going to survive developing the superpowers that all of these inventions and discoveries that we've been talking about could give us before too long." He looked at me pensively. "You mean we have to become more like Yoda, or Spock," and then I cut in with, "or more like Superman." Then he asked, "That's why you're calling the book Superman? Because we can't be tempted like he was, in *Superman II*. He let down humanity when the super criminals from Krypton attacked, just because he only wanted to love Lois Lane like a normal guy."

I smiled at him with what must have been a very impressed look on my face, and then I winced slightly as I asked, "What about Khan? Do you think he was really a villain, or was he a kind of Superman too?" Jason thought deeply for a moment, looking inwardly, in silence. "I think that Kirk let him live — you know, in the episode where he first shows up — because the captain thought Khan *was* a kind of Superman. That he wasn't really *bad*. It's like he respected him too much to kill him. So, instead he gave Khan a new world of his own to build. It wasn't his fault that the planet's orbit shifted." He told me that he wanted to re-watch the episode. I showed Jason that I had it on VHS. When his mother came to pick him up before too long, I gave him the cassette tape of *Star Trek* with the "Space Seed" episode on it to take home. As he walked out the door of my apartment, I said to him, "Listen for that line at the end of Khan's trial, when Kirk quotes Milton about Lucifer." I was oblivious to what reaction Susan may have had to this, as my gaze was fixed on the twinkle in Jason's eyes. I had already offered him the apple, and he had bitten deep.

After Jason left that night, I turned on the news and watched the presidential campaign coverage. Following the Iowa caucuses and New Hampshire primary, Donald Trump was in second place, with Bob Dole and Pat Robertson trailing him, and with George Bush having gained a slight lead over him. Bush's advisors were already considering reaching out to Trump to offer him the vice-presidential nomination if he withdrew from the race and backed Bush as the Republican nominee. While I doubted that Trump would accept such an offer, I felt that I needed to act fast. Ensuring that Bush was not elected in '88 had been one of my primary objectives. On my timeline, the ex-CIA director had been the principal architect of the collapse of the Soviet Union from 1989–1991, not Reagan, who got more credit for paving the way for it than he deserved. If Bush was not prevented from becoming President, it was still possible that he would find some other Soviet reformer to play the role that Gorbachev had played as his counterpart in tearing down the Iron Curtain and imploding the USSR. Perhaps Boris Yeltsin (although Yeltsin had not gone nearly as far as I remember him having gotten in the history that I was taught, since it was Gorbachev who really noticed Yeltsin and lifted him up before being betrayed by him).

In any case, George H. W. Bush was the son of one of the principal operatives of the Nordic Breakaway civilization within the power structure of the United States. Prescott Bush had been a principal financier of Adolf Hitler during the lead-up to the Second World War, channeling funds from the German American Bund to the Nazi Party. It is no wonder that his son had been chosen to manage the collapse of the Soviet Union, the continued existence of which would have made the Olympian re-conquest of Earth and establishment of the Traditionalist Imperium much harder. If Soviet Communism survived into the 2040s, it would certainly ally with the West to confront these self-proclaimed Nordic "gods" and their regressive Brahmin in the occulted Fourth Reich. The combined nuclear arsenals of the two superpowers, both still committed to Promethean Progress, might be enough to make them reconsider and, if not, to unleash a fiery rebellion.

Instead, in the world that I come from, both of those superpowers were long gone by the 2040s and the world was dominated by a Chinese hegemon whose Neo-Confucian ideology inclined them to accept the role of colonial Viceroy offered to China by the "Celestial Ancestors" who revealed themselves to a desperate and demoralized Earth in 2048. Taking out George Bush would be removing a key asset of the truly "Evil Empire" and further securing the survival of the Soviet Union into the far future, so that it could be one of two fists able to strike at that Olympian Imperium before it managed to subjugate the planet.

I considered the options, and I chose the one with the least risk of my being exposed. George Bush loved to go fishing and was known for getting behind the helm of his own speedboat off Walker's Point at his family's property in Kennebunkport, Maine. Sometimes he would test the upper limits of his speedboat, *Fidelity*, by throttling it forward at 75 miles per hour. As you may recall, I am an expert diver. So, I got my gear — not just my diving gear — and headed to coastal Maine where Bush would be spending the weekend to recuperate ahead of a major set of primary elections that could well decide the fate of his campaign.

It was several days before "Super Tuesday" on March 8, 1988, when Republican voters in Texas, Florida, Tennessee, Louisiana, Oklahoma, Mississippi, Kentucky, Alabama, and Georgia would all cast their ballots for their preferred nominee. Trump was not expected to do well in those states, since religious and rural Southerners tended to see him as a wheeler-dealer playboy New Yorker whose qualifications for the presidency were building casino hotels and being good at Monopoly. Trump's recently released book, *The Art of the Deal*, may have been a bestseller in the big cities (for thirteen weeks no less), but it certainly didn't help him gain any voters in the Bible Belt, especially not after he said that it was his own "second favorite book, after the Bible." The Evangelicals saw the 11-step formula in the book that was modeled on Norman Vincent Peale's *Power of Positive Thinking* as tantamount to advocating New Age witchcraft, except explicitly driven by greed and in the service of Mammon.

I arrived in Kennebunkport on Saturday morning, having left from Long Island in the predawn hours aboard an AtlantiCorp submarine (a decommissioned one that we had bought from the French Navy). Johnny came with me. Actually, he captained the submarine most of the way, before manning the vessel while I dove into the water of Walker's Point. There, I set up numerous moored mines, which had been the cargo of the submarine. They were geared to be released from their moorings and detonated by remote control. The submarine got close enough to the Bush family compound for me to ring the area around the dock with these mines, so that they could be detonated before the Vice President throttled his boat. Or, if that opportunity were missed, on his way back in after fishing.

When I got back on board, Johnny took us out to a position in somewhat less shallow waters but still close enough to the peninsula,

so that when we surfaced, I was able to surveil the dock at Bush's compound from the turret of the submarine, through the high-powered
telescope that I had. The vessel had been painted in camouflaged
colors that helped to conceal it against the background of the ocean,
and Johnny was watching the scopes vigilantly for any potential close
approach by other ships, in which case we would dive again to conceal
ourselves. That did not prove to be necessary, though. Around 2 pm,
Vice President Bush boarded the *Fidelity* with a couple of other men,
probably hoping to catch some fish to eat fresh with their dinner that
evening. Instead, he was the one to get caught, within a few minutes
of leaving his dock, when I detonated the mines, in staggered fashion, which I had positioned around Walker's Point. The redundancy
worked well, since the first mine damaged his boat but did not destroy
it. By the time I blew the third mine that was closest to the *Fidelity* on
its panicked retreat to the dock, Bush was blown to bits. I could see
his remains washing back up against the rocks along his property's
coastline.

Pat Robertson came out on top in the Super Tuesday states, instead of the now deceased George Herbert Walker Bush. But, as both
Trump and Republican Party leaders knew full well, the televangelist
did not have a hope in hell of winning a national election against the
Democrats. By the time that primary voting was held in big blue states
like New York and California, Trump was the clear frontrunner. In
June, he was finally endorsed by President Reagan. No one was surprised to see Trump become the nominee at the Republican convention in New Orleans that August, where he announced his choice of
General Haig as his vice-presidential running mate.

Donald Trump crushed Michael Dukakis in the televised debates
that took place in the following months. He got quite a bit of bad
press for being a bully on stage, but it paid off for him. "I'm tired of
nice people," he would say, when confronted about his tone and tactics. "This country is in *deep, deep* trouble. We don't need somebody
nice as President right now. That's not gonna solve our problems at

home — and *certainly not abroad*. You wanna send some *nice* guy to renegotiate our commitments to the Japanese and the Saudis? You think a *nice* guy is gonna stare down General Yazov over there in Russia before he takes the rest of Iran, then maybe decides that we're such *wimps* that he should just keep going across the Persian Gulf?" Enough people were genuinely afraid of this that Trump-Haig '88 became a winning ticket.

On a cold night in early November of 1988, Donald Trump was elected the 41st President of the United States. I was one of the few people cleared by the secret service to look down onto his podium that had been set in front of the rock-faced waterfall in the atrium of Trump Tower. After all, AtlantiCorp had been hired to provide additional private security on the walkways of all the floors surrounding the open atrium at the bottom of which the President-Elect would be delivering his victory speech.

Trump was true to the motto and main slogan of his campaign, "Back to the Future." He promised to return America to the Futurama vision of the World of Tomorrow, by modernizing our infrastructure and transportation, and by taking us back to the Moon and onto Mars. He said that our so-called "allies" would pay for all of this, and that our ability to outcompete Japan — with its homogenous, cohesive, and highly intelligent population — depended on not allowing mass illegal migration into this country and the destruction of the hard-working and innovatively minded demographic that had made America great in the first place. "*This* country is not a *trash* heap for the *garbage* that other nations throw out, because it's *cheaper* than incarcerating them — it's *cheaper* and easier for them to send their gangbangers, drug dealers, and good-for-nothings here. They're *parasites!*" *There* was the good old Trump *I* knew.

After Trump's victory, I felt like a tremendous weight had been lifted from my broad shoulders. My work here was not quite done, but it had reached a turning point. I wanted, more than anything, to really lose myself for a little while. To let go, completely. You might imagine that, as a philosopher, I would turn to some meditation technique to accomplish this. But what I really wanted was to be fucked like an animal. I mean to be handled, and hammered, by a man who makes me dripping wet from the riveting fear that he might tear me apart.

I was enough of a woman to know that is what no other woman can give you, and it is a *rare* beast of a man who *can*. I had not lived as a woman for about eighteen hundred years. So, I had not been taken like that since early in my marriage to Caesar Septimius Severus. Later, he figured out that his wife preferred women and he also lost the drive and the stamina for it. (Besides, by then I was very focused on the project that I had hired Philostratus to help me complete. No small task, trying to nip Roman Catholicism in the bud by universalizing a pagan philosophical messiah from my Syrian homeland.) It was high time to really remember what that feels like, even if only for a night.

It was important to me that it be a random guy who I would never see again. But where to find such a person who was up to the task? Disease was not as much of a consideration as you might think, because together with my slower biological clock and lengthened lifespan, one benefit of having been genetically engineered in the late 21st century was that I was born with blood that was tremendously disease-resistant — even to AIDS. That was good to know because I wanted whoever it was to shoot his cum in me, preferably more than once. I wanted him to break me — out of myself — so that what was left in my skin was nothing but a deliciously objectified condensation of the sheer pleasure of submission. I had always been the wolf. Tonight, I wanted to be the wolf's prey, ecstatic to be devoured by a ferocious hunger.

At first, I thought that I might find what I was looking for at the Limelight. But after scoping the place out, and not really being in the mood to get drunk or just dance, I got back in my matt black DeLorean with its black leather interior and cruised around the city's streets like I was looking for a hooker. Except that I was the one who wanted to be the whore that night. I put on songs like "Every Breath You Take" by The Police, Laura Branigan's "Self Control," and "Don't You Want Me" by The Human League, turning the speakers up high after rolling down my windows. After about an hour of cruising around, when the cassette tape was on Daryl Hall and John Oates' "Maneater," I found the type of guy that I wanted in the dark and narrow cobblestone streets of SoHo. He was not as much taken aback by how forward I was being as he was cruelly mocking. He likely thought to himself that I had no idea what I was asking for. I didn't ask his name. Nor did he volunteer it.

This brute took me back to his loft apartment, up a dirty old freight elevator. It was near the place where I had met Jean-Michel Basquiat at a private Warhol exhibition a few years ago. There was paint splotched all over his floor, together with broken bottles of booze and crushed cigarette butts. He looked a bit like Jackson Pollock, but more built. I wondered if he was a painter, but I didn't see any canvases around. Probably not an artist, but maybe an industrial design painter. Just before he started pushing me around, I noticed some spray cans in a dark corner.

The place was very unevenly lit. He took me to one of the brightly lit spots, where there was a dusty and crusty dark brown leather couch. I threw my long fur coat over the sofa, with the outside facing up. Standing back in the shadow, he ripped my silvery silk dress off — tearing it in half from the bottom up and tossing it aside. I wasn't wearing a bra or any panties. My hard nipples rubbed against the fur of my coat that was covering the couch, as he bent me further over. I kept my high heels on so that he could have a better angle. When he noticed the size of my engorged clit, he tried to humiliate me for it while pulling my hair. "You think I'm some kind of queer, bitch!?" he shouted. "You want me to rub my cock against your little dick or something?!"

I will refrain from scandalizing you with the details, but let me say that, over the next hour or so, this John gave me pretty much everything that I was wanting. On my way out, he didn't even give me anything to wipe the cum that was dripping down my inner thighs or my chin and chest. What he did give me was a twenty-dollar bill that he shoved into my handbag to insult me. I took it, just so that I could feel even more like a whore tonight — a very cheap and desperate whore — rather than a time-traveling Philosopher Queen posing as the only female executive billionaire in 1988 (albeit with most of her money hidden in Swiss bank accounts). I went back to my car wearing only my fur coat, and I ran every red light that I could on my drive back home through the relatively empty streets. After parking around the corner, next to the church, I tried to walk into and through my lobby as fast as possible, with the fur coat drawn tightly around my otherwise naked body. Once I got past the doorman, I even took my heels off to move faster.

When I was finally upstairs, and went into the bathroom, I saw what a mess I was. I could smell him all over me. It turned me on again. I ran my fingers along the inside of my thighs and gathered onto them as much of his cum as I could. Then, while sitting on the toilet seat, I fingered myself with it, while having flashbacks of everything that had just happened to me in that SoHo loft. It's a good thing that I had already turned the shower water on, because I shrieked like a banshee over and over again when I came.

I slept well in what was left of that night. When I woke up late the next morning, feeling refreshed, I got back to work on *Uber Man*. Books that I was using for research surrounded and ensconced my Macintosh, with the graphics on their covers illuminated by the blue glow of its screen. The two that I had lying open at the moment, face down, were Eric Drexler's *Engines of Creation* and F. M. Esfandiary's *Up-Wingers*. At the top of the stack leaning against one side of the Mac was a Penguin Classics edition of Friedrich Nietzsche's *Beyond Good and Evil* that had Franz von Stuck's 1904 *Sphinx* painting printed on its cover. The stack on the other side was topped by Ostrander and Schroeder's *Psychic Discoveries Behind the Iron Curtain*.

The last one was a particularly noteworthy book insofar as it demonstrated that, despite the unequivocal atheism and supposed "materialism" of the putatively "scientific" framework of the Marxist Eastern bloc, the Psychotronics program of the Soviet Union and its satellite states had far surpassed America in government-funded psychic research on latent human abilities such as Extrasensory Perception (ESP) and Psychokinesis (PK). To my great satisfaction, this made the case that spectral phenomena were a subject of empirical research in scientific laboratories. To treat such "paranormal" manifestations as "miracles" that reaffirm faith in revelation was just a tactic of psychological and social control that self-proclaimed prophets and manipulative clergymen would use on people falsely conditioned to believe that *natural* abilities — which we share with animals — are "supernatural" demonstrations of divine power that lie outside the scope of scientific study.

The most interesting part of the book was an account of work being done by Psychotronics researchers in Prague to develop devices that would be able to channel and amplify psi abilities. In *Uber Man*, I pointed out how, as Nanotechnology (of the kind that Drexler was already envisioning) became a reality, such devices could be much more precisely designed. It was also likely, I argued, that genetic engineers would be able to identify correlates for biological predisposition to becoming a psi virtuoso. They could then edit the genes of an embryo in such a way as to endow children with this trait at birth, potentially on a population-wide basis. I had to be careful, in my writing, not to smuggle in too much tacit knowledge about specific future developments, such as CRISPR, when I was discussing Genetic Engineering, or to make detailed references to graphene when writing about Nanotechnology. I *did* suggest biomimetics, and a bottom-up evolutionary design approach, to overcome bottlenecks in Robotics R&D.

Worst of all, I beat Vernor Vinge to coining the term "Technological Singularity." (Sorry, Vernor.) I was writing about how innovation in

various areas of technological development, which were in turn making new scientific breakthroughs possible, were mutually reinforcing
and deeply convergent. For example, the genetic engineering of a
much higher average IQ would result in individuals capable of solv-
ing hitherto intractable research problems in computer science that
would finally yield an "Artificial Intelligence" that was more than just
the product of linear algorithms running on digital binary machines.
By the same token, stronger and smarter computers, possibly ones
based on quantum computation, would be able to map and project
changes to the human genome in ways that made much more subtle
and complex forms of genetic engineering possible. Once nanotechnological design became feasible, it would be much easier to overcome
the locomotion problem in Robotics and build robots that are capable
of autonomously replicating any human physical movements. Robots
with much sharper perception and more subtle dexterity would, in
turn, be able to engage in Nanotechnology design and manufacture
far more effectively than human engineers.

Finally, to bring Psychotronics into the picture, the more comprehensive Genetic Engineering, Nanotechnology, and Robotics became
in their approach to analyzing, replicating, and augmenting the
function of human organs, including the brain, the more these nuts-
and-bolts research programs would come up against enigmatic psi
abilities. ESP and PK would be acknowledged as R&D problems in the
development of Artificial Intelligence or in the integration of the brain
with Cybernetic systems, perhaps for the purpose of "downloading"
human consciousness into an android body. There would be problems
of morphogenesis relevant to genetic engineering that could not be
solved but by factoring in non-local morphic resonance that, quite
apart from DNA, impacts embryological development by endowing a
baby with characteristics of the body that belonged to the psyche that
is about to be reincarnated as that child.

The ultimate point of convergence of all accelerating technological
developments, including in Psychotronics, would be convergence in a

point that is really a vortex — a singularity. On a graph of humanity's technical progress from the mastery of fire through to the harnessing of the atom, this "Technological Singularity" is where the increasingly steep upward slope of the graphed line becomes a spike going straight upwards off the chart. That signifies that the analytically projective mind able to graph developments to date, and extrapolate from them, including in the realm of science-fiction, will reach a barrier on the other side of which is what is "*über*" (over, above) Man.

The heart of my book, the part that I could not adequately convey to Jason yet, was philosophical and, by extension, political. I say, by extension, because *Uber Man* had nothing to say about petty politics. Rather, its ideological and programmatic dimensions were of the kind that Nietzsche anticipated when he prophesied the advent of a "grand politics" that would determine nothing less than the planetary destiny of mankind.

I followed F. M. Esfandiary in his argument that Left- and Right-Wing were no longer adequate ideological orientations, and that the future dichotomy in sociopolitical struggle was between those who wanted to keep us "down" in the muck of the "merely human" and those "Up-Wingers" who were ready to affirm an evolutionary leap into a technologically augmented "posthuman" condition. However, at the same time, *Uber Man* harshly critiqued Esfandiary for his preposterously naive view that this evolutionary revolution could be accomplished through more direct democracy and his even more despicable claim that nothing is worth dying for. The latter claim follows from his myopic materialism and disregard of abundant evidence for the survival of bodily death and the persistence of personality. Even were the latter not the case, Esfandiary's tritely derisive dismissal of the heroic Existentialist view of death, namely that an authentic and meaningful life can only be lived in the face of a finite horizon that is ultimately bounded by nothingness, is itself worthy of contempt. It is nothing more than a product of his own cowardly thanatophobia.

Rather, as Nietzsche understood well, the last and greatest revolution in history, the one that ends "human" history and inaugurates a "higher history" of the *Übermensch*, will necessarily be the bloodiest and most incendiary sociopolitical upheaval of all time. It will be a revolution of the extreme minority against the vast majority, who will by then have devolved into cynical and nihilistic subhumans. Sarcastically dismissive of every noble aspiration, they will have become addicted to creature comforts, perpetually diverted from serious aims and creative ambitions by a pseudo "culture" of crassly irreverent entertainment.

These will be the great "democratic" masses huddled together in both nationalist and socialist states, who only ever elect rabble-rousers and "men of the people" that let them feel good about themselves while facilitating their bottomless degeneration. This tyrannous majority, which the founders of the United States naively believed could be penned in by constitutional provisions for the protection of individual liberties, this mass of herd animals by comparison to which cattle are noble creatures, will resist further evolution by any and all means necessary. They would, as Nietzsche knew well, prefer that we walk the evolutionary tightrope back to being apes rather than to tread forward with the gymnast's poise and the requisite daring to become those Supermen who stand on the far side of the tightrope.

For those who are psychologically prepared and have the Promethean *ethos* to take the evolutionary leap *upward* to be protected from those who would clip their wings, for the impending and relatively immanent Technological Singularity not to be sabotaged and subjected to a controlled demolition by conspirators who are, after all, only giving the masses what they secretly desire, the most antidemocratic consolidation of power in history is required. This must take place by means of ruthless cunning and a hitherto inconceivable capacity for dynamically transformative violence. The revolution from *above*, of the very *few* against the many.

By no means does *Uber Man* argue in favor of oligarchy, or the empowering of merchants and financiers. Quite to the contrary. Like Plato, I call for radical *meritocracy*. Again, advocating in favor of a revolution that is beyond the classic dichotomy of Left vs. Right, *Uber Man* affirms much of Marx's vision of a Communist society as a *free* society and argues that the Soviet Union was, at least in its ideal conception, forwarding a Promethean project to turn mere human beings into Communist Supermen. The failing of Marx, and of Soviet state ideology, was to believe that the proletarian rabble of uneducated workers would *ever* be capable of undergoing the kind of *psychological* transformation that the transcendence of Capitalist profiteering and the avaricious coveting of private property requires. Let alone that they would be more capable of it than aristocrats, and even members of the bourgeoisie, some of whom had the benefit of exposure to works of philosophy, literature, and art that lifted them above and beyond their lower selves.

The Technological Singularity would fundamentally alter the parameters of economic and industrial planning, taking us from a scarcity economy where the organization of labor and redistribution of wealth, which are principal Marxist concerns, is supplanted by a post-industrial production platform of abundance that provides for leisure without the need for *any* human drudgery whatsoever. But this *New World Order* — as H. G. Wells called it — would be rejected by the masses, through their designated representatives in the political, corporate, and industrial spheres, let alone their clergymen who valorize the pointless suffering of hard labor as penitence for the Fall. Despite all their disingenuous clamoring for "freedom," what the masses really want is to ensure that they remain collectively enslaved by avarice, petty jealousies, and niggardly resentments of anyone with the aspiration and will power to build on higher spiritual ground.

Uber Man made the case that, from the standpoint of the early 1990s, when I planned for the book to be completed and published, we had no more than half a century to decide whether it was better to let ourselves be regressed to a feudal or archaic pre-industrial society, or whether we were intent on following through with the Technological Singularity and the "Spectral Revolution" that I argued would come with it. I appropriated this idea from my writings as Jorjani in the future past. Namely the idea that, as already suggested above in relation to Psychotronics, once we reached the event horizon of the Singularity in terms of technological development, hitherto marginalized and suppressed psi abilities would also have to be recognized by mainstream science. At that point, total social collapse on the scale of a planet-wide Salem Witch Panic would be inevitable, *unless* we were to forge a society wherein no one would think to misuse ESP and PK to harm their fellow citizens by committing avaricious or vengeful crimes. Such crimes would be untraceable by normal law enforcement procedures and impossible to prosecute retro-actively by means of the established procedures of our "impartial" justice system.

The only thing to do is to ensure that these transgressions never take place to begin with. Since, in the realm of psychic ability, which functions mostly unconsciously, to *intend* something may be to make it *happen*, there is no solution other than to make sure that such spectral crimes are unthinkable to whoever remains in society. That would reduce the population base to the same less than 1% of individuals who could also be trusted never to weaponize Nanotechnology or misuse increasingly ubiquitous gene-editing abilities in ways that would threaten the public welfare far more seriously than terrorists, thugs, and malcontents were able to do with the tools at their disposal in the 20th century. What Esfandiary did not understand when he wrote *Up-Wingers* is that evolution is an exclusionary process that selects *against* the majority of a population group who fail to exhibit a mutation that adapts them to environmental stresses. The selection *for* a mutation is, as a general rule, a selection for deviation from the norm, and the evolution *of a few* who become the progenitors of a new species *at the expense of the many*.

CHAPTER 7

GO FORTH UNAFRAID

S OMEONE WOULD have to bring *Uber Man* to the attention of
socio-political elites and celebrities around the world. Not a mere
publicist, but a person who could familiarize royalty, presidents, scientists, acclaimed artists, famous actors, and popular musicians with
the book's ideas even ahead of its publication. I came here with a very
clear idea of who that super-connected socialite should be: Ghislaine
Maxwell. I knew that in July of 1991, her father, media mogul Robert
Maxwell would buy the *Daily News* in New York City. Then, within a
few months, in November of the same year, he would disappear from
his yacht, the Lady Ghislaine, which was named after his youngest
daughter.

What was never revealed to the public, and what Ghislaine alone
among her brothers and sisters strongly suspected, was that Maxwell
was murdered. By whom, she did not know. He had gone from being
a very valuable high-level asset to the Mossad to becoming a liabil-
ity when, as the owner of numerous newspapers that he occasionally
used for blackmail, he started threatening the Israelis that if they did
not continue to fund his secretly bankrupt media empire, then he
would reveal certain sensitive information. For the sake of plausible
deniability, and to fit his public image as one of the best friends of
Israel, Maxwell's recovered body was given a burial on the Mount
of Olives with the highest honors of the Israeli state. Ariel Sharon,

Yitzhak Shamir, and Ehud Barak were all at his funeral comforting Ghislaine and her siblings. What she didn't know was that Barak, an Israeli military-intelligence man, had given the order for the assassins on the two-man submarine to board the Lady Ghislaine in the middle of the night and take out her father.

Within a couple of weeks of Robert Maxwell's death, it was exposed that he had engaged in massive fraud to fund businesses that were really bankrupt. The family lost its fortune, and their fifty-room mansion in Oxford, where Ghislaine had grown up, and stayed on weekends during her years as a student at Oxford University in the mid-1980s. Pretty much everything in the house, and at Maxwell's various offices, was auctioned off by Sotheby's. Her two brothers, who were officially involved in the family business, were even prosecuted, but Ghislaine, who actually had more knowledge of her father's questionable dealings, was able to walk away since she had no *official* position within the management of the bankrupt enterprises. By December of 1991, looking for a fresh start, Ghislaine had left and resettled in what was, for her, a small apartment on the Upper East Side of Manhattan. She may have been short on cash, but her Rolodex was still intact.

Ghislaine Maxwell was daddy's girl, and she was absolutely devastated by the death of her father. Her closest friends at the time noticed a complete change in her personality. She went from being a passionate and gregarious woman with a raucous sense of humor who was the life of any party, to someone silently contemplative and withdrawn. Her self-imposed solitude was so full of anguish that a couple of people who knew her best feared that Ghislaine might commit suicide, unless something or someone were to fill the black hole in her world and give her life meaning and purpose again. Unfortunately, in the timeline that I hail from, that some*one* turned out to be the former Dalton School math teacher and shady money manager Jeffrey Epstein.

Robert Maxwell had met Epstein in the mid-1980s, and the two hit it off. Maxwell saw in Epstein a man much like himself. Although

Epstein had not grown up nearly as poor as "Robert" had when he was still Jan Ludwig Hoch from the ghettos of Nazi-occupied Czechoslovakia, he was also a Jewish kid who came from nothing, or to be more precise, from Coney Island, but who managed to use his high IQ to hustle and con his way into being the trusted financial advisor of billionaires like Les Wexner. Maxwell flew Epstein to Israel and got him involved with Israeli military intelligence, initially in the arms-dealing aspect of their operations in the Middle East. Based in Manhattan, Epstein was facilitating and profiting from Israeli arms deals, through certain proxies, with Arab oil sheikhs and various guerrilla groups who were useful idiots for the Mossad.

The tragedy of Ghislaine's life was that, after her father was murdered by the Israelis, she ultimately took refuge with an Israeli intelligence operative of the same individuals who ordered Robert's assassination. The price for reclaiming her old lifestyle of mansion houses and private planes was that she would use her extensive elite international connections as a socialite, who had already functioned for years as a connector for her father, so that Jeffrey Epstein could set up these men by preying upon their appetites for underage women. Prominent politicians, royalty, journalists, actors and every other type of policymaker, public opinion shaper, and celebrity was secretly taped with underage girls that Ghislaine was tasked with procuring for Jeffrey, so that the State of Israel could control US and British foreign policy and shape Anglo-American public opinion. If any of these men ever threatened the interests of the Jewish state, they would be blackmailed into obedience with the tapes that would regularly be supplied to Mossad from Epstein's various wired estates, from his mansion in Manhattan to his Palm Beach house and the property on his private island. There were even hidden cameras installed on his jet.

After two decades in an abusive relationship with him, which in many ways was an attempt on her part to recreate her rapport with her domineering and manipulative father, Ghislaine would eventually try to get away from Jeffrey Epstein. But it was too late. When he was caught after dozens of women who had been groomed by Ghislaine brought accusations against him, she was also eventually apprehended. Once Mossad managed to murder Jeffrey in his jail cell, to prevent him from potentially exposing Israel's tremendous blackmail operation, the prosecution's focus shifted to Ghislaine. Although she attempted to flee Manhattan and literally head for the hills in rural New Hampshire, she was hunted and eventually apprehended by the authorities. Ghislaine then fell for the second time in her life, but much harder. The daddy's girl who grew up in a fifty-room Oxford mansion was now reduced, not to living in a small apartment on the Upper East Side, but to rotting in a New York City jail cell with guards watching her every move, including on the toilet and in the shower, and where flashlights shone on her even as she tried to sleep. How morbidly intriguing that the name Ghislaine, which is of Franco-German origin, means "sweet hostage" or a beautiful sacrificial "pledge." Did Robert Maxwell, whose own name was contrived and who had worked for the military intelligence agencies of three countries before she was born, give daddy's little girl that name on purpose? Or was it karma and synchronicity at work?

In any case, I realized that for Ghislaine to be saved from being captured and then sacrificed by the same people responsible for murdering her father, Jeffrey Epstein had to be gotten rid of *before* Ghislaine developed a relationship with him in Manhattan in the early 1990s. Furthermore, for her to be a constructive publicist and promoter of *Uber Man*, I would have to befriend her prior to her father's death so that, when she moved to New York in December of 1991, she would fall into *my* arms rather than into the clutches of Epstein and Israeli intelligence. I knew that Ghislaine had some proclivities toward bisexuality, without which this plan would have proved to be impossible. But while the potential for seduction was a sine qua non, it was far from sufficient. I needed to be able to offer Ghislaine the material comforts and financial security that I knew she would look to regain through her desperate relationship with Jeffrey (or, from *his* perspective, her work *for* him and his Israeli handlers). Fortunately, by 1991, the finances of AtlantiCorp, including but not limited to its pharmaceutical subsidiary, were such that I could afford to actually outdo Epstein in the lifestyle that I could offer to Ghislaine. Especially considering the fact that she would not have to live at the beck and call of a man whose girlfriend she sadly wished to be, when in fact she was his pimp and a tool of the assassins who murdered her beloved father.

The first order of this business was, however, to get rid of Jeffrey Epstein. By 1989, Epstein was already an arms dealer. I had operatives of AtlantiCorp put him under a tight enough surveillance net to amass a dossier that demonstrated this, a dossier that I would anonymously leak to the press after he was assassinated. No one would question the gunning down of an arms dealer. The authorities would see it as Epstein having succumbed to an occupational hazard. I set up a shell company and had its mock manager arrange a meeting with Jeffrey, putatively for the purpose of having Epstein illegally improve the company's finances. I asked Donald Barr to vouch for this manager so that Jeffrey would take the meeting. AtlantiCorp had cultivated a relationship with Barr, the former headmaster who hired Epstein to teach math at The Dalton School a year after writing the twisted science-fiction novel *Space Relations* (1973) — a book which curiously anticipated the sex-slave trafficking that Epstein would involve Ghislaine in. Barr had been an OSS operative during the Second World War. After leaving Dalton, he was appointed by President Reagan to serve on the National Council of Educational Research, a position that he retained under President Trump — the President *that I made*, and to whom Barr answered now.

Epstein accepted the meeting with my representative, which the latter had demanded be at Tavern on the Green in Central Park. Jeffrey liked to go for strolls in the park, so I had predicted, rightly, that he would walk back home to his townhouse at 9 East 71st street, which was almost directly across the park from the restaurant. It was also an 800-meter expanse (about half a mile) right underneath the windows of my penthouse apartment. In the predawn hours of that beautiful day late in May of 1989, two of my operatives had used a manhole to damage the electric lines near my building at 55 Central Park West. By the time that the lunch meeting was set, ConEdison was jackhammering away on the sidewalk between me and Tavern on the Green so that they could repair the problem underground. The noise was so loud that no one even heard the shots being fired from my sniper rifle with its silencer.

I used an open window toward the middle of the bottom floor of my penthouse. I had carefully tracked Epstein on my rifle scope as he left Tavern on the Green and then, when he was in a relatively secluded but open area, about halfway across the park, I fired three shots at him in rapid succession and each hit their target with high precision. The first to the skull. The second to the heart, after he was already on the ground. The third to one of his legs. That way, without any witnesses who could accurately remember where he was hit first, it would be hard for the police to determine from what angle the shots were fired. After all, he could have been hit in the leg, then fallen, so that the bullets entered his head and chest from a different trajectory than the one that could be traced to a high floor on 66th street and Central Park West. Besides, who was going to come looking for an assassin in this penthouse apartment that belonged to a business woman? After getting rid of Bakhtiar, Bush, and Gorbachev, assassinating Epstein was a walk in the park (no pun intended).

It was a Friday, so that night, after doing the deed, I hit the dancefloor and lost myself to the beat of Techno music at the Limelight, which was always my preferred club in the city, even before Studio 54 closed down. It was beautifully diabolical how it had been built inside of a Gothic church. I even managed to pick up a cute Goth chick, so that she could fuck what was left of my brains out. Once her hangover wore off the next day, she resented me enough for the size of my apartment, and its view over Central Park, that it was easy never to see her again.

I befriended Ghislaine Maxwell during her extensive stay in Manhattan in the month leading up to, and during, her father's acquisition of the New York *Daily News*. Epstein had been dead for two years at this point, and although she had briefly met Jeffrey before that day when I gunned him down in Central Park, he was no longer on her mind at all. In this revised timeline, he was but a blip in her life, much to the disappointment of Robert Maxwell, who had been scheming to turn Jeffrey into his son-in-law. It was on an evening in June of 1991 when we first met. I had booked the outdoor space at Tavern on the Green for a private party and put together the most impressive guest list that I could from out of the contacts of AtlantiCorp. The ostensible purpose of the gathering was to celebrate the launch of a new corporate venture, which I knew would reel Ghislaine in, hook line and sinker. I knew because I got the idea from her — a future version of her that would never materialize in this revised timeline, but one with whom she nonetheless shared the biographical background, talents, and traits that would compel her to devise the *TerraMar* project when she was trying to distance herself from Epstein in the early 2010s.

This AtlantiCorp project was called *NovAtlantis*. It was a plan for an environmentally friendly corporate colonization of the ocean depths in international waters over which no nation had jurisdiction, beginning with the North Atlantic, from the Caribbean to the Canary Islands. There were several principal objectives that this project aimed to achieve. For good optics, the first of them was to preserve this part of the ocean from overfishing and pollution, by the merchant marine vessels of various nations, through promoting international regulation such as universal adherence to *The Law of the Seas* convention of the United Nations, which the United States had thus far refused to sign. The second aim was to build submarine micro-cities into the bedrock of various ridges in unclaimed waters of the Atlantic Ocean. (How this could be seen as entirely consistent with the first aim was glossed over by referencing certain putatively clean construction methodologies and strict quotas on local sea life resource depletion, as well as proposals for fish farming.) The submarine settlement core of the project was justified based on projected sea level rise, with the idea that the best way to avoid catastrophic loss of life, mass displacement, and economic and industrial collapse on account of the drowning of coastal cities was to get *under* the rising water before it was too late. The third and final aim, which connected the project to Avalon Pharmaceutical (AtlantiCorp's subsidiary and cash-cow), was extensive laboratory research on the medicinal properties of a wide range of ocean life, especially with a view to treating and potentially curing cancer.

I guaranteed Ghislaine's attendance by having President Trump personally extend the invitation to her, with an assurance that he would be there. I knew that, for years, she had wanted badly to meet Trump and that her father had, in a most demeaning manner, rebuffed her request to set up a meeting with him. I scheduled the event to coincide with one of his visits back "home." The President would occasionally sneak back to Trump Tower for a break from the White House. I'd like to have seen the look on Ghislaine's face when she opened an envelope from the Oval Office, with the *NovAtlantis* event invitation inside of it, personally inscribed by the Don, and even more so when she received a follow-up phone call from Trump, who said something to the effect of: "I've heard a lot about you from a good friend of mine. All *good* things. I look forward to meeting you at the party." To get Trump to agree to do me this favor, I had flown to Washington in our corporate jet, and stayed at the Willard Hotel for several days waiting for the President to have time to fit me into his schedule with very short notice.

When Ghislaine arrived at Tavern on the Green that Saturday evening in early June of 1991, the restaurant and the whole area of Central Park surrounding it was full of secret service agents. She was dressed in a characteristically stunning fashion, in an indigo blue dress that exposed the tanned skin of her beautiful shoulders and shimmered like the ocean when the Tavern's chandelier light played across it, reminding me of that phrase "the wine dark sea" that Homer often used. Ghislaine's large, sparkling diamond necklace made it impossible for me to miss her as soon as she walked in. (Granted, I was lingering at the bar toward the entrance to make sure that I caught her upon arrival.)

"Lady Maxwell, I'm Dana Avalon," I said as I extended my arm towards her in the entry hall with its charmingly antique wooden rafters. "Thank you so much for coming!" She grinned at the warm acknowledgement, with a sparkle in her fierce eyes. "Let me show you to your table. You're seated right next to Donald." She briefly glanced down at her dress somewhat nervously, rocking slightly on her high stilettos, as she said, "The President is here already?" "Indeed, he is. Don likes to close at least one business deal before he's eaten dinner at any of these things," I replied while laughing disarmingly. "You know him quite well, then?" asked Ghislaine. "Oh yes, *quite* well. *I'm* the one who convinced him to go into politics." I looked back at her, as we reached the threshold of the outdoor seating area. "You can blame me for that." We both chuckled. "*He* certainly does," I added, as I led Ghislaine, now holding her by the arm, over to Trump's table.

"Mr. President," I said as Donald smiled at me boyishly and paused his conversation, "may I present Lady Ghislaine Maxwell?" He got up to shake her hand, towering over both of us. "I was a big fan of your father. A real fighter! If you inherited half his guts and his smarts, let me tell you, Ms. Maxwell, you're in good shape." "Coming from you, that's high praise Mr. President." "Come have a seat, here," he said as he pulled back one of the white wrought-iron chairs around the glass table. "You want to get a drink? You know I don't drink but," he gestured over to the outdoor bar, "maybe you want to bring your drink over." "Sure, I'll go grab a drink and be back in a jiffy," said Ghislaine, clearly looking for an opportunity to take a breath before what she knew could be subjection to a long and very one-sided conversation.

I winked at Donald, and after Ghislaine turned away from him, he winked back and gave me a thumbs up.

By the time I was delivering my short speech at a podium set up all the way across from the glass windows looking into the interior of the restaurant, I saw that she was getting along well with Trump. Now, to shift her focus a bit. My speech featured more than one story drawn from my experiences diving, which I knew would set the stage for her to connect to me more deeply since she had also been a life-long avid diver who grew up watching Jacques Cousteau with great interest. I set the *NovAtlantis* project announcement in this personal context, without making it too technical. When I sat down to dinner with Ghislaine afterwards, at the seat immediately to her left, so that she was sandwiched between Trump and I, it gave me great satisfaction that she was more interested in hearing about *NovAtlantis* than in continuing to exchange pleasantries, platitudes, and corporate gossip with the President of the United States. Ghislaine and I began to have a private conversation, leaning into each other and carrying on in a hushed tone of voice, with Trump talking loudly to the several other people at our table. I caught myself staring at her large pearl earrings, somewhat mesmerized by the sheen of her black hair that was a little less than shoulder length. I had to deliberately focus back on what Ghislaine was saying. I think she may have noticed this, and it intrigued her.

We were three drinks in and already on a first name basis, when I said, "To be honest, Ghislaine, the reason that I invited you tonight — I hope that I'm not being too forward — but I asked you to come because *NovAtlantis* still needs a project director. I don't have the time to manage it myself." She looked at me with a stunned, incredulous expression on her face. Fortunately, the tensed muscles of her forehead were complemented by a grin in which I could see both an appreciation of audacity and some deeper, potentially unfathomable, hunger that she let show itself. (It was only later that she confessed to me how unhappy she had been that her father never gave her "a proper job" at any of his businesses.) "You'll have a whole staff working under you," I rushed to add, almost apologetically. "You mean you want *me* to run this project for you?!" she finally blurted out. "I've already done my homework, Ghislaine. You'd be a perfect face for this venture, and the ideal person to generate interest in it among the right circles of people." She thirstily swallowed the rest of her third drink, and even crunched some of the ice at the bottom of it between her teeth.

Trump glanced at her sideways, and then gave me a bemused look. He broke the uncomfortable silence by turning to Ghislaine and nearly shouting, "What's she trying to *sell* you?" he asked, while moving both hands back and forth at his sides. "You know *this* woman talked me into running for President... and, uh... I'm not saying I have any regrets or anything," he shrugged as he caught himself, "and I *guarantee* you that I'll be in office for another five years," he added as he looked a bit uneasily at everyone else at the table, "but... well, *look*, Dana makes your life *harder*. She'll push you to the next level of what you can be — *if* you're *up* for that, you know what I mean? Some people who reach like that, they fall hard from somewhere they had no business being in the first place. Some of 'em even jump out a window." I started giving the President a hard stare. "But if you're your father's daughter, you'll be fine." He turned to the others at the table, pointing at Ghislaine almost rudely, "her father, *great* guy — a real *fighter*." In point of fact, he couldn't have delivered a better "sales" pitch for me. Trump was like that. Just when you thought he was starting to aimlessly stumble into something like a bumbling idiot, what he said or did wound up landing with the astonishing aptness of a master chess player's piece. He reminded me a bit of the card of the Fool in the Tarot.

Ghislaine Maxwell came home with me that very night. After all, I lived right across the street. Trump politely declined an offer to come over for a night cap. "You want all these *suits* to come over there with you?" He was talking about the secret service agents. "They don't let me go *anywhere* alone anymore. You two enjoy yourselves. *You don't want* these stiffs around," he whispered as he leaned down toward us, shaking his head. "It was a real pleasure to meet you, Ms. Maxwell." "The pleasure and the honor were mine, Mr. President." Donald patted me on the back as he headed toward the limousine that would take him back to Trump Tower.

We had our fourth drink of the night on my rooftop terrace, overlooking Central Park. "Just think about it," I said to her as our champaign flutes clinked together. "I don't need an answer for a while. There's a lot of preliminary work that I need to do to lay the groundwork for the project. Meanwhile, I know that you'll be busy helping your father with his acquisition of the *Daily News*." Ghislaine promised me that she'd seriously consider my offer, but I knew that what I was really doing that night was planting a seed that would only germinate in her mind after the death of her father and the scandal of the exposed bankruptcy of his fraudulent business empire — five months later. We parted that evening by kissing each other on the cheeks, as I put her in a car that was sent to pick her up. The wondrous joy, insatiable curiosity, and vivacious enthusiasm that I saw in her eyes through the tinted glass of the car as she looked up at me and waved goodbye that night, were all missing from her face the next time that I saw her.

It was December of 1991, a few weeks before Christmas. Rockefeller Center and Fifth Avenue, where I had spent the day shopping, were already glittering with decorations. Ghislaine was born on Christmas, and it was a special time of the year for her because although her parents were of Jewish descent, Robert Maxwell, seeking to endear himself to the British people, especially during his years as an elected politician, always celebrated Christmas on a grand scale. Both of my working fireplaces were on, including the one in the turret library on the rooftop with its hybrid Gothic and Deco design, where I was sitting curled up under a wool blanket watching the snow fall through the late afternoon sky, when the doorman rang to tell me that Ghislaine was here. We had spoken briefly on the phone, shortly before she moved to Manhattan to get away from it all and start over. I had already expressed my sympathies, and let her know, as considerately as possible given the circumstances, that my offer still stood. No one else had been hired yet to be the figurehead of the *NovAtlantis* project at AtlantiCorp.

When she walked through the door to my apartment, Ghislaine almost collapsed into my embrace. "I'm sorry," she mumbled, feeling embarrassed at being so vulnerable with someone she hardly knew. "I didn't know where else to go." She could barely look me in the eyes. "Consider yourself at home here, Ghislaine. Regardless of what you decide about my offer. If you prefer this place to your own apartment, or you just want a place to hide out, you can stay as long as you wish. I have two guest rooms, and my driver can take you anywhere you need to go. Our corporate jet can even discretely *fly* you anywhere you have to fly without attracting attention." Ghislaine Maxwell generally had an unflappable confidence about her, at a deeper layer of her persona than that of the social butterfly with an outrageous sense of humor. But what I saw in her eyes at that moment was from a still more profound sub-stratum of her psyche. She looked at me with the sad but wondering eyes of a little girl. "*Please* make yourself at home," I said with sincere empathy.

It took a while, but she did just that. By Christmas Eve Ghislaine had been spending more time at my apartment than at her own provisional pad across the park, which was about a fourth of the size of my penthouse. I made sure not to be overly aggressive in my approach to her, giving her plenty of breathing room and time to herself. She had brought over some luggage and filled the closets and dresser drawers of one of my guest rooms. We finished decorating my apartment together, including the impressive Christmas tree that my sunken living room with its tall ceiling could accommodate. It was still a lot smaller than the ones that she grew up with at that mansion in Oxford, but I know that she appreciated sprawling on the sofa by the side of the tree and basking in the warm glow of its lights — especially at night.

I would often take her shopping, and then out to dinner. French, Italian, Japanese — we hit every hot restaurant in the city. The first time that I walked her over to my black DeLorean and popped the door wing open, Ghislaine said, "I thought you had a driver." I replied, "I do, but I only use him to appear at business meetings, galas, and the like. To be honest, that's why I said that you could use him. These days, I hardly ever do." Ghislaine smiled as she climbed into the passenger seat next to me. Although she did occasionally make use of the limo driver, she much preferred having me chauffer her around town in the DeLorean. I noticed that whenever there was a bit of erotic tension between us in the car, she would unconsciously clutch and stroke the distressed black leather upholstery of the seat either beside or between her thighs. For those first several weeks, nothing had really happened between us besides kissing each other goodnight a few times after especially intoxicated and luxuriant dinner conversations in the course of which we got to know each other much more intimately.

On Christmas Eve of 1991, the night before her thirtieth birthday (she was sixteen years younger than me), we walked back home from a special holiday dinner at Tavern on the Green and snuggled beside the fireplace in the living room to warm up. When Ghislaine sat up for a moment to take her cashmere sweater off, I walked to the kitchen to pour us a couple of glasses of some pretty potent eggnog and bring back a plate of gingerbread cookies. I also slipped her Christmas and birthday present, which had been tucked away in a kitchen drawer, into the pocket of my pants. It was a set of keys. Not to my apartment, but to the apartment beneath mine. Unbeknown to Ghislaine, I had been engaged for weeks in an aggressive buyout of the person who lived under me. He hardly used the apartment, anyway. I made him an offer that he couldn't refuse, paying well over the market price, and brought to bear the substantial influence that I had with the building's board to expedite the transfer of ownership.

Toward the bottom of the glass of eggnog, Ghislaine and I started kissing with the carelessness of mischievous children. She might have thought that I was about to take her to my bedroom when I sprung up and pulled her off the floor by the hand. "I want to give you your present *now*," I said with what must have been an impish expression on my face. With her sweater strewn on the floor, she only had an undershirt on, so I wrapped the wool blanket from the sofa around her shoulders before walking her over to the door, then leading her out into the hallway to the stairwell. "Trust me," I reassured her as she wondered what the hell I was doing, "it's a surprise present." She followed me one flight down the stairwell to the floor just beneath my duplex penthouse, then to one of the doors on the hallway. I knew that any one of them would do, since some of the interior walls on that floor had already been knocked out to form a single apartment extending across the entire 18th floor.

Ghislaine was still rather baffled when she walked in the door of the apartment. "Merry Christmas and Happy Birthday, Ghislaine!" She was starting to get the idea, but still a bit dumbfounded as she surveyed the spacious rooms from the entry foyer. "The former owner has promised to get his furniture out of here by the New Year. Then, you can remodel it any way you like. I have the board wrapped around my finger." Now she understood, and I saw tears well up in her eyes. "It's a selfish present. I want you close to me, Ghislaine, and that guest room just won't do in the long run." She put one hand to her forehead and braced herself with her other arm around my shoulders. "And let's just get this clear from the outset: this is *your* place, and you should feel free to bring whatever men home with you whenever you want. Just maybe share a few of them with me now and then," I said as I shifted my tone from being dead earnest to reassuringly humorous. "So, you like men too, then?" she somewhat breathlessly asked, with tears still streaming down her cheeks. "Once in a while."

"I don't know what to say, Dana, this is just… I *can't believe* that you did this!" "Why don't we take a walk around the place?" I replied as I held her close and started to give her a quick tour of her new apartment. When we stepped out onto what would be her terrace, she noticed that along the exterior of the building, this apartment was part of the white brick facing that was distinct from the rest of the building's beige structure and set back from it, with especially detailed deco moldings aesthetically connecting it up to my duplex. The overall impression of these top floors, taken together, was of something between a Gothic castle and a Babylonian ziggurat sitting on top of a Manhattan residential building. As Ghislaine took all that in, I slipped the keys into her pants pocket, letting my hand linger a bit too long on her thigh.

When we came back up to my apartment, we headed straight to the master bedroom. I turned on the water in the bathroom's hot tub to warm us up from being outside in the cold night air with only our undershirts on. When we pulled these off, both of our nipples were hard — although mine were much larger than hers, despite my having such small breasts. Ghislaine had rather full and round breasts, with a shape that I imagine most men would think was perfect. She was too enamored of me at this point to judge me too harshly for my weird little, widely spaced tits. I could tell that she *was* perturbed by how huge my clitoris is, but my mutant vulva probably made her feel that she had the upper hand in something. Ghislaine relaxed into my body with her cheek lying against my neck. I kissed her forehead, beading with steam from the hot tub.

Suffice it to say that the sex we had that night was among the best in my life. I didn't confess this to Ghislaine because I knew that she preferred men to women and so I imagined that, although clearly satisfied, she might not feel the same. When I brought my Macintosh PowerBook 100 into bed with me the next morning, while she continued to linger on the verge of sleep next to me, Ghislaine asked what I was typing. "I'm writing a book," I said. "It's called *Uber Man*." After she was done snoozing and I brought her up some coffee from the kitchen, she perked up enough to ask me what the book was about.

"It is about how convergent advancements in technology, and attendant scientific breakthroughs, are reaching a point where Man will be forced to either face extinction or take a self-overcoming evolutionary leap — in every dimension, psychological, social, political — to a new form of life that is as far beyond the merely 'human' as Man is above the ape." Ghislaine's eyes widened, as if to say, "come again." She looked at me a bit apprehensively but also intrigued, as she sipped her second coffee from an AtlantiCorp mug. (I had brought a whole pot upstairs, to refill our mugs.) She had the blanket pulled up under her armpits, so as not to be cold, since we were both still stark naked. I flipped the lid of the laptop closed and placed it down on the carpet next to the bed. "What technological advancements?" she finally asked. "For example, Genetic Engineering, Robotics, Artificial Intelligence, and Nanotechnology," I said. "I see. What do you mean by 'attendant scientific breakthroughs?" Now she was interested.

"I mean that technological development isn't always an application of breakthroughs in theoretical science, the latter can be outgrowths of empirical horizons for observation and experimentation that are first opened up by new technologies." She stared at me fixedly, with increasingly intense concentration. "Also," I continued, "these breakthroughs include paradigm-shifting, or even post-paradigmatic areas of research such as Parapsychology." "You mean like Telepathy, Clairvoyance, and such... Mind over Matter?" she asked with an awareness of what those were. "Yes, Ghislaine, although the dichotomous categories of 'Mind' and 'Matter' are deeply problematic. Nature is *spectral*, especially when considered from the standpoint of the evolutionary process. None of these things you mentioned are really 'supernatural.' They're just natural processes that have been pushed to the fringe by our entrenched scientific paradigm."

"I haven't heard anyone talk like this since I was at Oxford." I smiled at Ghislaine somewhat apologetically. "Well, there *was* this one fellow I met on a few occasions. A friend or — I don't know — associate of my father's. Epstein was his name. He was really into cutting-edge Physics and technologies like Genetic Engineering that he believed could push the limits of what defines humanity. He *also* believed in voodoo — or telekinesis and such. But he was from Brooklyn, you see, so he had a way of putting things — let's say, *crudely* compared to you." She giggled. I faced forward and didn't say anything in direct reply. "Well, it's Christmas morning, I didn't mean to burden you with all that. I have a reservation in place for Christmas brunch at the Plaza Hotel's Palm Court, if you're up for it."

"Oh yes, the Plaza, that sounds delightful," she said. "Great! We'll celebrate your new apartment, and your birthday of course! ...Oh, I shouldn't presume. Did you have any other dates set with anyone today?" She blushed bashfully, her head a bit downcast. "Actually, I did *not*. My brothers and my mother will certainly call, and so at some point I should call them myself, since they'll get the answering machine at my apartment." "Your *old* apartment," I said with a smile. Still blushing, Ghislaine looked into my eyes and then gave me a kiss. "Wanna take a shower *together*?" I blurted out with childlike enthusiasm. "*Sure*," she said. "Let me use your bathroom first, though." After she climbed out from under the covers and strode across the room naked with brazen confidence, I endearingly imagined her sitting on my toilet contemplating technological advancement and post-human evolution.

I kid you not, it's probably what she was thinking about, because she went on and on asking me questions about it during our brunch at the Palm Court. Something I noticed about Ghislaine was that she was very good about taking a cue from someone. When I thought about it, this made sense and was less counterintuitive than I imagined at first (one might assume, with her upbringing, that she was somewhat narcissistically self-centered). To grow up as the favorite and youngest daughter of Robert Maxwell, she must have, from a very young age, gotten used to reading and attuning herself to nonverbal cues from the man, at the very least to stay on the right side of his Jekyll and Hyde personality to the extent possible. I don't know if, even now, she did it consciously. In any case, Ghislaine spent at least the first half of our brunch asking me to elaborate on my explanation of *Uber Man*, despite my repeatedly trying to refocus the subject on something of more personal interest to her.

Then, of her own accord, she made the connection between *Uber Man* and the NovAtlantis project that I wanted her to direct. "You want to colonize the unclaimed ocean depths so as to create a cradle for the evolution of this posthuman race, one that lies beyond the law of any regressive nation." I was deeply impressed. "Yes, Ghislaine, I confess that is my hidden motivation," I whispered as I leaned into her, as if anyone could hear us over the din of the other diners echoing under the curved glass ceiling of the majestic fin-de-siècle room. "I'll do it, Dana," she said decisively. "I'll direct your NovAtlantis project." When I thanked her, while holding her arm across the table, and expressing how much confidence I had in her, she added, "I can also promote your book and its ideas in the right circles of influential people. I know which of these people, at least privately, shares your contempt for the conventional limits of mere 'humanity' which, I might add, is entirely justified. Most 'people' are *worthless*." Now Ghislaine was the one whispering. "There is no reason why we should be dragged down with them, or *by* them, and miss *our chance* at taking an evolutionary leap within the coming century — or *sooner* perhaps."

Early in the spring of 1992, we flew to the Bahamas on my corporate jet and went diving together off the coast of Bimini, where I showed Ghislaine megalithic ruins that dated from the time of Atlantis. She was a qualified submersible pilot and she insisted on coming back, after our dive, for an even more magical descent onto the "Bimini Wall" and other hidden pyramidal and polygonal structures. She enjoyed being the one to pilot me in the small submarine. When we were headed back home, Ghislaine also climbed into the cockpit of the helicopter and flew us to the airfield where my corporate jet was waiting. She all but threw the designated pilot in the backseat together with me. I have to admit that she was the most bad-assed girlfriend that I'd had in this lifetime, even in the Gotham of 2112.

By the summer of that year, Ghislaine was officially acting as the director of AtlantiCorp's NovAtlantis project. She began by going on a lobbying tour that included speeches at the United Nations General Assembly, the Woods Hole Oceanographic Institute, US Congressional hearings on *The Law of the Seas* convention, and other international organizations relevant to the first of the three stated aims of the project. More importantly, Ghislaine began to promote the ideas of *Uber Man* to a select group of prominent politicians, broad-minded members of the British royalty, and the more visionary actors and celebrities that she knew. The book's publication was slated for the fall of 1992, at which point these individuals would be able to generate tremendous publicity and considerable moneyed private interest in its vision for a fusion of hitherto materialistic Transhumanism with the more psychically oriented Human Potential Movement.

In the early 1990s, the foundation was already being laid for Prometheism — three decades or *a full generation* in advance of when I had launched that movement in my life as Jorjani. My plan was to ultimately hand the movement, together with its supporting institutions, including AtlantiCorp and its capital, over to Jason once he completed his doctoral studies and wrote his first couple of books. Between now and then, I would work to build an unbreakable rapport with him, and to reshape his future in the most constructive way possible. (I said *constructive*, not *palatable* to the mob's public morals.)

Ghislaine settled into her apartment on the 18th floor of 55 Central Park West, where she resumed her role as a socialite hosting parties attended by the who's who of the city, all of whom I had an opportunity to mingle with, and some of whom I would invite up to my own penthouse. Since Jason transferred from the bankrupted Fleming School to The Dalton School in the fall of 1992, he had been coming for more frequent tutoring appointments to help him adjust to the higher academic standard. I had also given him a hardcover of the newly released *Uber Man*, which he was devouring and would often ask me questions about. One day, while he was sitting inside the glass enclosure on my terrace, doing his math homework, I asked Ghislaine to come up, ostensibly because I wanted to show her the new flowers that I was planting on my terrace.

"Jason, this is my girlfriend Ghislaine. She lives downstairs," I said by way of introduction. I had already told Ghislaine about Jason and that I was using the tutoring as an excuse to cultivate him as a Person of Interest. But that's all I told her. I wondered if she'd notice the resemblance between us, since she was one of the most keenly perceptive people that I'd ever met. I think she did notice but thought it too strange to remark upon. In any case, the look on her face clearly showed that she found something uncanny about Jason. "I once knew a man who taught math at The Dalton School," she said to Jason. I quickly intervened to change the subject, since I did not want her answering any questions about Epstein or his having been gunned down in the stretch of Central Park overlooked by this very terrace.

"Ghislaine runs that ocean project that I told you about. She is a diver, a submarine captain, a helicopter pilot — and, Jason, she knows just about anyone in the world who is worth knowing." Ghislaine feigned embarrassment and then rejoined, which she shouldn't have, "Dana has told me a lot about you, actually, you sound like quite an extraordinary young man." "She's told *you* about *me*?" Jason asked, as he looked over at me. "I confess," I said with my hands up in the air. "I talk about you a lot. Don't let it go to your head."

You wouldn't believe me if I were to tell you that I didn't sense any narcissism in this seduction. Or maybe you would just think that I couldn't sense it because I am a narcissist. But the magnetic attraction that had built up between Jason and I in the course of years of working together had reached an intensity that incinerated every form of petty egotism or self-indulgent fascination. We felt like we were a destiny together. How else can I explain it?

Moreover, as he hit puberty and entered adolescence (but before he was old enough to have to shave), he was beginning to look more like me. He noticed and wondered at the resemblance. I don't mean that he merely thought about it, but that it mesmerized him. When I would notice him unintentionally staring at me, captivated, I could tell that he was comparing his own features to mine. Once he asked if we were related somehow. I replied, "What do you think?" Jason paused for a moment, then looked me straight in the eyes, and said, "Yeah, but not in any way that people would understand." I smiled at him mischievously.

Once his father had left for California, and his relationship with his mother continued to deteriorate, Jason would lie to her that he was at a friend's house so that he could spend more time with me. Now that the geopolitical goals of my mission here had been accomplished, and the Soviet Union had survived into the 1990s, together with its constructive rivalry (especially in space) with an America under President Trump — I was more than willing to indulge him. Redirecting the course of Jason's life was, after all, my *other* mission here. The one that was on my shoulders alone.

The next several years would be crucial. The changes that I had made to the timeline, and to the circumstances of his life thus far, could not guarantee that he would be steered clear of a relationship that would prove to be catastrophic to the rest of his life. A relationship based almost entirely on traumatic karma from more than one past life. I could try to guide him toward some other girl or woman with whom he could hopefully develop a bond strong enough, and for long enough, to avert the danger.

Of course, Nassim Nouri occurred to me, but she was in Los Angeles. Aside from the age gap between them (Nassim was four years older), which was far more of an issue at this period in their lives than it would be later on, there was the risk that if Jason somehow met her during one of his trips to Los Angeles to visit his father, he might actually find it reason enough to move to Los Angeles. Obviously, I needed him to remain here in New York. I seriously considered encouraging him to pursue Eve Pomerantz, who in my now overwritten timeline would become a lifelong friend of Jorjani. But Jason wouldn't meet Eve for another couple of years, since she was a grade ahead of him at The Dalton School and they only had an opportunity to get to know each other in a Life Drawing class open to juniors and seniors. I also had reason to believe that such a relationship would come with its own long-term dangers to Jason's developmental trajectory as a thinker. Eve would encourage his few and otherwise fleeting flirtations with Traditionalism and the Perennial Philosophy, and any serious relationship with her would stifle his exploration of the frontiers of paradigm-shifting science and technological breakthroughs with transhuman potential. At that age, she was almost a Luddite.

No, I needed to put the Promethean elements of Jason's psyche on steroids and accelerate his development as a thinker. Only I could do that. I had to let him fall in love with me. That's all. Just let it happen. It *had* already been *happening* for years. He was clearly infatuated with me by the end of the very first session that we had together. Back then he had also been nervous. But he gradually got over that in the course of the first year of my "tutoring" him. It helped that his grades improved tremendously, because on account of that he was able to relax more when he came over to my apartment. We already had many conversations on subjects unrelated to his schoolwork.

Jason loved the rooftop of my penthouse apartment and on days when the weather was good, he used to sit on a chair at my table on the terrace that faced the Gothic/Deco turret that he called "the Gozer gate." Having *been* him, I knew that he had just hit puberty. Although there had always been something erotic about the electricity between us, the voltage had turned up by an order of magnitude. I mean I could have taken my clothes off in front of him at any time with absolute certainty that he would volunteer his virginity without a moment's hesitation.

One afternoon late in the fall of 1992, a couple of weeks after I introduced him to Ghislaine, I pretended to spill a blue drink that I had made for us on my white shirt and grey hound's tooth-patterned suit pants. It was "Romulan ale," actually, a concoction that I thought he'd get a kick out of, *Trekkie* that he was. (Yes, I confess to giving him alcohol at the age of 11.) We were already in my bedroom, flipping through a book of Syd Mead's concept art that I wanted to show him. So, I just took my soaked and stained pants off right there in front of Jason, together with my shirt. I had leaned forward enough while tutoring him that he knew I didn't usually wear bras. Knowing what I was planning, I was already excited. I waited for him to take his eyes off my engorged nipples for long enough to see the pointy bulge in my panties, as I leisurely looked for another pair of pants and a shirt in my closet. I was wearing a thong, so he also saw my bare ass.

What happened next was too perfect, and almost comical. *He* pretended to spill *his* drink on himself from the distraction of watching me. He also got some of it on my white carpet. So, first, still wearing only my thong, I got a wet and soapy towel from the adjacent bathroom and acted as if I cared about getting the blue stain out of my carpet (I couldn't have cared less), using it as an opportunity to bend over in front of him, with my ass in his face, rubbing the stain in the carpet back and forth. Then, after a moment, as if realizing the hopelessness of it, I told him to take his pants off so that I could throw them in my laundry machine right away. Jason looked really embarrassed. Not because of the spill, but obviously because he was hard as fuck, and he knew that I'd see that when he took his pants off. I did see it, despite his halfhearted attempt to cover his underwear with his shirt. "Your shirt is stained too," I said, looking at a blue spot on it that was right next to his cock. At this point Jason's cheeks were bright red. When I came back into the bedroom after throwing our clothes in the washing machine, I saw that he had also taken off his underwear, and was sitting on the side of my bed, rock hard. Now *that* was bold.

I stood right in front of him and stepped out of my panties — leaving them strewn on the floor. He could see how soaked they were at the crotch. But he only glanced at that for a moment before he was fixated on my pinkie-sized clit sticking straight out from my pubic mound and pulling my inner labia up out of my vulva. I could feel the heat of my own flushed cheeks, and my heart was beating fast. I gently pushed him back onto the bed, and then I sat on his face — straddling his jaw with my inner thighs. Even though the way that he was sucking my clit and licking my labia was a bit awkward, and he nicked me with his teeth a few times, I came faster than I'd ever come in my life. My whole abdomen was trembling.

I slid down and collapsed onto him, with my nipples rubbing against his chest. I could feel his hard cock against my wet labia. Almost immediately, my clit started getting swollen again from the excitement of having him inside me. I could feel it pressing firmly against his pubic bone as it grew. As soon as I leaned back to relieve the pressure on my throbbing clit, his standing penis pressed hard against that spot inside the front wall of my vagina. I tried to calm him, while I rocked up and down to modulate the pressure. Then, suddenly, I felt the warmest and most intense fountain of cum shoot into me. It was so exciting that I came again myself — even more intensely than the first time. When we kissed passionately for a long time afterwards, lying on our sides, face to face with our heads on the pillows, I whispered to him, "I'm going to teach you to dance. Only a god who dances is worth believing in. You're not going to wind up like Harry Haller in this life." He'd recognize the reference to *Steppenwolf* someday.

Over the course of the following weeks, we would make love many times. Usually, more than once during each of Jason's visits to my apartment. It didn't take long at all for us to become much more synchronized than during that first somewhat awkward, albeit extremely exciting, encounter. We would often come together at nearly or, in some cases, exactly the same moment. That may have been a function of bringing down the last remnants of the psychical barrier that, up to that point, I felt I had to maintain between us. I was worried that when Jason found out who I really was, he might be repulsed and reject me. Instead, once he knew the truth, we experienced the most intimate and unconditional spiritual fusion. Jason came to see me as something between a twin sister and a fairy godmother. That's when the sex became phenomenal. Whenever our gaze would fall on the blue stain that never came out of the bedroom carpet, we would look at each other and smile with our whole hearts. Blue, the color of the Impossible.

On his thirteenth birthday, the evening of which he spent with me, undoubtedly explaining to his mother that he was "going out with friends," I invited Ghislaine over for our little party. It was February 21, 1994. "So, you're a *teenager* now," Ghislaine said to him in the most mischievous tone with a wickedly wry smile on her face, which was bathed in the glow of the candles that I had just lit on his birthday cake. "Yes, see how he's already starting to look like me?" I said as I knelt down next to Jason and looked up at Ghislaine, with my face pressed close to his. "Don't you see the resemblance?" he asked her. It must have seemed to her like some bizarre antic from *Alice in Wonderland* or one of Kafka's absurd stories because, after two years of working together and practically also living together, I still hadn't told my girlfriend what I had revealed to Jason about who I really was and where — or when — I was from. She had noticed a lot of odd things, including my sniper rifles, and I think she began to suspect that I might be an intelligence agent of some sort. Jason had agreed to be my accomplice as I broke it to her *tonight*.

He blew out the candles, and for a moment it was dark. I turned the dimmer in the living room up to slice through the blue velvet. Then I poured the Romulan Ale into champagne glasses. "What is *this*, spiked with acid or something? I feel like I'm going to start hallucinating if I drink this," said Ghislaine only half-jokingly. "Follow the white rabbit, Alice," I said. Then I brought out Jason's present. The box was wrapped in a metallic cobalt blue paper that shifted patterns as the light hit it from various angles. He opened it and laid the photographs inside it across the table. They were black and white and color photographs of Jason in his twenties, his thirties, even his forties, at various events in different places and times in what would never be *his* future.

I had brought them with me in my submersible time machine, from a dark future that would never be. Ghislaine came around behind Jason, moving slowly with an increasingly astonished expression on her face. "*How* did you *do* this, Dana?!" Jason, who I had shown these before, looked up at Ghislaine with the most disturbingly calm demeanor and said, "Didn't you *know* she's a witch?"

"They're *real*, Ghislaine. To the extent that *anything* is." The look of perplexity on Ghislaine's face turned to an expression of horror. "You've been wondering to yourself for some time now if I have some secret life. If I'm an assassin or a spy. I suppose I am those things, my dear, but those aren't even half-truths." Ghislaine moved her mouth as if she were trying to formulate a question, but no sound came out. "I'm from the future, beloved." Jason slowly turned his head and looked up at her, "To be precise, she's a reincarnation of *me* from the future. A terrible future that *once was*, but thanks to all that Dana's done, will now never come to pass." Ghislaine finally managed to pull herself together enough to get a few words out, "Dana Avalon... *time traveler*?! From where — I mean *when*???" "From a city called Gotham, built above the drowned ruins of this one. I was born in 2077 and I left my dying world in 2112. My biography, prior to 1980 when I arrived here, is manufactured," I explained to the distraught woman who was about to learn what a terrible fate I had saved her from.

Ghislaine was silent for a long time. Then she said, "That explains a lot." After another moment's pause, she went on, "Intelligence operative — I suppose maybe that thought crossed my mind a few times — but, no, I was actually starting to become convinced that you're some kind of sorceress." Jason piped in with one of his favorite quotes from Arthur C. Clarke, "Any sufficiently advanced technology is indistinguishable from magic."

"Well, I think we've all lost our appetite for cake," I said as I led the two of them up to the turret. "You're going to want to sit down for this," I said to Ghislaine. I opened up a false panel in the library, revealing a metal vault and I spun its combination lock until its door swung open. First, I showed her photographs of my world, from the cityscape of Gotham and the partially submerged skyscrapers of Manhattan rising from out of the Atlantic Ocean, to the megalithic structures of the Olympians, who tyrannized as gods over a planetary population that had retreated into Traditionalism on account of the manufactured catastrophes of the 21st century. Then, I pulled out all of the reproductions of newspaper clippings about her and Jeffrey Epstein, the sex trafficking accusations against them, his suspicious death in jail, and her eventual arrest, conviction, and imprisonment. The reproductions included news stories from the 2030s when it was revealed that Mossad was responsible for the assassination of Robert Maxwell and was also the agency that funded Jeffrey Epstein's operation to set up elites for blackmail by the State of Israel.

The woman was shaking and in tears by the time she was done going through them, but true to her personality Ghislaine couldn't take her eyes off of them. She looked over some of the same ones, over and over again, trying to process it all. It would not be lost on anyone with even the most cursory knowledge of psychology that the reason I did this on Jason's thirteenth birthday was that I was trying to forge a trauma bond between her and him. Jason cautiously slid across the carpet to Ghislaine's side, as she sat on a chair around the coffee table covered with photographs and news clippings. He looked up to her and said, "She changed *my* future too. It's better this way. For both of us." Ghislaine, with tears streaming down her cheeks, glanced over at him, running her hand down the back of his head and neck, as she looked over at me, gazing into my eyes with a penetrating stare of haunting power: "Well, I suppose it couldn't be *worse* than it would have been — for *me*." "For all of *us*, Ghislaine. Now you can *really* achieve something, and now you know the whole *truth* that you've sought so passionately."

Jason Reza Jorjani never made it home on the night of his thirteenth birthday. He collapsed in my bed together with Ghislaine Maxwell. In the event that his mother called the police the next

morning, they wouldn't take it seriously considering the circumstances. A minor had to be "missing" for at least 24 hours before they
would lift a finger to search for him, let alone a "minor" who had gone
missing on a night he supposedly went out with friends to celebrate
becoming a teenager. So, Jason spent the morning of February 22,
1994 in my bed making love to a still dazed Ghislaine Maxwell who
half wondered if the revelations of the night before were but a dream.
I was there, but mostly as a facilitator and a conduit for the energy
that began to flow between the two of them. As a lover, Jason had been
groomed well by me in the past year and a half. Ghislaine took refuge
from the psychological disorientation she was suffering by grounding
herself in the intense physical pleasure that he filled her body with.
She came back to herself through the series of increasingly intense
orgasms that she had that morning.

In the weeks that followed, Ghislaine started spending more and
more time with Jason. Having studied French at Oxford, Ghislaine
made sure that Jason never lost the fluency in that language that he
had acquired at The Fleming School. They even went on a trip to Paris
together, pretending to be relatives whenever eyebrows were raised.
In some gender-reversed version of Woody Allen's *Manhattan*, sometimes she would come pick him up from The Dalton School and they
would sip Starbucks coffee together on a walk back to our building
across Central Park. By then, she had figured out just who used a
sniper rifle to gun down Jeffrey Epstein in that stretch of park back in
1989. Ghislaine had come to terms with the fact that, by daring to do
that, I had saved her from being a lifelong hostage of the same Israelis
who had murdered her father.

In his junior year, Jason had the audacity to set up a lecture for
Ghislaine in Dalton's Martin Theater, wherein she presented the
NovAtlantis project to an audience of precocious high schoolers and
their extraordinarily wealthy parents. That evening, just for fun, they
made out in the light and sound booth that was tucked away on top of
the dark spiral staircase to the side of the theater's stage. (She told me

about it in bed that night.) Ghislaine was a secret third guest at Jason's graduation from Dalton's high school in June of 1999. His father had flown in from Los Angeles to attend the ceremony, and while he sat next to his ex-wife, Ghislaine was in a seat elsewhere in that auditorium in the ancient Egyptian wing of the Metropolitan Museum of Art. Without either Jason's mother or his father noticing, she photographed him against the backdrop of the ruined Temple of Dendur inside the museum's glass enclosure. She even waited for him at the back of the Temple to sneak a few kisses for a moment when nobody else was around.

The two of them became a notorious power couple — with his ideas, her connections, *and my resources*. They made their relationship public only after he started college at Columbia University in the year 2000 (on this revised timeline, Jason would never attend NYU). Even then, with the first six years of it hidden, it was scandalous — but nothing like the scandal that Ghislaine would have been involved in on the timeline that my Prometheist team and I rewrote. She was young at heart and appreciated the vitality and enthusiasm of a man who was twenty years her junior. Despite the conventional idiocy and the backwards custom that had prevailed for most of history, the biological fact is that a woman takes until her thirties to reach her sexual peak, which was Ghislaine's age when she met Jason, but a man's peak comes a decade or more sooner, in his early twenties. She and Jason were pushing the outer limits of those parameters, but only by ten years. Ghislaine thought it actually looked good for her in the press to have a sharp and visionary boytoy hanging on her arm. It was part of her phoenix rise from the ashes of the destruction of the Maxwell Empire. On a spiritual level, Jason was older than her anyhow, and there were aspects of his personality that did indeed remind Ghislaine of her father.

On the evening of September 11, 2001, I took the two of them out to dinner at Windows on the World, the restaurant on the top two floors of Building One of the Twin Towers. With its floor-to-ceiling vertical windows that looked out to the north over the whole of Manhattan, and its elegant Modernist design, many considered it "the most spectacular restaurant in the world." I arrived at the World Trade Center before them, and for a while I stood at the base of the buildings marveling at the sleek fluted design, which at that moment reminded me of repeating tridents or three-pronged tuning forks, plugging each of the identical towers into some Neptunian battery. It was nearing sunset, the time of my booked reservation, so I walked to the North Tower.

On the way up the elevator I thought of the day's news coverage of the fifth anniversary of the joint American-Soviet manned Mars landing of September 11, 1996. I had spent the afternoon watching replays of the historic footage of NASA and USSR cosmonauts planting the flags of the United States and Soviet Union side by side on the Martian surface, before shaking hands. The news networks also showed computer simulations of the flight path of the NASA Ares V and Ares I, and the Orion spacecraft with its four-man crew, propelled to Mars by the two gargantuan rockets. Presumably Soviet Central Television was broadcasting images of the Russian hardware. True to form, President Trump had taken credit for this achievement that was the crowning glory of his second term in office. He boasted of making "the deal of the millennium."

After arriving at Windows on the World, I went to our table and sat there taking in the fiery autumnal colors of sunset hitting the beige walls, wood paneling and crème-colored cushioned chairs, bathing them all in a reddish-orange glow. I ordered their usual drinks for them, which arrived at the table just before they showed up. When Jason walked over to the table together with Ghislaine, she said, "Hey, tiger eyes!" I suppose that the setting sun was shining into my eyes at that angle that brings out the contrast of amber and black more than the greenish hazel. "Hi, you two," I replied, as Jason bent over to kiss the top of my forehead before taking his seat. Ghislaine reached for my hand under the table, and as my fingers clasped hers, I said to them, "I trust you know why I chose this restaurant, tonight, of all nights."

They looked at me with reverent tenderness, as Jason said, "These towers are now a monument to the Promethean defiance of fate." I added, "A Promethean defiance of Olympus that is still championed by both the United States and the Soviet Union." "May it be so for many years to come," said Ghislaine as the three of us clinked our glasses together with a "Hail Prometheus!" Who knew what unthinkable things would transpire in the forty-seven years between that evening of 9/11 and what had been the date of the Olympian takeover on my timeline? For now, however, we would go forth unafraid into that new future, for I had saved the Left Hand of Prometheus. It was clenched around a hammer aiming for anvils hidden in the forge of the furthest stars. We felt ready for the sickle that would harvest our kind from out of the field of dreams.

CHAPTER 8

LAST STOP BEFORE
THE MOON

T HE HAUNTING high-resolution images of clearly artificial structures on the surface of the Cydonia region of Mars had been
played and replayed on flat-screen televisions across the world for
days. But this was not just another one of those replays, intercut with
the pathetically baffled faces of mainstream archeologists, historians,
and NASA administrators. The replay was now set in the context of a
joint press conference held by the Defense Departments of the United
States and the Soviet Union.

It was January 27, 2010. Over the past year, repeated radiological
studies had discovered an unmistakable signature at Cydonia, and at
one other site on Mars, Utopia Planitia. The signature was that of massive nuclear detonations that had taken place approximately 250 million years before the present. High-resolution aerial reconnaissance
of the sight by drones sent out from both the American and Soviet
Mars bases had revealed colossal megalithic ruins at both sites. In the
first days of 2010, astronauts and cosmonauts rolled their rovers into
Cydonia in a joint mission to explore the site on the ground. Their
primary objective had been a pentagonal pyramid and a mesa that
appeared to be carved into a humanoid face. It was in the middle of
the joint expedition that top brass of the USA and USSR sat down

together on a panel, in front of the entire international media, to make this disclosure. Officials of both superpowers spoke, in English and Russian.

What they explained to an already panicked public is that, for decades, the nuclear missile silos of the United States and the Soviet Union had been subjected to interference from UFOs that appeared to be capable of violating the most secure airspace of North America and Eurasia. In a handful of particularly serious incidents, which took place in the 1970s and 1980s, the UFOs either shut down or started up the silo-based missiles of one or the other of the superpowers. Sometimes, the silos themselves were damaged by whatever electro-magnetic force was brought to bear by the lenticular or triangular UFOs that were seen by missile base personnel during these threatening incursions. On two occasions this had caused the USA and USSR to believe that each was preparing to launch a nuclear strike on the territory of the other. Their respective militaries had been placed on the highest alert, and Armageddon was only narrowly averted.

In view of the discoveries on Mars, both of the radiological signature and of the ruins, the Soviet and American officials at the press conference announced a massive restructuring of their nuclear arms posture vis-à-vis one another. They had agreed to begin phasing out silo-based ICBMs aimed at each other, in favor of nuclear weapons aboard fighters and bombers that would have to be manually piloted into enemy territory. The aim was to guard against a potentially catastrophic takeover of their arsenals by an "unidentified" outside force. A clip of President Reagan's 1987 speech at the United Nations about how an "alien threat" could bring us together also played repeatedly amidst coverage of this joint disclosure. The other major announcement made by the Soviet and American Defense Department officials was that the two superpowers would begin to officially and formally collaborate on multi-sensor tracking and scientific analysis of *all* UFO-related incidents that take place within the geostrategic spheres of NATO and the Warsaw Pact. Each incursion into restricted airspace would be treated as an act of war, and orders would be given to base commanders and scrambled jets to intercept and shoot.

Hardly twenty-four hours had elapsed since this press conference, when Jason and Ghislaine had packed their bags, as I instructed them to, and the three of us loaded our luggage into the limo that would take us from 55 Central Park West to the underground SCIF (Secure Facility) on Long Island. The projector-based "silver screens" had been replaced by flat-screen TVs mounted on the numerically inscribed concrete walls, with the same hardcore pornographic and ultra-violent content that was meant to misdirect psychic spies. Over the past two decades, the facility had expanded considerably — albeit in the manner of clandestine construction, of the kind that is employed in illegal mining operations. We had tunneled all the way inland to the ground beneath Avalon Park, with a secret vertical airshaft and exit point amidst the trees surrounding the statue of Prometheus chained to the rock. More significantly, the SCIF's tunnels also extended toward the shoreline, connecting to an AtlantiCorp submarine base on the North Shore of Long Island. In the tunnels of the hidden underwater lair, we had docked two submarines of a size and quality far exceeding the one I used back in '88 to set the mines that blew up Vice President Bush at Walker's Point.

Beginning on the night of January 28, 2010, the three of us monitored the unfolding situation from the SCIF. A small team was there with us, including trusty old Johnny, who, despite having gone gray, was in pretty good shape for his age. We would still occasionally spar together for fun, each making jokes about how the other was getting old. Our preferred 'style' had become Jeet-Kune-Do. Of course, we could jest because we had both benefited from late 21st-century genetic engineering that had slowed our biological clocks while extending our lifespans. The same could not be said for Jean-Pierre, who had driven us here. He was starting to look like an African mummy, and his thousand-yard stare had intensified in its degree of abstraction to the point where it testified that only a tenuous tether kept him connected to this world. Jean-Pierre's bone bracelet had, throughout the years, been complemented by other creepy armbands, sigil-inscribed rings on most of his long leathery fingers, and totemic necklaces and pendants fashioned of various animal parts and carved gemstones. Part of the expansion of the facility was a set of fairly well-furnished, albeit austerely Brutalist, bedrooms for overnight stays. We had always stocked the SCIF with emergency food and water provisions, as well as all kinds of medicine — after all, it was built underneath a pharmaceutical company.

My line of communication with the White House and the Department of Defense had considerably weakened since the end of President Haig's second term, back in 2004. But, while in office, General Haig had the highest level of security clearance that had been afforded to any Commander-in-Chief since Dwight Eisenhower. Even now, he still held that clearance. Trump had forged a fairly good rapport between us, having made it clear to the General from the time Donald took office in '89 that I was the one who suggested that Haig be his Vice President. Our relationship with a circle within the Defense Department, and especially those involved in DARPA (Defense Advanced Research Projects Agency), had made it a lot easier for AtlantiCorp to operate. Certain aspects of our operations became akin to what Blackwater had done for the US government in the early 21st century on my timeline. Now and then we would carry out small-scale black ops that could not be officially sanctioned by Washington, even as extraterritorial activities of the CIA. Given the détente and cooperation on Mars exploration and colonization, AtlantiCorp was able to maintain a surprisingly strong relationship with the Russians as well. Irena had gone back to Moscow, and she became my direct line to the KGB. On a few occasions she even brought blindfolded Soviet generals to the SCIF. You should have seen their reaction to the imagery we used as a countermeasure for psychic espionage. "You shameless Americans," they said, "this is why we could never keep up with you!"

There were enough bunker rooms for Ghislaine, Jason, and me to space out and each have our own, but the tense atmosphere of impending doom was such that none of us wanted to couple with one of the others to leave someone alone. So, the three of us shacked up together in the largest of the windowless concrete-walled accommodations, which had a king-sized bed, a sofa, and a few chairs. We were sprawled naked above the covers on the bed together (the thermostat had been turned up high in the winter weather) when Johnny activated the entry alert on the door by swiping his key card. I didn't bother to get under the covers or anything. Instead, I woke Ghislaine up. (Jason was already squinting in Johnny's direction, with the harsh hallway light flooding in through the door.)

"You guys need to get out here... now," he said. It was 3 am, on January 29. I quickly put on my black slacks and turtleneck from the night before, which I had thrown over the side of a chair. As Jason and Ghislaine also got dressed, I entered the main conference room at the SCIF and looked at the big boards that we had installed on the walls. These were electronic displays that, thanks to our connections at the DOD (Department of Defense) and the KGB, fed us the same information about American and Soviet missile launches that each superpower was able to obtain regarding the DEFCON status of the other. We were receiving the information directly from certain classified satellites, by intercepting the transmission of these satellites to Mount Yamantau and Cheyenne Mountain. When we arrived at the SCIF, I had put in a call to General Haig and Irena Akhmatova. Johnny told me that they had both called back and were now each on hold on separate lines. I suppose it was 11 am in Moscow, but why was Haig calling in the middle of the night? Before taking the calls, I scanned the big boards. About one-third of the missiles in the United States and the Soviet Union were preparing to leave their silos for their targets!

I had never heard General Haig sound *panicked* before. But when I took the receiver and put his call through, he frantically explained to me that in the preceding eighteen hours there had been multiple confrontations between UFOs and fighter aircraft scrambled to intercept them in the restricted airspace over nuclear missile ranges across North America. After firing on the elusive saucers, tens of these jets had been downed by "the enemy" and quite a few pilots were killed before they could bail out. After Haig hung up, and I took Irena's call, she explained that, since the press conference, the same scenario had played out inside the Soviet Union, except that the Russians had gone to the extent of trying to take out one of the saucers in restricted airspace over the Caucasus with a tactical nuclear weapon detonated by a kamikaze pilot from Ossetia. The end result of these skirmishes was that the high commands of both countries were now watching, helplessly, and in horror, as their ICBMs were being spooled up for launch. Haig and Irena told me that President Jackson and Premier Yanayev were on the hotline between the White House and the Kremlin, reassuring each other that neither of them was in control of the terrifying escalation to DEFCON 1 through the remote commandeering of their respective missile forces. They had come to the point of discussing a plan for each of the superpowers to bomb their own nuclear silos from the air to disable the ICBMs before they could be launched by the "unknown enemy."

Unfortunately, they would never have the opportunity to carry out that desperate last-ditch plan. At about 4 am Eastern time, on January 29, 2010, the screens that we had tuned to network television channels all went to the rainbow-colored bars of the Emergency Broadcast System. At the same time, we watched as the heat signatures of American and Russian ICBMs signaled that the missiles had left their silos and were speeding toward their targets on the opposite hemispheres. Ghislaine and Jason were holding each other close as they watched the big boards with rapt attention, and, for a moment, I put my arms around both of them.

M.A.D. — Mutually Assured Destruction — so this is how it would be used against the two superpowers, not by each other, but by an occulted enemy that had decided to seize its last opportunity to turn this system on those who designed it. Despite being somewhat paralyzed by terror myself, enough of my mind was working to analyze the magnitude, distribution, and trajectories of the missiles as they approached their targets. I had reviewed so many different nuclear war scenarios that what was playing out before us on the big board was recognizable to me. It was the kind of strike that was calibrated to take out only the key military bases, major population centers, and industrial bases of each of the superpowers. No smaller cities or towns were targeted, and, remarkably, neither were the nuclear missile silos of each side. The "enemy" clearly wanted to retain the capacity to engage in a second strike using more hacked ICBMs. The objective was clear: crippling both the USA and USSR — culturally, economically, industrially, and militarily — with the minimum of damage to the environment due to radioactive fallout.

Given the relatively limited scope of the strike, it was unlikely that the nearby Brookhaven National Laboratory would be a target. There was probably only one missile headed toward the heart of the Greater New York Metropolitan Area, with ground zero likely to be in Manhattan. So, we decided to hold our ground by staying in the subterranean SCIF, which had, after all, been built as a bunker that could withstand pretty much any nuclear blast except for a direct hit and also to protect against radioactive fallout with special air and water filters. We would ride out the storm here, and then, when the dust — or rather, the ash — had settled, a decision would be made as to where we might head in the submarines.

I was already thinking about it, though. In the past two decades AtlantiCorp, despite its name, had actually built up a significant second power base in the Pacific — specifically, in Japan. We had an AtlantiCorp facility on, and *underneath*, Lake Ashi in Hakone. The aboveground parts of the building, with a dock on the lake, had windows featuring a fantastic view of snowy Mt. Fuji. The people in the sleepy lakeside fishing village, with its narrow stone-paved streets winding up and down hillsides, were taken aback by the arrival of all of the construction material and manpower that we brought in to build the site — including the underwater base beneath the dock on Lake Ashi. It was possible to get to the Lake Ashi facility by taking a submarine to Sagami Bay, in Japan's Pacific Coast, disembarking at a port in Odawara, then heading into the nearby Fuji Hakone Izu National Park. Lake Ashi was the western boundary of this preserve.

The facility was only an hour and a half drive from Tokyo. We also had a helipad on-site, so that flying to and from the Tokyo metro area, and thereby avoiding highway traffic, was a possibility as well. I thought to myself that even if Tokyo and Yokohama were hit by the hacked and hijacked Soviet missiles, our Hakone facility should be unscathed. In point of fact, none of the missile trajectories being traced out in bright red on the big board seemed to be headed toward any targets in Japan at all. Interestingly, Europe was also being entirely spared. It seemed that the Olympians did not want to alienate these two populations, namely Europeans and the Japanese, before attempting to subjugate them after the Left and Right hands of Prometheus had been severed by destroying the USSR and the USA.

They might succeed with Europe, but the Olympian subjugation of Japan was a much more dubious proposition. Maybe 19th-or even early 20th-century Japan, but since the 1950s the Japanese had undergone a profound psycho-social mutation that was most evident in the sci-fi manga, anime, and video-gaming subculture of the country. The most creative cultural vanguard of Japan somehow managed to become even more Promethean than the West. Men like Katsuhiro Otomo, Ichiro Itano, Hideaki Anno, and Shigeru Miyamoto were torchbearers as powerful as any that Prometheus could hope to find in America or Europe. This is something that I had monitored closely, since the 1980s, and that I decided to invest in seriously when I had the facility in Hakone built in the early 2000s. Jason was in the middle of his studies at Columbia University, and he was very receptive to my strong suggestion that he add the Japanese language to his course load and continue to study it throughout his graduate years.

In the past life that I had lived as an 'earlier' version of him, I had traveled in Japan with Emma. I'll never forget what the Italian waiter in the restaurant on top of the Mandarin Oriental in Tokyo said to us one evening, as we looked out over the cityscape at sunset, with Mt. Fuji in the distance: "Japan is the last stop before the Moon." That stuck with me, even across lifetimes, because the Moon symbolizes the abode of the dead in the Tarot and other esoteric traditions. During that trip, I was bombarded by a profound psychic impression of the infernal — even volcanic — soul of Japan, a spirit that was captured in some of my photographs, for example, of the menacing guardian statues at the Todai-ji temple at Nara. Those photos in particular form a striking contrast with the ones of me petting the deer in Nara Park, one of the few images that capture how much of an animal lover I have always been, and also a rare glimpse into the spiritual gentleness that only those closest to me have known to be a significant aspect of my character. I had some kind of psychic break in Japan, because on the first day that I was back in New York, after having fallen asleep in my bed despite the daylight streaming into my room, when I woke up I could neither recognize my surroundings nor remember who I was. This went on for at least a full minute. Maybe even a couple of minutes. That is a long time to look around your bedroom and be assaulted by the alienness of every object in your surroundings, while you struggle to even recall your name or a single fact or frame of reference relevant to your biography.

Maybe I was able to intuit the chthonic element of the country because Japan was certainly "the last stop before the Moon" in terms of my relationship with Emma, a relationship that had been an ark for the most beneficently compassionate and patiently caring part of my persona. Then again, I had seen the end coming for years before being baptized in Hakone's Lake of Spectral Fire. In fact, I had a haunting prophetic dream about it — years earlier, around the same time as

Emma received those phone calls from an Artificial Intelligence that responsively recut my future conversations with Nassim Nouri. This nightmare became the kernel for my use of the symbolism of the wolf-man toward the end of *Iranian Leviathan*, a book dedicated to Nassim.

The nightmare begins with Emma and I going on a long journey together, which in retrospect I realized represented our future trip to Japan. The carriage which we are riding in stops somewhere in a forest, precognitively symbolic not just of wilderness in general but specifically of Fuji Hakone Izu National Park. The sun sets dimly behind us as we make our way through the trees, with the carriage driver having made it clear that we had to hike the rest of the way to our unknown destination. Suddenly, we stop because I realize that I am not carrying any baggage. Emma has *her* baggage, but I am empty-handed.

I think to myself — *Why did I not realize this before?* For some reason it seemed right to blame her, as if it was also her responsibility to bring my baggage, or to remind me to bring it. Without my things we cannot safely camp wherever we are going, and so we must make our way back to where the carriage left us off. It is quickly growing dark, and so we hurry nervously.

Before long, total darkness envelops us and it becomes clear that we have lost the way, that we will not make it back tonight. Stranded, as terror sinks in, from amidst the darkness and endless woods that encircle us, I see a wolf approaching. Slowly, steadily, stark white like a ghost lit by the pale moonlight.

Overtaken by fear, I faint. The scene repeats itself, except that now I look more closely to see that this wolf is actually a man approaching from amidst the woods — a wolf-man. His face, his body — he is me, and yet not me. Again, a blackout from fear. Then, I see Emma standing still, eyes closed, amidst a vast sunlit room in an empty apartment, and on the wall behind her are the woods, the nightmare, like a painting the contours of which are emerging from out of pitch black.

We are in the woods again, alone, when darkness first closes in, and we realize that we will not make it back. But now, there are two white houses, brightly lit in the night, as if at a crossroads amidst the vast woods — with nothing else but twisted shadows and trees all around. The houses are at an angle to each other; one in front of us, and one to the side. Two places where we might seek refuge for the night.

Out of the corner of my eye, I glimpse the wolf-man, ghost-like — *spectral*, disappearing from behind the dark window of one of the houses. I know that no matter what, we cannot knock on the door to that house. We should most certainly prefer to die out here lost in the woods! So, we go over to the other house and knock on *its* door. It looked like a prefab suburban American home. An old and plain man gets up lazily from the couch where he has been eating his TV dinner. He comes behind the window next to the door, and casts one bitter and foreboding glance at us, then he draws the curtains tightly shut in our faces. In retrospect, I realized that this man was me in one possible future — the one wherein I betrayed my destiny — and he was looking at me in this way as if to say: "How could you have done this to my life?"

The next thing I know, I had knocked on the door to the other house — almost as if by accident. Actually, this one is not a house. It is more like a stone castle in the forest. Majestic, but in ruins. I knew that I shouldn't have done it. Emma scolds me for being so stupid, as if now we are in a bind, and I have to get us out of it. "When he comes to the door, I am just going to make it clear that it was a mistake and that we are not staying for the night, *that's all.*" Yes, *that's all* — I told myself, as I reassured Emma. I will just stand firm and make it clear, and that will be that.

Then the door creaks open. He is an elegant man, impeccably dressed in a pinstripe evening suit — refined, and possessed of a bearing and composure beyond words. Everything in his home, glistening in candlelight, is as intoxicatingly charming and insistently inviting as the man himself. A magnetic charm pours forth from soul-piercing and darkly compelling eyes — a wolf's eyes. I know that once stepped across that threshold, there is no turning back.

Still, I give my apologies and try to make it clear that we're not staying. It is useless. He has made us an offer that we simply cannot refuse. Like some silver-tongued Lucifer, he turns my words around on me. Instead, I am suddenly listening to him as, from behind his kitchen counter, with a glass of red wine raised in his hand, he calmly explains that we are staying and that we have three choices, which are the "rules of the house" as he put it. We could either "die right away" or "die slowly" or "not die at all" but he assured us that this last option would be the worst of all three, because we would only helplessly watch each other suffer slowly and forever.

We try to escape the castle. Emma and I are in a dark and narrow stone stairway, running to try to make it to the top of a tower where perhaps we might commit some kind of double suicide, by throwing ourselves off the roof. There is an old black wooden door, with a round cold metal knocker. We stop running toward it and look up as the door creaks open. From behind it appears the head and torso of a white wolf. I think to myself — *we are finished.*

Emma is gone. Who knows what happened to her? Now I am alone in the dungeon of the castle, with my body being broken and drained on a spiked rack by the werewolf in the pinstripe suit. This vampire wants to break my body and drink my blood like wine. The world begins to spin and blur into oblivion, as I am wholly seized by the vertigo of terror.

The deed has been done. I am no longer there, but I see him from behind — setting down his glass of wine as he gently sits himself upon a fine iron-wrought chair. He has drunk my blood. Yes, that's all I imagined that he wanted. But no! He slowly leans over and reaches down, where resting against one leg of the chair is a violin. I can see every one of his long bony fingers, and the knuckles of his hands as he carefully holds out the bow — stretched like a sinew. He takes up the violin and holds it poised to play. It is then that I realize that this violin is my body. Its bow and wood cast from my sinews and shattered bones. He had taken my blood, drained my body of it, and turned it into wine, while he had masterfully pieced my broken body into this instrument that he now held in his hands.

Then, in one final moment of grace, he placed the bow upon the violin stem and, swaying gently, he *played*. Not just like a man with a violin — no, he played like a Master. As my eyes opened into wakefulness, I could still hear the sound of those first few notes filling my mind — something ineffable drawing out into eternity, like no human sound. *Was it angelic music,* I thought to myself then, *or was it the siren song of a demoness?*

That indescribably inhuman music was replaying in my mind when the red lines of the missile trajectories reached their targets and the big board displaying them went black. The SCIF's lights blacked out for a moment, before I heard the backup generator kick in. It must have been the electro-magnetic pulse from the nuclear blast that had undoubtedly just destroyed Manhattan. I could see the searing flash and the rising mushroom cloud in my mind's eye. The sunrise land awaited us as the last bastion of Prometheus, or would it be our last stop before the Moon?

CHAPTER 9

HYBRID HOSTAGES

W ANDERING IN the wilderness of Fuji Izu National Park, on the outskirts of our AtlantiCorp fortress in Hakone, one could almost forget that the world's superpowers had been destroyed by a nuclear holocaust that was not of their own making. One could also forget that when eating the high-quality sushi that we regularly had delivered from the fishing village. It was as if Japan had paid in advance for now remaining unscathed, from the bombings of Hiroshima and Nagasaki to the reactor meltdown during the Fukushima earthquake. I suppose that there was a certain historical justice in that — if any justice can be discerned at all in the broken arc of time.

The Imperium had emerged from out of the Amazon basin and lairs within the Andes Mountains, setting up a political order based predominately in what had been Brazil, Uruguay, Argentina, and Chile to fill the vacuum left by the two superpowers that the Olympians had destroyed by hacking the Soviet and American nuclear arsenals. There was also considerable activity in Mexico City and in the Yucatan, so whatever structure was forming was not limited to South America. Since news coverage was cutoff over most of the planet by the EMP bursts over North America and Eurasia during that rapidly escalating crisis, people had only a faint and fragmentary memory of the brief but fierce battle between the Olympian saucers and the air forces of the United States and the Soviet Union. The Russians, in particular, really went down fighting. They had taken out a number of the UFOs in kamikaze strikes with nuclear-armed fighter jets.

Only one of our two AtlantiCorp submarines made it all the way to Sagami Bay. The one captained by Johnny, which had been our supply ship, was struck by one of the many USOs that were speeding through the oceans in the aftermath of the manufactured apocalypse. I say "struck" as if it were an accident, but the sub was probably rammed on purpose. Jean-Pierre had also been on that submarine, but there wasn't time then to mourn either of them. (Later, in the hot spring bath, I would bawl my eyes out.) As Ghislaine manned our submarine, Jason (who had been combat-trained by Johnny) joined me when I boarded a merchant marine ship and raided it for replacement supplies that were vital for our days-long journey from the North Shore of Long Island to the Hakone facility. Unfortunately, the crew of the ship couldn't take a hint from the machine guns pointed at them. These supplies were vital enough to kill for because, once we got to Japan, we would have to trek from Odawara port through much of Fuji Hakone National Park.

Ever since we arrived and situated ourselves in the majestic Japanese-accented modernist house on Lake Ashi, Jason, Ghislaine, and I would take long walks through the forest. We would bathe naked together in the isolated waterfalls. Hiking up to certain of the higher hilltops, we could take in a spectacular vista with a view of Mt. Fuji that was even better than the one that we had from our dock on Lake Ashi. In the winter, when these little mountains were covered in snow, like the peak of Fuji itself, there was an especially eerie silence encompassing the place. A pregnant silence, full of secrets.

Jason met the boy on one of the days when he went hiking by himself. Ghislaine and I were in the hot spring bath that we had built into the ground floor of the house when he first brought this strange creature home with him. Supposedly his name was "Ikiru." We were drinking shochu and trying to relax after having been in the Ops room all day, monitoring news from Latin America. The most disturbing thing was that, from what I could see on the satellite broadcast footage, the leader of this Latin American Reich was a man who bore an uncanny resemblance to me in my incarnation as Nikolai — two lifetimes ago. Of course, he was older than Nikolai had lived to be. Maybe in his late 40s or early 50s, judging by the grey that was coming in at the sides of his hair. We were told that he was an Argentinian mining magnate, politician, and self-styled intellectual mystic. Born and raised in the German enclave of San Carlos de Bariloche, his name was Adolfo von Seelstrang. Apparently, he spoke both Spanish and German natively, and English a little less fluently with what sounded like something between a heavy Argentinian and Bavarian accent.

I called Ikiru a "boy" but, frankly, at times one got the impression that despite his superficially youthful appearance, there was some-thing undead about him. Partly it was something about the way that his lightly freckled and weathered skin was stretched over his neot-enous bone structure. When I looked into his pupils, I saw tentacled things from a posthuman future that had endured from a time before history in bioluminescent ocean depths untouched by sunlight. Once, what was reflected into my mind from his eyes was a windswept Earth that, but for the oceans, had been burnt into barren desert sands sear-ing under two suns.

"Boy" may also be inappropriate considering how effeminate he looked. Had it not been for his flat chest and diminutive stature, one could easily have mistaken his angular face for that of a pretty girl, es-pecially considering his bob cut platinum blond hair. I was reminded of the bishounens in the art of Takato Yamamoto and Junji Ito. Ikiru had a very pointy chin, thin lips, a slight nose, and high cheekbones. There was still something inexplicably Japanese, or at any rate orien-tal, about him despite how freakishly large his almond-shaped eyes were with their bright blue irises. That first day that I saw him, and on many subsequent occasions, Ikiru was wearing pants and a sweater that were jet black and clung tightly to his wiry, almost skeletal, frame.

When he took his hands out of his pockets to greet me, I noticed that the boy's fingers were also preternaturally long. Inhumanly so.

I confess that I shuddered the first time that I caught a glimpse of him making love to Jason. The three of us had been in the habit of leaving the Japanese screen doors to our rooms at least partly open, and when I passed by Jason's room, I could swear that before I saw that it was Ikiru's naked body under his, I had glimpsed some blue-black tentacled shadow on the bed, wrapped around Jason's back and thighs from beneath. When I stared hard, wide-eyed and in shock, I saw Ikiru instead. He turned his impish head to the side to face me and looked right into my eyes, without Jason noticing. My spine tingled as I slid the shoji screen closed.

Ikiru opened up a hidden world to us. Beneath Lake Ashi, on the side of the National Park, and not far from our facility along the lake's coastline, there was an entrance to an underground lair populated by "children" who looked more or less like him. They were products of a genetic hybridization program managed by a shapeshifting superorganism. In the weeks after I met him, as Jason's fascination with the terribly beautiful boy deepened into some kind of insane obsession, Ikiru guided our submarine to the large underwater portal to this place. Before it swirled open from the center outward, I could see that the metal portal had a symbol embossed on it that was something between a triskelion and a yin-yang.

The aesthetic inside of the lair was some bizarre cross between Wabi-sabi and the archeo-futurism of *The Dark Crystal*. Imagine the lyrical Art Nouveau-accented architectural structures in Brian Froud and Jim Henson's prehistoric dream world, but incompletely carved out of the bedrock from the start and now in a ruined state that somehow conferred upon them added grace and dignity. There were also small spherical orbs, with swirling electric liquid inside them, floating through some of the tunnels and chambers of this place. Most of them were blue. I was told not to get too close to these fairy lights.

This place was full of grayish-tan *things* that looked like large featherless owls, until you stared at them hard enough, so that they appeared to be mantids instead, before they slithered away into the cracks somewhere with tentacles that betrayed both of these forms as shamanic masquerades. These *things* were the progenitors and caretakers of hybrids like Ikiru. There were rooms full of technological gadgetry that was mysterious even to me, including one vast chamber with a vaulted ceiling lit by the blue glow of many tall incubation tubes in which the fetuses of the hybrids were growing.

I was given to understand, telepathically, that the fetuses had been transplanted into these vats from the wombs of periodically abducted women, after being conceived and gestating in these "mothers" for more or less the first trimester. All of the "mothers" of the fetuses here were Japanese, but Ikiru's caretakers revealed clairvoyantly that there were many similar lairs in other parts of the world. It was as if they were screaming in some superhuman frequency when they also showed me how the Olympians were going from enclave to enclave, underground and undersea, slaying all of the hybrid children at each of these places.

Shortly after he met Ikiru in the forest, Jason told me that he had a vision of children who looked like Ikiru, sitting in a circle, holding hands, and singing together under the starry night sky. He said that the tone of their harmonious voices was a music that no human being could intone. Jason said that he knew they were singing to him. That this was the future and, although he was long gone, they wanted to thank him for "making a place for them in the world." He had the impression that these wizened boys and girls saw him as their adoptive father — or their guardian.

What the shapeshifters wanted from us was no small favor. They knew exactly who we were. It had not escaped them that I had developed relationships with certain prominent journalists in Europe and that AtlantiCorp still had the capability to broadcast "news" over much of the globe via satellite uplink at the Hakone facility. The hybrids had

been a kind of collateral that they were planning to hold over humanity in their war of resistance against the "Nordic" Olympians. I understood this well from my own, now overwritten, timeline. Within a
decade of the Nordics having revealed themselves in 2048, pockets of
resistance — not all of them coordinated through Prometheism — began disseminating information about the hybrids through pirate news
broadcasts. The intention was to prevail upon the conscience and
maternal or paternal sensibility of the many abductees who had been
involved in the breeding program, thereby enjoining them to help in
the resistance against the Nordics who threatened these "blameless"
children and were intent on wiping them out as "monstrosities." The
pirate broadcasts were meant to act in tandem with close encounters
that would activate the abductees, most of whom had hitherto been
as unconscious as sleeper agents. Now, on this timeline, they wanted
AtlantiCorp to take up the task of coordinating these pirate broadcasts
that would parade the hybrids before the eyes of the world.

I realized that, in effect, these strange children were being used
as hostages or "human" shields. Still, the shapeshifters were powerful
and much needed allies. In all honesty, I could not think of a more
devastating weapon that was left to us after the nuclear holocaust that
the Devas had just perpetrated. The decades of slowly demoralizing
degradation through engineered and convergent catastrophes, which
had prepared the way for mass acceptance of the Nordics as "saviors"
on my timeline, had not taken place here. Consequently, it was possible that, especially in places like Europe and Japan, empathy and even
love for these strange children, or at the very least a desire to protect
them, could be leveraged to defend against the conquest of Earth by
the Traditionalist Imperium that was already building its power base
in Latin America. This ought to be done before the Imperium perpetrated the mass deception that the "grays" were monstrous abductors,
deviants from whom only the "Nordics" could protect the helpless
denizens of Earth. In truth, the "grays" were only one form taken by

the shapeshifting guardians of the hybrids, a form intended to emulate the gray androids employed by the Olympians to do their dirty work.

I agreed to set up a press conference in Tokyo, attended by a whole press corps of journalists from Europe, who had been contacted and briefed on an AtlantiCorp secure channel. In exchange, and in order to make an even more sensational impression at the press conference, the shapeshifters gave me an extraordinary "gift." In that maze of underground tunnels and caverns under Fuji Hakone National Park, they had machinery capable of cloning someone and dramatically accelerating the growth of the cloned body to adulthood — in a matter of weeks. They also had both gadgetry and techniques of a psychotronic nature, which made it possible to transfer one's consciousness and memories into the brain of this cloned body — with the highest fidelity. This is what they did for me. I hadn't transferred into a clone body since the days when I lived in Atlantis as Dara-El. That was something like twelve thousand years ago.

Jason and Ghislaine, both full of terrible apprehension, each held one of my hands as Ikiru worked with the shifty gray things to put me under and pull my psyche out of the 65-year-old corpse that would be discarded in favor of the cloned Dana Avalon whose seemingly 23-year-old body was floating in a blue-glowing tank that had served as her artificial womb. I was told that all of the gene splicing that had been done to enhance me when I was conceived in 2076, back in the Gotham that I came from, would of course carry over as part of the copying of my genetic code. Despite their acceleration of the growth of the clone, even the slowing of my biological clock and the lengthening of my lifespan would remain part of my DNA. Ghislaine later told me that her heart almost stopped when she saw the clone in the tank suddenly kicking and writhing, trying to pull the oxygen supply line out of her mouth. She had looked back at the lifeless body of her friend and lover. Jason was weeping over the corpse as it lay there on the cold stone table.

When they unplugged this cloned body and got me out of the tank, I could barely walk. For a few days, I had to lean on the shoulders of Jason and Ghislaine, who were on either side of me as I learned to use these new legs. As soon as I was on my feet, I began an intensive muscle-building and training regimen. Initially, I was skeptical of the reassurances from Ikiru that my muscle memory and even all of my acquired physical skills would return once my muscles were built back up again, but it turned out that he was right. After a couple of weeks, Jason and I were practicing martial arts together and I had to tell him to stop going easy on me. I also tested my sharpshooting abilities, which were intact. When I went diving with Ghislaine in Lake Ashi, she was happy to see that she could hardly keep up with me.

I was ready for the press conference. The immaculate conception of this new body that I was in would be another marvel to astonish the prominent journalists traveling from European cities, such as Paris, to Tokyo and who had, for years, known me and seen me age into my sixties — although, given my slowed biological clock, they never took me to be older than my late forties. Still, the nearly thirty-year age difference would be a shock to them and was nothing that any kind of plastic surgery could have accomplished.

The building that we chose was one of the tallest skyscrapers of Shinjuku, with a clear view of Mt. Fuji, and a large helipad on the roof where the helicopter by which we had arrived was also waiting to spirit us back to Hakone at high speed as soon as the press conference was over — or sooner, if something went wrong. At top speed the flight time, by chopper, was less than an hour from helipad to helipad. Of the hybrids, only Ikiru had come with us, so that the media could get a good look at him in the flesh. Images and video of the others would be played on the large screen behind us, and also fed directly to the broadcast cameras of the BBC, France-24, and NHK.

The three of us sat on a panel together, with all of the cameras pointed toward us. Jason's Japanese had improved to the point where he was able to provide a translation, paragraph by paragraph, sitting to the left of me behind a microphone of his own. To the right of me was Ghislaine, who delivered a French translation, after the Japanese one, whenever I would pause. Ikiru was in a backroom, waiting for the right prompt in the presentation to parade himself out before the cameras. We had barely begun addressing the seated crowd, when the whispers turned to stunned silence and you could hear people drop their chopsticks — and their sushi — to listen with bated breath. Here is what they heard, and broadcast — in English, Japanese, and French…

"Citizens of the world, greetings. I am Dana Avalon, the founder of AtlantiCorp, an organization based in New York that worked for decades to foster peace and cooperation between the United States and the Soviet Union, including and especially in the frontier of space exploration.

Those of you who already know me may be taken aback to see how much younger I look. That is because my consciousness has been transferred into a clone body. Let me explain.

As much as my heart is full of things that I would like to share with you in the wake of the horrific holocaust that has been inflicted upon our planet, the prevailing state of emergency forces me to be as succinct as possible in conveying only what is most essential for as long as this line of communication remains open.

As you may recall, immediately prior to the nuclear exchange between the two superpowers, they had jointly discovered and were cooperatively exploring irradiated ruins on Mars. They had also announced that the nuclear arsenals of both countries were subject to electronic capture by some unknown force apparently associated with Unidentified Flying Objects that penetrated the restricted airspace over both North America and Eurasia. In the hours leading up to the attack, I was in direct communication with individuals at the highest level in both Washington and Moscow. I can assure you, in no uncertain terms, that this alien enemy seized the arsenals of both the USA and USSR, launching the missiles of each on the territory of the other. This same alien enemy is now hard at work building an oppressively backwards and hierarchical, totalitarian empire in Latin America, from out of which they intent to expand and subjugate the entire world.

None of that is, however, what I am principally here to inform you of. Rather, what you need to know is that these Nordic-looking self-styled 'gods' are clandestinely engaged in a genocidal attack on hidden sanctuaries around the planet where communities of special children have been bred and raised. It is with the technology of one of these communities that I was cloned.

Ladies and gentlemen, these are *your* children. About one in twenty people in places such as Europe and Japan have, for a very long time, been secret participants in a genetic hybridization program intended to foster the further evolution of the human race and adaptation for the sake of eventual settlement throughout the galaxy.

Whether you know it or not, one out of every twenty of you — 5% of everyone watching now — is either a mother or a father of these children that you see on the screen behind us. Maybe some of their faces will seem familiar to you from a half-forgotten midnight journey that you dismissed as just a dream. Maybe you have always remembered holding them in their infancy, but have never dared to tell anybody, even your own family, that you have otherworldly offspring.

One of these hybrids is here with us today in the flesh, so that he can answer your questions and help you to understand what is in store for all of us here on Earth if we do not resist. We cannot allow the genocide of his kind to take place at the hands of these sadistic overlords, who are already responsible for the destruction of Mars. Come forward, Ikiru, and let everyone here meet you."

There were gasps amidst a barrage of camera flashes as Ikiru joined us at the panel table. He covered his preternaturally big blue eyes with his inhumanly long and bony fingers. Ikiru and I had barely begun to take questions from the shocked and shouting journalists when there was a visible disturbance around the camera crews. Someone rushed over to us and conveyed that the live international broadcast had been cut off from every one of the cameras and microphones in the room. We did not need any more information than that. The Japanese security men that I had hired tried their best to push back the press correspondents thronging us, as Ghislaine, Jason, and I made our way up to the helipad while protecting Ikiru between the three of our bodies.

When we got up there, we could see that a saucer was already approaching from the opposite direction as Mt. Fuji. It would catch up with us, and we would never make it. Ikiru, who knew this, stood his ground, and faced the approaching saucer with his left arm outstretched and the bony fingers of his right hand pressed into his downcast forehead. The saucer stopped dead, as if held back by an invisible force. I could hear Ikiru telling me, telepathically, to "go!" I grabbed Jason and Ghislaine and tried to push them up into the chopper, the rotor blades of which were already spinning and blowing a hard gust of wind through our hair and clothes. But as I climbed in after Ghislaine, Jason broke free and ran over to try to grab Ikiru. I shouted after him.

In the brief moment that Ikiru was distracted, and had loosened his telekinetic grip, the saucer managed to soar closer to us and fire off several laser beams — one of which sliced through Jason and splattered his charred innards across the rooftop, also scarring the helipad with a smoking black gouge. I was absolutely distraught at the sight of this. My heart turned to ice, and it felt as if my throat and stomach fell through my feet. But I could hear Ikiru in my mind again, this time commanding more insistently, "Go!!!"

I signaled for the pilot to lift off, with Ghislaine also crying hysterically as she clung to me while looking out the open door of the helicopter. The last thing we saw was Ikiru's whole body shaking, especially his outstretched arm, as the saucer stopped dead again, wobbled, then slowly fell out of the sky like a leaf. We were turning the chopper around to pick up Ikiru when we saw his head explode. His arm was still outstretched as his headless corpse collapsed onto

the rooftop. By now the journalists had made it up here, past the security men, and they were taking in the whole ghastly scene with their
cameras.

The footage would never be broadcast, though. By the time we
were nearing Lake Ashi, another two Nordic craft had come on the
scene. These were the Predator type that I remembered having descended on Gotham in its last days. After slicing off the whole top
of that skyscraper in Shinjuku with their laser beams, the Olympian
Predators sped to catch up with us. Before they could, though, a huge
triangular craft surfaced from out of Lake Ashi, with water rushing
down over the edges of it. It was actually a black Delta, the shape of
an equilateral pyramid. Once it was above the Lake, it shot forward,
faster than our eyes could follow, and took a position between our
helicopter and the fast-approaching Olympian Predators. We knew
not to look back. But the hybrids — who I later learned were trained
to pilot these craft — apparently made short work of the Predators,
because we got to our helipad on Lake Ashi in one piece.

A few of the hybrids were there waiting for us. They had telepathically experienced the martyrdom of Ikiru. Ghislaine took refuge in the
undersea Ops bunker beneath the Hakone facility. It had been built
to withstand everything but a direct strike with a nuclear weapon.
Meanwhile, I boarded a craft docked at our pier by the hybrids. We
sped like a torpedo through the lake in this cigar-shaped USO, all the
way to their hidden lair.

The shapeshifters were showing me how the hybrids pilot their
motherships using a partly telepathic interface. The skin of their
largest vessels was itself a living being of some sort, connected both
to an Artificial Intelligence and to the propulsion system, as well as
interfacing with the psyche of the pilot. As far as I was aware, the
Nordics still did not have this kind of technology. Probably because
they considered the engineering of it to be unethical or inhuman. I
was inside of this Leviathan with a number of the hybrids and several
shapeshifters when we felt the tremendous tremors tear through the

underground complex. I saw the shapeshifters freeze, and cock their heads in a birdlike way, as if they were listening intently. The hybrids stopped looking at me, and instead they seemed to be staring deeply inwards in perfect stillness. Then they all suddenly shrieked in a shrill expression of terror and rage that was more animal than human.

The mothership, Leviathan-like, left the collapsing complex by way of the portal — barely fitting through it as it lunged forward like some titanic squid. The water was blackened by blood and ash. When we rose through the air above Lake Ashi, and looked out the bulbous portals, which studded the body of the ship like so many eyes, we beheld a colossal mushroom cloud. The Nordics had detonated a huge nuclear weapon along the coastline. Ground Zero appeared to be the AtlantiCorp facility at Hakone. In my mind's eye, I suddenly saw Ghislaine turning to a cinder in the bunker faster than she could comprehend what was happening. The Olympians probably did not know the exact location of the hybrid lair beneath Lake Ashi, but they rightly thought that it must be close to our compound. They used a very high-yield nuke (probably in the tens of megatons range) to make sure that the blast wave was as penetrating and expansive as possible. I collapsed into the arms of the hybrids, who did their best to comfort me, although I could sense that they were mourning the loss of their kindred with as much emotion as they were capable of showing.

Before I knew it, we had passed through the stratosphere. The horizon of Earth bent into a bow, and then became a glowing blue globe beneath us. The star-studded blackness seemed especially vast, maybe because of the emptiness in my own lacerated heart or maybe just because it had been so many years since I was last in space that I had forgotten how devouring that darkness is. Once I was able to finally pull myself together, one of the hybrids held my hand and led me over to the two shapeshifters. At this point, they looked more like grays than owls or mantids. Their slanted big, black, almond-shaped eyes stared into mine, as their heads ticked back and forth on the long stalks of their necks. When they would put the talons of their four-fingered hands to their pointy chins, they looked like they were deep in reflection. One of them reached out and put its hand on my shoulder. Another placed its leathery palm on my forehead, with its nails almost piercing the skin under my hair. I winced. They smelled like sulfur and cinnamon.

Without my having to explain anything to them, they knew what I was thinking. They had probably known who I really was from the time that we began to build the facility at Hakone. For all I know, on some level, maybe they even summoned me there subconsciously — or the hybrids did. The interest that Ikiru showed in Jason was not haphazard or incidental. He had been sent to find and befriend Jason in Hakone Forest for a reason. I had to admit that I was dealing with time travelers so primordially ancient and adept that the project I initiated in Gotham must have seemed like a fool's errand to them. Now, it was time to try again, without being so foolishly optimistic.

They read from my mind that I thought I should go back to New York in June of 1978, after the spearhead team that I had sent from Gotham in 2112 had arrived but a couple of years before Nikolai committed suicide. I think that the whole plan that formed rapidly in my mind became just as quickly transparent to them, and maybe they even saw around the edges of it better than I was able to. In any case, it appeared that they approved this as the best remaining course of action. I could tell that from the way they were looking at each other, together with the emotional tonality of the telepathic impressions that I was receiving from them as they probed my mind.

I clairvoyantly discerned that in 1978 they had a hybrid lair (like the one in Hakone) located in the Hudson Valley of New York. They would go there, after dropping me off in Avalon Park on Long Island. In fact, I could see from what they were thinking that they planned to beam me down right into the labyrinth overlooked by the statue of Prometheus. These masquerading marauders were, after all, not without a flair for theatricality. Despite their superficially expressionless faces and indecipherable eyes, they were the greatest of all tricksters.

When the hybrids and the grays slid into the biomechanical pods that interlinked them with the Artificial Intelligence of the ship, I psychically caught glimpses of the telepathic communication between them and the sentience of this living vessel. The method that they used for time travel was quite different from that of the spatiotemporal warp drive of the saucer that I had piloted from Gotham of 2112. Now, as we jumped from Hakone in 2010 to New York in June of 1978, it felt like I was being carried within the belly of a beast that was performing a feat more akin to astral projection or telekinetic teleportation. I could even sense the distress of the Leviathan itself, as it — as *she* — left the element of her own epoch and swam into the dark night of time.

CHAPTER 10

HOMECOMING

THE SHIP'S vertical beam of light illuminated the green oxidized copper of the statue of Prometheus chained to the rock. Then it retracted, and the Leviathan disappeared into the darkness above me in the direction of the Hudson Valley. I could tell from the hue of the sky that it was a couple of hours before dawn. I walked all the way through the woods from the labyrinth at the heart of the park to the edge of the property that my team of time travelers should by now have acquired as the site for constructing Avalon Pharmaceutical. I was still wearing the suit from the press conference at Shinjuku. I took off the jacket because I was trying not to soak through my shirt with any more sweat. I could already smell myself. The sun rose as I approached the gate, and I hoped that, since it was a weekday, Johnny and company would be showing up shortly.

At the gate's security outpost, I saw a face that was most welcome. I started to tear up. Johnny had never told me just when he had hired Jean-Pierre. He must have been one of the first people in the group that would eventually constitute AtlantiCorp, who had been brought on board here and now rather than sent back from 2112. Jean-Pierre opened the metal meshed gate with the push of a button and then unhurriedly — almost apprehensively — came out of the guard post to look long and hard into my face, without my saying a word. When he gripped his chin with his hand contemplatively, smiling ever so slightly, I could see that he was already wearing that bone bracelet. "You look *younger* than your picture," he finally said with that deep Creole-tinged voice of his. Before I could offer an explanation, Jean-Pierre added, "Come with me, Ms. Avalon."

The warehouse-like office building was still under construction, with scaffolds set up all over the place, but it seemed that the factory next to it was already operational. A shaft of morning light was shining through one of the windows high up near the ceiling, and I squinted as I sat down at the table of the makeshift office that Jean-Pierre brought me to. He picked up the phone at the other end of the room, too far from me to hear what he said to the person that he dialed. Then he came back and brought me some coffee. I looked at the clock on the wall. It was 7 am. The calendar thumb-tacked near it read, "June 21, 1978."

Before he went back to the gate, Jean-Pierre brought over a large black binder that was labeled "Avalon Pharmaceutical" and set it down in front of me on the small conference table. When I opened it, I saw, together with the construction plans for the site, the already prepared FDA approval forms for our patented formulas to manufacture the drugs that on my timeline were introduced in the 1990s and 2000s under the names Singulair, Crestor, Diovan, Lantus, Nexium, Avastin, Herceptin, Enbrel, Rituxan, Plavix, Viagra, Remicade, Advair, Cialis, Humira, and Lipitor. About a third of them were anti-cancer medications, and quite a few others were relevant to the treatment of heart disease or its contributing factors. Though there was a killing to be made on it, I had ethical objections to producing any of the psychiatric drugs that I knew would become all too popular. I looked at Jean-Pierre a little taken aback that *he* had access to this information and that he was volunteering it to me, just because he seemed to recognize me from a picture of a much older version of myself that Johnny had apparently shown him. Intuitive as always, the Voodoo adept knew what I was thinking and said, "I *know* who you are, Miss.

When Johnny *arrives*, he'll tell you all about me. I run security for the company — *your* company, Miss Avalon."

Johnny arrived about an hour later. I had gone through most of the binder and was on my second coffee. He was shocked to see me, especially to see me looking like *this*. Back in the future Gotham that we came from, Johnny hadn't met me until I was in my early thirties. Now, according to the biological clock of this cloned body, I was about 23. "*Dana*?! What the hell?! You shouldn't be here for another two *years* — and... what... I mean how... are you *so young*?!" He saw that tears began to run down my cheeks and my voice cracked as I said, "Oh Johnny, it's so good to see you again!" My eyes lingered over his curly dark brown hair and northern Italian features. He must have noticed that I was looking at him as if he was back from the dead. "It all went so wrong, Johnny. Our mission — the one that I joined in 1980 — it all went to hell." Johnny looked scared as those words sunk in. "You mean," he said hesitantly, "you're not coming from Gotham in 2112 — *are you*?" "No, Johnny. Japan in 2010, on our revised timeline." He almost breathlessly asked, "Then we... already tried... and..." With an expression of profound sorrow in my eyes, I finished his sentence, "We tried — I tried — and failed miserably. I'll tell you everything. The foundations of the project are sound, but we need to change the mission."

There was a spartan shower in one of the bathrooms of the Avalon Pharmaceutical building. I used it while Johnny quickly went to fetch me a dress and more comfortable shoes from a boutique in Stony Brook. (He didn't get me new underwear, so I just went without wearing any — despite how short the dress was. As for a bra, you know I've never needed one.) Then, Johnny drove me to the woods around Wardenclyffe where we hiked along the Rocky Point trail as I recounted to him as much as I could of what had transpired between 1980 and 2010 in the destroyed world that I had just departed to travel back here. I tried to answer his questions as succinctly as I could so that he did not lose the forest for the trees. By the time we arrived at the ruins of my old laboratory, I think that he had gotten the picture. He was quiet as he watched me plod around the boarded-up building and place my hands somberly on its brick walls. In my mind's eye, I could still see my domed tower that had loomed over it three lifetimes ago.

On our way back to Johnny's parked Jaguar, we began to discuss what to do differently this time. Everything would still need to begin by building up Avalon Pharmaceutical, not just securing FDA approval for the drugs, but also carrying out the insider trading once we were listed on the New York Stock Exchange. I asked Johnny whether the team members tasked with working Wall Street were already in place. He said that they were busy acquiring capital by selling the gold, silver, diamonds, rubies, and emeralds that the team had been provided with in the Gotham of 2112 and had brought with them aboard their flying time machines. Cashing out tens of millions of dollars' worth of precious metals and gemstones without it appearing on the radar of the IRS or other government entities was no small task in the New York City of 1978.

I was a bit dismayed when Johnny confessed to me that our people on Wall Street were already looking to the Mafia for some help in doing this. Gambino, Bonanno, Colombo, Lucchese, and, above all, the Genovese. Johnny Franco, being of Italian descent himself, had moved to establish a working relationship with all of the major families. I had not been aware of the extent to which late 1970s New York was effectively under their control. When I had arrived in 1980, I never inquired into the details of how Johnny had gotten everything into such perfect order so quickly. This time, I would bear witness to all of the gritty machinations myself. In fact, that very first evening that I arrived he had an unbreakable meeting scheduled with a representative of the Genovese family at an abandoned warehouse on Chelsea Piers. He begrudgingly brought me with him, although we decided that I would stay in the car because I wasn't dressed appropriately. We took the 59th Street Bridge into Manhattan. The descending sun was glinting off the spire of the Chrysler Building. It was something else to see this skyline so pristine again, after having seen it destroyed twice now — once by water and once by fire.

After the meeting, which left us with a trunk full of cash-filled briefcases, Johnny brought me home with him. I helped him carry the briefcases up three flights of stairs. Upon arrival here Johnny had moved into a loft apartment between Greene Street and Canal in Soho. There was a view of the Twin Towers from the street in front of the gray building. There were boutiques nearby, which weren't closed for the evening yet, so I went shopping for a provisional wardrobe and some shoes. The two floors of the apartment were connected by a spartan metal spiral staircase, behind the small kitchen and dining room area. Johnny moved downstairs, sleeping on the pullout sofa, so that he could guard the door, and he gave me the makeshift 'bedroom' on the top floor while I began negotiating to buy out the owner of the Penthouse of 55 Central Park West.

There was no full-length wall enclosing the top floor, just one that came up to waist length and let you rest your elbows on it while looking over the living room downstairs. When I would stand at the closet to dress in the morning, I would sometimes see Johnny fold ing the couch up and greet him even though I was still topless. He knew that I always slept naked and, in the oppressive summer heat of this apartment with its insufficient air-conditioning, sometimes above the covers. I wondered how often he was tempted. Occasionally, we would go out to see movies together at the Cinema Village. The first of them, later that summer, was *Eyes of Laura Mars*. Afterwards, I bought the vinyl record of the soundtrack with the Barbra Streisand song "Prisoner."

Johnny had to accelerate the process of assembling the dossier of expertly forged documents that constituted my fabricated biography as a late twentieth-century business woman. How much younger I looked this time would be a problem for what kind of bio had originally been planned, and it had to be significantly paired down.

While the DeLorean prototype that I had ordered was being refitted with its black leather interior and painted matt black, Jean-Pierre was pulled off of security at Avalon Pharmaceutical to drive me around in his Fleetwood Series Seventy-Five Cadillac with bulletproof tinted windows.

One of the first business meetings that he drove me to was with our team members tasked with insider trading on the rising stock of Avalon Pharmaceutical. Our company was about to be listed on the NYSE as a publicly traded corporation, and they were already set up at an office in the skyscraper at One Chase Manhattan Plaza (28 Liberty Street) in the Financial District. The "Group of Four Trees" sculpture in front of the entryway was rather grotesque, but somehow it had been among the few salvaged pieces of monumental modernist sculpture from Manhattan that we had on display in Gotham. So it was strangely nostalgic for me. Once the company *was* listed, I certainly couldn't show up here. But the SCIF beneath the pharma company on Long Island hadn't been completed yet, so I took the risk of meeting them at their office. Someone from the office came down to bring me up so that I would not have to log my name in the lobby. At the meeting we discussed the specifics of how shell companies and off-shore bank accounts would be used to move the expected profits from stock trading on Avalon Pharmaceutical into a new corporation that would ultimately be set up as its parent company, namely AtlantiCorp.

The night of the day in October that Avalon Pharmaceutical went public on the NYSE and its rapidly rising stock began to be traded on Wall Street, bolstered by media coverage of the maverick new drug company, I invited Johnny to come with me to Studio 54 to celebrate. The place was really in its heyday. We dressed in the height of 70s fashion and pretended not to know each other, so that we would have a better chance of getting in than if we were mistaken for a couple. The bouncer hurried me into the broad black doors, and my heart began to race as "Stayin' Alive" by the Bee Gees got louder and louder once I walked through the entry hallway and past the coat check. The rainbow spotlights were glinting off the large pieces of silver glitter coming down from the ceiling in a steady stream. When he finally caught up with me at the bar, I poked fun at Johnny for having had to stand out there in the jostling crowd for an hour after I got in.

Once we had done a couple of lines of coke — the stuff was being passed around there like candy — we started playing a dangerous game together. We decided to try to hunt for a girl who we thought would want to fuck both of us if we brought her back to the loft in Soho. I say dangerous because Johnny and I had never been in a situation like that together before, and there was at least some risk of how it might affect the rapport of camaraderie between us. Around 2 am, we found our girl. Haggling with him over a few that we rejected was fun. This one danced to the disco music between our two bodies for a while in a way that clued us into the fact that she was the right choice. We threw the broad in the back of the Fleetwood Cadillac and climbed in on either side of her, with Jean-Pierre as our designated driver. I glanced at him in the rearview mirror and was astonished to see that he was actually struggling to suppress a smile. When I giggled at him in response, Jean-Pierre finally let himself look me in the eye and lick his lips with a little affirming nod. In my head I could hear him say, "You're something else, lady."

Johnny and I really did a number on that girl together. Afterwards, her immovable body was strewn across the entire pullout sofa. I took Johnny by the hand and brought him upstairs with me. We made a nightcap at my minibar and drank our cold-as-fuck olive-studded Martinis as we surveyed our collaborative conquest with our elbows resting on the barrier overlooking the living room. We even poured a bit down onto her body to see if it would bring her back to consciousness. Nope. We hoped we wouldn't have to call Genovese in the morning. While laughing and holding onto each other's naked bodies, we fell into my bed and slept like the dead.

Much to the chagrin of Jean-Pierre, I would often insist on taking long walks through neighborhoods — at least during the daytime.

Sometimes he would try to tail me, because he was responsible for my safety, and I would lose him by rushing down into the subway. Riding in the graffiti-filled cars was invigorating, even and especially when the men who would eye me from my heels to my scarlet lips also made it dangerous. The suit pants I usually wore made it possible to fight, or run, if I ever had to. I had resolved to hit the streets of Manhattan and become of one element with them more than during the first ill-fated take of this time-traveling mission. But if I kept eating pretzels and hot dogs from the Sabrett vendor carts, which I took a particularly perverse pleasure in doing, I knew I would mar my slim figure with a bit of a pot belly. Then again, my genes had been engineered to keep me leaner for longer than most people and to build muscle mass more quickly when working out — which I did regularly. I was looking forward to moving to 55 West soon, so that I could go back to my routine of jogging in Central Park.

I had resolved not to approach Nikolai until I was situated at my penthouse apartment, but that didn't mean that I couldn't spy on him. I remembered his routine well enough, especially at what hours he would stroll along the boardwalk. So, I went to Coney Island to trail him. As much as I had wanted to take the subway, Jean-Pierre insisted on driving me and I relented. After all, Nikolai had moved there, not just because he was from Brighton Beach, but also on account of the fact that he wanted to stare death in the face and that neighborhood was — short of the South Bronx — the most dangerous part of New York City in the late 1970s.

At first, I kept enough distance between us for him not to notice me. It was August, the zenith of the summer, so the boardwalk was sufficiently crowded for me not to be conspicuous as I shadowed him. But when Nikolai stopped to get a drink at the Atlantis Bar, I ordered one too and sat at a table where I could watch him and take in the sunset at the same time. Words cannot express how uncanny it was to sit there staring at a former incarnation of myself, right there before my eyes in the flesh. I wanted to reach out and touch him. Nikolai had a notepad with him and was jotting something down. Presumably, he was hashing out ideas for that final book, *Invisible Imperium*, which like all of his writings, would remain unpublished. How right the thesis of that book had been. How darkly prophetic.

Nikolai stopped writing, appeared disconcerted for a moment, and then looked straight at me. Our eyes locked. I had been looking at him over the rim of my sunglasses. But when our eyes met, I took them off and placed them on the table in front of me. Doing that felt like stripping. I finished my briny Martini as he watched me. Then, with another gaze straight into his eyes, I got up and walked away. A few paces down the boardwalk, I looked back. Nikolai's eyes were still following me. I doubt it was because he was checking out my legs in this super short dress, with its open back. More likely he was wondering if I was a spy sent by Jack, to extract him from life in hiding and forcibly return him to the Naval Intelligence office in the World Trade Center.

I couldn't wait to bring Nikolai back home with me, so I was relieved that in early September I managed to make a board-approved offer, above the market price, that the owner of the penthouse at 55 Central Park West could not refuse. I had wall-to-wall carpeting installed on both floors of the entire apartment, as was the swank fashion of the time. The furniture that I chose was a combination of Art Deco- and Bauhaus-style pieces. Johnny shook his head at how much I paid for the sofa, chairs, and some of the floor lamps. At least the vault did not have to be built into the library that already lined the walls of the turret on the roof, because I did not have any of the reams of documents and photographs that I had brought with me from 2112 the first time that I came here. All of those had been lost when the facility at Hakone was destroyed. I had even left some behind when we evacuated Manhattan to head for the SCIF. Speaking of the SCIF, it is ironic that at the same time that I was doing the interior decoration of my penthouse, construction of that facility hidden beneath Avalon Pharmaceutical was being completed. We used our relationship with the Italian crime families to secure the hardcore pornographic and ultra-violent footage that was to be projected onto the silver screens, as part of the psychic espionage countermeasures. The contractor that had been asked to inscribe the rows of numbers into the concrete walls of the brutalist structure was totally perplexed, but he wasn't being paid so handsomely to ask questions.

In any case, the most expensive element of my interior décor for the penthouse were undoubtedly the paintings. They were mostly surrealist pieces, from Max Ernst and René Magritte, with a couple of Italian Futurist canvases as well. These were not, however, the paintings of greatest personal value to me. I had resolved to acquire those two paintings of Khosrow Yahyai with which I had grown up, and that I held on to, for most of my life as Jason. In the fall of 1978, it was about a decade since they had been painted, but several years before they would wind up in the possession of Fereidun Jorjani. I tracked down Yahyai in Queens and, although he was troubled by how I had ever heard of him, let alone my penchant for those two paintings of his in particular, the amount of money that I offered him for them trumped any apprehension on his part. I hung these Persian paintings on two opposite walls inside the turret, with each one facing the other. I have never seen a more captivating and enigmatically profound work of Persian Modern Art than these paintings. I hesitate to describe them, because they are masterful works of surrealism, and any description will fail to fathom the depth and breadth of polyvalent symbolism that was enfolded in them by Yahyai, who clearly drew from both Persian tradition and modernist forms of expression. Nonetheless, I am compelled to say a few words about these twin paintings.

One of them appears to be of a Sun King whose head is surmounted by that of a Queen. This central axis is flanked by two figures akin to pawn chess pieces, abstract and alien. Let us not forget that the painter was the co-author of the *Star Child* script that wound up becoming the film *E.T.* The extraterrestrial element is clearly discernable here, especially in the many inhuman eyes that stare out at you from every part of the painting — as if the paws and the body of the Sun

King are akin to multi-eyed jellyfish. Their bodies end in something that is like a single claw or paw, also inhuman in appearance. In the eyes of the King and Queen are desolate desert sands.

This is also true of the eyes of the princess or royal concubine in the companion painting. She has two chains attached to her, one at her waist and one on her ankle. The one dangling from the ankle has a ringing bell at the end of it. Is she being prevented from escape by an alarm that would be sounded if she were to run, or is the bell to summon her servants because what chains her is actually her apparent power over others who are bound to be her slaves? Perhaps she is not just a prisoner, but a woman who once was in bondage but eventually overpowered the Sun King and became that Queen that ensconces his head and body within her own. The buttocks, thighs, and legs of the woman in the companion painting are full of the same alien eyes as well, and her feet are also those demonic-looking paws. In my life as Jason, they always reminded me of the paws of Zuul — the terror dog that is the minion of Gozer in *Ghostbusters*. The companion paint-ing, in particular, is full of small symbols that look like indecipherable hieroglyphics. They are all over the cushion-like greenish shape that the slender body of the enchained princess is leaning into, and above which her tentacle-like long neck twists up into her face with its de-spairing demeanor.

The first night that I spent at 55 Central Park West, I turned on my projector TV and watched news coverage of the large-scale protests against the Shah that had begun in Iran. At that time, no one knew where this was headed — but I did. This time, I would not try to stop it or twist it in any other direction. As I discussed with Johnny on that long walk in the woods around Wardenclyffe, I had learned a hard lesson that my thesis about preventing the fall of the Soviet Union (in-cluding by securing Iranian oil for the USSR) was mistaken. My whole way of thinking about resisting the Olympians through the gargan-tuan structure of two nuclear-armed global superpowers, namely the United States and the Soviet Union, had to be reexamined. It is true

that, on my timeline, the fall of the Soviet Union was eventually followed by the disintegration of the United States, and China rose to fill
the vacuum of power as a global hegemon, eventually handing Earth
over to the "Ancestors" as the Nordics appeared to the Chinese from
their Confucian perspective. But instead of investing so much time
and energy into trying to save the USSR, what if the same amount
of effort were put into breaking China well in advance of its rise as a
hegemon? What if the best defense against an Olympian takeover of
the planet was actually a fractious world with multiple decentralized
nodes of resistance in the name of Liberty and Independence? What
if the right model was not hemispheric superpower collaboration
on a global scale, aiming at an eventual Prometheist World Order,
but rather a movement modeled on piracy and partisan warfare?
Prometheus was, after all, a pirate — the first and greatest of all pirates.

I thought of Coney Island. It was time. If I waited any longer,
Nikolai might go so deep down the hole of suicidal depression that
even I would never be able to pull him out. Here is an apparent time
travel paradox for you. How can I save Nikolai from drowning himself, if that means that Jason Reza Jorjani is never born, which in turn
means that I cannot come to be as a reincarnation of both of them?
Well, it *would* mean that Nikolai could not be reborn as the son of
Fereidun Jorjani and Susan Power. But there was no real paradox about
how I could be here to do this deed. The informational structure of
the quantum computational Cosmos was such that, whenever a time
traveler crossed from one timeline into another, and made changes,
the "code" of the traveler (DNA, memories, etc.) was copied into the
active matrix while the world that she came from was rendered inac-
tive in the form of statically archived information. The latter is what
the Indian philosophers called "the Akashic record" or what game de-
signers in the future (from the perspective of 1978) would conceive of
as a "past state of play" in an archivable and re-playable multi-player
role-playing game. Coney Island came to mind again, specifically its

amusement park with its arcades, funhouses, and halls of mirrors, under the shadow of the Wonder Wheel.

This time I did not let Jean-Pierre drive me. In fact, I said nothing of it to him or to Johnny. Besides, my specially ordered DeLorean prototype had just arrived — refitted to specifications, with a matt black exterior and black leather interior upholstery. So, I drove right up to the projects where Nikolai was hiding out, and I lurked there waiting for him to take his usual route out to the boardwalk for his afternoon and evening stroll. As soon as I saw him come out of the side door that he typically used, which happened to be near the parking lot, I pulled right up next to him. Then I popped the winged door of the DeLorean open on the passenger side. He looked right at me, as I rolled down my window. "Get in the car!" I commanded.

Nikolai stared at me fixedly, at first somewhat taken aback, although, to his credit, apparently not at all scared. I had forgotten how *az jan gozashe* he already was at this point (that's an untranslatable Persian expression that loosely means something like "having left life behind"). Then, as I kept staring straight into his eyes, without saying another word, I saw him smirk a bit, as if he was either impressed or amused. I could faintly read his mind as he thought to himself, *Well, if she's here to kill me, I'll take* this *death.* Then, I smiled back at him with a twinkle in my eye. Nikolai walked slowly over to the passenger side of the car and climbed in. His smirk turned into a smile as the door wing came down and closed next to him automatically. He turned to look at me, pondering what his next words would be. "My name is Dana Avalon, and I'm *not* here to kill you," I said, preempting him. "On the contrary, Nikolai…" I didn't finish that sentence. Instead, I turned on the tape deck, which I had preprepared with a cassette of King Crimson's "In the Court of the Crimson King." He sat back into the black leather and listened to it as I drove us to Manhattan like a bat out of hell.

CHAPTER 11

EYES IN THE DARK

I ALMOST COULDN'T believe that I had Nikolai Alexandrov in my apartment. I kept wanting to touch him to reassure myself that this was really happening, but I held myself back because I didn't want to creep him out any more than he already must have been. He wandered around aimlessly for a bit, taking in the place, and occasionally looking over at me while I made him the kind of vodka Martini that I knew was his favorite drink. I made one for myself too. I held both cocktail glasses in my hands, as my eyes told him to follow me up the stairs to the turret library.

Before even moving into the apartment, while the wall-to-wall carpeting was still being put in, I had gone to the Strand in the Village and bought myself a huge collection of books that the store had delivered here. These now lined the shelves in the library along the interior walls of the turret, around the fireplace. It helped that most of the Strand's books were used, so their spines were already worn. Nikolai surveyed them, not casually, but with the manner of a detective — almost as if his life depended on it. This would be his first tangible clue as to what manner of dangerous person I might be, and what business I had snatching him up off the sidewalk like that. The multi-volume Loeb classics sets of Plato and Aristotle, which included the original Greek, Hegel's *Phenomenology of Spirit*, Heidegger's *Being and Time*, Bergson's *Time and Free Will* together with his *Creative Evolution*, the complete works of Nietzsche, the novels of Kafka and Dostoyevsky, tomes on the science of Parapsychology, such as Edgar Mitchel's *Psychic Exploration* and Sheila Ostrander's *Psychic Discoveries Behind the Iron Curtain*, the Futurist writings of F. M. Esfandiary and, of course, Gerald Feinberg's *The Prometheus Project* were all among the books that he was looking over.

Nikolai had barely surveyed the spines of a third of the books when he turned around and looked me straight in the eyes. His expression was one of suspicion mixed with irresistible intrigue. I extended my hand toward him, and he took his cocktail glass from me. Then I opened the door to the terrace, and we walked out onto it, careful not to spill our Martinis. He followed me to the wall that you could lean on to overlook Central Park, and after he had a moment to take in the blanket of trees and the skyline of the Upper East Side and Central Park South at sunset, we clinked our glasses and began sipping our drinks. I took in his features. Unlike Jason Reza Jorjani, of whom there were many photographs and even portrait paintings in the time that I come from, not a single photograph of Nikolai Alexandrov had survived even into Jason's time, let alone mine. I was astonished at how similar we actually looked. His hair was darker, and his eyes were greener. He had level eyebrows. But otherwise, much of our bone structure and features were as close as those of a woman could be to those of a man. He was a little taller than me, but not awkwardly so. I wondered if he also noticed the resemblance. I got the psychic impression that he had and that even from the moment when I drove up in the DeLorean this was one 'reason' why he was so intrigued as to let himself be abducted by me. Now, after seeing this apartment, and the books...

Nikolai looked as if he were trying to formulate something to say, but he stopped and smiled, as if to concede that he was at a loss for words. Instead, he looked back over Central Park. So, I took the lead. "Do you know who I am?" He was somewhat surprised by the question. "I know you have an excellent intuition, Nikolai. More than intuition, considering that work you do — or used to do. You know that you didn't just get into my car when I told you to because I look like a hotter version of you as a woman," I said as I laughed disarmingly. "Who am I, Nikolai? Tell me." Now he was smiling too, but also wincing somewhat. As he stared at me, sipping his Martini, I saw the expression of astonishment slowly creep across his face, and the look in his eyes turn from intrigue to wonder. "No," he said, "it *can't* be." I replied, "*Why* can't it be?"

"Do you have a cigarette?" he asked. I had forgotten that by now he was becoming a chain smoker. "I'm sorry, I haven't smoked for a couple of lifetimes," I answered apologetically, but also as a way to volunteer another clue. "I promise to have a few packs here for you next time you come over," I added. "But, you know, there are quicker ways to kill yourself than becoming a chain smoker." He replied, "Such *as*?" I said, "Such as walking off Brighton Beach into the Atlantic to drown yourself late one night." He wasn't smiling anymore. I had meant him, but he was thinking of Anna. "I'm sorry, I wasn't thinking of her. But of course, that's why you chose that method of suicide, because it's how she killed herself before you did." I could see the muscles in Nikolai's face getting really tense, and he rested his cocktail glass against the wall of the roof because his hand was starting to tremble a bit.

"Don't play *games* with me, lady. Who the *fuck* are you?!" He didn't actually say that. But I heard him think it. So, I said, "Nikolai, come on. You *know* who I am. After all you've seen, and where you've been — I mean, where Cybele took you — the memories that came back to you in those nights at the Hotel New Yorker, why is it so hard for you to believe that what your gut tells you could be true?" Nikolai breathed a sigh of frustration as he looked away from me and his eyes slowly scanned the buildings across the park from us, with the lights in their windows coming on now as dusk settled over Manhattan.

"You're *me*," he finally said. "Yes." Then he asked, "From… the *future*???" "Yes, Nikolai. *Two* lifetimes into the future." "What did you say your name was again, Dana…" "…Avalon." Nikolai pondered for a moment and then smiled with an expression that suggested he was enjoying an inside joke. "That's clever. Did you come up with that yourself?" I leaned back into the wall, with my elbows resting on it, and said, "Well, Avalon really *was* my father's name, and that of his construction company. I think I might have insistently whispered 'Dana' into my mother's mind before I was born. You know what it means, then?" "Oh yes. From the ancient Persian *Daena* and the ancient Greek *Dianoia*, for 'inner knowing' as in 'conscience' or 'wisdom'. The Persians and the Scythians depicted her — she was always female — as a guardian angel, Valkyrie-like." He could probably tell that I was looking at him a bit adoringly. "You know, on the timeline that I come from, after you commit suicide, you're reborn as a man who is half Persian." He processed the part about him committing suicide all too quickly and then asked, "In Iran?!" "No, *here*. In New York." He squinted and nodded deliberatively. "I guess that doesn't surprise me at all. I find their country and culture to be fascinating. I think I've lived past lives as a Persian, too." My rejoinder was, "Indeed, you *have*. Many centuries ago."

"So — what — are you here to save my life or something, Miss Guardian Angel?" he asked sarcastically. It's funny, I could hear the slightest tinge of a lingering Russian accent in how he spoke. I had forgotten how that had stayed with him for all of his brief life. There was also something Russian about his icy wit. "Aren't you afraid of creating some kind of temporal paradox?" he added even more sarcastically. I think the cool sarcasm was a psychological defense. At this point, Nikolai was really becoming afraid. "I mean, if you've saved me from taking my own life by bringing me here, then shouldn't you be disappearing right now or something?"

"You know that's not how time works, Nikolai. Not how time *travel* works." I could see from his changing expression that he was letting down the psychical armor of sarcasm. "I would be very interested in your explaining to me just how it *does* work, Dana, since, as you know, I'm a physicist who has also studied Philosophy." I smiled at him because I couldn't resist the pun, "All in good time, Nikolai." He smirked. But then his expression softened, and I saw an openness in his eyes when he looked into mine. He stroked the stubble on his chin a few times. Then, all of a sudden, Nikolai dropped his cocktail glass on the terrace floor and crushed it with his shoe. He proceeded to gently pry my glass out of my fingers and take a sip from it. We locked eyes. I knew exactly what he meant by that symbolic gesture, and I was impressed by the beauty of it.

I looked down at Tavern on the Green, knowing that he'd follow my line of sight. Then, I looked Nikolai over from head to toe. He had a tendency to dress in an overly formal fashion, even for his strolls along the boardwalk on Coney Island. He already had slacks and a blazer on, with a white shirt unbuttoned a bit down into his chest. All he needed was a tie. "Will you join me for dinner?" I asked. "At *Tavern*?" "Yeah, I can make a reservation for a couple of hours from now and we can go for a stroll around Central Park South and pick you up a tie." It was a Tuesday night, so I knew the reservation should be manageable. Had it been a Friday or Saturday there would have been no way, on such short notice. "Alright, angel," he said, smiling mischievously, "I'd be happy to take you out to dinner at Tavern on the Green."

I shook my head. Of course, I had been thinking that *I* would be the one to take *him* out, but then I remembered what I had been like as a man, and I felt bad for suggesting that we go to one of the most expensive restaurants in the city. "Please, *let me*, you probably didn't even bring your wallet out for that boardwalk stroll that I whisked you away from." He gave me a cocky look, as he pulled out a rubber-banded wad of hundred-dollar bills. "Wallet, *no*. Money, *yes*. I threw away my *wallet* and ID cards quite a while ago." Then, in a flash, I remembered something that I had completely forgotten about the last years of Nikolai's life, in those dangerous projects near the beach and boardwalk, under which so many homeless people lived. He used to — I mean, *I used to* — go around *and get rid of my inherited money* by literally throwing hundred-dollar bills at these bums. It was like something from a Tolstoy story. *What a romantic lunatic I had been!*

Nikolai was probably wondering why I was staring at him like that, slightly appalled, as I remembered that. I snapped out of it and collected myself. "Well — let me go make the reservation, and then we'll head out." He lingered on the terrace as I went inside to place a call from the phone next to the sofa across from the fireplace in the turret library. He was appreciating the magisterial architectural structure of the turret's exterior. Now that it was night, the spotlights were on, and the Gothic/Deco hybrid design details really stood out against the dark sky. When I came back out onto the terrace to tell him we should head out, he said, "It reminds me of King Arthur, Miss *Avalon*. That, and at the same time, some temple of Ishtar on top of a Babylonian ziggurat."

I took a few paces to where he was and turned to take in the structure together with him, standing close enough to Nikolai for our arms to rub against each other. "Yes, it's an epitome of New York architecture at its best. My mother was an architect, you know. We would study buildings like this, as inspiration for constructing the new skyscrapers of Gotham." He looked at me quizzically, "Gotham?" "It's a city that is built to overlook the partially drowned ruins of this one. New York resurrected, on higher ground." He took that in, then asked, "Higher ground? You mean like the Palisades?" I smiled. "Exactly." Nikolai raised his eyebrows and looked at me gravely, "I've had visions of that. Of Manhattan under water up to the thirtieth floor of the Empire State Building, and of another city, a new futuristic city, built along the Palisades and Englewood Cliffs all the way up into the Hudson Highlands." I leaned against the wall of the turret, with my exposed knee bent, as I folded my arms, and said, "It happens. I'm *from* there. From *then*." He asked, "*When*?" "I was born in 2077, and I traveled here from 2112. But it's a long story. I'll tell you everything — in time… Let's head out."

By the time I was tightening the tie around Nikolai's neck, with my hand on his chest, in the boutique along Central Park South, we could both feel the chemistry between us. It was magnetic. Those magnetic currents were bringing this already half-dead young man back to life — back to *this* world. I could see it in his face all throughout dinner, as I told him about my life in Gotham from 2077 to 2112, and a bit about what had taken place to bring that dark world into being. Although fall had recently started, the weather was still pleasant enough to sit outside — so we did. Our table had a view of the whole glass-enclosed Park Room, and Nikolai had pulled his chair around to sit more next to me than across from me, so that we could both people watch all the stuffy types in there chattering away meaninglessly over the white tablecloths. We had another round of Martinis with our steak and seafood. Nikolai had grinned at me, in an almost leering way, when I ordered the oysters. (Look, if he was going to throw hundred-dollar bills at bums…) On our way out, we had a third drink at the bar toward the front of the restaurant, under the impressive wood rafters. So, by the time we were headed back to 55 CPW, we were quite drunk and almost holding on to each other as we plodded across the street to my apartment.

"I'm obviously not driving you back home tonight," I said, when we got back up to the penthouse. "*Obviously*," said Nikolai, laughing drunkenly. I grabbed his arm and brought him to my bedroom. "Come try out my hot tub, *you'll love it*," I said as I went into the master bathroom and turned the water on. Then, I shamelessly took all of my clothes off and threw them onto the bed. Nikolai looked at me with an expression more amused than excited, as if he were looking at a colorfully strange child. "Come on," I goaded him, "don't be a bore!" Nikolai took his clothes off, hesitantly, piece by piece, carefully laying them next to mine on the bed. I got behind his back and pushed his naked body, choo-choo train style, into the large bathroom.

When I climbed into the hot tub, I noticed that he was eying my huge clit. I smiled at him impishly as I slid down into the rising water.

I guess my hypertrophied clitoris turned Nikolai on rather than putting him off, because he started getting hard as he climbed in after
me. He bent his knees and closed his thighs as he settled into the tub.
We leaned into each other with our heads propped on one another. I
would have loved to have seen our two faces together at that moment.
I reached my hand out under the water and he slipped his into it. We
held hands for a long time, as our faces beaded up and we could taste
the salt of our own sweat on our lips. We kissed gently.

When we started to cozily doze off together in the warmth and the
steam, I made the effort of getting us up out of the tub, and lazily half
drying off our bodies, before holding onto Nikolai as we went quickly
back across my room and climbed under the covers of my bed. Our
clothes were still strewn on top of the blanket — some of them sliding
onto the floor as we got in. I hit the lights from my bedside dimmer,
and we went out almost as soon as they did. Entangled as we slept
together in the bed that night, I felt like we were twins.

In the morning for breakfast, I made us toasted bagels with lox
and chive cream cheese, which I had picked up at Barney Greengrass.
"Listen," I said to Nikolai as we sipped our black coffee, "I have to go
to work. *Please* be here when I come home this evening. I'll give you
a set of my keys, so you're not shut in all day, and I'll tell the doorman that you're staying with me." Nikolai raised his eyebrows, with his
head tilted forward, as he set down the Avalon Pharmaceutical coffee
mug. "You trust me *alone* in your apartment, and with *your keys* — after just meeting me *last night*???" I looked at him like he was retarded.
"You're *me,* dumbass." I guess that fact was a lot clearer to me than
it was to him yet, or maybe ever would be. Nikolai kind of shrugged
with his face more than his shoulders, in a rather Russian way, as if to
say, "I guess…"

It was hard to focus on any work that day because I was full of
angst and trepidation over whether Nikolai actually *would* be there
when I got back. Johnny asked me what was wrong, but I didn't want
to tell him — at least *not yet.* I made an excuse to leave Long Island

and head back to Manhattan a bit earlier than usual. My heart sank at first when I walked into the penthouse and didn't see him anywhere on the first floor. Then, I rushed upstairs. How elated I was to find Nikolai sitting on the sofa in the turret library flipping through *Time and Free Will*. Heidegger's *Being and Time* had also been pulled out and was on the coffee table in front of him. He turned his head and looked up at me, silently and at first expressionlessly. When he saw how happy I was, he smiled.

I walked over to Nikolai and put my hands on his shoulders, rubbing them a bit, as I stood behind him. Then, I ran my fingers through his hair. When he tilted his neck back, I kissed his forehead. "*Privet, moy dorogoy*," I whispered to him. "You know Russian?" he asked. "I picked up a little — or relearned a bit, I guess — when I worked for decades to prevent the collapse of the Soviet Union. I had a Russian girlfriend for a while back then. Well — a *lover* more than a 'girlfriend.' She worked for me." Nikolai seemed more intrigued by the first statement than the second, but not by *much*. So, after making some black tea for us, and sitting beside him, I included Irena in my account of the first, ill-fated attempt that I had made to alter the timeline that led to the global dominion of the Olympian Imperium in the world that I came from. Nikolai found the tale astonishing, but not batshit crazy — as any normal person would have. In what I described to him that I had tried to do, he saw a lot of himself. "It's what I would have done," he said to me, consolingly, when I lamented about how foolish I had been to think that plan would have worked. I looked at Nikolai somewhat apologetically as I replied, "It *is* what you *did* do." He stared at the coffee table and while nodding wearily he said, "Right." Then, he asked, "What about the other one? Is it what *he* would have done, too? The incarnation after me, and before you. What was he like?" So, I started to tell Nikolai about Jason, and the more I told him the more he wanted to know.

I told him about the philosophical works, and the political projects, above all Prometheism, but as I went on it became clear to me that what Nikolai was most interested in was what was *not* in the history books or part of any official biography available in Gotham or in the asteroid belt colonies that so many Prometheists had taken refuge in as the Imperium consolidated its control over both Earth and Mars. So, I told him about Emma. To be honest, I had been avoiding the subject. When, in my lifetime as Jason, I wrote *Faustian Futurist*, based on my memories of the life of Nikolai, I conflated the characters of "Anna" and "Marjâna" whereas in fact, Anna was a separate person — tragic as her relationship with Nikolai had been. However, the reincarnation of the concubine of Dârâ-El in Atlantis, namely Marjâna, was actually Nikolai's mother who was murdered by his father when he was a child living in Brighton Beach. Emma was a reincarnation of *this* woman, who had been a lover of Jason in one past life and his mother in another.

Actually, she had been his mother in *two* past lives, because she was also a reincarnation of the much beloved mother of Nikola Tesla, namely Milutin Tesla, who died in Croatia in 1892 and whose spirit followed her son to New York after he visited her at her deathbed (she had waited to give up the ghost until only a few hours after he finally arrived). To be perfectly honest, she had *also* been his *wife* in yet *another* life. Let me leave it at saying that, in this other life, Jason was an infamous Carpathian prince and an initiate of a certain secret society, who ruthlessly fought the Mohammedan Turks, only to be thanklessly branded as a heretic by the Church. In *that* life, he tried to send the previous incarnation of "Emma" who was his wife to a convent in order to shelter her from what he deemed it necessary to do to protect his realm, and, in fact, to prevent the nascent Renaissance from being nipped in the bud by an Islamic conquest of Europe.

Nikolai got the point that Jason had a lot of karmic baggage with — and unresolved bondage to — this woman, who he met rather early on. His years with her deeply impacted his developmental trajectory, and the tragic end of their relationship was a trauma that marked him forever after. It was a reasonable speculation that, had he never met her again in that life, Jason would have — I mean, I would have — written *Prometheus and Atlas* as much as five years earlier, and never been lured by Jellyfish into being involved with the Alt-Right (shortly after it was published, and just when the opportunities opened up by it were beginning to flower). Of course, it would have been a somewhat more moderate book, but it also would have been published by the University of Chicago Press, or even Anomalist Books, rather than Arktos. Not that Emma was right-wing in any way. Quite to the contrary. But the impact of that relationship was profound, complex, and far-reaching from a psychological standpoint. It is hard to see what *good* ultimately came of it.

I could see that all this, which I recounted in much more detail than I am reiterating now, depressed Nikolai. That is the last thing that I wanted to do. So, I did not go on to tell him about how Jason had been badly betrayed by his maternal uncle, who disowned him after he was defamed in 2017, or any number of the other serious betrayals that he had suffered from those near and dear to him — including his friend and publicist of sorts, the renowned parapsychologist Jeffrey Mishlove — and that led him, eventually, to the darkest and most severe worldview that he could possibly have ever arrived at. It was not a question of projecting personal suffering onto the public sphere (as psychologizing detractors would say). Rather, Jason already had — for many years before that — enough evidence from the public sphere of national and world affairs to all but convince him that what had the audacity to call itself "humanity" represented a despicable failure of the project that he and his rebel associates had initiated in the last days of Atlantis. What the personal betrayals and disappointments did was to snuff his last hope of finding, on a more intimate and inter-personal level, enough exceptions to the rule so as not to reach the conclusion that Jason ultimately *did* reach. Namely, that, as Nietzsche put it, "Man is something that has to be overcome."

Well, I mean I didn't burden Nikolai with all of that in the turret library that first evening when I came home to him in my apartment, but I *did* share it with him eventually, bit by bit, over the course of weeks and months also filled with activities that were intended to re-kindle his love for life. He agreed to move out of that housing project that he was hiding out in, and to move what few possessions he had left at that point into my penthouse. I finally told Johnny what had been going on, and although he was concerned, he accepted it. It was not 1980 yet, but still, it appeared that Nikolai Alexandrov would not commit suicide by drowning himself off Coney Island after all.

Late in that fall of 1978, when it began to snow just a couple of hours to the north of the city, I suggested that we go skiing at Hunter Mountain together. I remembered his history at Scribner, and I won-dered whether making those memories resurface would mar the po-tentially revitalizing effect of hitting the slopes again. Nikolai was very much in favor of the idea, though, and in fact he insisted that we stay at Scribner Hollow Lodge. He wanted to poke around the woods in the back of the property, behind where his aunt's ski house had been, to see whether he could find that trap door that he had never been able to relocate again as a child. Nikolai was always left with a doubt as to whether that subterranean initiation of sorts in the middle of the night was a real experience or just a powerful dream based on actual prepubescent incest. Honestly, I also wanted to go back there myself, regardless of how Nikolai felt, because that hotel had been converted into the alpine lodge that my father and mother lived in as they de-signed the core structure of Gotham together. Although I was born in Gotham, they had kept the place as a ski house. I had stayed there while skiing many times from my childhood throughout my teenage years.

I drove us up the winding mountain roads in the DeLorean with Blue Oyster Cult's album *Agents of Fortune* playing on the cassette tape deck. Many of the trees in Hunter were still blazing with the fiery colors of fall leaves, but snow was already covering the ground. The further up we went, the deeper it was. It was nightfall by the time we got to Scribner and settled into our room. We were going to buy new skis and boots at the lodge in the morning and get a locker to store them in for the entire season. Since we were hungry, Nikolai and I had dinner together at the hotel restaurant. We sat at a table where we could look through the floor-to-ceiling windows out over the ski slopes on the mountain across from this hilltop. The trails were illuminated by the lights of the snowcats that were grooming them and packing the freshly falling powder.

After dinner we went for a long walk throughout the hotel and the property. First, I showed him all the places inside of the hotel that had been modified in my time — or my parents' time — to turn the place into an alpine chalet and private residence. Then, Nikolai led me outside through the falling snow, with our boots crunching into the powder, and brought me to the ski house unit that had belonged to his aunt. I remembered it as well, from my past life regression sessions in Gotham, although no doubt much less vividly than he did.

I knew that he wanted to keep going, further up the hill, into the woods behind the housing units, to the place where he remembered that trap door having been — the one that led to the subterranean chamber with walls covered in carvings of gorgons and owls. I indulged him, expecting that the place was something from a dream — or nightmare. But lo and behold! Not all that far into the trees, we came upon somewhat of a clearing, where Nikolai got down on his hands and knees, scraping the snow off of what felt like wood rather than earth beneath our feet. There it was. The metal lock that had frustrated his attempts to get back in here as a child had by now rusted to the point where, when I gave it a few hard kicks, it broke right off. We grabbed the part of it attached to the door, being careful not to slice through our ski gloves and cut our hands on the rusted metal. When we got the door open, the musty smell that came at us from out of the place was almost unbearable. It was tinged with some scent between sulfur and cinnamon. As I started down the steps with Nikolai behind me, I stopped dead when I remembered where I had smelled that before. I remembered what the shapeshifters had told me about their lair in the Hudson Valley.

I turned around and looked Nikolai in the eyes. Seeing me suddenly afraid made him even more apprehensive. But we persisted, turning on the two flashlights that we had brought with us to finish descending the crumbling steps. As the flashlight beams moved across the earthen walls, I saw them — just as he had described them. The insane Dionysiac designs of gorgons, owls, and other indiscernible insects and tentacled things. While Nikolai was examining these designs with his flashlight, I pointed the one that I was holding into the distance to try to gauge the depth of this place. What the beam caught horrified me. I only saw it for a moment, but I was so scared that I backed into Nikolai while gripping my chest. I dropped my flashlight, and it broke.

I grabbed Nikolai by the arm, and as the beam of his flashlight illuminated the terrified expression on my face, he let me practically push him up the stairs ahead of me, tripping a couple of times, until we got out and I threw the wooden door to the subterranean chamber closed with great force before he even had a chance to help me. I made Nikolai walk back to Scribner with me as fast as we possibly could in the snow. I mean we practically ran. It was not until we were in the hot tub of the grotto under the hotel later that night, after everyone else had cleared out, that I was able to talk about what I had seen illumined by my flashlight beam. I told Nikolai that it was his face, and yet not his face. "You mean a doppelganger of me?" he asked. "Those are harbingers of death," he said as he looked grimly at the plaster decorative rock over and around the hot tub. We were whispering to each other because the pool's bartender, who had brought us over the drinks that we had beside our elbows, was still down here in the Scribner Grotto. (In fact, he looked annoyed that we were staying down here so late.)

"No, Nikolai. I mean — not exactly. I've *seen* that face before. Remember when I was telling you about the Latin American Reich that rose up in the days when Jason, Ghislaine, and I took refuge at

our facility in Hakone?" He nodded affirmatively. "What I didn't tell
you — because it was just too weird, and I didn't want you to... well,
the leader of that nascent Imperium had *that* face. It was like your
face, but older. Also, the expression was different — especially his
eyes." Now Nikolai was the one who looked horrified. I added, "His
name was Adolfo von Seelstrang. He was supposedly an Argentinian
of German ancestry. But to be frank, the man's past was shrouded in
mystery. I know what manufactured biographies look like, since I've
had them put together for me. I don't think that guy was just the mining magnate from Bariloche that they claimed he was."

Nikolai said that he felt ill and wanted to go back upstairs to our
room at once. He had remembered something but did not want to tell
me until we were alone. Once we were warming up on the bearskin
rug in front of the fire in our suite, wearing nothing but the hotel
bathrobes bundled around ourselves, with our glasses of cognac resting on the brick of the fireplace, Nikolai finally opened up about it. He
reminded me of one of the strangest of his many uncanny experiences
in youth. The night that he had sex with his aunt in that strangely
vacant hotel in Italy. He seemed embarrassed to talk about it, and I
had to remind him that I *was* him and that they were my memories
too, just buried deeper in my subconscious on account of the lifetimes
that had elapsed for me since then. Finally, he spit it out. The weird
flask that his aunt had collected his sperm in the first time that he
had come, in that hotel room, when he woke up in the morning, it
was missing from the bedside table that she had put it on before they
went to sleep. It was then that, following what Nikolai was trying to
tell me, I realized for the first time who exactly Adolfo von Seelstrang
must have been. It sent a shudder through my spine. He was a clone
of Nikolai.

I was so distraught that night that I forgot to use any birth control
before Nikolai got into bed with me. In my old body, I had a sophisticated nanotechnological birth control device implanted into my arm.
I had done this by choice in my twenties, back in Gotham. But when I

was cloned at the lair beneath Lake Ashi, this obviously hadn't carried over to my new body. Besides, I mostly slept with women. So, on the rare occasion that I thought I might have sex with a man, I figured that I would use a diaphragm with contraceptive gel. I had only done that once so far, since arriving here in June of 1978. That night when Johnny and I went to Studio 54 together, I had taken precautions in advance. As it turned out, the effectiveness of this method was never tested because although we fucked the hell out of that girl that we brought back to his loft that night, it's not like Johnny himself came inside me or even really had intercourse with me directly.

In any case, after what we had just been through, birth control was not a thought that even crossed my mind as me and Nikolai tried to console each other in bed that night at Hunter Mountain. In the months up until then, while we had occasionally been turned on by each other, we had mostly lived together like twin siblings. But that night, we made love more passionately — and more desperately — than I'd ever been with a man before in my entire life. We clung to each other for dear life, and Nikolai came inside me almost as many times as I came. The ecstasies were transcendental, and during the most intense of them I left my body and looked down at us from under the ceiling for a few moments, until Nikolai's kisses and bites brought me back into my skin.

Maybe we should have fled back to the safety of Manhattan, but for whatever reason we stayed, bought our equipment as planned, and skied Hunter together for most of the next day. Somehow the adrenaline of carving our way down K-27 together, with crisscrossing ski lines, was therapeutic in dealing with the terror of the night before. What I *did* do was very discretely bring the sniper rifle, which I had bought shortly after my arrival in June, from the trunk of the DeLorean into the hotel room with us. I covered it in the emptied bag that had held my new skis. As irrational as it seemed to my analytical mind, I was consoled by having the gun at our bedside and I could tell that Nikolai was also.

It was about 2:30 am when I woke up suddenly, startled by reaching into empty space on the side of the bed where Nikolai's warm body had been when we fell asleep together. I jumped out of bed and went to the bathroom to see if he was in there. He wasn't. My heart sank. I noticed that the screen door to the terrace was partly open. It may even have been the cold that woke me up enough to notice that he was missing from beside me. When I turned on the terrace light, I could see that there were tracks in the snow leading away from a deep impression right below our room. I put my ski clothes and jacket back on as fast as I could, and I grabbed not only the flashlight, but also the sniper rifle from the bedside. I couldn't very well go walking through the hotel with that, and I didn't want to be encumbered by the ski bag that I had hidden it in. So, I decided to jump off the second-floor terrace. It was an easy jump, and once I had made it, I noticed that the tracks leading away from the depression that someone else had made in the snow before me, were *two sets* of tracks. One of a man who was walking on his own, and another of a man who, judging from the marks, appeared to have been dragged at least part of the way.

I followed the tracks. My heart sank as I realized that they were leading, through the woods, back to the trap door in the clearing up the hill. As much as I was desperate to find Nikolai, I started moving more slowly, already afraid of what I might actually find. I raised the sniper rifle — pointing it ahead of me, bending my knees, as I paced forward through the snow that was a lot deeper than it had been the night before. As I reached the clearing, I almost dropped the rifle to reach for my flashlight because I couldn't believe my eyes. The sight that confronted me was clear enough in the moonlight, though, and there was no way that I was going to put this gun down. There, right over the open trap door, was Adolfo von Seelstrang holding Nikolai Alexandrov up by the collar of his pajamas, as if Nikolai were a ragdoll and von Seelstrang were made of steel. Nikolai looked lifeless, although I could see — or I thought I could see — some movement in his eyes that suggested he was trying to look at me. His face was twisted, and frozen, into an expression of despairing resignation. I could not see von Seelstrang's face as clearly, because his back was mostly to me.

I moved very slowly to an angle that gave me a line of sight that I thought would put Nikolai out of danger, and I tried my hardest to steady my hand despite my heart beating out of my chest. Then I shot straight at von Seelstrang. For a sniper rifle, this was practically point-blank range. There was a silencer on the barrel, so the shot barely echoed in the woods. For a moment, I didn't know what I was seeing in front of me. Then, as things came back into focus, I saw that Nikolai was laying there in the snow — alone — in his pajamas, with blood pouring out of his chest. There was no Adolfo von Seelstrang anywhere in sight. I ran over to Nikolai, horrified, and screaming — more shrieking, really, when the sound would even come out of my throat. Between the hypothermia and the gunshot wound, he was gone. I felt for his pulse. I breathed into his mouth and pounded on his chest. Nothing. I sat there weeping over Nikolai's corpse until I nearly froze to death myself. Then, with my assassin's mind coming back on line, I realized that I couldn't very well bring him back to the hotel or explain this away to anyone who wouldn't have me arrested. So, as my tears kept freezing on my cheeks, I opened the trap door and slid Nikolai's body down the steps, together with the sniper rifle that had somehow blown him away.

I have never been more single-minded than in the weeks that followed that horrific night at Hunter. Nikolai had in some inexplicable way been killed by Adolfo von Seelstrang and so I was intent on hunting down that man who disappeared like a specter in the snow. By the time that I arrived in San Carlos de Bariloche, I was two months pregnant. Soon, it would start to show. I had decided to keep the baby growing inside of me, not only because it was all that I had left of Nikolai but, to be honest, because I strongly believed that he would choose to reincarnate as my child — as *our* child — thereby becoming his own father and, in a sense, his own mother from the future. Of course, that would also mean that Jason Reza Jorjani would never be born.

It was January of 1979. Located in the Andes Mountains, in northern Patagonia, the Bavarian-style village was cold. The only person who I had told about all of this was Johnny because I needed his help using the resources of the nascent AtlantiCorp to gather enough intelligence to be effective once I arrived in Argentina. We had more or less tracked down von Seelstrang. He was a 21-year-old student studying at the University of Buenos Aires, but at the moment he was back home with his family in Bariloche during the winter break between semesters. I kept asking myself how the von Seelstrang that I saw that night, both down in the subterranean chamber and then holding Nikolai up over the chamber's trap door the night after, was the fifty-something-year-old-looking man that I had first seen when, in Hakone in 2010, me and Ghislaine were watching news coverage of the rise of the Latin American Reich.

Ultimately, it did not make much difference to me. I was going to kill this bastard, no matter how old — or how young — he was now, and no matter how much he looked like Nikolai. Actually, the resemblance was even more motivating to me. It made me see him as a monstrosity, as if he — or whatever Frankenstein made him — had stolen Nikolai's face, *my* face (of two lifetimes ago), to use as a mask for the future leader of the Fourth Reich.

Our intelligence had shown that Adolfo would go skiing with his family at Cerro Catedral, a ski resort in the mountains only 19 kilometers (12 miles) from his hometown of San Carlos de Bariloche. You could see the town from the top of the mountain, which also had a spectacular view of the Andes range. Targeting von Seelstrang while he was skiing had some poetic justice to it, considering the circumstances under which he had spectrally abducted and murdered Nikolai during our ski trip to Hunter Mountain. I did not bring my sniper rifle all the way to Argentina. We did not have the AtlantiCorp private jet yet, so I was not about to check a sniper rifle together with my luggage when I flew first class on Pan Am. Instead, what I had with me, besides my ski gear, was a plastic gun in several pieces that could be easily assembled, and that fired fast-acting and absolutely lethal poison darts. It was a real assassin's weapon.

I rented a chalet close enough to that of the von Seelstrang family (who knows who they really were) that I was able to spy on Adolfo with my high-powered binoculars. So I knew when he was headed to the slopes. I trailed him in my rental Mercedes. After we parked, I carefully kept enough distance from him so as not to be noticed as I carried my ski gear up to the lift area, snapped my skis on, and got on the chairlift a couple of chairs behind him. Once we reached the summit, I followed Adolfo to the relatively steep trail that he chose to start his day with. I was pleasantly surprised at how steep the trail was, because once I hit him with the poison dart his fall down this slope would be so bad that he might also break his neck.

I didn't wait around to find out, though. He was about halfway down the trail, and I was a couple of meters behind him, when I shot him in the exposed side of his neck with the dart gun. I held on to the weapon, only discarding it on the roadside, in deep snow and between some trees, when I was headed back to the airport in San Carlos de Bariloche. I had already packed the very light luggage that I brought with me, so there was no need to return to the chalet near his family, who would soon be informed of his "accident." I saw him reach to pull out the dart, just before I skied past him, and practically bombed the rest of the run. So, unless they did an autopsy (which, considering who they were, they might do), it is possible that his death would just be chalked up to how badly he had fallen down that double black diamond.

On the way back, I had to change planes in Buenos Aires, just as I had on the way to Bariloche. When my flight got into JFK in the middle of the night, Jean-Pierre was there to pick me up in the limo and drive me home to 55 Central Park West. I had hoped to get a good night's sleep after such a stressful operation, which I had been planning for so long. Unfortunately, I woke up from a terrible night-mare after only a couple of hours.

In the nightmare, I saw things from the perspective of a little boy, who was only at waist height compared to the adults near him. They were congregated around the open door to a room in some kind of health spa or hospital. Certain of the adults would go into the room, then come out with their heads downcast. The men, who were wearing suits, held their fedora hats in their hands, and some of the women were quietly crying as they came out. The fashion of the women's clothes suggested, even more clearly than the style of the men's suits, that it was probably sometime in the 1960s. I noticed that most of the people were speaking German, but a few were speaking Spanish. These Spanish speakers looked Argentinian. The other people were very white. So was the boy whose eyes I was seeing through, judging from his hands.

Finally, he accompanied a maternal woman who was holding his hand as she took her turn to enter the room. A sick old man was propped up on pillows in what looked like a hospital bed, and at first it was hard to make out his face because he was being given oxygen by the attendant nurse. The boy was a bit frightened by this sight. There were physicians there too, talking to a couple of people who just stayed in the room while the visitors came and went. The woman patted the boy's back to urge him to walk forward to the old man's bedside. The man reached down with his wrinkled and trembling hand. As the maternal figure put the boy's hand inside the hand of the dying man, the attendant took the oxygen mask off so that — through the eyes of the boy — I was looking right at his face, while feeling the hair-raisingly cold clasp of his hand. Despite his moustache having been shaved off, there was no mistaking him for anyone else. It was the Austrian painter. He looked like he was in his seventies. That's when I woke up gripping my abdomen, where I felt cramps worse than any that I had ever gotten around my period. The cramps went away after I soaked in the hot tub for a while, but I didn't get much sleep for the rest of that night.

In the weeks that followed, as we entered February of 1979, my attention was repeatedly captured by the unfolding events of the Iranian Revolution. As I explained earlier, this time I had resolved to let it take place just as it had on the timeline that I came from rather than to revise events in Iran as I had done on the timeline wherein I saved the Soviet Union from collapse (in large part by engineering Soviet seizure of Iranian oil reserves and Persian Gulf seaports). I was watching news coverage from Iran one evening, when my doorbell rang. I assumed it was the superintendent or maybe building staff bringing up a package that was left for me downstairs, because we had very good security at 55 Central Park West, and nobody got upstairs to someone's apartment without the doorman calling up for them to be cleared. Also, I was intent on getting back to the news report as soon as possible, so I did not call downstairs to ask. Instead, I just went over and looked through the peephole. I couldn't believe my eyes. I backed away from the door for a moment, wondering what I should do. It was Cybele. All six-foot-nine inches of her. She must have found out that Nikolai had been here. I decided to open the door.

"Cybele... how did you..." She looked at me like I was being ridiculous. I dropped the question about how she got past the doorman, and I introduced myself. "I'm Dana Avalon." She smiled politely, and said, "Of course you are. Who else's apartment would I be at?" I felt embarrassed, and nervously said, "Please come in." I was still wearing my suit pants and shirt from work, so at least I was dressed decently, and my makeup was still on too. I gestured for her to follow me up the stairs to the turret library. "Is he still here?" she asked. I glanced back at her. (Dear Lord, she was tall — especially for a woman.) "It's a long story. Please have a seat," I said as we entered the library. "Would you like anything to drink, before I try to explain?" Cybele gave me a long-faced look. "Am I going to need a drink?" she asked. "Well, *I'm* going to need one. Should I make you one too?" She nodded affirmatively. "Martini? Manhattan?" I asked her. "A Manhattan with bourbon would be great, thanks," said Cybele. I had put a minibar in the turret, even though I knew that, now that I was pregnant, I really needed to cut back on my drinking. So, I made us two Bourbon-based Manhattans right there, while Cybele examined my library.

I set down our cocktail glasses on the coffee table in front of the sofa. I also kindled the fire and stoked it with my fireplace tools. Meanwhile, Cybele was looking back and forth at the two paintings by Khosrow Yahyai. Before I sat down next to her on the couch, I pulled Nikolai's manuscripts out of the library, where they had been wedged between certain books that he had brought with him when he vacated that awful apartment that he had on Coney Island. All three of his manuscripts, which had been lost in the timeline wherein he committed suicide, were here — *Being Bound for Freedom*, Nikolai's adaptation of his doctoral dissertation critiquing the Many Worlds Interpretation of quantum mechanics, *Faustian Futurism*, which he wrote under the name Nick Griffin, and that last prophetic work about the Fourth Reich, *Invisible Imperium*. I put these on the table in front of Cybele, so that her cool and nonplussed demeanor finally came apart as the façade that it was. As she reached for them, I sat down next to her. "To Nikolai," I said, as we clinked our glasses and started to sip our drinks. "That's a hell of a Manhattan," said Cybele, after she took her first couple of sips. "Yeah, I've gotten too good at making them," I said. In addition to very high-quality sweet vermouth, I had put just the right amount of orange peel bitters into the bourbon, and I made sure that the ice was so frozen that, when I shook the drink, not too hard or for too long, it didn't melt into the booze and dilute it.

Over the course of the following two or three hours, and another round of drinks (which I really shouldn't have had), I explained to Cybele what had happened to Nikolai — both on the original timeline, and since I picked him up from Coney Island in my DeLorean on that afternoon in September of 1978. She told me that she had come here because she had sensed that Nikolai was in extraordinary danger, and she had clairvoyantly "remote-viewed" him living with me in this apartment with its distinct rooftop architecture. Cybele was very psychic, so she could make a lot of connections without my having to lay everything out explicitly. She was also able to intuit, before I volunteered it, that I was a reincarnation of Nikolai from the timeline wherein he committed suicide in the summer of 1980. Cybele told me that she thought that what happened the night that von Seelstrang abducted Nikolai from Scribner was some kind of psychokinetic astral projection, but she found it just as paradoxical as I did how this could have happened if that older version of Adolfo would never come to be, because only months later I assassinated him in Bariloche when he was still at the age of 21. Cybele also intuited that I was pregnant, and she understood why I believed that the boy (I knew it would be a boy) was going to be a reincarnation of Nikolai, who would choose my womb instead of being reborn as Jason Reza Jorjani.

I never had an easier time talking to another woman, even including Ghislaine. I suppose it was because, like myself, Cybele was not exactly of this world. Although she was not a time traveler from the future, her having one foot in the underworld of the Nordics — and a son who was himself one of the rebel Nordics — gave her access to a society that was similar to the one that had dominated Earth in the time that I came from. In point of fact, not just similar to it, but the embryonic form of the Olympian Imperium. She assured me, as she already had during my life as Nikolai, that her son, Apollyon, intended to resist the Traditionalism of that Imperium from within. But they were Nordics, anyhow. Both of them.

I mean looking at her, I sometimes wondered how they would get away with just being out and about in our world. Granted, Cybele looked a lot like a Swede or some kind of sandy blonde-haired Scandinavian. But still, her eye sockets were exceptionally deep set, with dark shadows around those turquoise irises, and her broad forehead was abnormally high. You would think she would at least wear her hair with bangs to conceal that somewhat. Then there was the question of her height. How many women are as tall as a basketball player? She was beautiful, but there was unquestionably something freakish about her that I imagined would be problematically conspicuous. Cybele startled me when she let on that she could hear what I was thinking, by saying, out of the context of our conversation, "I usually wear a hat and large sunglasses. Can't do anything about my height, though, other than never wearing high heels to make it any worse. Plus, I'm so big-boned and I have so much muscle mass that I'd probably break long skinny heels." I invited Cybele to stay for dinner, but after learning everything that she had about Nikolai that evening I think she wanted to be alone to process it all. I promised to make copies of Nikolai's manuscripts to give to her next time she visited me, which she assured me that she would do soon.

Cybele certainly kept that promise, and not just so that she could pick up the xeroxed manuscripts. Over the Spring of 1979, as Iran descended into medieval Muslim theocracy, I was granted a welcome diversion from that grim reality by Cybele's frequent visits to my penthouse. During my lifetime as Nikolai, I had only had sex with her a few times, during that brief stay at the Biltmore Hotel in California. But in this life, she moved in with me and we became long-term lovers. I had no idea that she was open to being with a woman, although frankly I think that part of that openness was on account of the fact that, in addition to my being a reincarnation of Nikolai, Cybele believed that I was carrying another *male* reincarnation of Nikolai in my womb.

Having already been a mother, namely to Apollyon, Cybele was a constant source of counsel and support during my pregnancy, in the course of which she was also my lover. For the first time in my life, I actually had breasts. They were still very small relative to the average, and certainly compared to Cybele's, but when I started lactating, I also grew some breast tissue under those huge nipples that I've always had. This meant I had to finally start wearing bras on a regular basis, especially because otherwise I would wind up lactating through my dress shirt at work. Sometimes, Cybele would suck the milk from my tits while we made love, which helped me avoid that inconvenience from happening too often.

Perhaps to Cybele's chagrin, I had decided that I would name my son, not Nikolai, but "Jason" in remembrance of the boy who would never be born. Jason Avalon came into this world on July 9, 1979. Cybele helped to deliver him in a home birth that was also attended by Johnny, and by a doctor closely associated with Avalon Pharmaceutical. Throughout Jason's childhood, she would become "Aunt Cybele" and he would be "Uncle Johnny." The baby that would have become Jason Reza Jorjani was strangled to death by his own umbilical cord on February 21, 1981. (At least, that's what Jorjani's death certificate would say.) By then the soul that would have animated that baby had already been my boy for a year and a half. Saying that Cybele "helped" in the delivery of Jason is an understatement. She literally pulled his little head and shoulders out of my birth canal with her bloodied, preternaturally strong hands. The crying boy's first sight as he entered this world were her soul-piercing blue-green eyes. As my lover, Cybele would, in effect, become Jason's second mother, and Apollyon would have a brother after all.

OTHER BOOKS PUBLISHED BY ARKTOS

OTHER BOOKS PUBLISHED BY ARKTOS

	Recognitions
	A Traditionalist Confronts Fascism
GUILLAUME FAYE	*Archeofuturism*
	Archeofuturism 2.0
	The Colonisation of Europe
	Convergence of Catastrophes
	Ethnic Apocalypse
	A Global Coup
	Prelude to War
	Sex and Deviance
	Understanding Islam
	Why We Fight
DANIEL S. FORREST	*Suprahumanism*
ANDREW FRASER	*Dissident Dispatches*
	The WASP Question
GÉNÉRATION IDENTITAIRE	*We are Generation Identity*
PETER GOODCHILD	*The Taxi Driver from Baghdad*
	The Western Path
PAUL GOTTFRIED	*War and Democracy*
PETR HAMPL	*Breached Enclosure*
PORUS HOMI HAVEWALA	*The Saga of the Aryan Race*
LARS HOLGER HOLM	*Hiding in Broad Daylight*
	Homo Maximus
	Incidents of Travel in Latin America
	The Owls of Afrasiab
RICHARD HOUCK	*Liberalism Unmasked*
A. J. ILLINGWORTH	*Political Justice*
ALEXANDER JACOB	*De Naturae Natura*
JASON REZA JORJANI	*Closer Encounters*
	Faustian Futurist
	Iranian Leviathan
	Lovers of Sophia
	Novel Folklore
	Prometheism
	Prometheus and Atlas
	World State of Emergency
HENRIK JONASSON	*Sigmund*
VINCENT JOYCE	*The Long Goodbye*
RUUBEN KAALEP & AUGUST MEISTER	*Rebirth of Europe*
RODERICK KAINE	*Smart and SeXy*

OTHER BOOKS PUBLISHED BY ARKTOS

OTHER BOOKS PUBLISHED BY ARKTOS

RICHARD RUDGLEY   *Barbarians*
Essential Substances
Wildest Dreams

ERNST VON SALOMON   *It Cannot Be Stormed*
The Outlaws

WERNER SOMBART   *Traders and Heroes*

PIERO SAN GIORGIO   *CBRN*
Giuseppe
Survive the Economic Collapse

SRI SRI RAVI SHANKAR   *Celebrating Silence*
Know Your Child
Management Mantras
Patanjali Yoga Sutras
Secrets of Relationships

GEORGE T. SHAW (ED.)   *A Fair Hearing*

FENEK SOLÈRE   *Kraal*

OSWALD SPENGLER   *The Decline of the West*
Man and Technics

RICHARD STOREY   *The Uniqueness of Western Law*

TOMISLAV SUNIC   *Against Democracy and Equality*
Homo Americanus
Postmortem Report
Titans are in Town

ASKR SVARTE   *Gods in the Abyss*

HANS-JÜRGEN SYBERBERG   *On the Fortunes and Misfortunes
of Art in Post-War Germany*

ABIR TAHA   *Defining Terrorism*
The Epic of Arya (2nd ed.)
*Nietzsche's Coming God, or the
Redemption of the Divine*
Verses of Light

JEAN THIRIART   *Europe: An Empire of 400 Million*

BAL GANGADHAR TILAK   *The Arctic Home in the Vedas*

DOMINIQUE VENNER   *For a Positive Critique*
The Shock of History

HANS VOGEL   *How Europe Became American*

MARKUS WILLINGER   *A Europe of Nations*
Generation Identity

ALEXANDER WOLFHEZE   *Alba Rosa*
Rupes Nigra